Praise for *Dark Pines*

'The tension is unrelenting, and I can't wait for
Tuva's next outing.'
Val McDermid, author of the Tony Hill and Carol Jordan novels

'Memorably atmospheric, with a dogged and engaging
protagonist, this is a compelling start to what promises
to be an excellent series.'
Guardian

'The best thriller I've read in ages.'
Marian Keyes, author of *Grown Ups*

'Atmospheric, creepy and tense. Loved the *Twin Peaks* vibe.
Loved Tuva. More please!'
C. J. Tudor, author of *The Chalk Man*

'A remarkably assured debut, *Dark Pines* is in turn, tense,
gripping and breathtaking, and marks out Will Dean
as a true talent. Definitely one to watch.'
Abir Mukherjee, author of *A Rising Man*

'Dean never lets the tension drop as his story
grows ever more sinister.'
Daily Mail

'Bravo! I was so completely immersed in *Dark Pines* and Tuva
is a brilliant protagonist. This HAS to be a TV series!'
Nina Pottell, *Prima* magazine

'Will Dean's impressive debut shows that
Nordic noir can be mastered by a Brit.'
The Times

ALSO BY WILL DEAN

Dark Pines
Red Snow
Black River
The Last Thing to Burn
First Born

BAD APPLES

WILL DEAN

A Point Blank Book

First published in Great Britain, Australia, and the Republic of Ireland by Point Blank, an imprint of Oneworld Publications, 2021
This mass market paperback published 2022

Point Blank would like to thank sensitivity reader @deafgirly for her tremendous help across the Tuva Moodyson series.

A CIP record for this title is available from the British Library

ISBN 978-0-86154-198-0
ISBN 978-1-78607-982-4 (ebook)

Typeset in Janson MT 11.5/15pt by Geethik Technologies
Printed and bound in Great Britain by Clays Ltd, Elcograf S.p.A.

Oneworld Publications
10 Bloomsbury Street
London WC1B 3SR
England

For all the English teachers. I know it's not always easy but we appreciate you. For helping young people fall in love with stories and language. For your enthusiasm and heart. Your dedication. And for introducing fiction to the kids who need it most.
Thank you.

1

I slam my foot on the brakes and come to a halt a metre behind the black car.

My Hilux shakes on its axels.

Thick fog.

My seatbelt digs in. The 4x4 in front has its hazard lights flashing. Wisps of fog drift between my bonnet and its rear end, illuminated by my headlights. Is the driver in trouble? I open my window a crack and mist pours in like smoke billowing around a closed door. Why would you stop your car on this hillside road? It hasn't broken down, the exhaust fumes are drifting out into the forest air.

I switch on my hazard lights and that's when I hear the scream.

Then another scream. Fainter. Or perhaps just an echo.

My head jolts to the left, to the dense pines hidden by the fog. Sweat starts to drip down my back. I check my phone. Good reception. Another scream, this one weaker: lost to the mists.

Did the driver in front leave the relative safety of their car to wander through the trees?

As I open my door to get out, the 4x4 in front jerks back and its rear lights shine bright in my face. I fall onto wet ground, my hands sinking into leaf sludge. Are they reversing into me? I scramble to my feet.

'Hey!' I yell.

The black car has rolled back a little because of the steepness of Visberg hill, that's all. More like a mountain than a hill. Almost a cliff. The car gains traction and its tyres squeal as it accelerates hard and disappears uphill into the murk.

My heart's thumping.

Cold air and exhaust fumes.

'Help me,' says a woman's voice. Someone in the forest.

I climb back into my Hilux and pull over, half on the road, half off, and switch on my hazards. I don't know this hillside forest, I have not stepped into its trees before. But I must check on this screaming woman. How can I not?

'Hello?' I shout out.

Nothing.

Chill around the back of my neck.

I jump a ditch that's October-full of stagnant brown water, and enter the treeline. One tree deep. Three trees deep. Five.

'Hello? Are you okay?

She screams again. No answer, just a guttural plea.

I turn and I can't see my Hilux anymore, can't see the road. No hazard lights, no headlights, no tarmac. The fog is rolling through on the breeze. It *is* the breeze. Misty waves stroking my face, dampening my hair. I use my hands to cover my hearing aids and then I yell, 'I'm coming!'

I walk. I cannot run. I'd fall into a ravine and die. I'd slip on a rock and plunge headfirst into a freezing river. I walk and I focus on where I think the woman is, and let me tell you I am not well qualified for this task. Not in twilight. Not in autumn. Not in fog-riddled woodland.

Sobbing. One of my hearing aids is damp and it's giving me feedback.

'Where are you?' I shout.

'Over here,' she says, and I could almost laugh if this situation wasn't so desperate.

I trudge past stumps and trip over moss-crusted boulders. There are boggy stretches that hunger for my boots and my shins. I try to step on roots. Dry land.

I find a path of sorts and start to jog. My chest feels like it'll explode; cold mist pumping down into my lungs and out again.

The slimy caps of wet mushrooms glisten in my peripheral vision.

She screams again. Unintelligible. Is she trapped by a bull elk? Held down by a man? Injured in some kind of animal trap?

I have no bearings. I could be anywhere. Nowhere. I turn on my heels and the next scream sounds like it's from the other way. Is she moving around in this forest? Am I going round in circles?

I almost run face first into the house.

A damp, wooden structure with no windows at all on the ground floor. No door I can see. A painted doll's house that's been damaged in a fire rests on a tree stump. It's sat a little way from the main building. The kennel-size roof is blackened and the tiny furniture inside is singed. I look around at the real house. Lots of windows upstairs but no way in or out. What is this place? Some forest-ranger station? Green pollen and mould rising up from the forest floor, trying to reach up to those high windows. A bronze clock bolted onto the gable end; a clock with no hands to tell the time with.

'Please,' says the voice. 'You have to come.'

The voice is close. Is she inside the house?

I turn a quarter circle and listen to her voice and then I run. To where I *think* she is. I have my phone and the knife Benny Björnmossen sold me last year. I run.

'Keep talking,' I yell, gasping for breath. 'I can't see you in the fog.'

And so she does. She whispers continually. Droning. Chanting. Is she injured? Or is this whole thing a trap?

I dash through birches and around pine trees, their dead lower branches scratching at my neck, drawing blood on my wrist.

She's whispering now.

I can barely hear her.

'I'm nearly there,' I yell, but I have no idea where 'there' is, just as I have no notion of where 'here' is either. Drop me in a forest and I'm likely to fall down and give up, but throw in thick fog and I may as well…

An arm catches round my neck.

I fall.

Wet moss and pine needles.

A body on top of me. Heavy. Smells of waxed jacket. A forearm to my face.

'Get off me!'

'Please,' she says.

I roll away and she is staring at me, her eyes bulging and red, her fingers bloody.

'Please.'

'Who are you?' I ask, the fog managing to drift between us, her face breaking up behind the static.

She gets to her knees and stands and I see her jeans are red. Stained. Splattered.

I pull my knife from my bag and she says, 'No,' and puts her palms to her face, and she says, 'No, no, no.'

I take a deep breath of forest air, dense with spores and rotten leaves. It's thick autumn air laced with the tang of rot and decay.

'Over there,' she says, pointing into the mists.

I swallow hard and stand up and move to where she's pointing.

A fallen pine, its root system flat and sprawling like a metro map. A dash of colour behind. A coat?

I clamber over the pine, its rough bark scratching at my trousers like the nails of a grasping hand.

Two boots.

And two legs.

'Dead,' she says.

I look back and see the woman properly for the first time. She's shaking her head. No coat. Just a haunted expression.

'What happened here?' I ask. But she just points harder, her blood-tipped index finger stabbing into the fog.

She doesn't come to where I am. She stays back.

My foot plunges into a deep pile of leaves and brown, acidic water fills my boot.

'Call the police,' I say.

'No phone.'

I take out my phone and dial Gavrik police. 'It's me, Tuva Moodyson. Halfway up Visberg hill. You'll see my truck. Fifteen minutes into the forest on the north side. Near a house with no ground-floor windows. A body.' I end the call because what more is there to say.

The woman keeps back and I don't trust her yet. I don't like the look of her scarlet hands.

The body is resting on granite, not earth.

Covering the rock is a thin layer of saturated, bright-green moss. A blanket.

The head is hidden by a coat, probably the screaming woman's coat, but I can tell this is a man's body. From his boots, his hands, his shape.

I turn back to her. 'The police are on their way.'

She just looks at the coat covering the top half of the body, at the reflective patches now red with fresh blood, and she chews on her lip and shakes her head from side to side. I'm losing her to these mists. She's two metres from me and she's now just a ghost of a person.

The dead man's wearing black jeans. Rubber boots. His coat is open to reveal his blood-soaked beige sweater. No wedding ring. His palms face up. A single fallen pine needle rests along one of his lifelines, nestled in the crease of his motionless hand.

I kneel down.

Next to my knee is the crisp curve of a copper beech leaf and sitting within its cupped form is a pool of human blood. No animal is troubling it. There is no ant or fly arriving to fulfil a basic destiny. It's perfect. Obscene.

I reach out to lift the corner of the coat covering him, and the woman lets out a ghoulish bark.

A warning.

'I need to check for a pulse,' I say, although looking at the wound on this man's chest, the amount of blood loss, I know it's a preposterous notion. He is lifeless. But I must. Even here in this hillside forest, we must hope.

'No,' she says.

The fog drifts past her and I see the dread in her eyes, the blood on her face now that she drags her fingers across her damp cheeks.

I turn back to her coat, careful not to disturb the bloody beech leaf.

I hold the coat by the zip toggle and lift it a fraction.

My fingers automatically connect with his skin so I can take a pulse.

I move the coat higher and throw it to one side.

No pulse.

And no head.

2

I scrabble away from the body and come to rest with my back against a rotting birch trunk.

I pant for air. Desperate for fresh air, my chest convulsing.

The woman is sobbing somewhere behind me.

What happened to this headless man? A bear attack out here in Visberg forest? A wolf attack?

I swallow repeatedly to stop myself from throwing up but there is acid in my mouth. I lock my jaw and look away from the scene.

The woman's shaking her head and rocking back and forth on her heels.

I step over to her.

'What happened?' I ask.

She just shakes her head more vigorously.

I reach out to comfort her but she pulls back and her head lifts. The woman's eyes are wide, her focus darting this way and that.

'The police are on their way,' I say. 'I'm Tuva Moodyson.'

She nods and I urge her to step further away from the headless corpse. I don't touch her or get too close, I just smile and signal with my head that we could move away.

The woman takes a few strides with me.

We don't talk. We've seen too much for chitchat. But the air is better here. It's too heavy back by the body. Dense with death. It's suffocating.

'What did that?' she asks, with a strong accent I can't quite pinpoint. Lebanese? Syrian? 'What could do that?'

She's pointing over at the body and her fingertip is red.

'I don't know. How long have you been here?'

She just stares at the man on the moss-covered granite. At her coat concealing his gaping neck wound.

'How long have you been here?' I ask again, louder this time.

Her eyes snap to me. 'Half an hour, maybe,' she says. 'I don't know. I was out looking for mushrooms when the clouds came down. I got lost. On the way back to the road I almost fell over him.'

I offer her some spearmint gum and she takes it.

We both chew and the mint helps.

'I saw it. The wound. The skin and the…'

She trails off. Her Swedish is excellent but I have to focus to understand.

'Did you see anyone else around?' I ask.

She shakes her head.

'I screamed for help. I couldn't just leave him out here all alone, but I wanted to. I wanted to run away.'

'I'm sorry,' I say.

She doesn't cry. We don't touch hands or arms. We just stand very close in this wild place. A gunshot rings out and she ducks.

'Elk hunt,' I say.

'I know,' she says, standing up straight once again.

Her teeth start chattering.

'Wear my coat for a while.'

'No, I'm okay.'

I look back at her coat. The neon fabric and the growing darkness and fog affording this headless man some modicum of privacy, some tiny shred of dignity.

I take out mittens from my pockets and offer them to her and she takes them without looking at me. To cover her red fingers more than to protect her from cold. To distance herself from the blood.

'What's your—'

'Alright, what's the situation here,' booms a loud voice from somewhere in the fog. A torch beam swings over us and then a man steps closer. From his demeanour I'd say he's police.

'Officer, over there.'

He's not in police uniform. Must be a plain-clothes officer or some kind of park ranger.

The man shines his torch over at the body. The reflective patches of the coat shine back. A wet slug climbing up the dead man's boot shines back. The drying blood shines back.

'Please move away,' says the man. 'Move back now.'

We do as he says.

The cop uses a stick to lift the corner of the coat and then he stumbles back in much the same way I did. Except he staggers away from the scene and starts to gag.

The woman covers her eyes with her hand.

More voices from the murk. Words I can't make out. Torchlight. A radio.

Thord steps through the fog and says, 'Are you okay, Tuvs?'

I nod.

'She okay?'

'Yeah.'

He walks over to the other guy and they chat and then Thord gestures for the plain-clothes cop to come and stand with us. Chief Björn and Noora arrive. We're told to move further back and wait.

Noora takes down the woman's name and contact details and then she tapes up the scene. She doesn't look at me, she just sticks blue-and-white striped police tape from pine tree to birch, from stump to boulder.

Others arrive and the fog lifts some more.

Lights are erected on tripods. The scene is photographed. There are people here putting on white zip-up suits.

Through the mists the striped police tape looks like lasers at a nightclub.

The Chief walks to us.

'Are you alright?'

The woman and I both nod.

'We're going to need statements from you both. Can you accompany me to Gavrik police department.'

'I need to make a phone call,' she says.

'You can do that from my police vehicle.'

'I'll follow in my truck.'

He nods and sighs. 'Terrible business.'

We walk together through the trees and there's a dull ache at the back of my jaw. A molar or a wisdom tooth. The path is even and the air has cleared to the point where I can see at least ten metres ahead. With the Chief here it's not like walking through a dark place. He has a gun on his hip and he gives off the kind of confidence you have when you've been raised in forest country. Like nothing bad could ever happen to him.

Visberg hill is a line of police, coroner, and other emergency vehicles. The blue lights strobe up into the wet pine canopy and dance off the surface water of the ditches.

I follow Chief Björn and the woman down the hill in my Hilux. My legs are tired. I'm not hungry, just exhausted. The hazy image of that rough, severed neck will be engraved on my mind until the day I die. I will try to delete it, or at least archive it, but I already know I will fail.

The forty-minute drive back to Gavrik passes in seconds. A blur. A bad dream. We take the long route back because of the driving conditions, I guess. The Chief always prides himself on doing things the correct way. The safe way. I get a pain in the pit of my stomach as we pass between McDonalds and ICA Maxi, the two gateposts of Toytown. A pain and an ache all in one.

Gavrik is deserted. October. Drizzle and fog. Why wouldn't it be.

I park up in my space behind *Gavrik Posten* and walk over. The shadow of the Grimberg Liquorice factory is lost to the mists.

Inside the cop shop things are warm and bleached and predictable. Bolted down seats and safety posters. Vertical strip blinds. Humming radiators. A copy of the *Gavrik Posten* left folded on the pine counter.

The woman is hungry and feels faint, so she gets looked after while I go through to the back and give the Chief my statement.

'Sorry you had to see that,' he says.

'Me too.'

He takes his notepad and switches on his recording device and slowly unscrews the lid of his fountain pen.

I tell him how I heard the scream. About the black 4x4 that drove away up the hill. How I found the woman near the house with no ground-floor windows. Saw the body. Lifted the coat.

'You notice anyone else in the area?'

'No.'

'Any other vehicles parked on Visberg hill? Anyone up near the derelict train tracks?'

'No, but it was so foggy I couldn't see much.'

He makes a note. Dark green ink.

'Notice any noises in the forest out of place? Quad bike? Any fresh bootprints?'

'No.'

'Did the woman say anything to you?'

'Just that she found him. Asked me if an animal could have done that to him.'

'An animal?' He looks up.

I nod.

'Was she wearing a headscarf when you found her? A yellow headscarf?'

I shake my head.

'She mention Pan Night or Halloween?'

'What's Pan Night?'

He ignores that. 'Did you take any photographs of the crime scene?'

'Why?'

'Just answer the question, please.'

'No.'

'Can I check your phone?'

'No.'

He takes a deep sigh. 'I'm going to ask you to keep any photos or specific details out of your newspaper for the time being. We need to keep all the information tight until we know what happened tonight.'

'No photos,' I say. 'I'll agree to that.'

'Or specific details.'

'Chief, you know as well as I do, if I don't print what I found then someone else will. Fast. You can't contain this. People have a right to know.'

'Do they, now?'

I nod and clear the corners of my eyes. My mascara has clumped.

'I'll be sensitive,' I say.

'Mind you are.'

He photographs my boots, the treads.

I walk out of the cop shop and past Benny Björnmossen's gun store. His shop's still open and it's full of customers. Brisk business. That's elk-hunt season for you. Ammunition and high-energy hunt dog-food and GPS trackers. Camouflage jackets and gutting knives. The bell tinkles as I open the door to the *Posten.* Empty office. The clock on the wall says 7:40pm. Three desks in here looks wrong. It's one too many. But we're managing.

Lena steps out from her office at the rear left.

'Just got a call from Ragnar Falk. A dead hunter?'

She steps toward me and reaches out her hand and places it on my wrist.

Suddenly I feel faint. I steady myself.

'Lena, the man had no head.'

3

Lena locks the door and takes me back to her office.

'Shit, I'm sorry,' she says.

'I feel for his family. Imagine having to identify the body? In that state, from the neck down?'

She squeezes her eyes together and shakes her head.

I take a deep breath. 'I'm going to write it tonight.'

'Get the details down then go home. Food and sleep, Tuva. Need you strong for tomorrow.'

I work for twenty minutes at my new desk, my fingers still shaking. With Sebastian and Lars in here with me during the day it's ridiculously cramped. I'm next to Seb's desk. He's adopted my old one. His microwave-size PC is surrounded by photos of his family sailing, and one of him with some half-famous American singer I don't recognise. My desk has no photos. One fancy new laptop that Nils won't quit complaining about, and no photos whatsoever.

I say goodnight to Lena and drive to my new apartment. A little further out of town than I'm used to but I have a small balcony and an extra bedroom. Benefits of getting promoted.

Once inside I lock my door and peel off my wet outer clothes and heat up a microwave ping meal for one. Chicken tikka masala. Hardly any chicken. Not much tikka masala. The neighbours are arguing again next door. I've been here ten days and so far there have been ten very vocal arguments. Her talking sternly. Him shouting. I can't make out the words through the wall but I get the gist. And I feel each door slam and each stamp of a boot. They have a young kid but I've never heard him make a noise. Hardly even seen him.

I throw the food carton in the bin and their argument escalates. I want to scream, 'I saw a dead man today lying on a layer of wet moss. I saw his blood on the leaves and his hands curled up into claws.' I want to yell at them about how I couldn't find a pulse. How I couldn't even find a face. But instead I remove my hearing aids and drop them in a tub of desiccant on my bedside table to dry out. Yeah, I may have a fancy new job, but these still cost almost a month's salary.

Silence.

The relief is all-consuming. No screaming, although I can still feel my neighbours' fury through the walls. Their frustrations and disappointments and exhausted, repeated, never-changing, never-compromising arguments. But all is quiet.

I think of their kid.

Their quiet boy.

I shower and sleep and wake with a dark and heavy realisation.

What if the killer was watching us last night?

Behind a shield of fog, what if he or she was still out there? What if they saw us? What if they watched the whole thing? I check my windows and my door. Would he recognise me if he saw me again?

I grab two thin supermarket pancakes, douse them with sugar, fold them up, toast them until the sugar inside turns to caramel and the pancakes start to crisp. I dig them out of my toaster with a wooden butter knife, eat them and leave.

Gavrik's busy. Hunters and mushroom pickers. Cross-country skiers stocking up on wax and new poles before the snows arrive. Tired men on parental leave, wheeling around their babies, each kid lying on a sheepskin blanket under a mosquito net. Protected from all angles. Guarded from the multifarious dangers of Toytown.

I came back because of Lena's job offer. But also because I realised I need her and Tammy and Thord in my life. I even need Nils and Lars and Benny Björnmossen from the hunt shop, although it feels strange to acknowledge it. Sometimes you spend all your energy getting away from a place only to realise you have to go back.

I park and walk past the roofless ruin of St Olov's church. A black crow sits atop the lichen-covered drystone wall and it tracks me with its shiny beak.

The office bell tinkles and I push the door open.

'Look who it is,' says Nils from inside. 'Fancied a lie-in, did we?'

He's still unzipping his coat. The shithead probably arrived a full thirty seconds before I did.

'Found a decapitated corpse on Visberg hill last night, what's your excuse?'

'Thord told me about it in ICA,' he says, pulling off his boots and placing them on the rack. He slides into his new Crocs, not a great look with white socks, and moves so I can peel off my autumn gear. 'You heard the rumours?'

'Rumours? Already?'

'Spreading faster than a wildfire through Norrland,' he says. 'You should see Facebook.'

I slide on my indoor shoes and walk into his office-slash-kitchen and pour myself a coffee.

Nils checks his gelled spikes in the mirror hanging on the wall, the one sponsored by Svensson's Saws & Axes, and sits down at his desk.

'Marie from the Kommun heard it was the Austrian clockmaker, the one from Visberg square. Heard he'd blown off his own head with an antique shotgun.'

I sip coffee and say, 'Incorrect.'

'Alright, then. Benny Björnmossen got told by one of his customers it was the Yugoslav, you know the one.'

'Care to narrow it down?'

'Don't know his name. Some kind of commando-marine green-beret type; war criminal, owns the pizza place in Visberg. Never been myself, my pappa told me to avoid that hill town at all costs. Accident black spot, it is.'

'War criminal?'

'Yugoslav,' he says.

'You're not a man of nuance are you, Nils?'

'Nobody calls me a nuisance to my face.'

'What about innocent until proven guilty?'

'Just sharing what I heard. Helping you out now you're back with your big job title and your ultra-slim metal laptop.'

'Thanks, pal.'

He runs his tongue over his teeth.

'Watch out in Visberg, though. That steep hill. I'm serious. Take Sebastian with you and keep slow on that twisty road. It's a black-spot.'

'You ever hear about something called "Pan Night", Nils?'

He puts both hands up to his hair and perfects his spikes again with his fingertips.

'It's what the hill people call their Halloween.'

'Hill people?'

'Visberg people. They have their own version of Halloween is all.'

Lena appears in the doorway, a pencil stuck in her afro.

'It's not Halloween,' she says. 'It's one week before. Totally their own thing, started by whatever iron and steel family dominated Visberg centuries ago. But it's got a lot darker since.'

'You been there on Pan Night, boss?' asks Nils, removing his Crocs from his desk, leaning in.

'Only locals welcome,' says Lena. 'Nobody from Gavrik goes. It's a Visberg thing.' She turns to me. 'Ragnar Falk can fill you in. He ran the *Visberg Tidningen* for forty-two years so if anyone knows, Ragnar knows. A one-man newspaper that whole time.'

'I'll get in touch with him,' I say.

'No need. He called this morning. Ragnar's expecting you at Visberg town square in forty minutes. Better get going. And, Tuva…'

I look at her.

'Watch out for that road. It's a death trap.'

4

I pass by the sewage works and keep on going.

Marginal farms and clusters of bright white birches. Houses built in the '70s with little or no foundations. The kind where you can't really sell them or even get a mortgage. You have to leave them to rot down or sink.

My dash reads nine degrees and there's a glow to the Kommun. Low sun heating up damp land. Mists rising from granite boulders as big as town halls. And that's just the part of the rock visible above ground.

I drive past Svensson's Saws & Axes. Big client of the *Posten.* Lots of advertising space this time of year. I overtake a cyclist with a leather rifle bag.

The town of Visberg is built on top of the hill. A small mountain, really. As I approach I can feel the elevation. The thinning of the wet October air. The change in temperature.

The road winds up. The hill's so steep in places that it snakes one way and then turns back on itself like a beginners ski-slope, so it's hard to get a good look at the town. You might glimpse it out of the corner of your eye, but then you have to refocus so as not to drive off a steep cliff or into a deep ditch full of ice-cold forest water.

But the town is there. You sense its presence long before you get a good look at it. Visberg might be half the size of Gavrik but it has twice the stature. And ten times the wealth.

I approach the white memorial bike on the side of the road. The place I stopped last night. The spot where I heard that ghostly scream through the fog. There's a pair of official-looking cars parked up. The ground has been pummelled to mud. Churned. The body will be gone by now. Some highly qualified woman or man will be sharpening their bone saws. Preparing their Dictaphone. Checking their scalpel.

That poor man. The ultimate dehumanising act. Without a face, what are we? Without a brain? The detachment of a soul, or else a bank of memories, from a heart.

Medieval.

I get chills just thinking about it. That quivering beech leaf. The pool of blood held in its curve. The unlikeliness of it all.

I pass a cross on the far side of the road. Fresh flowers either side of it still wrapped in cellophane. Carnations and tight-bud roses. Another death. Another troupe of broken friends and family left behind.

My truck shudders as I drive over disused train tracks. A relic from the old days when Visberg was part of a thriving, centuries-old Swedish iron and steel industry.

And then the town begins to reveal itself.

The winding road ahead. The incline. The town disappears from view again as I turn. Pines either side of me like sharpened barriers erected by ancients. Unsophisticated perimeters to keep me in, keep me on track, keep me heading higher and higher.

My dash falls from nine Celsius to seven. Then down to five.

The Hilux sounds different on this hill. The transmission. Or the engine straining.

I head up higher.

The town appears again atop the mountain, like some Italian monastery. Like Monte Cassino before the bombs rained down out of the sky. Like the construction of Visberg was an act of defiance. A *fuck you* to the world.

The road straightens up. Was the dead man from this isolated place? Is his killer still walking these streets?

A town square up ahead, one I recognise from Google images. Three-sided.

In front of me, beyond the bandstand and the bronze statue at the centre of the square, is the main structure in the town. Originally a home for disturbed minors. Three storeys. Wooden. Long and flat, like the side view of a club sandwich. Lots of windows. The building is painted black with yellow window frames. But the main event is up on the roof. It's the huge rotating bee that really draws the eye. Moving round at a speed so slow you have to look twice. Thrice. You have to keep on looking.

I arrive in the square itself. Prettier than any part of Gavrik. More money here. More greenery and thoughtful town planning.

On the left side is a row of shops with dwellings above. Visberg Grill, the local pizzeria. Then some kind of café with blacked-out windows. Then an *Apoteket* pharmacy. Then Konsum, a small supermarket. A town this size doesn't justify an ICA Maxi or a Co-op Forum. The row of shops to my left is bathed in sunlight. Which is more than can be said for the ones opposite.

I drive on. Slowly. Trundling, really. Not another car on the road.

I turn right at Konsum and pass the Hive. A thriving self-storage business. Biggest in the Kommun. Bigger than anything in Gavrik. I almost stored Mum's things here – and Dad's, although I think of those as Mum's now – but instead I keep them all in a rented lock-up in Karlstad. It took me a whole weekend to move them from the hospice and her old flat. Her sewing machine. Her favourite blanket. Her photo albums in year order. The white shoes she wore on her wedding day. I donated most of her clothes to charities, but kept a few items. I've stored them in suitcases, even though I doubt I'll ever revisit them. I cried all my tears that weekend. Alone in a windowless storage unit.

Past the Hive is the dark side of the square.

First, a dental surgery. Tammy told me she came here one time for whitening but she didn't like the place. Never came back. Then two empty shops, and then some kind of watch shop with a huge, heavy clock jutting out from the wall. Looks too big for the building. Too heavy. Looks like it might pull the whole block crashing down into the square.

So, this is Visberg.

Hill town.

If you mention this place to a Gavrik local they might say, 'airs and graces' or 'mind that road' or 'some of us got to work for a living'.

My GPS tells me, 'you have reached your destination' and sure enough, Ragnar Falk is standing on the pavement waiting for me. I wonder how he feels about Lena and her husband buying his failing newspaper and giving me his town to cover. How does a person come to terms with that?

I get out.

'Welcome to Visberg,' he says, holding out his hand.

White beard. Blazer and elasticated jeans. V-neck underneath.

I know Ragnar a little from police conferences over the years, but he's aged significantly since I last saw him at Midsommar. Back then he was asking Chief Björn about Tammy going missing. Now he's introducing me to his town.

'Thanks, Ragnar,' I say.

'Although I wish I was welcoming you with a better news story. Lena told me you were right there in the forest last night.'

'It was a shock,' I say.

'Of course it was, my dear. That kind of awful business is a shock even for the most seasoned journalist.'

He sticks out his chest. He's my height and still looks strong, despite having seventy years on the clock. But his face has changed. His beard is white and soft, with some ginger still in his moustache. His eyes are sky blue.

'Come in, come in.'

He ushers me over to a closed-up shop. The *Visberg Tidningen* sign is still visible on the window through the whitewash.

The office smells of old paper and coffee.

'Sit, sit,' he says.

I do as he asks and he moves behind his massive oak desk. The walls are full of framed front pages of old *Visberg Tidningen* issues.

'Forty years of stories up there,' he says, following my gaze. 'These are just the highlights, just a few of the highlights.'

'What do you think about the corpse found last night? The beheading?'

He peers at me with those light blue eyes.

'Coffee, my dear?'

I shake my head.

'Dreadful business, a beheading,' he says. 'Makes such an awful mess. I always feel sorry for the next of kin having to identify the body of a loved one in that state, even if it's just from a photograph, the wound concealed. That's a horror you never walk away from.'

'And a shock for the town,' I say

'They're scared,' says Ragnar, nodding. 'People are afraid.'

'It's natural.'

'It's not natural,' he says. 'Over the years Visberg town has seen more than its fair share of decapitations.'

5

'This isn't the first beheading?'

'Oh, goodness, no,' he says.

'No?'

'When you've been a professional journalist for as long as I have you see everything. It's all cyclical, my dear. Is this your first story working on your own?'

I bite my lip. 'No, it isn't.'

'All news is cyclical in a hill town like Visberg, you see. A corruption scandal at the town hall. Wait ten years. There will be another. Some kind of youth pregnancy at the high school. Wait two years. Another one, you see? There is no new news and eveyone's related to everyone else.'

'Beheadings, though?'

'We had one in '83. A motorcyclist. Head came to rest well down the hill. Rolled down like a soccer ball, it did. Another one the year after, an arborologist. That means—'

'Tree surgeon.'

'An amateur. Not a complete decapitation, but as good as. Dead by the time he hit the ground, or so I was told. Local man, but not an Edlund.'

'Edlund?'

'The family.'

'What family?'

'The Edlund family. How do you take your coffee?'

'No, thanks.'

'When you've been doing this a few more years you'll be drinking strong coffee like me. Sign of a professional.'

He taps his nose and pours from a thermos.

I'll give Ragnar Falk one more pass on the patronising bullshit then I'll call him out. I'm mellowing, I guess.

'And then there were the animal beheadings. Much more recent.'

'Animal?'

He sits back down and takes a sip of his coffee and lets out a pleasure sigh.

'Well, not strictly beheadings. Rather, three boar brought down in the hunt last year. The men left the hooves and guts and skins and heads. A day later they reported all the heads missing.'

'Wolves?'

'Ahh, I take it from that you're a city person.'

'What?'

'Wolves would start with the organs, my dear. Not the heads. I can recommend some nature books if that might be helpful. And I think I have an old manual on journalism.'

You just stood on a landmine, mate.

'First of all, my name's Tuva, if you don't mind. Second of all, as you well know, Ragnar, I've been a journalist for years. In London, in Malmö, in Gavrik. I covered the Medusa killings, Ferryman, and the two missing women over Midsommar. I appreciate you introducing me to the town but we're on the level here. You and me. Both journalists.'

He studies me.

Then he looks over at his wall. Forty years of stories. Almost half a century of Visberg town life documented, investigated, reported.

He looks back at me.

'I'm out and you're in.'

'I didn't mean to be a bitch, it's just that—'

'No, you're right. I sold my business. Too old, too frail. Bad leg. And you're a good journalist, I'll give you that. I've read some of your work. Now, Tuva. How about a fresh start. Can I show you around?'

'I would love that.'

He smiles and nods and shows me out the door.

'What can you sense?'

'Autumn?'

'Yes, yes. But what exactly?

'Rot?'

'What is it that's rotting?

I look around. Take a breath.

'Apples?'

'Bingo.'

We walk out and cross the street, past my Hilux and into the square itself. Grass. A hundred or more mature apple trees. The bronze statue and the freshly painted bandstand.

'The locals ask for the apples not to be cleared away until past Halloween. For the atmospheric aroma.'

'Fair enough.'

'The whole town smells like a cider press.'

He smiles and walks on.

'This is Adolf-Fredrik Edlund, founder of Visberg town.'

It's an old dude in bronze with a bad moustache, resting his boot on a massive anvil with a sharp front end.

'Steel magnate?' I say.

'Iron, and then steel. Used the river networks to transport to the coast. His family still own shares in the company – one of the oldest in Sweden. That's why so many locals here are independently wealthy, you see. All from this one man.'

'Nice.'

'Not really,' he says, pointing to the road leading between the Hive and Konsum on the sunny side of the street. 'If you live down that street you'll most likely own a large mortgage-free house and play golf at the club and be called Edlund. If you live down there,' he points to the road passing from the square between the Hive and the dark side of the street, 'then you'll not be part of that team.'

'You live over there?' I ask, pointing to the cheaper, darker side.

'I do.'

'Interesting.'

'It means there's a constant divide here in Visberg. A tension between the Edlund clan, who don't need to work, and the rest of us, who do. They keep their golf club extremely closed off.'

'Just for Edlunds?

'There are a lot of them, Tuva.'

A car drives by slowly. It's an old American Chevy. From the '80s, I think. Squared-off corners. It's painted up like a sheriff's car in a movie. Beige with stripes and rooflights. On the doors it says 'Sheriff' in large font, and then underneath, in much smaller font, is the word 'Taxi'.

'Is he a sheriff or is he a taxi driver? I ask Ragnar.

'That, my dear, is a very good question.'

6

Ragnar Falk waves his hand and the car pulls over to us.

'Morning, Sheriff,' says Ragnar.

The man gets out of his taxi. He's dressed like a state trooper in a movie.

'Morning, Falk,' he says, then turns to me. 'Don't believe we've met.'

'We met last night in the forest,' I say, holding out my hand. 'Tuva Moodyson.'

He grimaces and shakes my hand vigorously and says, 'Of course we did. I'm Harry Hansson, people round here call me Sheriff. Awful sad business last night. Even for us officers, but for you, a civilian. Horrendous scenes.'

'Do you know the ID of the victim?' Why am I asking this guy? He's a taxi driver.

'Anything official like that, it's best to go through Chief Björn at the Gavrik police department.'

'Do you work with them?'

'You could say that, Tuva. I'm neighbourhood-watch community-liaison officer. Visberg is my district. Has been almost ten years, now. So finding that last night was a shock. On my watch, you see. My patch.'

Ragnar interjects, 'Sheriff Hansson is very well respected in Visberg. Keeps order, even with us being so far away from the actual police force. He'll be important for you to keep in touch with.' He turns back to Hansson. 'Tuva will be covering all Visberg stories for her paper now the *Tidningen* has closed its doors.' He looks over mournfully at the office on the dark side of the town square. 'Tuva, Sheriff. Sheriff, Tuva.'

'I'll be increasing patrols in light of the incident. There's residents afraid to go outside their houses, all sorts of gossip starting to circulate. It's my job to keep this town safe. My duty.'

He straightens himself up. Brown trousers, beige shirt with lots of pockets and shoulder straps. A star on his brown tie, another on each shoulder. Badges on his upper arms that look like my swimming badges from school but say 'Sheriff' in large print, with 'Taxi' barely visible underneath.

'Is Sheriff an official Swedish law-enforcement role in Värmland?' I ask.

He gives me a broad smile and says, 'It sure is in Visberg town, wouldn't you say, Falk.'

'I would,' says Ragnar.

'Well there you go then,' he says to me. 'There you go.'

'Can I interview you in the next day or so about the killing?'

He reaches inside his taxi and pulls out a card and gives it to me. 'Anytime. I'm always around here on patrol. You just call that number.' He turns to Ragnar. 'How's the hip, Falk?'

'It is what it is,' says Ragnar, rubbing the top of his leg.

'That's the ticket,' says Sheriff Hansson. 'Positive mental attitude. Who you introducing Moova to next?'

'Tuva,' I say.

'That's it,' he says.

'The Hive,' says Ragnar. 'Margareta and her boy.'

'Swell,' says the Sheriff. 'Give Marge my best.'

He drives off in his '80s American car with the windows down and his elbow sticking out.

I smile and stare at Ragnar.

'He's a bit of an oddball,' says Ragnar. 'But he's good. Locals do what he says, he keeps order, keeps Gavrik police in the loop. We're so far from the rest of the world up here we need someone like him. Do not underestimate Sheriff Harry Hansson.'

'I won't, I mean—'

'He'll be one of your best sources in this town.'

And suddenly I realise this really is my town now. Along with Gavrik and thousands of hectares all around. Smaller towns and villages. Forests. But Gavrik and Visberg will be my priorities. This is my patch. Expanded.

'Let's go see Margareta and Emil.'

We walk through the square and each apple tree is surrounded by lazy buzzing wasps. The apples are falling or rotting on the branches. The smell is sickly sweet. The air is thick with it.

We cross the road.

The sign next to the door says, 'The Hive. Lowest self-storage prices in all of Värmland. Open 9am to 9pm. Discretion guaranteed.'

Ragnar pulls on the door but it's locked.

We both peer through the window.

Ragnar rings the bell.

A boy approaches. I can't see him clearly through the security door – the glass inside is crisscrossed with wire.

'Emil,' shouts Ragnar. 'Emil, open up. It's me.'

The boy isn't a boy at all. He's a very short man with a full moustache. He looks at us from a distance, from over by the counter in reception, and then he puts down his bucket and mop and yells, 'Closed today, try back again tomorrow!' I can read his lips from here.

'It's me,' says Ragnar. 'I need to talk to your mother.'

Emil smooths his moustache, then sniffs his fingertips, then hurriedly picks up his bucket and turns and again yells 'Closed!' and walks away through an internal door.

'The Hive is never closed,' says Ragnar. 'I do hope Margareta isn't unwell.'

I check my phone as we cross over to Konsum on the sunny side of the square. Text message from Lena: *Gavrik police press conference at 4pm.*

'I'll introduce you to the dentist instead. He's an Edlund, twelfth generation.'

'I can't stay long, I need to cover the police presser.'

'Tell me, does Lena give you an expense account?'

'Yes. Why do you ask?'

His face breaks out into a broad toothy smile. 'Why don't we talk over pizza?'

We walk past Konsum and past the pharmacy, some new kind of wisdom teeth flossing-stick is advertised in the window, and on to Visberg Grill. The dull ache in my jaw intensifies.

We step inside the Grill. Bolted-down plastic seats, a backlit menu, and there's an open hotdog-takeout hatch on the far side, overlooking the view down the hill, over the vast forests, but it's not used at this time of day. Most of the tables are occupied. I make a mental note to bring Tammy here for a well-earned pizza feast. I think she'd like it.

'Fillet steak, mushroom, onion, béarnaise, peanuts and banana, please. Thin crust.'

What the hell?

'One of whatever he just said,' I say to the handsome guy behind the counter. 'And one Spicy American sausage for me, please.'

'New face in town,' says the man. Thick accent. Deep voice and blue jeans. Tight white T-shirt. Gym body. 'You're very welcome here, my name is Luka Kodro.'

He doesn't shake my hand or pat me on the back or kiss my cheek. He just looks at me, but he's one of those guys with a *look*. There's some kind of power to it that makes me feel like a teenager again.

'I'll secure us a table,' says Ragnar.

I pay and take two portions of pizza salad, it's a Swedish thing derived from a Balkan thing, and two glasses of tap water.

'Luka is from Bosnia, but now he's a Swedish citizen,' says Ragnar, lowering his voice. 'He was a soldier in that dreadful war. An elite soldier of some description. I've tried to interview him about it but he doesn't talk to me. He says he only likes to look forward, not back.'

The boom of gunshot drifts through the hotdog hatch and mingles with the pizza aromas.

'Bloodlust,' says Ragnar.

'The hunt?'

'Our forests aren't as big as Utgard but our quotas are better. The Edlund family pull strings, or so some people suspect.' He taps the side of his nose. 'I don't hunt myself, can't stand the sight of blood, but I've heard the ponds and rivers and bogs around Visberg, in the forests covering the hillside, are excellent territory for elk and wild boar.'

'Visberg special and a hot Yankee sausage,' says Luka, putting down two plates.

The pizzas look excellent, even Ragnar's fruit-salad abomination. Who the hell puts peanuts, steak and bananas on a pizza?

We eat and Ragnar fills me in on more of the town's history. How the Hive used to be an institution for unwanted children, and then for those juveniles of a criminal disposition. Some kind of hospital facility. And how since the '70s it's been self-storage.

A customer walks in carrying his motorbike helmet under his arm. Except it's an awkward carry because the helmet has large deer antlers attached to it.

'One thing I'm curious about,' I say. 'What exactly is Pan Night?'

Everyone, every single customer inside this place stops eating, stops chatting, and turns to face us. Ragnar puts down his knife and fork and chews, and his sky-blue eyes bore into mine. The antler-helmet guy looks at me with his mouth wide open.

Ragnar swallows and wipes his mouth with a paper napkin.

They're still looking. All of them. Waiting. They've stopped chatting, and most of them have even stopped chewing.

'It's...' he begins, and then he clears his throat. 'Whatever you've heard from outside Visberg I can tell you categorically that there is no such thing as Pan Night. Not anymore.'

7

The other diners resume chewing their crayfish pizzas and their kebab-meat pizzas and the volume in the room returns to normal levels.

Ragnar gives me a look that says, *Hurry up and eat your bloody pizza. And whatever you do, don't ask anymore questions about Pan Night.*

The whole room watches as we leave.

Sunshine outside: cool October sunshine. It picks out the pigment in the apples. Apples on the grass and apples on the trees. Greens and reds and the burnt oranges of fruit on the turn.

'I have an important appointment later, so let's get on with it,' says Ragnar, his tone curt.

He opens the door to 'Mind Games.'

We pass through a black curtain. Another. Down a short corridor. More black sheets hanging from every wall. The floor is painted velvet-black. The kind of specialist paint that absorbs light. The sun cannot penetrate back here. They should have taken a lease on the shady side of the street.

I know what this place is. Mind Games is my kind of place.

We pass through another black curtain. Round tables with illuminated keyboards. Monitors with moving Mind Games screensavers. Headphone sets complete with microphones draped over each flat screen. The place is empty save for three men.

'This is a video gamer café,' says Ragnar.

I know exactly what it is. I'm excited just knowing it's here. My opinion of Visberg, the forgotten place up the mountain, just shot up. I like this place. Pizza and gaming. My kind of town.

'David,' says Ragnar in a loud voice.

The young guy Ragnar's addressing doesn't look up, he just points at the man opposite him, who throws his headphones down on the table and says, 'What?'

These two are twins. Identical twins, a few years younger than me. Early twenties.

'David, this is Tuva Moodyson. She's a reporter, she'll be covering Visberg now I'm retiring.'

David looks down at his screen then back at me.

'Hi,' I say, offering my hand.

'Hi,' he says.

I move closer and glance at his computer.

'My second favourite *Call Of Duty*, I say. 'Prefer *Black Ops*.'

Both he and his twin look up at me and they both smile. Dark, cropped hair, athletic, two sets of deep brown eyes. David's brother says, 'Daniel.'

Then the other man in the room yells at his screen, like the computer just told him he was fired and his parents have both been kidnapped and his girlfriend's left him. A guttural, manic scream.

'He's the town accountant,' says David, looking over. 'Some kind of auditor. On his lunchbreak. Blowing off steam I guess.'

'We don't want to keep you from your shooting games,' says Ragnar, already backing out of the room.

'At least we keep the shooting to the screen,' says David. 'We heard the victim was killed by a .338, so I'd say it was a moose hunter responsible.'

'Who told you that?'

'Forum. Chat on the forums. They said it was a moose gun, a Winchester Magnum.'

I make a note of that on my phone.

'I'll be back,' I say.

We leave and the sun hits my eyes as we step back into the cool town square. There's a violinist setting up in the bandstand. She's wearing an orange hunting cap and she's tweaking her instrument. Tuning it.

Ragnar introduces me to the staff in the pharmacy and in the Konsum mini-supermarket. One cashier asks Falk if police have found the severed head yet. Asks him if we're to have a curfew in the town. He tells her to talk to the police over in Gavrik. By this point the smalltown gossip will be spreading like a virus. I need to tap into it, like I do in Gavrik and like I did in Malmö. The rumours and amateur theories are my way in. We check the Hive again but the door's still locked. Looking through the reinforced glass I can see a Husqvarna cardboard box on the counter, the photo on the box is of a bearded dude felling a pine tree. We step away. White smoke's billowing out of their chimney and Ragnar says, 'Haven't seen them have a fire here before.'

We walk over to the shady side of Visberg town square. The dental surgery is busy – I can see four or five people in the waiting room. One man walks out holding his jaw and cursing under his breath. He has blood on his collar.

'That one's a pop-up shop,' says Ragnar, pointing to the shopfront between his old office and the clockmaker's on the end of the row. 'It just popped up. Two sisters running it from your neck of the woods.'

I peer through the dirty glass, but all I can see is a mask. It couldn't be them, could it?

'Halloween?' I ask.

'If you say so,' says Ragnar.

He limps over to Wimmer's Clocks and stands in the shadow of the heavy clock. Looks like something you might see bolted onto a huge department store. Looks like it could fall and crush Ragnar.

There's a musical tune when the door opens. Something baroque. Every square metre of this place contains multiple grandfather clocks and carriage clocks and wall clocks. These ones are all set to the correct time: a little before 3pm. But there's nobody here.

Glass cases full of Seikos and old mechanical watches, and another with digital alarm clocks plugged into a damaged extension cord wrapped in black tape.

There's a staircase in the middle of the room leading down to a basement. A chain blocks the way and a sign in cursive script reads, 'Museum: Strictly Invitation Only'.

'Hans?' says Ragnar, his hands cupped around his mouth. 'Hans, are you here?'

A bang from downstairs.

Ragnar looks at his watch.

Not sure that's really necessary in here, mate.

A head appears down in the basement. The man walks up to our level and steps over the chain. He's as tall as a grandfather clock. Pale. Fine mousy hair. Balding. He has a magnifying eyepiece on a metal band and it's resting in the middle of his forehead like a third eye.

'Ragnar Falk, my friend.' He moves his eyepiece. 'Well, what have we here then.'

'This is Tuva Moodyson. She's taking over my beat.'

The two men shake hands but there's a warmth here. A slap on the shoulder. The tall man turns to me.

'Hans Wimmer. A pleasure to meet you, Ms Moodyson.'

He offers me his hand. Each fingertip has a latex covering. Like a row of tiny condoms.

'I have an appointment at the golf club, I'm afraid,' says Ragnar. 'I'll leave you two to chat. See you again soon, Tuva. Thanks for the pizza.'

Ragnar leaves and the same baroque tune plays as the door closes.

'I have never seen him more excited,' says Hans Wimmer, looking down on me. 'Ragnar's like a schoolboy. It's not about the golf course, though that is a particularly fine example I'm told. It's about the acceptance, you see.' He looks out the shop window as Ragnar crosses the town square. 'Very few non-Edlunds ever get membership. He's moving from outside the circle to inside. He's about to become a true hill person.'

'And you're not?'

'Goodness, no.'

He looks at the clocks on the wall.

'You're using hearing aids, I see. Just a polite warning: in a few moments the clocks will strike the hour and you may wish to adjust your volume settings.'

I'm taken aback by this. What a kind thing to say.

'Thank you.'

'So, you will be writing about Visbergians. How interesting.'

'I cover Gavrik as well. The whole area.'

'And now you have an important story. A story that requires a delicate touch with the local population.'

I think back to that gaping neck wound. Flesh exposed. The red earth all around. The woman's coat, soaked.

'Do you have any theories, Mr Wimmer? Any help you can offer?'

He smiles and I notice how perfect his teeth are. They must be veneers: the uniformity of them, the squareness, the glint.

'Please call me Hans. This is usually a quiet town in my experience. That's what attracted me to it.'

'Where are you from?' He sounds German. As he's being polite I'll try to reciprocate.

'Austria,' he says. 'Central Vienna. Via Geneva and Moscow and Estonia. I never seem to stay in the same place for too long. At the moment this hill is where I call home.'

He checks the time on the nearest clock face.

'Is there anyone you think I should interview about the body? Anyone you find suspicious?'

He smiles but this time he shows no teeth.

'Well, you just ate his pizza.'

'Sorry?'

'Mr Kodro, our friendly, local war criminal. There's only one person in this town who's killed before, multiple confirmed kills, decapitations, torture, killings in cold blood, in hand-to-hand combat, slaughtering his own neighbours. And you just ate his pizza.'

8

Silence between us.

I look past Hans Wimmer through the shop window and see an apple fall from a tree and burst on impact.

Clocks tick all around us and then one starts to chime. We both look at it: a pendulum-powered grandfather clock made from walnut. Another one dongs. Then another. Soon they all start chiming and ringing together. Manic cuckoos jab in and out of concealed doors. A pine clock with a waterfall starts to play a tune, actual water powering the tiny wooden wheel. The sound is too much. Others chime. Bells and cheeping and music and beeping. A wave of chaotic sound.

'I have to go,' I say, pointing to my ears.

He shrugs and says something I can't read on his lips, then turns to head back down to his private museum.

The cider-scented air is a relief. I can still sense the last chimes from inside the stuffy shop but I'm outside now.

The drive back down the hill is soothing. I had to hand in my last Hilux to the dealership in Malmö when I quit. This one is better. More bells and whistles. Bluetooth. Better seats. Better speakers. More power to get me out of dangerous situations. I love this thing.

The hill feels even steeper on the way down. Like the upper part of a ski jump, only this one is lined with pine trees as tall as air-traffic-control towers.

Two vans are parked on the side of the road. I have to indicate and swerve to get past them. A national from Stockholm and some other outfit from Gothenburg. Satellite dishes on their roofs. One well-lit woman is speaking into a camera as I pass by, an assistant holding an umbrella well above her head to keep it out of shot.

I don't like the way everyone in Visberg points at the pizzeria owner. If he was an active soldier, a special-forces fighter, and that's a big 'if' that requires substantiation – I've interviewed enough special-forces veterans who turned out to be no such thing – then he'd have been active almost thirty years ago. And even then, it doesn't mean he'd be capable of killing a man in peacetime. Dad would have said, 'Everyone deserves to be believed. Always try to give the benefit of the doubt, Tuva.'

But Dad's lessons are fading in my memory. If I'd been older than fourteen when he died, I'd remember more. He never knew me as a woman, or as a journalist. I look up at the grey sky and smile. He seems closer to me up on this hillside.

I get to Gavrik and park in my space behind the *Posten* offices.

'Presser in ten,' says Sebastian from behind his desk.

His nose is out of joint since I started back here on Monday. He was the sole full-time reporter for a while and Lena reckons he has the potential. Then, yours-truly returns and he's stuck with the school ice-hockey grand slams and the bread-and-butter elk-hunt quota stories or the hairdresser getting sued because she almost cut someone's earlobe clean off.

I collect my digital Dictaphone and my pad and we head over to the cop shop.

Thord puts Sebastian in the second row. It's a small room and they want to give some of the prime spots to the nationals and big regionals. They don't want those journalists to stop coming. Reporters are reluctant enough to revisit Gavrik as it is.

Noora's standing by the door and she won't make eye contact.

Chief Björn walks in from the back and the camera flashes light up to his face. He still has some of his tan from the summer. He stands behind the microphones and clears his throat. He adjusts his tie, but today there is no tie-pin and he looks like he regrets its absence.

'Ladies and gentlemen, I'd like to thank you all for coming.'

Someone's phone rings and the Chief gives them a three-second death stare.

'Last night at approximately seventeen-hundred hours two local residents discovered a deceased male in the forest of Visberg hill, approximately 45km east from here. The deceased male was found to the north of the main road in dense vegetation. The said male was pronounced deceased at the scene. I can share some information with you today, but as our investigations are ongoing I will be unable to take many questions pertaining to this case.'

We all sit forward a little more in our plastic stackable chairs.

'The deceased man has been identified as Mr Arne Gustav Persson. Mr Persson was a long-term resident of Visberg town. He was a well-respected local plumber and member of the church choir and chamber of commerce. I can tell you at this time that Mr Persson was the victim of a gunshot wound to the torso area.'

Camera flashes. Hands shooting up.

'There were other wounds but I cannot go into details at the present time and I'd ask you not to speculate until we release an official statement. I'd like to take this opportunity to appeal for information regarding this crime. If you know anything, no matter how seemingly inconsequential, then I'd urge to you contact the Gavrik police department.' He runs through the contact details I memorised years ago, and, for the first time ever, gives social-media contact details as well.

I put my hand up.

He points to me.

'Chief, do you have any suspects for this crime?'

Chief Björn sticks out his lower lip and says, 'We are following up on multiple leads and keeping an open mind at this time.'

A woman behind me with thick, glossy hair, magazine hair, says, 'Chief Björn, was this a hunting accident?'

'We're not ruling anything out. Like I say, we keep an open mind. However, there are some specific details I cannot currently divulge that suggest this was not an accident, hunting or otherwise.'

A man behind me with a rich Leonard Cohen voice asks, 'Chief, what do you say to the rumours the victim was decapitated and the head was displayed on a nearby tree stump.'

More flashbulbs.

Tree stump? Did I miss that? Have they found the severed head?

The Chief puts out a spread palm and says, 'That's all I can say for the time being. Now, once again, I'd like to appeal to your viewers and readers for information. Please get in touch if you know anything or suspect anything relevant to this investigation. Thank you.'

More flashbulbs and questions. One young guy asks, 'Chief Björn, what do you say to the allegations that this ritualistic killing is related to Halloween, and will Visberg be afforded extra law-enforcement officers on October thirty-first? Sir? Chief, will you comment?'

The Chief walks out through the door he came in.

Sebastian and I leave and he pulls me to one side outside the *Posten.*

'I've found something similar from ten years ago. Hunt season, late October, gunshot wound, decapitation.'

'You did?' I ask. 'Where? Who?'

'Not local,' he says. 'I was going deep on a Google search when I found it. Wasn't an elk hunt, it was a wild-boar hunt. Four men decapitated in total. One each year for four consecutive years.'

'Jesus. Was the perpetrator ever caught?'

'No,' he says.

'Shit.'

'But it's probably not relevant,' he says.

I frown.

'All the deaths occurred deep in the forest.'

'Okay?'

He looks at me. 'In Bosnia.'

9

I tell Sebastian that if you widen your net enough you'll find similar crimes all over the world, not only in Bosnia. Humans are the same everywhere. I ask him to find out what he can about Arne Persson's surviving relatives and try to schedule me an appointment to interview whoever was closest to him.

Lars is inside sitting on his inflatable haemorrhoid cushion – it looks like the face of Homer Simpson – rewriting a piece on Gavrik transport improvements. Cycle paths for him, psychopaths for me.

'Pan Night,' I say. 'You've been living here since the last Ice Age, Lars. What's Pan Night all about?'

He looks up from his screen and I count the seconds. The adjustment of his glasses and the thinking time. I'm patient because the man is an invaluable font of local knowledge.

'Edlunds Bruk,' he says. 'Oldest industrial family in the area, much older than the Grimbergs, even.' He gestures in the direction of the salt liquorice factory across the road. 'One of the Edlunds set up Pan Night hundreds of years ago, if I remember correctly. Before all the modern American Halloween nonsense. As I recall – and Visberg was never really my patch, I've only visited once as a boy, and after that Ragnar Falk was always a territorial so-and-so, from what I remember – it was like a thank you to the local people. Modern employers may take their staff out for dinner, or even away for a team-building outdoor activities weekend.' He shudders. 'Thank goodness Lena isn't interested in that kind of thing. The Edlunds asked the Visberg locals to leave a single, empty pan outside their front doors after the sun went down. A saucepan or similar. Then the family grandees, the board and so on, the most wealthy and powerful of the senior Edlunds, they'd walk around and drop money in each of the pans. A few silver coins, that's all. But it evolved over the years to a net of coins and a riddle. Sometimes a sketch or a carved bone for the children of the steelworkers. Each generation of Edlunds put their own twist on it.'

'Okay.'

'Some twists were stranger than others. I'm not sure when the practical jokes started to overtake the kindnesses. But in the late nineteenth century, the Edlunds distanced themselves from the whole enterprise. Locals took it upon themselves to surprise their own neighbours. Feuds were settled on that very night each year. And the pans grew in size, I'm told. Some of them cauldrons or feeding troughs. From what I understand, the whole thing fizzled out in the '80s as Halloween became the groovy new thing. Why do you ask?'

'Because so far nobody in Visberg wants to talk about it.'

'Hill people,' says Lars, like that explains everything.

I squeeze behind my new desk and Sebastian comes back in. He's lost some of his pretty-boy shimmer but he still looks like he's here by accident. Got lost on the E16 and never found the route out again.

I write up my notes and order my stories for the next issue. Sebastian starts making calls and Lars has a frog in his throat so I pull out my hearing aids to focus.

Blessed relief.

I draft a few headlines and map out a comprehensive timeline of the murder investigation. The autopsy has now been completed. It may take some time for the body to be released for burial. I'll attend if possible. If it's a public affair I'll attend and write it up in a respectful manner. It'll help give the town some closure. Vital for them but also good for me if I'm to live among these Visberg hill people in the years ahead. Public burials, and I don't mean this to sound disrespectful or morbid, but they can offer valuable insights into the locals. In exchange for those insights I'll write a good story. Local journalism is a two-way thing. They help me and I help them.

At five I get an email from Sebastian, who's sitting all of two metres to my left. This is normal in Sweden. Minimal real-life interaction is the norm. You see a person leave their apartment in the morning and you make damn sure you dash back into yours. Better to be two minutes late for work than to have to exchange coffee-breath small talk that neither of you wants. But Sebastian's also emailing me because he knows my aids are out. And I'm grateful to him for that.

The email details a meeting with the victim's ex-wife, Annika, tomorrow at 10am in Visberg. He links the address and her details. She's still using her late ex-husband's surname, Persson. I reply, 'Thanks.' I'm still not used to this – being able to ask people to do things for me. The 'Deputy Editor' title will take a while for me to grow accustomed to.

At six I head home. Noora texts to ask if she can come over at seven and I reply, 'Can't wait.' And it's true, I can't. She's one of the best things in my life right now. I made a conscious decision to move back to Toytown and that feels good. This isn't an accident or an imposition. I want to be here this time.

I get home and shower. When I open the door to my new balcony the smells of autumn pour into my apartment. That earthy scent. I'm not keen on these smells in a forest or valley, but here in my apartment block – concrete and electric light all around, door locked, roof over my head – I'm fine with it.

I pull on a white cotton dressing gown. Tie the belt loosely.

A knock on the door.

I open.

She steps forward and kisses me on the side of my mouth. Her hair smells of coconut. She looks at my dressing gown and then at what I've arranged on the kitchen table.

'Cheese?' she says.

'Cheeseboard deluxe,' I say.

We step over to the table and I take water biscuits from the cupboard and put them down next to a brick of parmesan. I can't cook but I can still prepare a delicious feast.

'Muffallo Bozzarella?' she says, pointing to a creamy Burrata topped by a drizzle of nutty olive oil and a sprinkle of sea salt crystals.

I smile. A stupid in-joke.

She pinches the end of my dressing gown belt between her fingers.

I lean in closer.

Her breath on my neck. The fine fuzz of her cheek against my chin. The scent of her.

I sense her sigh. A good sigh. And I kiss her. My teeth dragging gently on her lower lip, as gently as anything could ever drag. A glance of her tongue.

We step away from the kitchen table as one.

The pressure of her hipbone against mine. She slowly pulls my dressing-gown belt and the gown opens. She doesn't pull it apart. She kisses the skin beneath my earlobe. Her breath warm against me. She puts her hands on my waist and I push my fingers into her hair.

We lock tighter and tighter together. The room is hot. My lips caressing down the perfect slope of her neck. Her hand inside my gown. The pressure of her palm at my waist.

A door slams nearby.

Noora and I look up.

Nothing.

Just the draught from an open window.

We kiss harder, and move to the bed, and fall on each other. But then another bang, one from outside my own apartment door.

We disengage.

'I'll just check,' says Noora, standing up. Her face back to police mode.

I wrap my gown's belt tight around myself.

Noora looks through the security lens, then opens the door.

There's a young boy sitting alone on the building stairs.

The boy from the flat next door.

He's holding a tartan sausage dog the size of a courgette.

Noora and I step out.

'You okay, kid?' asks Noora.

I sit next to him as Noora looks around for his parents.

'I'm Tuva,' I say.

He looks at me with huge brown eyes.

'Nice dog. What's your name?'

'My name is Dan.'

'You live there, Dan?' I point to the door in front of us. 'Next to me?'

He nods his head.

'Your mum or dad home?'

'Mum's at the shops. She's angry.'

Noora knocks on the door but nobody answers.

'How old are you, Dan?' she asks.

He answers her but he's looking at me.

'Seven.'

'Do you like cheese, Dan?' I ask.

He shakes his head and makes a disgusted face and Noora and I both smile.

'Come inside if you like. You can wait for your mum with us.'

'Mum's angry now,' he says.

'I'm sure she's not angry with you,' I say. 'You want to come in for a bit?'

He nods and I lead him by the hand. He's exceptionally thin and his nails are long and dirty. His clothes are stained. His trousers are too short for his legs.

'I'm sure she'll be back home soon,' I say. 'You want a sandwich?'

I make him a ketchup sandwich because that's what he wants. Excellent choice, kiddo.

Noora passes a note under little Dan's door.

Three hours later his mum still hasn't returned.

Dan's watching *Aladdin.* Noora takes me aside, 'I should contact child welfare.'

I let out a big sigh. 'Can that wait for a bit? Just in case this is a one-off? Let's give her the benefit of the doubt this one time. Give her another hour.'

Forty minutes later Dan's mother returns with no shopping bags.

We intercept her outside her door and tell her we found Dan, gave him a sandwich and a glass of milk, then a banana. He's watched *Aladdin.* He's tired.

She looks at us both and I have rarely seen so many emotions flash in one pair of eyes: gratitude, relief, fury, angst, confusion, fear. She nods and mutters something, 'thank you', I think, and takes him into her flat.

When I wake at seven Noora's already showered and dressed in her uniform. She's checking her phone.

'You okay?'

'Results back from the autopsy,' she says. 'Sorry, sorry, you don't need to hear this on an empty stomach. I'll make coffee.'

I sit up and rub my eyes. 'Tell me.'

'It's not for the newspaper though, Tuva. Not yet. This is strictly off the record.'

'Understood.'

'The decapitation of Arne Persson. The evidence suggests,' she pauses, looking at me, 'that the victim's head was severed by a chainsaw.'

10

The drive to Visberg takes over an hour on account of a lumber wagon picking up felled pine trunks close to the sewage works.

I'm lost in thought. The awful facts as presented to me a few hours ago by Noora. The chainsaw theory. And now the realness of me talking to the victim's ex-wife. It never gets easier. I try to prepare, to be mindful of what she must be processing right now. Shock morphing into disbelief morphing into acceptance and loss. I tap into my memories of when Dad died. Me, a fourteen year-old. An only child. Being told by a policewoman that my father had been killed in a head-on collision with an elk. The impact that had on Mum. The impact it still has on me to this day.

My truck begins the ascent. Gradual at first, almost imperceptible. I pass Svensson's Saws & Axes and its sign says 'Out felling! Back in 10'.

The road winds higher and higher.

There's a tractor up ahead with a special attachment you probably wouldn't see in many other corners of the world. The tractor is stabbing down sharp orange poles into the soft earth either side of the asphalt. Like slalom ski poles. Orange sticks with reflector stripes to stop people like me driving straight into an icy ditch when the white months arrive. Which they will. Soon.

Higher. No fog today but low clouds sit over the town like a malevolent breath from above.

There aren't any vehicles close to where I parked that night. Just the white bike. That ghostly memorial to an anonymous fallen cyclist. A pedal bike spray-painted white and left on the side of the road for all eternity. A reminder to us all. A vision so stark we take a moment. Lose a breath. Rethink our priorities.

I pass a bus shelter with two teenage girls sitting side by side, each one wearing a bobble hat. Yellow and blue. I pass a cross on the opposite side of the road. Another memorial. With fresh flowers and a slice of pizza ejected from some truck window I don't know when.

Visberg square is empty.

Apple trees creaking, an unoccupied bandstand, that giant bee rotating on top of Hive self-storage. The pizzeria owner is taking a crate of fresh tomatoes from a guy in a van. There's a mobility scooter parked outside the pharmacy, small dog attached. But no pedestrians.

I drive on past Konsum and beyond the square. A barber shop with two chairs and two cylindrical glass jars full of bright-blue barbicide; the black combs inside like coral from some deep-sea trench. Two barbers, one in each chair. Zero customers. Two copies of the *Gavrik Posten.*

My GPS tells me I have reached my destination. Or rather, 'Your destination, you have reached,' because I downloaded a new Yoda SatNav package.

Number 36.

Grey-painted door. Grey-painted house.

I knock and the door immediately flies open.

'Are you Tuva?'

Blonde woman, hair almost as fine as mine. Narrow shoulders, a large beauty spot above her upper lip. Tired eyes. A pained smile.

'Yes, Mrs Persson. I'm so sorry for your loss.'

'Come inside off the street.'

She's wearing Nike Air Jordans. Either originals from the '80s or reissues.

'Coffee?'

'Please.'

We sit down at her kitchen table. Four chairs. A rubber polka-dot cloth. Thermos. Plate of digestives.

'Your colleague said you wanted a few words for the newspaper,' she says. 'About Arne.'

She puts her palm to her eyes. No sobbing or appreciable tears, but she is hiding her gaze and holding tight on the side of the table.

'If you feel up to it. I wanted to give you a chance to say a few things. To remember Arne to the town.'

She nods, her palm still clamped to her face. Then she removes it and says, 'I'm sorry.' She smiles a broad, beautiful smile and says, 'We weren't even married anymore.' Her smile breaks out into a stunted laugh. 'But I still loved him. That doesn't go away so easily.'

I take out my Dictaphone.

'I'm deaf, you see. I don't want to mishear your words.'

'Of course.'

'Arne took up walking in the boar forests earlier this year. He wanted to get fit, even though he's been pretty fit all his life. Soccer and plumbing.' She looks at me. 'That's why he was in Visberg forest that day. On that steep hillside.'

'What do you think happened, Annika. I mean, do you have any theories? Did Arne have any enemies you know of?'

She looks up at the ceiling. 'I've told the police all I know.' She looks at me again. 'He had scuffles and scraps in the past. He spoke his mind, you see, didn't back down from an argument. But most people liked Arne. He helped people out if they were in a fix. Generous with the money he had. Always very generous with his tenants and friends. He'd help out if he could.'

'Did he have any fights or arguments recently?'

She sips her coffee.

'Not recently that I know of, but we haven't been speaking regularly. The divorce only went through last year.' She glances out the window. 'Arne never got on with Dr Edlund, the town dentist. They played off in a charity golf competition over near Torsby a few years ago, not the Edlund's course, a public one. Sven was there in his plus fours with his 50,000-kronor clubs, each one monogrammed. All the latest gear. He's part owner of the local private course, see. And Arne beat him with his father's old bag of clubs. Wooden things and old broken tees.' She chuckles and a tear appears on her lid. 'Sven Edlund never lived it down.'

'Any other run-ins? Any rivalries or bad blood?'

She pours us both more coffee.

'It's probably nothing.'

I stay silent. One of Lena's tricks.

'He's had an ongoing issue with Hans Wimmer, the German clockmaker on the square.' Hans is Austrian, but I let that go. 'Arne inherited an old pocket watch from his father. It was a Longines. Over a hundred years old. Not terribly valuable but it was his prized possession. Anyway, Arne took it to Hans for a service because it had stopped working. Hans Wimmer told Arne it was a fake, a re-dial or something, the parts had been messed around with, probably fifty years ago. Not original. Arne took that as a slur on his father's legacy. They never spoke again after that.'

'Thank you, Annika. Is there anything else? Any other detail?'

'I don't know if I should say.'

I wait.

'I heard he had a thing with a woman in the town, after we were divorced, I'm certain he was faithful when we were married.'

'Go on.'

'I never found out who the woman was. But it ended badly, that's what I was told.'

'Who told you?'

She shakes her head. 'I'd rather not say. Doesn't matter who.'

'You have any idea who he was seeing?'

'Well, I was talking to Sheriff Hansson about this, not about her exactly. But I do find it odd that the killer stole Arne's wedding ring.'

I did not know this. I sip the coffee and try to look like I did.

'I mean,' says Annika. 'I know it's strange that he still wore it after we divorced, but really it has no financial value whatsoever, so why would the killer take it off his finger?'

'Are you sure he was wearing the ring?'

'He always wore it,' she says. 'Sheriff reckons his finger was scratched up, pressure marks from someone pulling it over his knuckles.'

She squeezes her eyes together and wrinkles up her face.

'That's terrible.'

'And people round here will try to point the finger at Luka Kodro, the restaurant owner, but they're just narrow-minded.'

'Why would they point a finger at Luka?'

She frowns and swallows hard and says, 'Luka and I…' she pauses. 'We had an affair a few years ago. I'm not proud of it, but it happened. We broke it off after a couple of weeks. We told our partners. Arne couldn't accept it, despite the fact he was no angel, always had an eye for the ladies. Luka's wife did accept it, I suppose. But Luka wouldn't hurt a fly, he'd have no reason to do something horrendous like that to Arne.'

We finish up the interview and she shows me to the door.

'Thanks again for the coffee and for talking to—'

'I still loved him, you see,' she says. 'Arne was a good man, really. Better than I ever deserved. It didn't work out between us but I still loved him.'

I leave my Hilux where it is and walk over to the Hive self-storage building. Its door is propped open with a black cinder block.

I peer in.

An apple drops to the ground behind me with a thud.

'Anyone here?' I ask.

The guy from yesterday approaches slowly.

'How can I help?'

Emil Eriksson is a whole head shorter than me. Thick bushy moustache that doesn't quite fit his face. Side parting. Plimsolls. A candy bracelet on his wrist.

'I wanted to introduce myself. I'm Tuva…'

'Who's this, Emil?'

A woman strides in wearing a fitted maroon dress and high heels.

Emil looks at me then back to her.

'I'm Tuva Moodyson. My newspaper over in Gavrik just merged with the *Visberg Tidningen* so I'll be covering the town news from now on. I wanted to introduce myself.'

'Taking Ragnar's job more like it,' she says. 'Ragnar Falk, smells of talc.'

I frown. 'No, it was more like he sold—'

'I'm just having a laugh. The name's Margareta Eriksson, pleased to meet you. This is my son, Emil. Say hello, Emil.'

Emil says, 'Hello, I'm Emil.'

No shit, Emil.

'We've owned the Hive since 1989. My late husband found this fascinating historical property,' she looks around her, 'advertised in Dagens Industri. We're proud to say we're the leading independent self-storage business in all of Värmland.'

'Are you here about the dead plumber?' asks Emil, looking up at me.

'Ah, yes,' says his mother. 'Of course you are. I'm sleeping with a carving knife under my pillow from now on. Can't take any chances.'

'I'm just introducing myself to the town,' I say.

'They cut off his head and his hands,' says Emil, adjusting his bracelet. 'With a chainsaw. No prints, you see. No way to identify Arne with no hands or head.'

I frown again and say, 'But Arne has been identified.' I want to explain that the hands were not removed, but I'm in no position to divulge those details. That's police business. Maybe if his hands had been cut off he wouldn't have been identified so quickly.

'Killer underestimated the Feds,' says Emil. 'That's what I'm trying to tell you.'

'Would you like to run a story on us?' asks Margareta. 'A feature, perhaps? Ragnar Falk smells of talc always despised us. Never so much as let us in the paper unless it was a paid-for advert. Would you like a feature? An exclusive story?'

'What about?'

She turns on the spot and spreads her arms and bellows, 'What about? Just look at this place, the stories in these walls. Centuries of history. The things I could tell you, Tuva.'

'Always happy to listen,' I say. 'Once we've got to the bottom of the murder on Visberg hill I'd love to chat.'

I hear the theme tune to *Cheers* in the distance.

She points at my face and says, 'That's more like it! Now I must go and open up a unit for a customer. Emil, show Tuva out, please.'

Margareta smiles and totters off with a set of keys in her hand.

I head for the door and say, 'Nice to meet you, Emil,' but he rushes past me and stands in my way, his small frame silhouetted in the doorframe, the whiskers of his full moustache backlit by the light from the street.

He starts to remove the candy bracelet from his wrist.

'Please,' he says, offering it to me.

'No, thank you.'

He's still blocking the door.

'Please, it's a custom here. Everyone gets one.'

I take the candy bracelet. The individual candies are coloured pastel pink and blue and green. There's fluff stuck to them.

He moves aside.

As I pass by Emil to leave he raises his fingertips up under the shadow of his moustache and sniffs them.

11

I head outside into the sunshine.

The Hive is so long it covers one side of the square. A whole block, I guess. Like a shit version of Harrods or Macy's. With my back to the yellow-and-black building I can see the dark side of the street to my left, the sunny side to my right, the descent straight ahead of me. I walk toward the dark side of the square.

Margareta's unlocking a large drive-in self-storage unit on the far side of the Hive. I wave and she looks away.

I deposit Emil's candy bracelet in a bin.

The breeze is cool on my skin. I cross and stand outside the Visberg dental surgery. The window has a large cardboard sign inside, taped to the glass. It reads, 'No Refunds.'

I open the door.

A reception desk with a woman sitting behind it reading a book. A fish tank. Two leather-clad benches. Two mannequins posed as if they're reading magazines, the faded periodicals taped to their plastic hands. A coffee table stacked with copies of the *Visberg Tidningen* and *Dam* magazine. A kid's play area consisting of a wooden box stuffed full with mangled dolls in various states of undress.

'Good morning,' says the receptionist.

'Hi, I'm Tuva Moodyson. Eleven o'clock with Dr Edlund.'

She smiles and puts down her copy of *Anna Karenina*.

'Let me just find your appointment.'

She puts on a pair of glasses and uses the computer. Her name badge says 'Julia Beck'. She's around my age, maybe a few years older, maybe thirty. Red hair's up in a messy ponytail that suits her. Freckles. A relaxed demeanour.

'Eleven o'clock it is. Take a seat, Tuva, and if you could fill out one of these please.'

She hands me a form on a clipboard with pen attached.

I sit down next to a mannequin and look at the receptionist.

Julia Beck smiles and says, 'Susan and Linda are here to put people at ease.'

Well, Julia, that ain't working.

I complete the form and hand it back to her.

'You live in the big city?' she says, checking my address on the form.

'No, just in Gavrik.'

'The big city,' she says.

'Small town.'

'Oh, you're too modest.'

'Are you from here, Julia?'

'Born and raised on this here mountain,' she says.

'Sorry about the awful news.'

Julia's eyes open wide. 'What's happened now?'

'No, I mean the murder. In the forest.'

'Oh,' she looks relieved. 'That. Yes, terrible. My neighbour's installing CCTV. Even thinking about buying a Rottweiler pup.'

She says something else but it's a mumble and her mouth's covered with the clipboard, so I say, 'Sorry, I'm deaf. What did you say?'

'I said I could tell you one or two things about this town. I could…'

'Tuva Moodyson,' booms a deep, clipped voice from deeper inside the building.

'Dr Edlund will see you now,' says Julia.

I walk through the doorway and along a corridor. Four closed doors and one open one.

He says, 'Come in and take a seat' without even looking at me.

Sven Edlund dresses like a wealthy aristocrat. Short, neat hair. Black with some grey. Dark red trousers, a tweed waistcoat, a tie with a deer-head insignia. He's wearing a monogrammed pinkie ring and tortoiseshell glasses.

I sit back in the dentist's chair and he pulls on a white coat and a face mask.

'Lie down and open your mouth as wide as you can.'

No small talk with this guy.

'Not that wide,' he says.

I close my mouth a little.

His face is on mine. His coffee breath filtering through his mask. He says something but I can't hear and I can't read him through the mask.

I make a noise like, 'Eh?'

He looks irritated. 'When was the last time you visited a dentist?'

'About a year ago,' I say. 'I'm deaf so it's hard for me to hear you.'

Hard to talk as well with my mouth wide open.

'I'm not interested in your ears,' he says, standing straight, pulling down his mask. 'Only your teeth.'

Thanks for clarifying, dickhead.

'X-rays.'

He asks Tobias, the dental hygienist, to complete the X-rays because apparently the dental nurse is off sick having eaten some bad mushrooms. It's that time of year, I guess.

The hygienist is clean-cut with a nice jaw. His breath is minty fresh.

'Bite down on this, please.'

He inserts something between my teeth and then he retreats behind the safety of a lead screen. The machine beeps. He repeats the procedure.

'Awful news,' I say, once my mouth is empty. 'The body, I mean.'

He shakes his head. 'Last thing this town needed. You hear about this kind of crime in New York or Cape Town. But not Visberg. My girlfriend wants me to add extra locks to her doors. She's even talking about a reinforced steel door.'

'Can never be too careful,' I say.

Dr Edlund comes back into the room and Tobias leaves.

'You've lost part of a filling, I'll repair that today. And you need root-canal surgery on your lower-right back molar. The one before the wisdom tooth. It'll take two separate appointments.'

'Will it hurt?' I ask.

'There will be some discomfort,' he says.

He gets to work on the filling. Injecting my gums with local anaesthetic. He doesn't have a sensitive touch – feels like he's rushing to get me out of his surgery so he can play a round of golf with his cousins. Scraping. Probing. I look around the room. Computer with keyboard, covered in a fitted transparent-plastic protector. Nobody wants blood and plaque on their spacebar, do they? A digital SLR camera with flash. He sucks my mouth dry with that tube thing. And then the drill starts up. I should have put my volume down before this all started. The drill whine, that high-pitched squeal, is a bad sound for me. I feel the drilling in my mouth but the noise of it is even worse. He builds up the filling and gets me to bite on it, then grinds it down and asks me to spit.

The chair goes back to upright position.

'Make an appointment at reception for the root-canal procedure.'

'Thank you. Mr, Edlund, can I ask you a few quick questions.'

'It's Dr Edlund.'

'Sorry, of course. Dr Edlund, do you hunt the forests on Visberg hill?'

He bites his lip. 'Of course. My family have hunted these woods for three hundred years.'

He removes his white jacket.

'I need to ask – as your family have been in the town for centuries and you're an elder figure – do you know who might have killed Arne Persson? Could that have been an elk or boar-hunt accident?'

He looks over at the wall beside the computer. Two certificates. Some kind of dental qualification. One says 'Sven Edlund', the other says, 'Eva Edlund'.

'Your wife?'

He clears his throat. 'Yes, but Eva doesn't practice. She's too busy with her charities and so on. The Edlund foundation. No, no. I don't think the death was attributable to the hunt in any way. Possibly a transient. Two berry pickers fighting over their patch. I heard they use machetes to cut through the undergrowth, imagine that, machetes in Sweden! Could have been mushroom pickers, even; we have Eastern Europeans working around these parts. Some even ask for work at our golf club.'

'But why Arne Persson, and why in such a gruesome manner?'

'There's no rhyme or reason with those kinds of people. Now if you'll excuse me, I have a meeting.'

He picks up a golf glove and leaves the room.

I rub my jaw. There's some numbness on one side but it's not too severe.

I make an appointment with Julia for the root-canal work, and she tells me she'll book me in with Tobias for a deep clean. I agree because I'd quite like extremely clean teeth, and also I need to grill as many locals as I can and this is as good a way as any.

I pay and walk out past the mannequins and into the town square.

A kid wearing a Batman cape picks up an old apple and throws it at a motorbike. The apple explodes on impact, juice and pith covering the seat of the bike.

I pass the old newspaper office and check in on the pop-up shop.

One mask displayed in the window.

Candles lit within, but no electric lights.

I open the door.

It squeaks on its hinges and I have to heave to get it open. Like the door is too big for the frame. Cool inside. At the rear of the room are two shadowy figures. Their chins and the undersides of their noses are lit by flickering candles.

'Close the door, girl,' says a familiar voice.

12

I close the door behind me.

Cornelia and Alice Sorlie have opened a pop-up shop?

'Keep the heat in, girl.'

'I had no idea you were in Visberg,' I say.

'Ain't permanent, is it, Alice.'

The quiet one shakes her head.

'Poppin' up shop, ain't it, Alice.'

'Pop,' says Alice. 'Pop-up.'

'It's good to see you both.'

Alice just snorts at that and the candles flicker in her snort-breeze.

I walk further inside. The trolls are displayed on mounts and columns and stands like prize orchids in a fancy Stockholm florist. There's a troll here perched on a black shelf. It's as tall as a newborn baby, if a newborn baby was to suddenly stand bolt upright. Possessed by a demon, perhaps. Controlled and consumed by a dark force. I can't see the troll's features clearly in this murk but it looks slightly different to the others I've come across before, all of them carved by these sisters.

'Special,' says Cornelia, the talking one. 'We don't pre-carve specials as a rule but we do some for this week. Always sell out in Visberg last week of October.'

Alice nods and I see she's completely bald now. She used to have patchy home-cut hair but now she's shaved, apart from the left hand side of her head where she has some kind of ponytail sticking out at an angle. No hairband required, the hair is as stiff as wire cable.

'That special's got some real good skin, ain't it, Alice.'

Alice puts her hand to her own neck.

I step closer to the troll. Its eyes are at exactly my eye-level. One glass eye, either from a doll or else a reused glass eye. The second eye is smaller. It's more animal.

'The right eye?' I ask.

Alice smiles broadly, showing me her missing teeth.

'Glass,' says Cornelia. 'From Belarus. Pre-war.'

'The other eye.'

'Utgard weasel,' says Cornelia. 'Snared it myself. Only had one decent eye, more's the pity. Still, it cooked down well enough. That special looks a bit ratty but someone will want it in this town, mark my words. Rattier the better for hill folk. Alice lacquered it beautiful with birch resin and pike fat. Should last them generations.'

The weasel eye has a sheen to it, like a varnished painting. The eye looks too small for its pine socket.

In hill town, in this dark and unsigned shop, with these two, the smell of animal decay and sawdust, I feel like I'm surrounded.

'How many are here?' I ask, looking around into the shadows.

'Twenty-nine, including Alice,' says Cornelia.

'Including Alice?' I say.

Alice nods but she does not smile.

The troll in front of me has human hair on its carved pine fingers. Each digit ends with a human fingernail, half moon and all. It has big, rubbery lips.

'Lips? I ask.

'No touching, girl,' says Cornelia. 'You touch it, you buys it.'

I turn on the torch function of my phone and almost fall back into a troll stand.

This one has oversize teeth behind its fleshy lips. Yellow teeth with chips and dark metal fillings. Teeth with plaque. Gums?

'Gums?' I ask.

'Window putty,' says Cornelia. 'If it keeps your window glass in, it'll keep his gnashers in, won't it, Alice.'

Alice bares her teeth at me. She has only three left from what I can tell, one on top and two on the bottom.

'You get the teeth from the Edlund surgery down the road?' I ask.

'Don't be stupid, girl,' says Cornelia, the talking one. 'Those days are long gone. These are all from overseas, we get them by the gram.'

'Teeth,' says Alice, nodding.

When I shine my torch around I see other trolls in various positions. These 'specials' are usually made to order. They're hugely expensive. One has four legs and is cocking one of them like a dog taking a pee.

'No price tags?'

'If you gotta ask the price then you ain't a troll person, truth be told,' says Cornelia. 'Hill folk wander in here. They see one of Alice's trolls they set their little hearts on and they buys it. Cash only. We got masks if they can't afford one of the specials.'

Alice covers her face with her hands and then spreads her fingers so I can see her eyes.

Some of the trolls have hair sticking out of their noses. Hair so long it brushes past their mouths. Some are bald, polished pine, like an oak ball on top of a stair spindle. Some have thick, matted hair. Others have painted hair, like black treacle poured over a polo ball.

'Look,' says Cornelia, walking over to me.

She hands me a mask and one of the candles in the shop dies. Its wick splutters and the smoke rises vertically up to the dark ceiling above.

'What is it?'

'Mask,' says Alice.

It feels like leather or hide. Animal skin where the flesh beneath wasn't removed properly and it's still there in clumps. Rotting meat and sinew. The mask I'm holding has two eye holes and a fringe of black and white fur.

'Badger?' I ask.

'Badger hair and boar hide,' says Cornelia. 'You need a mask for the big night, girl?'

'What do you know about Pan Night?' I ask.

Alice shudders and grimaces.

'I know we ain't welcome after dark, none of us are except hill folk.' She points to the trolls in the room. 'It's not our thing. We're usually here selling till dusk then head back to Utgard, aint it, Alice.'

'Home,' says Alice.

'Any idea who killed the man in the forest? Why they took his head?'

Alice narrows her eyes.

'Alice saw a young man with a saw late last night, didn't you Alice,' says Cornelia.

Alice keeps her eyes narrow and nods slowly.

'Have you told the police?' I ask.

'What do you think?' says Cornelia. 'Course we told 'em. Man with a saw ain't uncommon though, not in these parts.'

'Did you see what he looked like Alice?'

Alice scowls and waves her hand in the air like she doesn't want to discuss it.

'They found a shell casing, that's what we heard from a hill man,' says Cornelia. 'Shell casing out in Visberg woods. Decent calibre, kind to put you down and keep you down. So Björn will find the killer soon enough, I reckon.'

'Do you think Pan Night and the murder in Visberg forest are somehow connected, Cornelia?'

She looks to her sister. 'What do you say to that, Alice?'

Alice blows a raspberry.

I point to the black lightbulb-size helium balloons affixed to the trolls' pine hands.

'The black balloons?'

'Ah, they're just for the likes of you and me,' says Cornelia. 'Outsiders. Alice has seen the *real* balloons, just a glimpse, but I ain't been near them. Pan balloons, I'm talking about. You go ask the timekeeper man about them balloons, girl. You leave us be and go bother the timekeeper man.'

Alice stands up slowly and then widens her eyes.

'Go,' she says.

13

I will not let this pre-Halloween bullshit spook me. Investigating the murder of Arne Persson is the task at hand. Helping to bring his attacker to justice. Finding some closure for Annika and the others Arne left behind. Visberg locals might think I'll stay back, keep a respectful distance, leave the town to its own devices, but I won't. Push me away and I'll push back twice as hard.

Wimmer's clockshop is closed. There's a sign on the door that says, 'Timex' and then underneath is scribbled 'Closed today for private museum visit'.

When I exit the square and start my descent down the hill, I pass by Harry Hansson in his sheriff car. He nods his head like a real sheriff might do.

I drive over the disused train tracks still embedded in the asphalt. The level crossing is here, but the barriers and lights are long gone. Tammy once told me there's an old train carriage somewhere in the forest. A place where local teenagers used to congregate to flirt and smoke and escape the realities of hill town for a few hours.

The sky is the colour of an old faded tattoo. Blues stretching into mauves. Whites fading across the wrinkled horizon as the sun drags itself from east to west.

The two at the bus stop are still there. Still waiting.

Down past the cross and the white-bicycle memorial and on.

The trees either side of me contain killers. Men and women with rifles built for war. Telescopic sights and knives and fresh ammunition. Is this the future our forefathers saw coming? The execution of a hundred-thousand elk each and every autumn. Dogs and bullets. The slicing and eating of flesh. Disembowelment. Skinning. The celebration of so many deaths regulated, ordained, desired by the state.

I pull up at Svensson's Saws & Axes. It's a hut on the side of the road with a window display and car spaces for five. If the killer did in fact use a chainsaw, and he bought that chainsaw here at the base of Visberg hill, then he's a fool. But sometimes, often, some would say, they are.

There's a cardboard cut-out of a man behind the glass. He's wearing a Husqvana cap and he's wielding an axe. The thing is motorised so the axe moves up and down slowly. The cardboard guy is grinning like a child. Three chainsaws each side of him, all varying sizes. Petrol, but also a lightweight lithium-battery-powered model. I open the door and it bleeps.

'We ain't got no toilet in here,' says the man at the counter, by way of welcome.

'I don't need one.'

'Well, what do you need?'

'Maybe an axe.'

'*Maybe* an axe? You either need one or you don't need one.'

I ignore that and check out the axes. Haven't got a clue of the differences between one or another but I stand and study them.

'Splitting or felling?' he asks, moving my way, with his shoulders so far back he's bent like a boomerang.

'Splitting.'

'Wood or man-made?'

'What do you suggest?'

He sniffs and looks me up and down.

'Lightweight polymer model. Suited to a female frame.'

I pick up a wooden axe. It weighs a ton.

'How much?'

He almost smiles.

'That there is a felling axe. You gonna be felling some pine, young woman?'

'Most probably.'

His almost-smile spreads across his face.

'1,900 kronor.'

For a stick with a shard of metal at one end?

'What about your chainsaws?'

'What about them?

'You sell any recently?'

He straightens up and frowns.

'You from the special police force, young woman? That it? You a detective in plain clothes from Stockholm or someplace? Säpo, is that it? You got a badge or a warrant or whatnot?'

I step over to a chainsaw.

'I'm a reporter. Just started in Visberg and this terrible murder happens. I heard there was a chainsaw involved.'

'I'd say there was a rifle involved,' says the man. 'You hassling Benny Björnmossen in Gavrik gun store with this fancy routine of yours?'

'You bet. Do you advertise in the *Gavrik Posten*?'

'Twenty-two years.'

'Maybe I can talk to Nils and get you some kind of discount, as you've been loyal for so long.'

He smiles and scratches the underside of his bristly old chin.

'Nils wouldn't piss on a nun if she was on fire in his kitchen.'

'I'm his boss.'

The man's eyes bulge slightly and he smiles some more.

'I'm all ears, young woman.'

'Tell me everything you can.'

'Everything I can?'

'Have you heard any rumours about the victim?'

'I heard some.'

I wait.

'I don't want to talk disrespectful about the dead.'

'Any motives, then? Do you have any personal theories?'

'I don't know if I'd use a fancy word like theories about what I think. Just got the thoughts in my own head for what they're worth.'

I gesture for him to keep talking.

'I don't know,' he says. 'I gotta get started with my stocktake.'

'Do you think a chainsaw could do a thing like that?'

'Lop off a man's head, you mean?'

I nod.

'Young woman, a chainsaw can slice through a hundred-metre-tall hardwood tree like it's a stick of butter if the chain's oiled and kept sharp. A human neck ain't nothing to it.'

'You can call me Tuva.'

'Well, you can call me Lennart Alfredsson.'

'Alright, Lennart. Theories. Motives. You have any ideas?'

He steps back behind his counter and keeps his eyes on me the whole time.

'How much of a discount should I be expecting, then?'

'I'll do what I can. I'm Nils's boss now.'

'Yeah, you said already.' He grins and shakes his head. 'Bet he ain't too fond of that notion.'

'He's getting used to it.'

The man snorts.

'Edlunds,' he says.

'What about them?'

'Too much money makes your brains go soft, my old mamma used to say, God bless her soul. They got far too much of it, all of them have. Not even cash really, they got real wealth. Generations of it. Whole town stinks of dirty old money and rotten apples. Feel free to quote me on that.'

'You're not a friend of the Edlunds.'

'Friend?' he says. 'Not one of them's ever lifted an axe or a chainsaw in their lives. Too busy playing golf over at their country club in their expensive clothes. Look down on the likes of me and you. Well I don't look up at them, I can tell you now. If you don't need to work a day in your whole life you'll find trouble, mark my words, Tuva. They're riddled with affairs, infidelities, drug using, and the games they play when us working folk ain't looking...'

'Games?'

'We got a tradition this time of year, but it's not something for your newspaper. Anyway, we use it to mark the harvest, a town event. Part of Halloween, if you like. But they take it to some ugly places. Perversions, my wife used to call them. You can hear them Edlunds in the streets after dark, but like I said, none of that's for your newspaper.'

'Okay.'

'You keep it out, you hear me?'

'I said, okay.'

He wipes his nose on his sleeve.

'And then there's the Yugoslav. He doesn't hunt but he's a better shot than me or Benny Björnmossen. Some people say the policemen should go talk to the Yugoslav, have a quiet word in his ear.'

'Anyone else?'

He thinks about that.

'Only person I see park up that stretch of the big hill recently is Dr Edlund in that black wagon.'

'Sven Edlund, the dentist? I just met him.'

'Nope, I'm talking about his wife,' says Lennart. 'Makes us call her "doctor" even though she plays golf and drinks gin cocktails most days.'

I remember the black 4x4 from the night of the murder. The car that sped off.

'I'll do some more research before I decide,' I say gesturing to the axes. 'Thanks for your help.'

'Keep what I said about the town customs out of your newspaper.'

'I said I would, Lennart.'

'And watch out for the hill. Road ain't safe this time of year. We been lobbying the Kommun for decades to get it rerouted. Too many freak accidents. You watch yourself. Got a decent car, have you?'

'Brand new Hilux with stud tyres. Still got that new car smell.'

'Smart young woman. Good for you.'

I drive off and call Thord via my Bluetooth hearing aid.

'Tuvs.'

'We need to talk.'

'Don't have much time. Coffee at the hotel?' he says.

He doesn't need to specify as there's only one hotel in all of Gavrik. And Visberg doesn't have a single one.

'McDonalds in twenty. The coffee's better.'

'It's a date.'

I pass through the twin shadows cast by Gavrik's salt liquorice factory and head down Storgatan. McDonalds has been modernised since I left for the south. The tills have been replaced by giant touchscreens. When I get inside, Thord is tapping a screen with his knuckle.

'I just want two cappuccinos. It's like goddam *Minority Report* in here.'

I haven't seen the film but I understand the reference.

We sit down away from everyone else.

'You okay?' he asks.

'Not easy building trust in a new town, especially in a town like Visberg. Like I'm starting all over again.'

'Hill people,' he says.

'Is Harry Hansson a real sheriff?'

Thord almost spits out his coffee.

'I'm sorry, Tuvs.' He wipes his mouth. 'No, no, aint no such thing as a sheriff in Sweden. He's neighbourhood watch, but he takes his role real serious. Does every course he can, gets every certificate available. In actual fact, he does a good job up that hill. Chief calls him our "eyes and ears". But he's got the same powers as you or Ronnie from the bar, or my dear old mamma.'

'What's happening with the murder case?'

He sips and looks at me.

'What?' I say.

'You give me what you've obviously found out, and then I'll oblige,' he says.

Oblige?

'Rumours a chainsaw was used in the decapitation.'

'Shhh,' says Thord, looking around the room, moving closer. 'Keep your voice down.'

'Visberg locals gossip about the Bosnian pizzeria owner. Say he has previous, although not in Sweden, not for years, not in peacetime. Others say the Edlund family are extreme hunters and that the boredom created by their wealth leads them to games. Strange rituals. And then there's the Austrian clockmaker who lives closest to the scene of the crime.'

'Alright.'

'Have you found the spent shell-casing at the crime scene?'

He frowns at me.

'Have you found it?'

'Anybody mention Margareta Eriksson at all? Hive storage lady?'

'No, why?'

'No reason.'

I give him a look.

'Just that her husband died in a chainsaw incident back in 2011. Got ruled an accident at the enquiry but people talk. They weren't in a good marriage, so people said. Rumour she was having a long-running affair with a local man but nobody's saying who that was. Anyway, according to the Chief, the boy, Emil his name is, he was helping his dad lop a dead branch off some kind of beech tree. Ladder slipped. Son was apparently holding the base of it. His dad, Margareta's husband, well, he wasn't shot with a rifle but he ended up in the same state as Arne Persson.'

I make a mental note.

'Forensics? Ballistics? Physical evidence? Fibres? Anything you can share?'

'Early days, Tuvs,' says Thord, sipping his coffee. 'And don't go grilling Noora neither, she's under strict orders from the Chief to keep things to herself. He told her there needs to be a Chinese wall between the two of you when it comes to police business.'

'Why do you think I'm here talking with you?'

He grins and winks and wags his finger at me.

'Gun?' I say.

'Not recovered yet. A 6.5x55mm, or so I'm told, which is pretty standard this time of year. Shot from roughly twenty metres away in thick fog. Which suggests Arne Persson was dead for a while before he was discovered. Considerable blood loss. The…' he whispers, 'the head has still not been located.'

'His ex-wife told me he would have been out exercising in the forest.'

'Not always good for your health,' says Thord.

I widen my eyes at the gallows humour.

'I'm sorry.' He rubs his chin. 'Tough week. Listen, no fingerprints so it's possible the shooter never touched the victim. Or could be he was wearing gloves.'

I think back to Wimmer's latex watchmaker finger covers.

'Bootprints are a complete disaster. Too many, a muddy mess this time of year. Churned and then destroyed by the never-ending rain. Victim's wedding ring was taken, which suggests to me this could have been personal in some way. Not much value in that ring. We got the boys from Karlstad homicide assisting. Any major developments I'll give you the nod, if I can. Best guess, in those conditions – thick fog, elk hunt in full swing, that far away from any other town or city – I'd say it's most likely a local resident's responsible. Some kind of bad blood.'

Thord gets called away on his radio so I walk over to Tammy's food van on the far side of the ICA-Maxi parking lot.

The rear of her van now has CCTV installed. The end door has been reinforced and locks from inside. Two bolts not one. I reach the serving hatch and look in.

She's in there on her stool watching something on her iPad.

'This is a hold-up,' I say, a McFlurry ice cream in each hand.

She springs up and sticks her head out the hatch and kisses me on the cheek. 'Dessert of the gods,' she says, taking a Daim McFlurry. 'Processed-dairy full-fat goodness from pudding McHeaven.'

14

Tam switches things off and shutters up her food van. 5:10pm. Her prep is done. Twenty-minute break until she opens for dinner.

Being able to hang out with Tammy is the biggest perk of Gavrik life. Sure, the place is an epic downgrade from Malmö, especially when you factor in my new hill-town responsibilities, but she makes it all worthwhile. Her and Noora do, but in different ways. Tam and I are easy together. Always easy. Never a cross word or a strained meal. She's the kind of friend you always look forward to meeting, even if you're tired or cranky.

We hug. It should be awkward, the two of us in a car park, each holding an ice cream, but it's never awkward with Tam. It's the most natural thing in the whole world.

'Your place or mine, Tuva Moody?'

'Mine's parked over by McDonalds,' I say.

'Get in then,' she says, unlocking her Peugeot with the aftermarket bleeper she's had installed. Tammy is security conscious. Understandably.

'It's the texture,' she says, her elbows by her steering wheel. 'The creaminess. It's a whole other dimension of smooth.' She looks at me. 'And then there's the Daim pieces.'

'They do not go soft,' I say, using my own spoon-straw.

'No they do not,' she says. 'Ronald freakin' McDonald. Give that creepy old clown three Michelin stars and retire him off someplace hot for his troubles. A motherfucking Grade-A Master Chef, but does he get the recognition?'

I shake my head, a basic grin plastered on my face.

'They laud praise on the same old dudes with their foams and emulsions and soufflés. Wake the hell up and give Ronald his stars.'

'How's your new guy?'

She looks over at me with a glint in her eye. 'He a sweetie,' she says. 'Remembered our one-month anniversary.'

'That even a thing?'

'Fuck knows. It is for him. I went along with it.'

'Good of you.'

'How about you and Noora?'

'I'm happy,' I say. 'She's perfect. But it makes liaising with the police over this chainsaw beheading case a little more complicated. Boundaries and no-go subjects all over the place. When we share a day off, which is rare, or when she stays over, it's always nice, but it's also complicated.'

'Never seen you this happy. They find the head yet?'

I take a moment to digest that segue.

'Not that I'm aware of.'

'My customers have been talking about it all day. One of them bought a personal-attack alarm, keeps it on her keyring just in case. A loose head,' she says. 'How horrific is that.'

I nod and stare out the window. We're facing away from the van and the supermarket. Out onto an open field and the forest fringe beyond. The sky is darkening to granite and the top fringe of the forest looks like a ripped piece of black paper, its edge serrated.

'Police know who did it yet? Who had it in for Arne Persson?'

'Don't think so,' I say. 'I'm sure they're working hard on it. Thord tells me Karlstad homicide are in charge, but that hill, that strange little town, seems like there's no real police up there. And I used to think this place was cut-off.'

'They got money up that hill,' says Tam. 'That's the difference.'

'Some of them do. I need to develop sources. I must apply the same work ethic and the same enthusiasm as I would starting a new beat in LA or Sydney.'

'You'll do amazing.'

I punch her shoulder gently in thanks.

'Do you get counselling or whatever because you saw the corpse up close? Because of the state of it, I mean. Otherwise the trauma can catch up with you later on. You should check that with Thord.'

'No, I don't…'

'Don't dismiss it, Tuva Moody. I had sessions after Midsommar and it helped me, it really did. For weeks I couldn't go in confined spaces – lifts, even small bathrooms – or I'd have panic attacks. You go through something and you think you're fine, but sometimes you're not. Helps to talk to someone trained. Doc Stina can hook you up.'

I remember those first few weeks. Tam was not herself, she was subdued, didn't want to go out, didn't want to leave her apartment. I'm so happy she got through all that and came out the other side.

'I'll never unsee it,' I say. 'The gaping neck wound. The way his orange cap was there and then there was a space and then his severed neck. But I'm more haunted by the woman who found him. Her voice through the fog. The look in her eyes when she saw me. She's the one who needs counselling.'

'Where is she?'

'Police can't locate her. She's not a suspect but they want to talk to her again.'

'You want takeout for the team later?'

Tam knows. She remembers how Thursday is print night and Lena, Sebastian and I will be in the office till nine or ten. How Lena usually treats us all to takeout.

'Affirmative,' I say.

'I'll make sure I don't sell out of the good stuff. I'll keep some aside.'

'And crackers,' I say. 'The spicy ones, not the white ones.'

'Have I ever let you down?'

My phone rings.

I sync it and gesture an apology to Tam and answer.

'Tuva Moodyson.'

'*Hej*, Tuva. This is Hans Wimmer speaking. Hans Wimmer of Visberg Clocks and Watches.'

'Hello, Hans.'

'I noticed you approach the shop earlier when I was downstairs with a museum visitor.'

How did he know that? He wasn't in the shop? Was I on camera?

'Oh, I was just...'

'I have a proposal for you, Ms Moodyson. A bargain.'

I frown. 'I'm listening.'

'Here it is: I'll let you in if you let me out.'

'Sorry?'

He chortles to himself.

'I'll explain in person. Meet me at six-thirty when I close the shop?'

I can't say no to this kind of request. Every journalist, no matter how junior or senior, must exploit every available lead. Every source. Every 'in'. Most of my *Posten* stories are already written. I can polish them later when I get back to the office. And I can lean on Sebastian.

'On my way.'

I say bye to Tam and we hug, I mean a real tight embrace, the kind of thing friends do when they know they might not see each other for a while.

'Watch your back, Tuva,' she says.

I walk away to my Hilux and drive off up Storgatan. A man steps out of Benny Björnmossen's shop carrying a brown leather rifle-bag. It's Sven Edlund, the dentist. The rifle bag is monogrammed, his initials flash in my headlights. He climbs into the passenger side of a waiting black Audi 4x4. The Audi from the hill. The Audi that drove off.

The road darkens with every minute.

Part of me wishes I was still hanging out with Tammy in relative safety. Most of me wishes that.

My dash reads five degrees and half a tank of gas. This autumn has been unseasonably warm so far and even wetter than usual. That means two things: more mushrooms and more bloodthirsty critters.

I stop at a red light past the sewage works and there's a tree lying horizontal in the field. Looks like it's been felled. The branches have been lopped away by a chainsaw. Each one now a nub. The trunk has bleached white over the summer and the tree, after its amputations and its whitening, now resembles the ripped-out spinal cord of some mythical beast.

This Hilux came on winter tyres but I still slide on Visberg hill. It's not ice or snow, it's leaf slime. The autumn fall. Needles and leaves and fungi lying over the road like a film of sludge. Not enough traffic to shift it. This place is more wilderness than human. Like we've never really been welcome. Like we're fighting a losing battle.

Up the hill. Past the white bike, past the cross, past the now-empty bus shelter. Over the derelict train-tracks, cresting the summit. The scent of rotting apples drifts through my heating vents. The bandstand's uplit by powerful lamps hidden down by the apple-tree trunks.

I park outside Visberg's Clocks and Watches. Wimmer's there, behind the window, wearing a yellow pocket-handkerchief, removing all the plastic alarm clocks from the display, like this is a flagship Cartier boutique and they're 100,000-kronor diamond-encrusted horological works of art. Each one's worth two or three pizzas. Why remove them?

'Good, good. Excellent,' he says, opening his door. 'Shall we?'

'Shall we what?'

'The Hive,' he says. 'Self-storage. I'll explain everything.'

I see the wood-carving sisters in their pop-up shop next door as I pass. Two masks in the window now. A brown animal-skin mask with a tiny nose. From a rat? A shrew? And a white papier-mâché mask with badger-fur trim.

'Yes,' says Hans Wimmer. 'I'll explain why they're here as well. I'll explain what I can. From one outsider to another.'

Then he says something I can't pick up because he's looking away and it's dark.

'Say that again, please. I didn't catch it.'

'You should get a cochlear implant attached to your skull,' he says.

What? Screw you, clockman.

'That's none of your business,' I say.

He stops. We're outside the dental surgery now. That 'No Refunds' sign visible over Wimmer's shoulder.

'I apologise,' he says. 'My Swedish lacks nuance sometimes. I don't have the words. I should have said my niece uses a cochlear device and finds it satisfactory overall.'

'Happy for her,' I say.

He walks round the back of the Hive. There are no streetlights back there. The wind picks up.

'Just wait a minute,' I say, looking around.

He shows me his key. 'You don't trust me?'

The giant bee on the roof squeaks as it turns in the murk. A car engine revs on the other side of the square. A crack. Was that rifle fire from the forest? Shouldn't be hunting after dark. Against the rules.

'What exactly is it that you're going to show me, Hans?'

He stands there, a head taller than me, and breaks into a broad smile. His teeth glow so that's all I can see.

'It's a local thing,' he says, walking off.

I check my phone – thirty-four per cent battery. Full reception. I enter 112 but don't hit call.

Behind the Hive is another door. The sign says 'Hive Premium'.

Hans unlocks the external door. We go inside. He flicks a switch and a row of lightbulbs illuminate the corridor. Lots of other doors.

Like a prison, but painted yellow and black. He unlocks another door. A staircase. We walk up.

'Where are we going?'

I'm glad I told Lena and Seb I was heading here. I'm glad they know where I am.

'Hive Premium,' he says, looking back over his shoulder. 'Discretion guaranteed. You pay more, you get more.'

Top floor. Another locked door. We go through.

The units up here are larger. There are perhaps twelve or fifteen doors covering the whole floor, so each unit must be the size of a classroom.

'Don't tell them I brought you up here.'

'Don't tell who?'

'Anyone. Now, here's my bargain, take it or leave it. I show you inside this unit. Explain what I can about the upcoming festivities. Then you write a long and detailed article focused on my watch-making. Photographs and references, etcetera. Perhaps a series running over several papers.'

'Advertising your shop?' I ask.

He looks disappointed with that. 'I have watchmaking friends all over the world, from Switzerland to Japan to Argentina. I want them to know what I can do. For posterity, I'd like to showcase all that I have learned.'

'You let me in and I'll let you out?' I say.

'You see,' he says. 'Now you understand perfectly. Is it a bargain?'

'Sure,' I say, hungry for insights into this town, its hidden truths, something to explain why Arne Persson was killed and mutilated. 'It's a bargain.'

He unlocks unit 33.

He opens the door.

We both go through.

He flicks the switch.

Lights buzz on the walls. The room is larger than I thought. As big as two classrooms. There are hooks all over the ceiling. Metal hooks. Meat hooks. The floor is lined with sheets of brown packing-paper and the air is cold. Attached to each ceiling hook is a length of twine. The lights buzz louder. The glare pulses. There's a clock in here on the wall. Something winding. On the bottom of each length of twine is a balloon. Or, more accurately, some kind of balloon-size sack. Some are skin coloured, others are glossy black. Under each one is a red, circular stain on the brown paper. In the corner is a bench with two gas tanks and a vice.

'What the hell is this?' I ask.

The clockmaker is nowhere to be seen.

A loud click.

The lights go out.

15

I fumble with my phone in the darkness.

Think straight, Tuva.

No window in the room.

And I can't get the torch on my phone to work. I start to dial 112.

Something at my shoulder.

I jerk myself away and drop my phone. When I reach down I hit one of the hanging balloons with my head and it's softer and bigger than I expected. Reeks of dead animal.

A groan from somewhere in this building. In this room?

I get to my phone and the screen is frozen. I retreat to where I think the wall is, where I think the corner is.

The smell has intensified somehow. The balloons are decomposing.

Another loud click.

And then the lights come back on.

The balloon I head-butted is swinging back and forth, and the liquid oozing from its base has splattered an intricate pattern on the floor.

'That Margareta Eriksson,' says Hans, flustered. 'Penny-pinching so-and-so. Lights don't stay on more than a few minutes unless you rest something against the switch.'

'Do it,' I say, cancelling my emergency call. 'Rest something.'

He leans a rifle against the light switch then half turns and smiles at me. 'What do you think?'

The smell is overwhelming – like a butcher's shop on a hot day, but also aerosol cans.

'I think you need better ventilation.'

'Very true. You try telling Margareta this.'

'She knows you do…this?' I gesture to the obscene balloons, each one three or four times larger than a standard balloon. Each one irregular. Deformed.

'We pay triple price for units on this floor. Discretion guaranteed with Premium Hive storage. Only *we* have the keys, you see. No copies. No master keys.'

'We?'

'The customers. The Premium customers. You can bump into all sorts up here. People from Karlstad and Torsby. I saw a senior politician from Munkfors here one time. The nurse from the dental surgery: the young man, he keeps his medicines here. He's a prepper, that one. The Hive is better than safety-deposit boxes. More secure and less visible.'

'And you use your secure unit to…blow up balloons.'

'Come, see.' He points over to the workbench. There's a bowl of chicken breasts or turkey breasts next to the vice. 'Watch me.'

He takes a bag from his jacket pocket. He removes tiny rubber balloons. But they're not balloons, they are his watchmaker's finger gloves; single latex covers for each digit. 'Old habit,' he says.

He sinks his hand into the steel bowl and picks up a turkey breast. He pulls off membranes and veins. He manhandles it onto the end of a nozzle attached to a tube, attached to one of the gas tanks.

'What are you doing?'

Hans Wimmer pulls the turkey breast further onto the nozzle and secures the neck with a metal clamp and a knot of string.

He looks up at me and smiles and I notice he has two eye teeth growing over each other. 'Cross your fingers, Tuva.'

I don't do it.

He opens a valve and air rushes through the nozzle. The breast grows slowly in size to Dolly Parton proportions and beyond. Well beyond.

I stand back.

'This one's a moose,' he says. 'Cow moose. It can grow very large indeed before it goes bang.'

The thing enlarges. Bigger and bigger. An irregular, lumpy skin-coloured beach ball.

'What is it?'

'It's a moose bladder,' says Hans. The rest are pig and cow. For the big night.

'Pan Night?'

He ties the end of his new moose-bladder balloon and I once again question what shitty life choices led me here, to this hill town, this secret storage unit, with this Austrian watchmaker, and these dozens of inflated bladder-balloons. Which God did I disappoint? How many of them?

He uses a long stick to hang the moose bladder from a ceiling meat-hook.

'The black ones are already dry.' He points to the painted balloons. 'All pig bladders. The others are bovine, cow as you might say, and will get painted later tonight. The moose aren't for Pan Night, in fact, they're for Halloween, for a private function next week.'

'Lovely.'

'You don't approve?'

'Whatever ticks your boxes, man.'

'I was speechless when I discovered this tradition back in the mid '90s. My master watchmaker used to perform this very task for the town. He wasn't an Edlund but he was in their inner circle, he was even a non-voting member of the golf club by the end. And now all this is my responsibility.'

'Isn't it secret?' I ask.

He steps toward me and the bladders all move in the breeze he generates.

'I would use the word *discreet*,' he says. 'Nobody visits Visberg so it's not too complicated to keep it under the radar. Tonight I'll finish the elk balloons, and the spraying, and the other adaptations. All ready for tomorrow night.'

'Will I be able to attend Pan Night? As a bystander?'

He laughs and moves the rifle away from the light switch.

'The Sheriff will close down the town sometime after seven. It's been that way for centuries. Like a curfew. If you want in, and that's not what I'm recommending to you, then make sure you get here well before then. You'll need a mask, you'll need to fit into the scene, you see, and you'll need to stay hidden until proceedings begin.'

'When's that?' I ask.

'When all the little kiddies are tucked up safely in their beds,' he says, smiling. 'I can't stop you from coming, but I will warn you. It's not like Halloween. This is quite serious for many in the town.'

'I need to go buy a mask,' I say, eyeing the exit.

'Don't forget our bargain,' he says. 'I'll let you in if you let me out. A high-profile article, Tuva. In the *Gavrik Posten* newspaper.'

I nod and make my excuses and bolt down the stairs.

Outside it's dark and there's frost in the air.

The screeching of a crow on the roof mixed with the squeaking of that rotating bee sign. The tang of fermenting fruit.

I get to the sister's pop-up shop.

'Clockmaker man said you'd come back to visit us tonight, girl,' says Cornelia, opening the door. 'Clockmaker was right.' There's a single three-wick candle lighting the place and all I can see of Alice is the whites of her eyes glowing in the far corner.

'I need to buy a mask, please.'

'Think we can help with that, don't you say so, Alice.'

'Yep,' says Alice, stepping closer. She's already wearing a goddam mask, her face concealed behind paper-thin boar hide. Like a cosmetic sheet-facemask with slits for her eyes and mouth. A semi-translucent thing with a flaccid rat's nose.

She takes a more substantial mask from behind the counter and grins and hands it to her sister who hands it to me.

'That boar had a tusk the size of a mink's tail. Just one left.'

'How much?' I say, holding it. The fur, the weight of it, the animal's skin against my own.

Alice sucks air through the considerable gaps between her teeth.

Cornelia says, 'Call it a thousand. Cash only.'

'Cash? In Sweden?'

'We live by our own rules out here, girl. Take it or don't take it.'

'I'll take it. Can I drop by with the cash tomorrow?'

Cornelia looks at Alice for her decision. Alice mulls it over then looks back at Cornelia and nods.

'Your lucky day, girl. See you tomorrow.'

I throw the mask in my Hilux and cross the square. The apple trees creak in the wind and the place feels more like a forest than a built-up area. Thank God for the streetlights and the welcoming pizzeria lit up in the corner of the square. I kick cooking apples as I walk. The bandstand smells of varnish, like someone's cleaned and prepared it.

I text Lena about dinner. Ask her not to order Thai tonight after all. Tam will understand.

Visberg Grill is empty. Just Luka Kodro sitting at a table playing a game of Go with himself. There's a chessboard laid on the next table.

'Are you open?'

'Welcome, please. Do come in.'

'Takeout pizza?'

'Of course. What can we get you?'

There's another man behind the counter with an apron on.

I check my phone and read Lena's message.

'One Vegetarian.' That'll be Sebastian – my-body-is-a-temple – Cheekbones Newboy the Third. 'One Hawaiian, and one Spicy American sausage.'

'Excellent choices,' says Luka. 'Please take a seat and my chef will get right on it. Would you like a drink? It's on the house.'

There is no bar here, no alcohol, no licence, but I want a rum and Coke. Just to take the edge off my nerves. The headless man, the Hive, the sisters, that membrane of a mask. Just need a generous dose of gold rum to steady myself.

'Coke, please.'

He opens a glass bottle of Coke and gives it to me, together with an Ikea tumbler. I have the same ones in my new apartment. I remember what Annika told me about her ex-husband. The affair he had with Luka Kodro's wife.

'You play Go?' I say.

'Nineteen by nineteen board,' he says. 'I learnt in the military. I just dabble nowadays. You play?'

'Chess,' I say.

His eyebrows rise up.

'Ten-minute cooking time, ten-minute game?'

'You're on.'

I don't particularly want to play chess right now but it's a suitable cover to grill him, excuse the pun.

'How long have you been here in Visberg?'

He offers me the white side of the table.

'Since the war, 1995.'

'That must have been awful.' I move my king's pawn two places.

'It was hell on earth,' he says, mirroring my move.

'I heard you were a soldier?'

'Not by choice.'

'But you fought?'

'We all fought our own battles in our own ways. My father, my mother, my grandmother. And we all lost.' He pauses and looks up at me. 'Everyone lost.'

I move out my knight.

'Where did you live before?'

'Bosnia,' he says, smiling, looking up, moving another pawn. 'In a small town. I was training to be a schoolteacher. But then the whole world turned upside down. My neighbours, many of whom had been my parents' neighbours, their friends, suddenly became my sworn enemies. Laws disintegrated. The rules of etiquette changed more in a day than you could imagine them ever changing in a whole lifetime. Unacceptable things became acceptable. Or invisible. There was no Geneva convention in those small towns at that time, on those quiet country roads. There was no time to consider the consequences for your soul and the souls around you.'

I move out my bishop.

'Why are you here in Visberg?' he asks. 'I heard you are from Stockholm?'

'I am. I moved out here to be close to my mother.'

I don't usually open up like this but his monologue about war and souls and neighbours means nothing is off limits. Once you go there you can go anywhere.

'Good daughter,' he says, moving his queen four spaces.

'No,' I say. 'Not good. Just present.'

He looks at me for a while then nods and checks on the pizzas.

'Terrible about Arne the plumber,' he says.

I move my rook to defend against his amateur queen offensive.

'I saw the body.'

He looks at me with pain in his face. Not shock or curiosity like other people. I can tell he doesn't want a vivid description or a blow-by-blow account of the lifting of the coat. That severed neck. The blood pooled on the beech leaf.

'It's so vulnerable, no.'

I frown.

'Life. Our lifelines. We might feel strong but we can be ended in the blink of an eye. Once you see a spirit turn into flesh and bone you can never go back. It's like you have new eyes. Different eyes.

The fragility of our own existence here on this planet. The fleetingness. The way we can all be destroyed in an instant.'

He moves his queen and looks up at me.

'Check mate.'

16

I take the three pizza boxes and walk through the square to my truck. There's a black rat over by the bandstand gnawing on a hot-dog bun.

The air has a chill to it up here that we don't get down in Gavrik. Something to do with the altitude.

An old woman with a yellow headscarf is filling a cast-iron fire basket with logs. Another woman outside the Hive is doing the exact same thing. She bends up and I see she's also wearing a pale yellow headscarf.

The pizza boxes go down in the passenger side footwell. I put the blower on max to keep them warm, and use my wipers to move a fallen, sunken, half-rotten cooking apple from my windscreen. The apple falls off but I'm left with a pectin-smudge rainbow covering half the glass.

I leave hill town behind.

Over the train tracks, past the cross, past the white bike. My Hilux smells of the good things in life: grease sinking into cardboard, melted cheese, hot sausage, caramelised onions, crisp pizza-crust. One section of the scent, one distinct aroma, takes me back to Dad. I think it's the cardboard. Hot, full of pizza steam. Back when I was thirteen, in the months before he died, a pizza place opened up in our Stockholm neighbourhood. A Korean couple and their shy niece. Their thin-crust pizzas were spectacular. Dad used to pick up two on his way home from work. We'd always choose the same toppings.

I remember him smiling as he divided them up. Two triangles each of each pizza. He always wanted to eat them straight from the box but Mum would say, 'not on my watch,' and we'd eat from pre-heated plates. She never did heat a plate again after his accident. She hardly ate at all.

I reach the base of the hill and speed up.

My headlights are full beam for much of the journey because no other fool is driving around this part of moose country on the eve before Pan Night when there's a psychopathic killer still on the loose.

I round a bend and my headlights pick out a field of stationary cows. Each one glows in my halogen glare like a plump ghost hovering over the churned, chilled land. Their eyes shine back at me. A field of unmoving spirits. I can't see their legs. You wouldn't know there was anything in that field but there is. Dozens of them.

Past Svensson's Saws & Axes, and for whatever reason, now, at 8pm, there's a queue out the door. A queue of axe buyers? Or chainsaw buyers? Or is the shop owner selling something else on the side?

I hand out the pizza boxes in the office and Lena and Sebastian grunt and start eating as they type. I pull out my aids and eat and work on fixing my stories. This will be my first issue since moving back up from Malmö. My first paper with 'Deputy Editor' written in print. There's even an actual story about it. How meta is that? Lena wrote it herself. She won't let me read it until I have a copy on my desk.

After I email my stories over to Lena I say goodnight and drive home. I open my apartment door and there's a note on the floor.

'Thanks you for my Sand Witch. From Dan.'

He's even drawn a sandwich on the note although it looks more like a sponge cake. Decent kid. Shows promise.

Next morning my pillow alarm shakes me awake at seven. I pranked a boyfriend with this in London back in my student days.

He was a good person, maybe I shouldn't have done it to him, but I did. He was asleep on my pillow and I changed the setting on my alarm in the early hours of the morning without waking him. The way he jumped out of bed and rolled underneath it when the shaking started almost made me die from laughter. He thought it was an actual earthquake. I mean, he was from Tokyo so maybe I should have been a little more sensitive, but he saw the funny side after a day. Alright, a couple of days. Shake, rattle and roll, baby.

I dress in black skinnyish jeans that are getting bobbly between the thighs and a black roll-neck. I look like an apprentice burglar.

In the *Posten* I write up the story of Arne. His life. It's one of those moments where I don't feel qualified for my job. Because I never knew Arne Persson and because I only have a vague impression of the man from the interviews I've conducted. His hobbies, his school history, his ex-wife. I try to do him justice but it's not easy. And then I realise the killer hasn't been given a nickname and I'm happy about that. Means there's less focus on the perpetrator and more on the victim, and those he left behind.

Seven calls to various prosecutors, lawyers, the coroner's office, and then Karlstad Homicide. Diddly squat. Nada. Zip. This is the way it is sometimes. I find I can get more insights from a gossiping shopkeeper or kindergarten teacher or neighbour than I can from officials with knowledge. I help Sebastian rewrite a story on tick-borne diseases. Encephalitis and Lyme disease. Animals the size of a grain of rice that have the power to kill a full-grown human. He interviewed Doc Stina for the piece, and some professor from Lund university. It's a good meat-and-potatoes *Gavrik Posten* piece, but he wants help so I oblige. I suggest he also interviews someone who's recovered from Lyme disease. Get the human angle, the pain, the suffering, the recovery, the lessons learned. Less academic, more relatable. He nods and gets to work. Smart kid asking for help. Lots of guys his age, with his looks, act like they know it all pretty much from birth. Props to cheekbones.

Lena steps out and asks me what I'm doing tonight, if I fancy coming over to her place, nothing fancy, taco night and a movie?

'Thanks, wish I could, but I'm heading uphill again.'

'Tonight?'

'Oh, yeah.'

Sebastian looks over. 'Mind if I tag along? I need to get to know Visberg too.'

I look at him with his blond hair and cheekbones and broad shoulders and cupid-bow lips. 'No,' I say, and then I soften it. 'Pre-arranged meeting. Next time, yeah?'

He looks disappointed and who could blame him. He'll be stuck in Toytown with Netflix at home or else Ronnie's Bar. I happen to adore both but I don't reckon he feels the same.

I step into Lena's office and close the door.

'Pan Night,' I say.

'Peter Pan?'

'Nooooooo.'

'Deep-pan pizza?'

I scowl.

She shrugs.

'Stop messing. You heard of it?'

She nods and smiles. 'Course I have. Something to do with Halloween. Thought it ended in the '80s?'

'I'll let you know tomorrow.'

'Stay safe, you hear me.'

I give her a thumbs up and leave for the newsagent across the road. A packet of cheese doodles, a bag of wine gums, a bottle of Coke, an open meatball-sandwich. All the major food-groups covered.

As I drive further away from civilisation, the light leaches from the landscape. The sun sets over hill town in the distance. Melts into the mountain. Then a cooler, bluer light replaces it. The temperature reading on my dash falls from nine degrees to four. Visibility worsens. Drizzle. I use my wipers but there's not enough rain so they squeak like pigs getting their tails pulled off. The drizzle morphs into fog. I slow down. Past Svensson's Saws & Axes. Closed. The door bolted. I reach the base of the hill and the fog's almost as bad as it was that awful night. My engine growls as I begin the incline. Past the white-bike memorial. I get too close to it with my studded tyres and have to swerve into the middle of the road to correct my line. Past the cross; fresh flowers all around it now. I move my head forward to focus, my chin almost touching the steering wheel.

And that's when I notice the flashing blue lights.

The cop car.

The bus shelter, destroyed. Debris everywhere. The contents of a suitcase spread all over the road. An old truck down in the ditch. Smoking. It's bonnet dented.

Two body bags laid out on the asphalt.

17

The scent of diesel in the air.

I stare at the body bags.

The Sheriff saunters over to me like a cowboy in a western. Are his thumbs actually through his belt loops?

'Don't get too close, Tuva. Stay back.'

He looks flustered.

'What happened here?'

'Road-traffic accident. I'm forced to close the road so you'll have to head back I'm afraid.'

Instead of a gun or a Taser on his belt there's a row of pens, a mobile-phone holster, a small multi-function knife, and a pair of driving gloves.

'Is an ambulance on its way? The coroner?'

'Thord Pettersson's organising everything.'

I look at the body bags. Feels wrong to photograph them.

'I need to get into Visberg.'

'Not tonight, you can't.'

'Just for an hour, then I'm going on to Falun.'

'Falun?'

I nod.

He shines his torch into the cab of my Hilux.

'I'll let you get past, then. Take care of yourself in Falun. Odd people.'

Oh, sure.

'What happened here tonight?' I ask.

'Truck crashed into the bus shelter. Nobody hurt so we must count our blessings if truth be told.'

'But, what about...?' I point at the body bags.

'Chimney sections.'

I frown. Like, *what?*

'Driver had two lengths of double-insulated pipe in the back of his truck. Got people installing it this weekend onto his log-burner so he's organised someone to pick the lengths up later this evening. They're quite valuable, see. That's why they're protected.'

I let out a deep sigh of relief. 'I'll see you later.'

'Oh, no, you won't,' he says. 'Road will be closed till tomorrow now. Whole town's shut off. Only one road in and one road out. You head back on the river route when you're done in Falun. Visberg's closed for the night.'

'I can do that. Mind if I take photos of the bus shelter?'

'No harm, no foul,' says the Sheriff.

I get out and the fog is rolling down the hillside and through the pine trunks either side of the asphalt. I photograph the truck because it's a story but also I want the number plates so I can check out what exactly is going on here. I photograph the shelter. Then I carry on up the hill.

More fire baskets have been placed around the town square. The giant bee on top of the Hive is still squeaking, and a man with an extendable ladder is inspecting the streetlights. I need to find a suitable place to hide my Hilux. If I'm to blend in on Pan Night, observe, photograph, get a grip on this place, eavesdrop, then I need to keep my truck out of sight. I drive past Konsum and on towards Annika's place and see a 'Road Closed' sign in the distance. I pull a U-turn and head back the other way, between the Hive and the dental surgery. Smaller houses, some Radhus semi-detached, some detached. But nowhere I can hide this hulking pick-up truck.

The fog's thickening so I drive slow. Trundling along in the hope I'll find a distant car park or scenic picnic spot. Somewhere I can pull off the road.

There's a young woman up ahead holding two Konsum carrier bags. I wind down my window.

'Excuse me, can I ask…'

'Hello again,' she says.

'Sorry? I…'

'It's Julia.' She smiles a goofy smile. 'From the dentist? I checked you in.'

'Sorry,' I say again, tapping my head. 'I'm terrible with faces.' Actually I'm great with faces but she's wearing a large orange hat and I've only ever seen her for ten minutes. 'Is there someplace round here I can park?'

'Not tonight. Town's closed. You should leave as soon as you can.'

'Just for an hour, then I'm heading onto Falun.'

'Oh, that's okay then, I guess. I thought you meant for the whole night. For an hour, sure, you can use my garage if you like.'

That's not going to work but at least it'll buy me some time. I can ask her for more locations.

'That would be great.'

So she jumps in my truck. I was not expecting that, I was expecting an address or a number. We drive away together.

'Nice van,' she says, and then she puts on a Southern US accent. '*Fancy*.'

'Where do you live?'

'Just over there.'

We drive for literally three minutes to her house. I'd say something acidic about it but she's helping me out so I swallow it down.

'It's Friday night and I never get to meet new people here,' she says. 'Quick drink before you drive off to Falun? What do you need to do in your hour here?'

What do I answer? What do I need to do? 'A drink sounds fantastic if you don't mind.'

Her eyes light up like there's not many people her age in this town who want to drink with her. I'll break my rule. Since returning to Gavrik I've only drunk on weekends. That method has worked out pretty well. I tried the same thing in London years ago and one time I started drinking on Saturday lunchtime and powered through till early Wednesday morning. That was quite a weekend.

She unlocks her front door and I notice she's wearing a candy bracelet like the one Emil tried to give me. We go in.

It's a bombsite. Clothes on the floor, food all over the table, carrier bags in the kitchen sink. Good for her. I'm instantly at peace in this place. She's even messier than I am.

'Martini or bag-in-box wine or a beer or…' she inspects a bottle from behind her toaster, 'bourbon?'

'Mixers?'

She empties her Konsum carrier bags in front of me. Biscuits, tampons, Coke, milk, sliced ham, coffee granules, carrots. My kind of shopper.

'Coke alright?'

'Whisky and Coke. Just a single as I'm driving later,' I lie. 'Thank you.'

'Anytime. I need a double, what with the week I've had and the night ahead, I need a strong frickin' beverage.'

She mixes the drinks and I make some space for myself on the sofa.

Julia brings over a bag of Cool Ranch Doritos and the pack of ham. She doesn't decant into a fine porcelain bowl. She tears the crisp packet open and displays it on the table. She peels back the ham wrapper.

I look around and say, 'Nice place you have here,' and then we both burst out laughing and honestly I needed this. There could be a killer in this town, eating takeout crayfish pizza or buying condoms in the pharmacy right now. Not just a killer, but a person capable of beheading another human being. Taking that lifeless head away for God-knows-what purpose. So sitting here with this relaxed redhead receptionist drinking lukewarm whisky and Coke is a relief.

'I understand you have to get away,' she says. 'I know you're important around here.'

'Important?'

'Reporter and all that. Newspaper writer. Everyone in town's talking about you. My boss is talking about you constantly.'

'Sven Edlund?'

'No, his wife, Dr Eva. She runs the place really. Runs him.'

'Haven't even met her,' I say.

'And yet she knows all about you, Tuva. Watch out for that one.'

I take another sip. It's delicious.

'What are they like? The Edlund family.'

'Rich as fuck,' she says. 'Eva's got one of these on her shoulder.' Julia holds up a Dorito.

'A crisp?'

'A massive chip. It's because she hasn't practiced dentistry, you see. All that time getting good grades, all that money spent going to medical school, and she's never actually practiced.'

'Why not?'

'Four kids and a golf club, I guess,' says Julia. 'Except it's more like a country club really. They only had the kids because it's a status symbol among the Edlunds, that's what I reckon, anyhow. They're a different breed to you and me. Money for life, from the moment they're born. Lots of them have three or four or even five kids. Show them off like diamonds or sports cars.'

'Did Eva Edlund know the dead plumber?'

She almost spits out her whisky. 'Dr Eva know Arne? Are you kidding me?'

'No.'

'You don't know?' she moves in closer. 'Arne Persson installed all the sprinkler systems and plumbing at the golf club a few years back. Lots of underground piping, I heard. Only it never worked properly. It wasn't the money that pissed off Dr Eva and Sven, it was all the gossip. Other Edlunds said they'd gone for a cheap option. Started gossiping that the dental surgery wasn't making money, that they'd employed a shoddy workman.'

'Bet Eva didn't like that.'

Julia folds a piece of ham and inserts it into her mouth. She's pretty in a way. Redhead, freckles, broad easy smile. Her eyes dart around like she's always looking for fun.

'Dr Eva hated Arne. Not because of the money she lost, like I said. Nor the gossip, really. You see, those fairways and greens look like fields to you and me but they're her pride and joy. She was very much involved in the design process, in the landscaping. They had an Instagram account showing off the greens and bunkers, and then they had to go dig up half the course to replace piping and so on. It was a real local scandal. And then there's the rumour that she fancied him back in their schooldays, back in the dark ages, and he rejected her advances.'

She makes a face like, *I'm sure you can read between the lines here, Tuva.*

'Did Ragnar Falk cover any of this in the *Visberg Tidningen*? The golf-course problems, I mean. I'd like to read more on it.'

She bursts out laughing and a small piece of ham or saliva, I'm not sure which, flies out of her mouth.

'Ragnar wouldn't say boo to a horse.'

'Goose.'

'Wouldn't say goose to a horse?'

We both fall about laughing again like idiots, the whisky loosening our Nordic inhibitions, although I doubt Julia had many of those to begin with.

'So it wasn't in the paper?'

'Ragnar had a very respectful arrangement with the Edlunds,' she says. 'And that's why he'll be a member of the golf club by the end of the year. You mark my words. Biggest prize in all of Visberg if social climbing gets your juices flowing.'

'What about the Hive self-storage. Margareta and Emil.'

'What about them?'

'Any goss?'

'For your newspaper?'

I shrug.

'No, no,' she says, looking down at her drink and then her floorboards. 'I need to watch my mouth.'

I look at my watch. 'And I need to get going soon.'

'You really going to Falun tonight?' she says. 'Or are you here for some fun?'

I pause and reflect and then hold my hands up and smile. *Guilty.*

'I can read you like a book.'

Can you, now?

'You got here too early. Doesn't kick off until the town kids are all in bed asleep. Sometime after nine.'

'Are you going, Julia?'

She shakes her head. 'I'll put my saucepan outside the door like everyone else, but I'm not traipsing around in the cold late at night just to see my neighbours dressed up strange, walking around backwards. I'd rather trick-or-treat next week with the children and the old folk. Much more fun.'

'What is it exactly?'

'Pan Night?'

I nod.

'Better you see for yourself than I tell you. My words couldn't do it credit.' She rubs her tummy. 'You hungry? I'm cooking pasta if you fancy some?'

I nod and she gets to work, chopping shallots and portobello mushrooms and flat-leaf parsley.

'You look like a pro,' I say.

'Nigella, Jamie and Gordon taught me everything I know,' she says. 'Food is my third biggest passion.'

'Second?' I say.

'TV.'

'First?'

She looks at me with her knife in her hand and a parsley leaf affixed to her lip. 'Men.'

'You got your priorities straight,' I say.

'People say unconditional love is unrealistic. I say it's the only sort. You have a boyfriend?'

'Girlfriend,' I say.

'What's her name?'

I like that she didn't squirm or close up or say something cutesy.

'I call her "N".'

She smiles and drops pappardelle ribbons into boiling water.

'If it's Nigella then I'm officially very fucking jealous.'

Ten minutes later we're eating from large white, asymmetrical bowls. Steaming tangles of pappardelle, flat and shiny with oil. Caramelised mushroom slices, each one fried off in butter and then garlic. My pasta is hot and covered with parmesan shavings and cracked black pepper and fresh parsley. It is excellent food.

'Thanks for this, you didn't have to.'

'I'm just glad you didn't drive off to Falun. There will be nothing much to see there tonight.'

'Had to tell your local sheriff I was headed there. The road's closed. Truck crashed into a bus shelter on the hill.'

'Course it did.'

I frown at Julia.

'Last year on Pan Night, a lorry jack-knifed on the road. The year before it was an oil spill that closed it.'

She looks at me.

'They shut down the town every Pan Night?'

'They try,' she says. 'My mum used to hate this night. The way the Edlunds impose themselves on the rest of us. Take it over even more than on a normal night.'

'Did your mum move away?'

Julia looks down at her pasta and the candlelight dances over her eyelids.

'I lost her two years ago.'

'I'm sorry.'

She looks up, smiling. 'You weren't to know. No need to apologise. She wasn't in a good place. My dad left before I was born. She fell in love eventually, but it didn't work out well. She told me she loved the man despite him lying to her that he'd divorce his wife. All the usual bullshit excuses. She waited and waited and then she got sick. It was almost a relief at the end, to be honest. For her and for me.'

'I lost my mum last year,' I say. 'Just before Christmas.'

'I'm sorry to hear that,' she says. 'Dad?'

I shake my head.

'Two orphans eating Visberg-forest mushrooms on Pan Night,' I say, lifting my glass of whisky and Coke. 'To you.'

'To us.'

Julia agrees to keep my Hilux locked away in her garage for as long as I need it there. She helps me put on the mask I bought from the wood-carving sisters. I pull on a black ski hat and she checks the coast is clear before I head out the front door. She places her rinsed-out pasta saucepan by her step and looks back to me and winks and says, 'All clear.'

My mask smells of goat skin, even though the sisters told me it's boar. I adjust the eye slits and try not to let my lips touch the fleshy side of the leather.

'Thanks, Julia,' I say.

She pushes me toward the road.

'Don't let them bully you. Don't eat anything. And don't, whatever you do, do not go inside the Hive tonight.'

18

The streetlights have been covered over with rough sacks. There are slits and holes cut into the sacks so they let out some light, but it's weak and it moves around with the breeze.

Visberg town square is a dark place tonight.

The next thing I notice as I approach the side of the dental surgery is the smell. Bonfire smoke and grilled meat and rancid old apples. The air is thick with the sickly sweet smells of autumn.

I adjust my mask and walk past a fire basket and on towards the Hive. The wood spits and hisses. The bee on the roof is illuminated like it normally is, but it's spinning at least twenty times faster. I'm mesmerised as it turns. Blurry. Its squeak has sped up to a buzz. A low hum. The thing looks like it might fly off the roof at any second.

No cars around. No vehicles of any description.

I'm twenty metres from the square when I hear it.

The howls. The cackles and the chanting and the manic laughter. How many locals have gathered for this? There are three-thousand residents or so in this town. Take away the kids, and the grandparents looking after the kids, and that must leave almost a thousand souls.

I walk past empty pans. Saucepans with glass lids and cast-iron cauldrons as tall as my knee. Bowls of peeled eggs left beside some of the pans. Peeled and white and sat in clear liquid.

My vision is impeded by the fog and the wood smoke and the darkness but most of all this hog-hide mask. It smells of the wilderness. Of rotten meat.

A couple walks toward me.

A man wearing a dark business suit and a head mask made from bear. The headdress covers his head and hangs down his back; thick brown fur. His partner is blonde. Short. Her face is hidden beneath a black welders' mask. She's wearing a grey sweater and a grey miniskirt, only they're not grey anymore, they're red. She's covered herself in red paint or synthetic blood. Just a guy and a girl out for a stroll. He's pushing a pram, an old-fashioned pram with four spoked wheels. I can't see what's inside. It's completely dark. As they pass me she rubs his crotch with her hand and he lifts his bear head and grunts.

More fire baskets. I turn into the square and there are perhaps a hundred small fires, each with a healthy stack of birch logs next to it. Mist mingles with smoke. The air is heady. The atmosphere is electrified like an inner-city estate just before a riot.

Another couple approach. The woman is a backwards walker. He's facing me with a simple black sheet-mask and she's pacing in reverse, holding his hand, her brown-leather mask facing forwards, her eyes looking back; her body facing back, but her mask looking forwards. Her black balloon is small, the size of a lightbulb. It's helium-filled. Rising into the sky on a three-metre string. His is larger, like the ones Hans Wimmer showed me inside his premium storage unit. Larger than a human head and spray-painted black. Misshapen. Bulbous. It's on a short string. It bobs around as they walk. They stumble past me and I hear him mumble, 'And I shall fear no evil.'

Manic laughter from the bandstand.

Plumes of smoke rising vertically off this stunted mountain.

Shrieks of delight and pain from the locals. I get the feeling they've been waiting all year for this. For their private night. A very grown-up event they probably heard rumours of as children. Like Midsommar, this is a brief moment where they get to loosen their modern Swedish morals and shake off the twentieth century and delve back into their dark past. The middle ages. The Viking period. And beyond.

Stretching back to their animal heritage. Pre-Christian. Pre-Sweden even. A thousand savages for one night.

People are picking the rotten apples and sinking their teeth into the soft and wasp-infested fruit. A man lies under a tree dressed from head to toe in a leather sheet, stitched roughly with long staples. He writhes into the mud, into the apple slurry, and he moans.

I look into the dental-surgery window. No lights on. There are no lights in any of the shops or offices. Even Konsum is dark and locked. When the mini-supermarket is closed on a Friday night you know something is seriously wrong. My stomach is tight with unease but also adrenaline.

There's something hanging from an apple-tree branch so I walk over to investigate. Howls erupt from all around the square as more locals arrive. A drum beats in the distance, from the direction of the forests. Locals have tucked their kids into their IKEA beds and thanked their elderly parents, parents who did all this themselves back in the '80s, who know the score, and they have creeped out to gather in this dark square.

I get closer to the tree. To the thing in the tree.

It's a troll.

A carved pine figure. Humanoid with rope coiled around its timber neck. Swinging in the wood-smoke breeze, its animal tongue, maybe transplanted from a shot hare or a snared badger, falling limp from its painted pine lips. This troll is naked. I've never seen one quite like it. Scars and cuts all over its wooden torso. Its breasts are acorns complete with stalk nipples. I walk closer, my mask stinking as the moisture from my breath softens it. The hanging troll's feet are covered with troll blood. Its fleshy penis hangs low by its ankles.

A man approaches me. Does he know me? Can he see my face through this mask?

He's dressed in black leather trousers and a black T-shirt. He's wearing an oversize Mickey Mouse head. He reaches his hand out slowly. Black fingerless gloves.

I retreat. 'No…'

He places his finger up to his Mickey Mouse lips and says, 'shhh.'

And then he reaches out for me again, this time with two hands, his huge Disney eyes and Disney smile and Disney ears bearing down on me. He opens his palms and places them centimetres from my chest, so I push him. A short jab. Not sure if it's his oversize head or what, but he topples backwards onto the wet grass and starts cackling. Laughing like he's high on something.

I move away but there is no safe place here. No well-lit corner. No open store. When I've felt threatened before I've headed into a busy café, into a Burger King in London, into a well-lit street with CCTV. None of that here. Just a town square with shrouded street-lights and closed businesses. Hundreds of moaning, howling locals drifting through the fog. Pans outside doors. Bonfires and a giant spinning bee. And now the sound of a single violin.

It makes things worse. I stand beneath an apple tree, this one free of executed trolls. In the bandstand are now two violinists. They are both wearing tuxedos and black gimp masks, complete with shiny rubber balls in their mouths. They are playing violins facing each other, not out at the square. And it's not music exactly. More like high-pitched squeaks and squeals.

The statue of Adolf-Fredrik Edlund has two masks tonight; one on the man himself and one skewered onto the pointed end of the anvil. A tall woman speed-walks past me. She's wearing a thick grey-fur outfit of multiple layers. It looks like rough elk-fur, but there's a gap beneath her neck to show off her cleavage, the only human skin visible. I hear her say, 'As I walk through the valley of the shadow…' as she speeds on by.

A couple, or maybe two strangers, are kissing furiously against the next apple tree. They are groaning and scratching at each other as they rub against the rough bark of the tree trunk. Moans of pleasure and pain. I'm transfixed. It reminds me of a kiss I witnessed in a McDonald's outside Madrid one time. Two high-school kids, both around seventeen years old. A handsome boy with short black hair and a handsome girl with long black hair. The heat between them. The intensity of their kissing and their bodies. Their obvious lust. The craziness of it. The way they carried on regardless of us all. These two are the same. And then they're not. They go further. The shorter one turns around so he or she is facing the tree. The taller one howls and then they start biting at each other, moving on each other. A rhythm begins. I watch them through the fog and smoke, and then I pull my gaze away.

What is this? Shopkeepers and auditors and consultants and digger drivers. Let loose. Bringing the wild back for a night.

'Why aren't you in Falun?'

I turn on my heels. Around the other side of the tree is the stern face of Sheriff Harry Hansson.

'I'm… I'm…'

He shakes his head.

'I'm…'

He takes a deep breath. 'Well, you're here now,' he says. The Sheriff's wearing a black version of his usual outfit, but hanging off his belt is a metre-long truncheon or cosh. He has black paint all over his hands and he's carrying a large, black bladder-balloon. 'Safe word is "bee sting",' he says. 'I'll need a word with you about all this tomorrow. Don't forget. Bee sting.'

He walks off toward a pram left on its own beside a park bench.

The violinists pick up their tempo but it's still not music. Sounds like a high-note aria played backwards at high-speed. Like the shop-front windows might shatter at any moment.

This is going to make one hell of a story but I have no idea when I'll be able to tell it. Probably not until I've moved on to some big city in a few years. Maybe Stockholm with Noora. God, I hope that's in our future somehow. But right now I have to focus on the task at hand. If there's one thing I've learnt about a party atmosphere, it's that people let their guards down. Especially when costumes are involved. If I can glean anything about the grisly Arne Persson murder tonight I may be able to help save another life.

Four fire-breathers roar and exhale flames up into the night sky and the whole square illuminates. I see things I didn't notice before. The man with the horned mask sitting on a bench, masturbating. The huge, broken clock on the side of Hans Wimmer's shop isn't broken anymore. Well, I guess it is. The hands are rotating anticlockwise as fast at the bee on the Hive is spinning. Whirring. Time reversing.

A pan outside the old newspaper office has a troll in it stuck down, head first.

Two women approach each other. Each one is holding a large udder balloon, each talking in chants or tongues. They turn and offer me an egg so I take it. Soft boiled. Soaked in vinegar. A pickled egg? Feels wrong in my hand. Too flaccid. One of the women sees me hesitate and places her hand over my hand and squeezes gently so the undercooked albumen oozes between our intermeshed fingers and then the yolk bursts. Warm protein spreading over our thumbs and down our wrists. She leans in and I think she's going to kiss me. A rush of butterflies in my stomach. Moths. Small birds. But she lowers her head and licks from her hand and from my hand, and her partner howls and they scamper off into the murk.

There are lanterns in trees, and they swing in the breeze. The shadows are unreliable. This whole damn town is unreliable.

A man in a fur coat and pointed wooden clogs squats in the middle of the road and relieves himself.

The two violins screech and more people fill the square to the point where there aren't many free spaces for me to keep myself to myself. I wipe my eggy hands on the dew-dampened grass. I look around me and I am hyper-aware now. Locals are more drunk or more high. The noises mess with my hearing aids and the darkness and weirdness turns me twitchy.

A group of powerfully built men walk past and ignore me and they are all chanting, as if in church, 'The shadow of death, the shadow of death, the shadow of death.' I can see the veins and membranes of their udder balloons clearly in the bonfire light.

In the back of a parked pick-up truck there is a seething, heaving mass of naked bodies. They all have bags over their heads but they are moving to the violin noises and they are pulsating like a singular mass of pale maggots.

More wild howls and screams. Cackling. The gimp-masked violinists walk away from each other, leaving the bandstand, stepping among us. Some people sit on the grass. Calm. Masked spectators. But others are kissing, leaving in groups of two or three, heading to the open door of the Hive.

And then someone else screams.

A different tone.

Not playful.

Fearful.

Two women in animal fur and latex Elvis masks rush to the clockmaker's shop. A man in a full bearskin, complete with a saggy bear head, holds a cast-iron pan high above his head.

The violinists stop playing.

The bearskin man roars. 'Get the Sheriff!'

19

A small crowd of us runs over to Hans Wimmer's clock shop but most people just ignore the roar. They carry on groping each other, kissing, bobbing for rotten apples, and walking backwards round the square.

Twenty people circle the bearskin man and the pan. A herd of beasts.

The Sheriff comes through and people make way.

'Give me some space.'

The howling and chanting still fills the square. But the violinists are silent.

There's a huddle. Three people remove their masks. One is Luka Kodro, the pizzeria owner. One is Ragnar Falk, his white beard glowing in the din. One is a woman I don't recognise. She's wearing furs and red face paint.

The Sheriff has his hand on the radio affixed to his shoulder.

The woman sifts through the contents of the pan and nods and then looks up at the Sheriff. 'Definitely human teeth,' she says, adjusting her minks, each one whole, each one hanging limp from her body. 'Not animal. Human.'

'How can you be so sure?' asks a man still wearing a black carrier bag over his head.

'Because I studied these.' She holds up a molar, its root obscenely long in her fingers. 'I studied these for longer than you were in full-time education.'

It's Dr Edlund. Eva Edlund.

The Sheriff takes the tooth from her, and then he takes the pan.

He still has his hand on his radio. Hesitating. Thinking.

A man opposite with a moose head, not a mask, an actual hollowed-out moose head complete with antlers, shakes his head from side to side. It's a small gesture but his antlers magnify the movement.

The Sheriff swallows and takes his hand off the radio and walks away with the pan. I hear the contents rattle as he moves. Sounds like grit or glass beads.

'Plumber's teeth?' asks a woman beside me with grey make-up and a rough sackcloth hat similar to the ones wrapped around the streetlights.

I run after the Sheriff.

He sees me out the corner of his eye and says, 'I'll call this in. We got procedures to follow, even tonight. You run along now and let me do my job.'

But two hours later the teeth are forgotten about and there's no sign of any police. I've been waiting for them to arrive. Nothing. More and more people are heading into the Hive. A troupe. A queue of hideous misfits drawn to the block-size building. The bee on the roof is whirring now, and the clock hands are spinning so fast I can hardly keep up with my eyes.

Pans are full to bursting. Stuffed with rotting fruit and coins and bloody loins of deer. Some people leave their masks in a pan. Others drape silver-charm bracelets from the pan handles. I see one man stagger to a pan and urinate in it, but he's reprimanded by a gang and sent away.

Were they really human teeth in the clockmaker's pan? Teeth from that severed head? Arne Persson's teeth? One part of me wants to call Chief Björn myself but I know that action would finish my career in this town stone dead. They'll never trust me again. And I won't get to the bottom of the Edlund's secrets that way. So I'll wait it out. Keep looking. Bide my time.

A man in loose animal skins comes up to me. He's wearing a Baby Björn-style sling on his chest. There's a cross-eyed troll sitting in it. He asks for a light.

'Don't smoke, sorry.'

He leaves me be.

There's a darker tone to the square now. The crowds have thinned out, some to return home and relieve their elderly babysitting parents, others into the Hive to do God-only-knows. What's left are writhing couples and more backwards walkers than before. Huddles and small groups all trekking anti-clockwise round Visberg square, their boots caked in rotten-apple sludge and ash.

I have that feeling you get at a good house party in the early hours of the morning when you know you have to go home. When you're exhausted but you can't quite face the night bus. Or in my case, getting back to Julia's garage and driving all the way back down to Gavrik. I can't leave yet, the road must still be blocked.

A man passes by, his chest bare. He's wearing a wolf mask and he's beating a kettle drum. Pan Night has a heartbeat now. The violinists start playing again. Beats and screeches. Bass and treble. The bee spins. A man sits on a bench, his legs crossed, oblivious to a couple underneath ripping at each other's clothes. The man on the bench is holding a rat. Its tail must be as long as my forearm. Brown fur. Lifeless. The man holds it out in front of his face and looks at it, shows it off to the crowds. He's salivating. He opens his mouth and takes a bite and fluid dribbles down his neck and stains his chest. Rivulets streak down past his nipples. The rat isn't a rat, it's a rotisserie chicken, the kind with dark sugary-brown skin, and it has a tail adornment skewered into the flesh. Genuine rodent or quality imitation, it's difficult to tell in this light. The bonfire smoke intensifies and I watch the man gnaw the imitation rat carcass and pick his teeth with the bird's-wing bones as the couple under his bench start to groan with pleasure.

More beating of drums. More demonic string section accompaniment. A man in a straitjacket and bright-red lipstick shuffles over to me. He's almost comical but then he starts cackling and trying to rub himself against me so I kick him in the shin. He comes back harder, puckering his scarlet lips so I say, 'Bee sting,' and he deflates and walks off in the other direction.

The Sheriff's patrolling the square. Walking around with a worried look in his eye, his hand close to his radio.

A woman passes by Konsum with two Irish wolfhounds, each one wearing a high quality 'bald man' mask. They look appalling.

I approach the bandstand because people are talking there. Not wailing or dry-humping or howling, just talking. I might learn something. There may be gossip.

But actually they're not chatting, they're each chanting, 'As I walk through the valley of the shadow of death I shall fear no evil,' at double-speed, on a loop.

All around the square people pull burning logs from fire baskets. The man next to me, a man with curled ram horns adorning his rough-stitched leather mask, whispers, 'Hydrogen.'

The people with the burning pine logs hold them up and others step to them. Clusters of large, black bladder-balloons form. Elk bladders, mostly. Some cow. The logs are held close to the clusters and the balloons flare and burn and light up the square in bright light and the man with the ram horns points at the bronze anvil upon which Adolf-Fredrik Edlund is standing resolute, and he says, 'That's not a mask.'

20

Everyone in the bandstand goes quiet and looks over at the statue.

At the anvil.

At the mask. But it's not a mask, it's too bulky to be a mask.

It's a head.

The square is still full of noise; the shirtless drummer, the wolf howls and chanting. But more people come closer. To look at what we're looking at. The Sheriff arrives and gets flustered.

Hush.

One woman screams and the noise of it fills the square.

The Sheriff steps closer to the head and then takes off his hat and places it on his chest. Like he's praying. He looks over at us.

'You see who left this?'

We all shake our heads.

The Sheriff climbs up onto a bench and sticks his thumb and index finger in his mouth and whistles.

The drummer stops.

A man lets go of his bladder balloon and it floats haphazardly, diagonally, up through the fog until it disappears.

'I've called Gavrik police,' says the Sheriff. 'If you all know what's good for you, you'll clean up, pack up, and bug out.'

Everyone stands still, like statues. Black statues with masks and fur – and prams, some of those packed tight with troll triplets, wrapped in blankets against the cold.

'Go on, now.'

The Sheriff climbs down. He presses the button on his radio and it crackles and he speaks into it.

I see faces pressed against the glass windows of the Hive. Steamed-up glass and eyes.

The crowd in the square turn back into civilised modern Swedes within minutes. Masks are pulled off. Front doors are unlocked and pans snatched inside. I can see Eva Edlund the dentist's wife and Ragnar Falk. The clockmaker is removing black balloons from apple trees and someone else who has chosen to keep their mask on is waking a half-naked couple asleep or high underneath a bench.

Some people try to sneak a peek, like motorists slowing down beside an accident to observe the carnage and bloodshed from the corners of their eyes. Not so despicable that way. Just a glance, not head-on. A peripheral half look at death and destruction.

The backwards walkers start walking normally again.

The bee on top of the hive slows to its normal pace.

The clock outside Hans Wimmer's shop stops dead.

Someone walks around with an extinguisher and puts out all the fires in the fire baskets. The town square is heavy with steam and cold fog.

The Sheriff drags over a menu board from outside the pizzeria, the kind that's hinged at the top. He takes another from outside the gamer café and another from Konsum and he cordons off the severed head the best way he can, I guess, the way a neighbourhood-watch, taxi-driving, bullshit sheriff might do.

The head has no teeth, that I can see. Its jaws are spread wide and its gums shine in the weak light of Visberg town square. The skin is grey and the neckline ragged. The eyes are bulging and red. I look away.

I'm tired all of a sudden. Exhausted. You might expect the electricity in the air to heighten with the discovery of Arne's lifeless head. Displayed. Flaunted. But the electricity has gone. The hill people leach out into the side streets, like black treacle finding the paths of least resistance. Figures run out of the Hive, and they flee whatever action was going on inside their secure units, their premium top floor. The fires are all out. The unattended antique prams are gone. Electric lights start coming back on as the sacks covering the streetlights are pulled off and people switch on their indoor lamps as they get home and kiss the foreheads of their innocent, sleeping children.

There are four of us left in the square. Me, the Sheriff, and the two gamer-café twins, Daniel and David. They have a wheelie bin each and they're wearing latex gloves and filling the bins with masks discarded in the panic and used condoms, neatly tied, and half-empty jars of pickled eggs and burst bladder-balloons, sagging and lifeless.

The Sheriff says something into his radio and then waves his arms around to prevent a crow from getting too close to Arne Persson's severed head. The crow is trying. She is persistent. The Sheriff starts saying, 'Go on, scram…' Swinging a sandwich board up at the dark-eyed bird.

And then a boom rings out through the square and the twins drop to the ground like well-trained professional soldiers.

The crow flies away, unhurt.

Luka Kodro is backlit from his bedroom above Visberg Grill. He's leaning out in his white T-shirt and the muzzle from his rifle, pointed up into the sky, is smoking.

The Sheriff docks his hat and Luka closes his window.

Ragnar Falk delivers the pan full of teeth to the Sheriff and then he looks at me disapprovingly and heads back to his apartment over the old newspaper office on the shady side of the street.

The sun isn't coming up yet but it's thinking about it. Grey pre-twilight washes over the town square and picks out the giant bee.

It's like none of this ever happened.

A thousand people. Gone.

The prams and trolls and cauldron pans. Gone.

The sex and the chanting. The whispered psalms. The bearskins and papier-mâché Disney masks and screechy violinists. All gone.

Blue lights. Sirens.

Indoor lights switch off all around the square, like kids caught reading after lights out.

Two cop cars pull up close to the statue.

Chief Björn steps out of the lead car. Noora steps out of the other.

They huddle for a moment with Sheriff Hansson and then a pizza menu board is moved to one side and the Chief inspects the head. He does not remove his hat. He kneels. He stays down there a while. He walks back out. I overhear him say crime-scene specialists are fifteen minutes away. More words are said but I can't get them and I can't read lips in this low-level light.

Chief Björn walks over to me and Noora chats with the Sheriff.

The square is empty but it smells like bonfire smoke and the ground is a slurry of mud and fermented apple puree.

'You here the whole time?'

'Yes, Chief.'

'Did you see who left the head here?' he points back toward that anvil without taking his eyes off mine.

'No.'

'You see anyone suspicious here tonight?'

Where do I begin?

I shake my head.

He looks at me, narrows his eyes, then glances over at the clock-maker's shop.

'I cannot emphasise enough how important this is. Did you see anything out of the ordinary here tonight. Anyone approaching the statue area.'

What do I say? The Chief must know about Pan Night, at least the headlines, the general idea, he must tolerate it. I see the Sheriff behind the Chief and he's shaking his head almost imperceptibly.

'I don't think so,' I say.

A van arrives and four people step out. I retreat a little way and watch them suit up and take photographs of the head and the area immediately surrounding the anvil. They erect proper screens around the statue but it's too tall and awkward-shaped for a tent. They go about removing the severed head from the anvil point and bagging it up. I can't see them do it and I'm grateful for that. There are some things you don't need to see to understand.

The pan of teeth is handed over to the crime-scene guys and they bag the teeth and tag them.

'Will need a statement from you in the morning,' says the Chief, glancing over at the broken clock on Hans Wimmer's shop. 'Later this morning.'

'Okay, Chief. Who do you think did this? Is it Arne's head?'

I expect him to dismiss me with a patronising off-the-shelf police-chief remark but he looks weary and says, 'Something like this? Truly I do not know.'

The sun comes up and bathes the rooftops on the bright side of the square with white forensic light.

Konsum opens like this is just any other day.

I trudge back to Julia's house. Her garage is unlocked. I get into my Hilux and drive home. Numb. Too many impressions. Too much to take in.

What the hell is wrong with this town?

21

Usually I'd stop by McDonalds before home, but I have no appetite. I'm too tired to eat. Too pensive.

Why would a person shoot a man dead, sever his head with a chainsaw, then remove his teeth? Leave the body in the forest, the teeth in a pan, and the head skewered on an anvil. Is this some kind of sick game?

I park next to my building and go in.

When I stop to unlock my first-floor apartment, my neighbour's door swings open. Wealthy-looking guy with a dark suit and black high-polish shoes and dyed black hair. Piece of tissue on his chin stuck on with blood. And little Dan by his side looking up at me, smiling.

'We're late,' the man says to Dan.

Dan whispers something to the man and the man shakes his head and Dan says 'Please, Pappa.'

The man sticks his tongue into the side of his mouth and nods.

Dan runs back inside the apartment.

'Bye,' I say.

'No,' says the man, pointing at me. 'Wait.'

Dan runs back out, his gloves dangling from his sleeves with string. He puts his hands behind his back and says, 'Which hand?'

I point to the left hand.

He switches hands and shakes his head.

I point to the right hand.

He hands me a piece of A4 printer paper. His face is proud and embarrassed and excited all at once.

I take it and turn it over.

'That is my sand witch,' he says.

It is a sandwich, and it's also me and Noora and little Dan. In the picture Dan is smiling and his face is bright pink.

'It's a great picture,' I say.

'We're going to be late,' says his dad.

'Thank you, Dan.'

The man drags his son away, his expensive leather-soled shoes clicking and clacking down the stairs. Over his shoulder, Dan's face is looking back up at me, his eyes smiling.

I lie down for twenty minutes then shower. I use the fresh-mint-and-lime shower gel, the one that's like drinking five espressos. Honey loops with fridge-cold milk, Twix ice-cream bar – do not judge me, not after what I saw last night – and then I dress and leave the flat.

Outside it's trying to sleet.

I arrive at the office.

The bell above the door tinkles and I feel half hungover, even though I haven't touched a drink since Julia's single-measure whisky and Coke. Lena comes through and says, 'What happened?'

'Coffee?' I say.

We walk through to the kitchen at the back. Nils has put a note on the coffee jug reminding us to rinse it thoroughly. Lena sits on his unoccupied desk – this is Saturday and ad salesmen don't work weekends – and I pour us both coffee from the percolator. She gets a chainsaw-store freebie mug, which is probably inappropriate this week, and I get a Grimberg-Liquorice anniversary mug.

'It was strange enough before,' I say. 'Visberg is…'

'I know,' she says. 'I heard they found the victim's head by the town statue?'

'On the anvil.' I take a sip of coffee but it's too hot. I blow into the mug. 'Skewered onto the sharp end of the anvil.'

Lena cringes.

'I have to give a police statement and that won't be easy.'

'How so?' she says.

I pause and rub my tired old eyes.

'Imagine Halloween but darker and weirder. Adults only. R-rated.'

'Pan Night?'

I nod. 'Not sure how much detail I should tell the police.'

She sips her coffee and puts down her mug.

'Well, don't get yourself into any trouble. But remember, they know all about Pan Night. Been tolerating it for years. Decades, even. What they want is witnesses, any relevant suspicious activity, a timeline leading up to the discovery of the head.'

'Alright.'

'Any theories in Visberg as to who killed Arne Persson? Police talking to anyone in particular?'

I down my coffee, the burn to my throat some kind of strange comfort, and pour myself another.

'Shade on the Bosnian grill owner. Ex-soldier. People talk about the clockmaker but that's just because he's an oddball as far as I can tell. Then there's the sisters.'

'Utgard sisters? Wood-carving sisters?'

'The very same.'

'In Visberg, now?'

'Pop-up shop,' I say. 'And from what I saw last night they're doing brisk business. Then there are the gamer twins, who people gossip about because non-gamers always think video games turn us all into homicidal maniacs with no impulse control.' She watches me top up my coffee again with a look in her eye like *maybe they've got a point.* 'Woman who owns the Hive self-storage. Her late husband died in a freak chainsaw accident years ago.'

Lena shudders.

'Partial decapitation,' I say, looking her in the eye.

'Shit,' she says.

I nod. 'I'm told the neck wound was extensive. Cut more than a third through.'

'You plan on going anywhere dangerous, anywhere off the beaten track, you take Sebastian with you as back-up, okay? Make use of him.'

'It's all off the beaten track,' I say. 'All of it.'

The phone rings in her office so she goes off to answer it.

I sit down at my desk and the caffeine hits. Acid reflux and hyper-alertness: the two consistent states of any good reporter.

Six stories. Bare-bones layouts and sub-headings. A list of people I need to probe now I'm better known in the hill town. Word spreads, and last night will have helped. I was there when they experienced a watershed moment. There on the inside. They'll talk more freely now and I can help break this case, because from what I saw last night, that closed-community mentality, that violent rewind to ancient traditions, they will not open up to the Gavrik police. It's got to be me who bridges that gap. Me, who works things out. For the sake of Arne Persson and his ex-wife, Annika. For the sake of every other surviving resident.

Lars walks in at nine. This is odd because Lars is part time and doesn't work weekends. Also, even on work days he gets in at around eleven. He pulls off his outer coat like a T-Rex might struggle with a tight sweater. Or any sweater, I guess. He hangs it up.

'*Hej, hej*,' he says.

'*Hej, hej*? It's the weekend, Lars. Your calendar malfunction on you?'

He shows me his little wheelie case, some kind of hand-luggage expandable thing, and says, 'Working on my book.'

Ah, yes. Lena did mention Lars is writing his memoir. If you have any trouble sleeping, you may want to look into pre-ordering it.

'Nineteen seventy-seven to nineteen eighty-three,' he says, sitting down slowly on his chair and rearranging the haemorrhoid cushion. 'Including the time the Karlstad mayor visited the town.'

'You hear about last night, Lars?'

He looks over with a blank expression and adjusts his bifocals and says, 'The head?'

I nod.

'I heard.'

Gathered that.

'Absolutely horrific. I've never been to Visberg town as an adult.'

'You've lived here forever. Never been tempted?'

He smiles and powers up his computer.

'Looks like I was wise to avoid it,' he says. Then he trudges into the kitchen and brews a fresh pot of coffee. His Velcro indoor shoes squeak on the linoleum. Down in Malmö I missed the sound of that squeak.

When I get to the cop shop there's already an out-of-town journo van here. They're not filming, they're drinking something hot from disposable McDonalds cups and chatting among themselves.

'Tuva,' says the slick-back journo from *Aftonbladet*.

'I'm going inside.'

'I heard you were there when the severed head was found early this morning.'

I look at him and say, 'You need new sources, mate.' And then I go inside.

Thord's at the counter.

'Thanks for coming in.'

'I want to help.'

He's eating cereal from a cardboard bowl with a plastic teaspoon.

'That so your hand looks bigger?'

He looks down at the spoon and drops it in the bowl and says, 'Come on through to the back.'

I give him my full statement. We go over the discovery of the body on Visberg hill earlier in the week. The woman who found him. I talk in great detail about the head, describing the man who noticed it, and then I give reasonably accurate descriptions of where I was standing and the exact time of discovery. But he doesn't ask about the hours before. Why would he, I guess? I probe him about leads and he says, 'Not now, Tuvs.'

The outside-broadcast team are filming as I walk out. There are probably three more of them in Visberg town right now. Women and men with good hair standing in front of a cordoned-off statue holding microphones and saying, 'In the early hours of this morning the head of a deceased male was discovered on or around the statue of legendary local industrialist Adolf-Fredrik Edlund in the quiet ex-steel town of Visberg.'

I spot the stationery-store woman walking toward the camera, adjusting her red beret and licking her lips. The gossip queen of Toytown has come out of the woodwork.

Slick-back approaches her. 'Madam, can I ask you about the awful news coming out of Visberg town this morning?'

'You surely can.'

Broad smile. She shuffles closer to the camera and slick-back intercepts so she doesn't get too close.

'What do you make of the discovery of a severed head in the town square?'

'My Auntie Else used to live up that hill before her divorce and she said there was black magic up there this time of year.'

'Care to explain?'

'Not on your life, young man.'

He frowns ever so slightly then smiles.

'What do you think the impact of this news will be on such a close-knit community?'

She ignores the question. 'It's your kind up there, that's why it's so hushed up if you ask me, I'm not one to gossip, but...'

'One of us?

She lowers her voice. 'The old man from the *Tidningen*.' Her volume returns to normal. 'Whole town knows he was caught as a boy with his mice.'

'With his mice?'

'Pet mice, you know, the little white ones, not the black mice, not rats or shrews or voles. Clean mice you keep in a cage. Cut all their tiny heads off, he did. Used a cutlery knife or so I was told, not sharp, you know the sort, so those little mice must have gone through agony at the hands of Ragnar Falk.'

Noora walks out of the station and ignores the reporters desperate to talk to her. She looks at me, and I know that look. I follow her round the back of *Gavrik Posten.* We sit in my Hilux.

'I can't tell you much right now, Tuva. I have to keep to my boundaries.'

'And…'

'Just. You know you went to the dentist in Visberg last week and they want to do follow-up work for you. Root-canal. I can't tell you why or share any details, but do not go back to them yet. You'll understand why soon.'

'What is it?'

'I can't talk yet, I have to stick to my bound—'

'Fuck the boundaries. It's me you're talking to, Noora. What is it?'

She looks over at the direction of the cop shop, then back at me.

'The loose teeth discovered in the pan in Visberg. They *were* Arne Persson's teeth.'

'As suspected. And?'

'His teeth had four fillings and a crown, completed within the past seventy-two hours. All post-mortem.'

22

'Shit,' says Noora. 'I shouldn't have told you that yet. Keep it to yourself, Tuva. That's off the record. Promise me.'

'Don't worry.'

'I'm serious,' she says.

'And I said, don't worry.'

'I have to get back to work. I'll try to see you later.'

I'm left to try to process this new information. Why would someone kill Arne Perrson. Cut off his head. And then do dental work on his teeth? Is that some kind of sexual kick? It wasn't to disguise the identity of the victim, because we already know the identity of the victim.

The office is subdued. It usually is on weekends but today even more so. Lars in his loose-knit cardigan, typing out his memoir with two manicured index fingers. Lena's behind her closed door. People are passing by the window wrapped up in coats they've taken from their winter storage. Possibly from their private unit at the Hive.

I can't drink more coffee, I already feel sick.

Sebastian walks in.

'*Hej, hej*,' Lars says to him.

Sebastian slips off his winter boots and puts on his indoor espadrilles. Somehow he looks good in slip-on shoes. We're all in Crocs or sandals or, in Lars's case, Velcro ICA Maxi sneakers, and here comes new boy with his cheekbones and his sailcloth beach shoes.

'I've been out in Utgard forest,' he says.

Lars says, 'Why would you do that, Seb?'

'Couple from Norrland bought the Carlsson place at the centre of the forest. They're knocking it down and building the biggest new house in the Kommun. Serious planning dispute, so I was there interviewing the new owners and their architect.'

'Paulsson?' says Lars, one of his eyelids twitching.

'The other one,' says Cheekbones.

'Alfredsson?' says Lars.

'That's him.'

Lars nods to himself. The man is an encyclopaedia of local information. He has org charts in his head. He has family trees and lists of architects and an archive of old *Posten* articles, the ones *he* wrote at least, and most likely an underground-sewer map imprinted on his memory.

I pick up my phone and place the octagonal foam attachment on the earpiece close to my hearing aid.

'Gavrik police, Thord Pettersson speaking.'

'It's me again.'

'Call you back.'

I unplug my aids and put them on my desk to show Lars and Cheekbones I'm working. I search for post-mortem dental work but I get nothing. In the whole world. Nada. Zip. Rightly so, in my opinion. There is no record of people working on the teeth of dead people. Jesus, I hope my Google history never gets made public. Then I look into dental students studying on human cadavers. Happens in some dental schools but not all. Usually the larger ones attached to teaching hospitals.

My eyes get blurry from lack of sleep but I snap off a line of Marabou milk chocolate, the one with excellent salty crackers hidden inside, and keep on searching. Some war-crime files I'd rather not look at too closely. Reviews of *Marathon Man*, the Dustin Hoffman movie. Law suits and criminal cases against dentists who removed multiple teeth from children unnecessarily for financial gain. My rear molar starts aching again out of sympathy. I do a search of Värmland and sketch out a map pinpointing the location of all dental surgeries. But it wasn't necessarily a qualified dentist who did this heinous thing. Back in my London student days I once helped a flatmate repair his own filling. He couldn't afford a dentist and couldn't get into an NHS surgery. So he did it himself. DIY filling-repair kit from Boots in Bethnal Green. He drank some of my rum before he started. I was just the mirror holder, really. And he managed it. Replaced the chunk of broken filling with a new one. I print off the map and check the results. Visberg Tandklinik is the closest dental practice to the location of the murder, we know that already. That surgery has two registered dentists: Sven Edlund and his non-practicing wife, Eva. Then there's Tobias the hygienist and Julia Beck the receptionist. In Gavrik we have the Folktandklinik. Other practices further afield in Torsby, Falun, Munkfors and so on.

My phone rings and I put my aid back in. The jingle plays and then I can hear.

'Tuva Moodyson.'

'I haven't got long,' says Thord.

'Talk over a quick lunch?'

'How quick?'

'Twenty minutes?'

'Fifteen. The Hotel. I'm leaving now.'

He hangs up.

I grab my coat and boots and cross the road. He's there coming out of the station. If I walk with him I might get sixteen minutes. Seventeen if I walk him back after.

'The morning I've had,' he says.

'The head?'

He nods. 'And the paperwork. Got my mid-year appraisal next week and I did not need this.'

We're already outside Hotel Gavrik. Small town. Short distances. The hotel is backdropped by the twin chimneys of the factory. The hotel's sign is wonky as usual and the entrance is flanked by two carved pumpkins.

I hold the door for him.

'Lunch, is it?' says the owner-receptionist-waitress.

What do you think? Double room for a quick lunchtime shag, the local journo and second in command of the cop shop in full uniform.

'Yes, please,' says Thord, because he's a better person than I am.

She shows us to a table but we opt for a quieter one in the far corner.

Paper tablecloth, paper napkins. Photocopied menu says pumpkin soup followed by meatballs and mash followed by fruit salad. Vegetarian option for main course is mash and salad. Welcome to Gavrik.

Thord gets us water. His winter skin is coming off him in flakes.

'You look tired,' he says.

'Oh, thanks.'

He smiles.

'A source told me the head is...'

'Shhh,' says Thord, leaning closer. 'It ain't Halloween yet, keep your volume down.'

'Told me the head was Arne Persson's. That the teeth were his too and they've had fillings done.'

'Source?' says Thord, scratching his eyebrow.

I nod.

He puffs out his cheeks. 'Not just fillings, Tuvs. The teeth had been *whitened.* Autopsy doc says within the past seventy-two hours. Still had some whitening gel present. They'd been flossed and the calcifi... the calculu... the plaque had been scraped off.' He leans closer. 'I don't even know what to say about that. The Chief surely doesn't, either.'

'Motive?'

'What motivates a lunatic?' he says, tucking his paper napkin into his collar.

Our soup bowls arrive. Bright orange soup with a single ICA Maxi mini crouton floating on top.

'Heard you was there for the local festivities,' says Thord, an orange glow to his lips.

I nod.

He slurps his soup.

I drink mine. It's not spiced. Not seasoned even. Lukewarm. Tastes like boiled potato water.

'You interviewing the dentists?' I ask.

He swallows and puts his spoon back in the bowl. 'People talking about Sven Edlund on account of him being a hunter, being a woodsman, being a dentist.'

'Open and shut case,' I say.

'Golf club gives him a solid alibi. Of course, he's a partner in the golf club and most of the snobbos up there are his direct relatives, so there's alibis and there's alibis, if you know what I mean.'

I do, Thord. I do.

'His wife?'

'Ain't a dentist no more.'

'Studied though.'

'Yes, she did. As did another couple of dozen in the upper Värmland region. More, if you count the retirees and the ones who dropped out of tooth school before they graduated.'

The meatballs arrive. Brown sauce made from beef stock and cream and soy sauce. Lukewarm mash. Best food this place serves.

'Tobias the hygienist?'

'Solid alibi, a local of good standing. We already checked.'

'Any other leads?'

'Now wait a minute, says Thord, a meatball hovering on his fork in front of his mouth. 'All these questions, Tuvs. You were the one there in the square last night. It's time for you to fill me in.'

'Fill you in?'

He nods and chews. A speck of brown sauce on his napkin.

'Weirdest night of my life, Thord. Like Halloween on LSD. Masks and howling and fires.'

'All legal that, apart from the LSD.'

'Yeah, nothing seriously illegal. Just Weird. Cultish. Like that town plays by different rules to everywhere else.'

'You identify anyone close to that anvil?'

'Masks,' I say, shaking my head. 'Masks and costumes.'

He checks his watch and eats three meatballs all at once.

'I heard Margareta's late husband died from a chainsaw wound.'

He nods rapidly and points to his bulging cheek; the international code for *wait a sec, mouth full.* 'Accident,' he says eventually. 'Years ago. Just a freak accident.'

'Who would want Arne Persson dead?'

Thord turns his fork to activate shovel-mode, and clears up the remainder of his mash and sauce. 'You tell me. That's why I'm here. You feed me information and I feed you some.'

'Link to the Medusa murders?' I push my half-finished food away.

He shakes his head and takes a meatball off my plate with his fork. 'There is no serial killer story here, Tuvs. Also: Medusa never flaunted body parts in a public place. Quite the opposite. And Medusa never taunted us police.'

'You think this guy is taunting you?'

He nods. 'Playing games with us. Or with the Sheriff. I never seen anything so flagrant in all my police days. Chief's furious. He reckons it's personal, that someone's got it in for him.'

'Chief needs to keep his head.'

Thord starts to nod and then he looks at me and points his fork at me and shakes it and grins and nods.

'No time for fruit,' he says.

'I'll walk you back.'

We split the bill and leave and Thord lowers his voice and says, 'Ruger rifle, got the ballistics back an hour ago. Bullet lodged in a

Scots pine, seven metres behind the victim. Serious weapon but common in the elk hunts. We're checking our database.'

'Did the body fit the neck perfectly, if you know what I mean?'

'It did. Nothing removed. Nothing missing apart from a bucket full of blood. And that came back all linked to either the victim or an animal. Probably an elk.'

'Could it have been a vet working on the teeth?'

Thord nods. 'We already thought of that. Could be. We're also looking through lists of any professions with pliers strong enough to pull teeth out of a man's jaw. Ain't an easy thing, so I been told. But with YouTube and Google, anyone can get access to pretty much any how-to guide these days. White coats told me teeth got blood flow all of their own. Did you know that? I thought they was just sitting there, bone in bone, but apparently they got blood and veins. Whoever pulled them teeth and worked on them surely was meticulous. White coats told me they brought in a university tooth-expert to assist them. Told me it was some of the finest dental work they ever seen.'

23

Saturday-afternoon shoppers dawdle down Storgatan like they're relieved there's no murderer in their town. Of course, the truth is the murderer could well be based here. Could be their next-door neighbour or their poker buddy. Could be their husband.

Tobias the hygienist disappears into Ronnie's Bar so I follow him.

I step inside and the light levels drop. Could be any time of day or night inside this place. The only way you can tell the time of year is by looking at the coat rack on the way in. Overladen in winter. Lightweight coats in spring. Almost empty in summer. Full of camouflage gear and orange, waterproof hunting-caps in autumn. I count five such caps as I go past. One of them has 'KILLER' scrawled on in black Sharpie.

Ronnie looks up and acknowledges me with an upward nudge of his head. I'm local now, I guess. By choice, not by circumstance. I chose to come back and make this part of Värmland my home for a while longer. Maybe I'm the first outsider ever to do that. Maybe I'll be the last.

The pool table's lit up but nobody's playing. The lamp hanging above the blue baize advertises the STP Pulp Mill on one side and an extra-strong beer brand on the other. There are about fifteen people drinking quietly at tables. A woman in a leopard-print top reads a novel as she nurses a large glass of red wine. A group of elk hunters, with hands both muddy and bloody, laugh and clink their beer bottles in the corner. Looks like they got lucky. Looks like they made their death quota.

I step up to the bar and sit next to Tobias.

He looks over at me like, *don't I know you from somewhere?*

I smile at him. 'Tuva Moodyson.'

'Deep clean,' he says.

Ronnie shrugs behind him.

'What are you drinking?' I say.

'Me?' he says. 'Just a lemonade. But I'll pay for it.'

'I got them,' I say. 'Ronnie, two lemonades, please.'

'Really,' says Tobias. 'I'd rather pay for mine, if you don't mind.'

'Doesn't mean you have to sleep with me,' I say. 'Not if you don't want to. Don't get your boxers in a knot.'

Swedish guys.

He smiles and we clink glasses.

'What are you doing all the way out here, Tobias?'

He scratches the top of his back. 'Surgery's closed for the weekend on account of the crime scene in the town square. Police here in Gavrik wanted us three to give statements.'

'Three?'

'The Edlunds and myself. Everyone with formal dental training. You hear that the teeth in the severed head had undergone dental procedures?'

I nod. He's good looking, this hygienist. And he looks hygienic, I mean he really lives up to his job description. Very clean. Too clean for me, to be honest. Looks gleaming and smells minty fresh.

'You think your boss did it?'

He almost spits out his lemonade. 'Sven? Hell, no. He's one of the most passive people I've ever met. Sven's more *Mahler* than murder.'

'His wife?'

'Stop it,' he says. 'I'm serious. Don't go spreading rumours like that. Eva and Sven are aloof, yes. Some people find them a little arrogant but they are not capable of anything so awful, I can assure you. And I just told your local policeman the exact same thing.'

'You, then?'

'Me?'

I shrug. 'Frustrated hygienist who always dreamed of becoming a dentist proper but never had the grades. You do it, Tobias?'

He pushes his wrists together. 'You got me.'

'Someone told me you're a prepper.'

'No. Just prepared, there's a difference. I worry about winter storms, mainly, up there on the hill. I like to keep food stocks and antibiotics. People think that's crazy but it gives me a sense of security.'

'Any theories, then? About Arne Persson?'

'I don't know,' he says. 'Gossip can lead to lynching in a small town like Visberg. Hill people, you know.'

'You're not a hill person?'

'I'm a Karlstad person.'

'Okay. So who killed your town plumber and then fixed up his teeth?'

Tobias sips his lemonade and then coughs a little, like it went down the wrong way. He turns from me and coughs some more and then turns back, his eyes watering.

'On paper at least, Kodro is the most dangerous man in the town.' His voice is hoarse. 'But personally I think he's also one of the most intelligent.'

'Grill owner?'

'A very erudite man. Reads a lot.' One more cough. 'Listens to podcasts on all sorts of subjects. But it is true that he was a killer back in his home country, and I'm not sure you ever lose that ability.'

'Luka Kodro get on well with Arne Persson?'

'His wife sure did,' says Tobias, giving me some side-eye. 'But we can't blame her for all that. Arne Persson broke a lot of hearts in Visberg town over the years. He played games with Margareta over at the Hive, strung her along for years after her husband died in that accident. Some people think Arne Persson wasn't the saint he's being made out to be.'

'*You're* saying that?'

'Not what I meant.'

'He break any other hearts I should know about?'

He takes a sip of his drink. 'I heard Luka Kodro and his wife went through counselling and extensive couples therapy afterward. Sex can be a strong driver to action.'

I frown at him.

'Are you flirting with me, Mr Robinson?'

He looks at me then looks away then looks at me again and we both laugh. The sound of it cuts through the tension and my tiredness. The table of hunters look around to us. One man, with a patchy beard, camo cap and mosquito bites all over his neck, perks up and presses his bloodstained finger to his lips in a silent warning.

'It was probably an out-of-towner,' says Tobias.

'Why would they be deep in the elk woods on Visberg hill?'

'That must be the least weird thing about this nightmare.'

I notice Tam walk in so I jump off my stool to greet her but then stop myself. She's with a guy. With her new guy. I fix my hair and rub my cheeks to try to get some colour into them and then I go see them.

'Tuva Moody,' says Tam. 'I'd like you to meet Julian. Julian, I'd like you to meet the best thing about Gavrik town, Tuva Moodyson.'

We shake hands. He's cute. Tall and skinny with scruffy, brown hair and brown eyes.

'Tammy's told me all about you,' he says.

I think about saying, *don't believe any of it*, but I resist because I'm not quite that lame.

Tam whispers, 'Date?' so quiet I can't hear her, but I can read it on her lips.

'No, no,' I say, looking back at Tobias. 'Just work.'

'Pool?' she says. 'After?'

'Bed,' I say. 'Exhausted.'

They leave to play pool and I sit back down on my stool.

'Nice that you have this place to hide out in,' says Tobias. 'We could do with something like this in Visberg. Maybe one day we'll have a bar of our own.'

'At least you have the Grill and the gamer café.'

'Gamer café isn't really a café, though, is it,' he says. 'Mind Games is more like a crèche for angry, frustrated young men who want to kill each other on screens. They launched a game on the first day of the elk hunt called *Hunted 2.0*, you hear about that? So while the locals are out actually hunting elk in the great outdoors, fresh air and exercise, obeying a code of conduct and maybe culling a few on the first day, these boys were slaughtering hundreds if not thousands of pixelated creatures onscreen. Elk, bears, mountain lions, condors, polar bears, Siberian tigers, the lot. And then, in the later levels, I heard they turn on each other in the virtual forests.'

'Sounds like I should check that game out.'

'You game?'

I drain the last of my lemonade. 'Sure do.'

'They don't hunt each other with guns in the final levels,' says Tobias, his face stern. 'They hunt with their bare hands.'

'Onscreen,' I say.

'Yeah, but still. Their avatars are augmented versions of the photos they upload. It's that realistic. They strangle each other in this virtual world. They fight their own neighbours, realistic faces and all, and they tear out each other's spines and organs. Trophies like scalps and earlobes get them extra points. The players even rip limbs off and beat other hunters to death with them. And…'

'Go on.'

'Decapitation. That's what gets you to the top of the local leader board. You only win if you completely sever the other players' heads.'

24

As I drive home from Ronnie's Bar I pass an elderly couple walking awkwardly, each one carrying a brand-new snow shovel. The handles are covered with ICA Maxi plastic bags as if they needed any extra protection. That's late October for you. Change your tyres. Top up your log pile and your stocks of antifreeze. Change the oil in your snow blower. Freeze your elk haunch. Ready yourself for the potential killer that will surely come.

In my post box I have a Happy Halloween card from Aunt Ida, Mum's sister, my only living relative on planet earth. It shows a carved pumpkin on a skeleton's body being chased by a ghost. This is how Aunt Ida and I communicate. In August I sent her a birthday card. Now I get this. In two months we'll exchange Christmas cards. We haven't seen each other since the funeral but at least we have this.

I walk up the stairs and unlock my apartment door. No arguments from my neighbours, which is a relief. Maybe they've gone away on holiday? Had counselling? Signed a fucking peace armistice?

Down on my mat.

I frown and bend.

A newspaper? No, just a front page. *Visberg Tidningen* dated October 15.

The last ever issue.

The headline says 'Thank You' in large print, but someone's ringed random words in various articles and columns. A person has highlighted words or parts of words, then neatly cut out the front page, travelled here to my apartment, and slid it under my door. Meaning they got inside my building. My address is public, this is Sweden after all, but everything beyond that door should be private to us tenants.

I drop my handbag and place the front page on the kitchen counter.

Loud voices from next door.

First line in the paper they've circled 'Do not' in red ink. Some kind of kitsch 'Do not worry, the news will still keep happening even after we're gone' local-paper bullshit non-story. A tiny word is marked under a photo. Part of the credit. It's the word, 'Talk'. Then the word, 'Panic' is half ringed to form the word, 'Pan'. That was a story about panic-buying of a particular grade of ammunition, now that the manufacturer has gone out of business. A short piece on the autumn equinox clock-change has the word, 'Night' picked out in broad red marker. Later in the same article it's an 'Or' that's ringed. Story about an Iraqi kid getting the best grades in the local school with the word, 'boy' used. And then, at the very bottom of the page, a piece on the annual elk hunt. It mentions quotas and stats from the national wildlife survey. There's a quote from Benny Björnmossen himself, and another from Sven Edlund, the snobby dentist. But it's not a word that's circled, it's the bloodied, bent neck of a cow elk. An argument booms through the wall from next door. I hold the paper out at arm's length.

Do not talk Pan Night or boy...and then the dead elk image.

Acid in my stomach. Someone's making a threat with this front page. Is this Ragnar Falk's work? Doesn't seem like his style but maybe that's the whole point? Or one of the other three-thousand hill-town locals who received a copy of the paper. More, maybe because it was the last one ever printed.

I double-lock my door and check my apartment. Under the bed, in the wardrobe, in the bathroom, in the box room. I pull the blinds and the racket from next door intensifies. High-pitched screams and low-pitched staccato yelling.

The sinister threat of the annotated newspaper front page and Aunt Ida's Halloween card sit next to each other by the sink. The boy? Which boy are they referring to? Sebastian? Or do they think I have a son? A boyfriend?

A knock on my door and I almost jump out of my skin.

I just stare at it. I do not move.

Another knock. Impatient.

'Hello?'

A woman's voice.

I open the door. It's the tenant from next door. I half expect her to have a black eye but she looks fine. Coat, bobble hat, leather handbag. And her son hanging onto her leg.

'Can you do me a huge favour, Moa.'

'Tuva.'

'Sorry. Just this once, I promise. I'll pay you back.'

'How much?'

She makes a pained expression. 'No, I mean, yeah, I wish I could. But, no, that's not what I mean. Can you watch Dan for me. An hour – two, tops. I have to go do something and his dad…' she looks down at her son, 'he's…busy. Would you mind? He'll be no bother will you, Dan?'

Dan looks up at his mum but says nothing.

'Erm, sure,' I say. 'I have to work later, but two hours max should be okay. Do I need anything special for him? Food? Toys? Wouldn't it be easier if I sit him in your place?'

'No,' she says sternly. 'Sorry. I mean…' Her tone softens and she forces a smile. 'The flat is a real mess. Go on, Danny, go play with your new friend.' She mimes over his head and I can understand both words, over twenty years of practice. 'Thank you.'

The door closes.

Just me and the kid, then.

He sits down meekly on the end of my sofa and looks at the back of his hand. He's basically me from twenty years ago. Awkward, shy, an observer of life rather than a participant. My mum never palmed me off to neighbours, but there was one woman I'll never forget. When I was fourteen, the same year Dad was killed, the year from hell. She was a school-dinner lady, with frizzy hair and beautiful green cat eyes. She could see what was happening to Mum. She could tell. Once a fortnight she'd ask if I wanted to go over to her place for cod in boiled-egg sauce or meatloaf with mash. She'd do what some mums do every day, but she'd concentrate all that simple quotidian love into a single evening. How's school? What music are you listening to these days? Isn't the ice on the lake thick this year? Do you need a new coat, because I know a great discount place just outside town? Simple questions. Parental questions. Nothing showy. Never, 'How are you coping without your dad? Or, 'Is your mum okay?' Or, 'What's it like being deaf?' Never any of those. She must have known I didn't have the strength or the distance or the vocabulary for them. Just practical questions that made me feel safe. Made me feel like a fourteen-year-old again.

'I said, can I have some water, please?'

Shit.

'Sorry, Dan. I didn't hear. I'll get it for you.'

I run the tap and then I turn and say, you sure you don't want a Sprite? I have Sprite.'

'Yes, please. Thank you.'

I pour us both Sprites.

The dinner lady down the hall let me drink Sprites. Let me watch TV, even through there were only a few channels in Sweden back then. She let me eat Marabou chocolate. Always the orange-crisp version, always cut up into squares with a boning knife, always placed on her IKEA coffee table in a small floral bowl.

'You want to watch something on TV?' I ask.

He nods. 'Captain 'Merica.'

'Not sure about that one. Let me see.'

Kids need TV and to hell with anyone who says otherwise. All the best people I know loved TV and movies and books as children. Stories are the escape that all young humans crave.

I flick through Netflix and decline about seventeen of his suggestions.

'What about *Dumbo*?'

'Looks boring.'

'Negative, Danny boy. *Dumbo* is one of the finest movies ever made. Buckle up.'

He frowns at me.

'Chocolate?'

He nods.

We watch the opening scene. The music and the train working hard to get up the hill. The elephants knocking in tent pegs with mallets, and the stork flying in with the big-eared pachyderm baby. Dan's transfixed. He's crossed over into that world.

I lean back on the sofa and Dan doesn't get too close but he moves his arm so it's next to my wrist and suddenly I get the same sensation you have when a stray cat lets you stroke its head. That trust.

The movie plays on and I almost fall asleep. From the nightmare of last night, that severed head, the most disturbing town rituals I have ever witnessed, to this. I close my eyes and think back to Dad and me watching *Dumbo* together.

There's a bang onscreen and I snap out of my daydream and remember what Tobias the hygienist said.

The gamer twins.

Hunted 2.0.

I sit up and ask Dan if he's hungry and he tells me he's not. Stomach full of Marabou with digestive-biscuit pieces and Sprite will have that effect. I google *Hunted 2.0* on my phone. It's rated R18. I check the Wikipedia entry even though I'm no fan of pundits in the media casually linking video games to violent acts in the real world. The evidence is tenuous at best. I click down to the 'Controversies' sub-heading and find more sub-sub-headings and footnotes. Japan, Mexico, Ireland, and South Africa. Two attacks by students in a school, one in a gaming competition, and one at home. All mutilations. I YouTube-search the game. Shit, it looks nasty. Shoot 'em ups and beat 'em ups I'm used to, graphic beheadings I am not.

'What's that?' says Dan, peering at my phone at an angle I hope to God ensures he didn't see anything.

'Work.'

'Is it Captain 'Merica?'

I smile.

The movie ends.

Then the two-hour limit ends.

Then another hour goes by.

'Where do you think your mamma went?'

'To find my pappa.'

'Where did he go?'

'He was very sad. He goes sometimes. He broke our kitchen table.'

I stand there nodding. Feeling unqualified to comment.

'Things will get better at home soon, Dan. It's Halloween next week. Will you get a party at school or something?'

'Can I watch Captain 'Merica now?'

'You want dinner? Pizza okay?'

He nods. 'I like pizza.'

We watch *Aladdin* for a second time while the frozen pizza heats up in my hardly used oven. By the time it's ready, the Robin Williams genie character is in full-swing and I'm enjoying it again as much as Dan is.

'This is a funny one,' he says, ketchup on his chin.

My phone rings and I pick it up immediately hoping it's Dan's mum.

'Tuva, it's me,' says Sebastian. 'I've just been chatting with Benny Björnmossen outside Ronnie's Bar. He says the hunt-team leaders are calling a meet. He says the elk they shot and butchered in Visberg forest over the past weeks...'

'Yeah?'

'Benny Björnmossen says the hunters left all the inedible parts in the forest. One big pile, just like they always do. And now all the heads have been taken from the pile. They're missing seven elk skulls.'

25

I end the call and look at the skinny kid on my sofa.

'Dan.'

He turns to face me.

'What's your mamma's phone number?'

He looks puzzled and then says, 'Seven.'

I type 07 into my phone.

'And?'

'Eight.'

I type 8.

'Nine, ten?' he says.

'Do you know her number, Dan?'

'No.'

Shit. I can't leave this kid here on his own but I need to get to the forest, take photos of the hunt team, get quotes, work out if the missing elk skulls are connected to the Persson case. I need to piece this whole thing together.

Still nobody home next door.

I'm about to call Sebastian to ask him to drive to Visberg when someone knocks on the door. I pass Dan to his mum and run out to my Hilux.

Thank God I didn't have to send Cheekbones on this assignment. He needs to shadow me, I don't deny it, it's just hard to know when's a good time to start. This time last year I went to see Mum in the hospice. I was in the room when a senior doctor visited her with a medical student. I know this is an essential part of their training. I understand it completely. In theory. But them discussing the reasons why they wouldn't resuscitate my own mother if her heart stopped was too much. Maybe they'd heard I was deaf and thought I couldn't hear what they were saying. Me, sat there, unable to breathe, my hand gripping her tube of rose-scented hand cream so hard it lost its shape. Oozing from the screw top. Scent of wild roses filling the room. The doctor and the student turning to look at me. At the cream I was rubbing into my own skin to make it all go away.

I pass by the steaming sewage plant and keep on going.

Sebastian will do just fine. It's just that he's so obviously a city kid. And he's too bloody handsome for his own good. What he needs is a broken nose and ripped fleece.

The world passes by in a blur. My wipers are on intermittent. The dash reads seven degrees.

Four trucks parked on the side of the road. No space for me so I keep on going uphill until there's a safe place for me to park.

I bring the truck to a halt and pull hard on my hand brake.

The mist wheezes horizontally and wets my face in a way that only Swedish drizzle can. No discernible rainfall and yet I am getting completely soaked. I pull my hood to cover my aids and I walk with my head twisted round against the incessant spray.

I get to their Volvos and trucks and head into the darkness of the trees. My shins ache from the extreme gradient. Bootprints and churned mud. A tiny packet of snus tobacco, the kind that looks like a teabag and is designed to be tucked under a lip for hours to inject tobacco straight into gum blood, sits neatly on a lichen-covered rock.

A gunshot. Two more.

I head deeper into the forest and although I'm shattered from not sleeping last night, I feel alert from the cold and the wet. Not thinking of Dan now. I did the best I could for him. Just focus on the job at hand, Tuva. Survive this. There are seven missing elk skulls and one maniacal killer still on the loose.

Autumn. Sitting water, squelchy earth and old bonfire smoke.

I keep on going, following the prints. More rifle shots. I can find my way out if I need to, I have the trail. And I have a charged stungun in my pocket.

I walk on around a pine tree, wet lower branches soaking my face, the needles dragging across my cheek like hundreds of microscopic fingers. I find myself in a small clearing. A fire smokes and spits at its centre. Six men sit at a picnic table, three on each side. Four hunt dogs underneath it, gnawing on bloodied bones.

'Well, look who showed up,' says a deep voice I recognise.

I step over to them, relieved they're still here but I'm on my guard. Six men and me. Four dogs and me. Six rifles against my stungun. Six proven killers and one dumb-ass reporter.

'*Hej*,' I say.

All six men just look at me and chew.

The fire crackles and flares. There's a big cow elk strung up behind them, its bloodstained legs tied with blue rope, the rope looped over a branch, the bulk of it heaved up. When the wind catches the carcass, the branch squeaks with the strain.

They continue staring at me. Swallowing. One man drinks from his beer can.

The elk's guts lie on the ground along with its fur and its head and its hooves. The guts are pale blue and they look like sacks of fluid and strings of pale sausages. They are steaming.

'Liver,' says a man with a full, red beard. 'Warm moose liver. You want some, girl?'

The other five grin at that.

I stand up straighter. 'Got any bear meat, old man?'

One guy whistles and the rest just laugh and pat the red-beard dude on the back like *she got you, she got you real good.*

Sven Edlund walks over to me.

'Why are you out here? This is private. We're eating.'

'I heard multiple elk skulls have gone missing.'

He shakes his head.

'Probably just wild game. They take the heads sometimes, drag them away into the deep brush.'

But he doesn't look convinced by his own words.

I address the other five.

'You know who or what would take elk skulls from the forest? Skulls with no antlers?'

'Could be Little Bo Peep,' says one man.

'Could be Little Red Riding Hood,' says another, biting into a shiny slice of fresh liver.

'Go back to the big city,' says the red-beard guy. 'These woods ain't for your type.'

The biggest guy on the table throws a stringy piece of liver down by his boots and his dog swallows it whole. The dog has some kind of GPS tracker device tethered to its collar.

Another guy says something but he's got an overgrown handlebar moustache and he's eating so I can't make out the words.

'I'm deaf,' I say. 'What did you say?'

The man takes off his orange hunt cap and he's bald underneath. He says, 'I...I didn't know you was deaf. Don't think none of us did. I'll pray for you.'

Where the fuck do I begin.

'I don't need your prayers. Have you seen anyone in the forest? Non hunters? You think this could be linked to the murder of Arne Persson?'

They all start talking at once. Group chat, the worst kind. The kind where I can't decipher a single thing and the voices melt into noise.

'Can I take a photo?'

Sven Edlund walks over to me. He smells terrible, like the hunt vest he's wearing has never been washed. He leans in close and says, 'Edlunds have been hunting this land for three-hundred years. No, you cannot take a photo. Men...' He turns to the table. 'Clear up, let's get back to it.'

The handlebar-moustache guy clears paper plates stained with blood and liver juice and throws them on the fire. It flares and spits. He places empty beer cans and uneaten bread into a black bin liner. He hangs the bin liner on the branch next to the dead cow elk.

Sven says to me, 'We have reports of a cow elk with young back that way.' He points to the way I came. The well-trodden trail through to the cars. 'You don't have a gun so we cannot guarantee your safety that way.'

'I'll walk with you guys.'

'No,' he says. 'No, you will not. We're hunting. We're going to the old pines. An elk would smell you a mile away.'

He sniffs the air around my head.

'You will go that way.' He points in the opposite direction, deeper into Visberg forest. 'There's a trail. Walk for five minutes, past both big beech trees, then take a right at the cliffs. Double back, follow the blue tape on the trees, and you'll get back to Visberg hill, back to the ghost bike.'

I look that way. Dense trees, packed so tight they block all the light.

'Think I'll go back the way I came. Take my chances.'

'We won't let you do that,' he says. 'We will not allow it. I'm not playing games here. It's life and death. That way…' he points to the trail I came on, 'is dangerous. That way…' he points to the dense trees, 'isn't. We're not giving you a choice.'

I walk a few paces, turn, and use my phone to take a low-key illicit photograph of the hunt scene. Then I run through the pines, my heart pounding. Nobody saw me. One large beech. I keep on going, my face slick with sweat and mist. A mosquito buzzing around by the back of my neck, looking for its next meal. Hunting. Everyone here's hunting something.

Another large beech. Broader than the first. Does this qualify? Is this the second beech Sven Edlund mentioned? I can't see any cliffs. I check my phone. Hardly any reception but there is some.

I stop dead when I hear a rifle shot.

Then two more, the booms ricocheting through the endless pine trunks and echoing inside my own head.

Did an elk just die? A wolf? A wild boar?

I walk on and get to a twenty-metre-high cliff of craggy granite. Trees sprout from its cracks and moss covers any surface that's not completely vertical.

But there is no blue tape flickering on tree branches. I've seen what they look like, I've written articles on them. Hunt teams tie plastic ribbons of varying colours so they can locate their own elk-hunting towers the next year. Did Sven send me the wrong way? Intentionally? Some kind of test? I check my phone. No reception here, seventeen per cent battery. And then I check the cameral roll on my phone for the last photo I took. Five hunters clearing their bench, all looking this way and that. But the sixth man is different. The sixth is the big guy with the red beard and he's staring straight into my lens. He saw me take the photograph.

I switch my phone to airplane mode to preserve the battery and I slip it in my inside pocket. I learned this trick last year. Battery life is extended if you keep the device at room or body temperature. A lithium battery will drain much faster at seven degrees than at thirty-seven. Is it even seven degrees still out here? Feels closer to zero.

There are no blue ribbons so I try to get back to the cliffs, back the way I came. All I need is that cliff, the beech, the other beech, then the clearing, the butchered animal, then the muddy path. I'll take my chances with the mother elk. Better her than a night in this unlit forest all alone.

You might think a twenty-metre-high granite cliff would be easy to find in a forest but you'd be wrong. I can't see up and I can't see across. No view to speak of. I try to stay calm, to breathe slowly, but I know I'm lost. I have no idea what direction is what. Two bites on my wrist and a scratch on my neck where I killed the mosquito, a wet smudge across my hairline.

No cliff.

No pair of beech trees.

No nothing.

The forest thickens up and it darkens. No more sounds of gunfire. Have the hunters left me here? Did they assume I found the trail and now they think I'm back in the safety of my truck?

I push through a dead bush and on up over a rocky escarpment.

A house.

A place I have seen before.

No windows or doors at ground level. Plenty upstairs. No lights on. No signs of life. Okay, so, worst comes to worst I break in and sleep inside tonight. At least I've found something man-made out here. Somewhere safe.

I scramble down past dead currant bushes and a compost bin with its lid missing.

Stacks of firewood all over the land like tiny shrines.

More logs leaning up against the house itself. But no discernible way in. No door or steps.

I retreat a little way and look up at the first-floor windows. There's a line of clocks on the sill. Mickey Mouse clocks and carriage clocks. All pointing out rather than in. There's a small, black, lightbulb-size balloon in the other window, its ribbon attached to the latch.

The wind picks up.

I can hear a chainsaw in the distance.

Breeze cooling the back of my neck.

The scent of kid's shampoo.

'Hello, Tuva.'

26

My hearing aids distort his words.

Feedback and white noise from the moisture.

I turn round.

Hans Wimmer's standing there. Looming a whole head taller than me.

'I just dropped off my daughter for choir practice at the Lutheran church. Did you want to see me?'

He's carrying logs and kindling. It doesn't look like he just dropped off his daughter.

'I got a bit lost out here. I was talking to the hunters, Sven Edlund and his friends, they're close by.'

'Barbarians,' says Hans. 'Bloodthirsty simpletons. I get no peace from autumn through spring living here. Marauding redneck executioners.'

'How do I get back to the road, Hans?'

He looks one way then the other, as if trying to figure it out himself.

'I have your old boss inside the house if you'd like to come inside for a coffee? It's still fresh in the pot.'

Lena? Or Anders, my old Malmö boss? All the way up here?

'Anders?'

'Who?'

'Anders, from Malmö.'

'Who?' he says again. 'I have Mr Ragnar Johannes Falk inside the house. Come in and warm up, if you like, before you trek back to the main road?'

There's no smoke coming from the chimney. The house doesn't even look occupied. Is Falk really here? With the lights switched off? Is he okay?

'No, no. I should be...'

'What a lovely surprise, Tuva,' says Ragnar, walking from behind the house, his limp more evident than before, his white beard glowing in the damp, forest air. 'What an unexpected surprise.'

'Go back in, back in,' says Hans. 'Nobody's watching the *dammsugare*. The house mice will surely eat the lot.'

But Ragnar walks toward us. He's wearing a yellow pocket handkerchief just like Hans Wimmer. They both turn and head back toward the house and disappear behind it.

I follow.

There's a set of outdoor concrete stairs up to a first-floor door. They're hidden unless you approach this dark side of the building. Ragnar's taking his time to get up the steps.

'Come in, come in. Make yourself at home, Tuva. Please sit down.'

The house is wooden on the inside, like a sauna, and it's almost as hot as one. There are kids' toys all over the place: dolls and doll's houses, racing-car models and tin soldiers. There's a jigsaw of *Frozen* fully completed on the timber floorboards.

He steps over to the fireplace. 'Let me light this.'

Ragnar sinks down into an old, fabric armchair. There's a sofa with lace antimacassars, and a low coffee table with a cracked glass top. Three sets of coffee cups and saucers laid out, like they knew I'd be arriving. And a plate of *dammsugare*: little cake rolls wrapped in poison-green marzipan and dipped in chocolate. Named after an old-fashioned design vacuum cleaner. The name literally means 'fluff sucker'.

The fire crackles and spits in the hearth and Hans blows air at it with a creaky pair of leather bellows.

'Where was I?' he says, before pouring us all coffee.

Ragnar says something but I still can't hear. My aids need a night in desiccant. *I* need a fucking night in desiccant.

'I'll be out of your way soon,' I say. 'Nice to dry out and warm up.'

Ragnar wipes sweat from his brow and says something but I can't make it out. My lip-reading isn't *that* good.

'What?' I say.

'Why are you out here?'

'Hunters,' I say, sweat dribbling down my back. 'They reported some elk skulls missing. Seven of them. So I had to come out here to report on the story.'

'Barbarians,' says Hans Wimmer. 'Primitive heathens.'

One of my aids starts working clearly again.

'You know,' says Ragnar, fanning himself with his hand. 'Hunters round here take their lifestyle so seriously that their year starts on day one of the elk hunt. There is no January to December for Visberg hunters. They plot their whole year around this savagery.'

Suddenly I'm exhausted. Sleepy. It's like I'm being drawn back to this infested hillside. The mass of it, the darkness within, the spinning bee perched on top, keeps drawing me closer.

'Police are talking to those sisters two doors down renting the shop,' says Ragnar. 'They got wind of the rumours.'

'Rumours?' I ask.

'That the mute one had issues with Arne Persson. That they'd had some kind of fight and Arne scared her.'

'First of all, Alice isn't mute. Second of all, I doubt anyone could scare her or her sister.'

Hans loosens his collar, then pours coffee from his cup into his saucer and sips it. Ragnar does the exact same thing.

'I don't know all the facts,' says Hans Wimmer. 'But they were definitely having *issues*. Lawyer letters and so forth. The license on the pop-up shop was informal on account of the short term, you see. I have a twenty-year lease on my shop.' He looks proud of himself. 'Arne only gave them a one-week rolling-term licence.'

'Arne Persson was their landlord?'

'Inherited the place from his uncle. His uncle was a wealthy man in these parts. I heard Arne was in the process of evicting the Sorlie sisters. Trying to, at least.'

'Those troll creations,' says Ragnar, his cheeks reddening.

'Quite despicable things,' says Hans.

'One even had a…' Ragnar Falk makes a ring with the fingers on one hand and takes his index finger of the other hand and jabs it through the hole.

'A…?'

Ragnar and Hans Wimmer both nod and slurp more coffee from their saucers. It's a thing in Sweden, mainly with the older folk. Cools down the coffee.

The room is hotter than ever. It's stifling.

'I need to be getting back before the woods get too dark,' says Ragnar. 'Don't want to be mistaken for a tasty deer, do I?'

'Me too,' I say. 'Can we walk together?'

Ragnar says, 'I'd like that very much indeed. We can talk about the newspaper business.'

We say goodbye to Hans and set off. Feels totally different walking in the woods with Ragnar Falk. He was a journalist here for over thirty years. I trust him. An old man with a limp and a good standing in the community. He's not a hunter and he did a deal with Lena. She knows him. I guess, in a way, she vouches for him.

The pines glow grey in the murky twilight. This is elk o'clock, the most dangerous time of night. Ragnar can keep up a surprisingly good pace considering his leg. I follow behind and focus on the orange, reflective stripe on the hood of his waterproof jacket.

Two gunshots in fast succession. A cloud of birds squawk and lift from an oak tree. They scar the pale sky as they flee.

I take my phone off airplane mode. Twelve per cent battery.

We pass the smouldering bonfire left by the hunters. Hooves and entrails and curled, half-burnt paper plates. The skin left on the ground like a dishevelled rug, stained with bile. Fluids leaching into the pine-needle floor.

Noises ahead.

Car engines.

The safety of a tarmacked road.

We reach the ditch and I help Ragnar cross it. As I leap across I see my own reflection down in the still, brown water. A woman leaving the realm of the wild things and rejoining safe, predictable civilisation. From uneven ground to flat. From nothingness to a route away.

Ragnar looks over at the white-bike memorial. At its spray-painted saddle and handlebars and brakes. At the white bell. The basket. He waves me away and sets off in his Saab. I walk up the side of the road to find my Hilux.

The hill is so steep my calves start aching.

Six per cent battery on my phone.

I think I can see the bee on top of the Hive in the far distance up the hill. But it could be a plane flying over. Or a streetlight. It's difficult to judge the angle from down here.

I find my truck and break out into a broad grin.

A crow rises from the treetops.

And then there's an explosive crack in the air and the pine immediately behind me shatters, covering me with splinters of wet bark.

27

I freeze.

Is there an elk or deer behind me somewhere? A creature that just escaped death? Or am I that creature?

I run toward my truck, and that's when the next bullet almost hits me.

I drop.

The sound ricochets off the trunks all around me. Ragnar's gone. No cars. No help anywhere.

I start to hyperventilate. My heart pounding against the wet ground.

Something took the impact back in the treeline – granite, I think. Something splintered. I'm not sure I heard it but I could sense the impact.

I swallow hard. Searching everywhere with my eyes.

Is this a hunt? Am I in someone's sights right now?

I crawl on my hands and knees along the lip of the ditch, loose chips of gravel biting into the flesh of my palms. I try to drag myself flat but I don't have the strength.

No more shots.

It's like I'm pinned down by a sniper in a video game.

No cars pass by.

I keep low, wet grass brushing my chin.

My pulse thumps in my temples. Is he reloading? You are not going to die out here on this godforsaken hill, Tuva. This is not how it ends.

Six more metres to my truck. Do I stand up and dash for it, or stay low and take my time? They might be gone now. Whoever had me in their sights probably left already. They missed and then they left.

My Hilux looks like a reinforced fortress as I approach. I take my key from my pocket and hold it between my teeth. I don't unlock, I want as little signal of my position as possible. I crawl. My jeans are caked in mud and I have dirt up inside each sleeve. No more shots. No bullets. I'm almost there.

Three more metres.

Silence.

I look across the road. A wall of spruce. No hunters to look at. No elk-shooting tower or plastic ribbons. No beam of red light from a laser sight.

The sound of a car. The vibrations. From downhill or uphill? I can't get up or cry out for help. I want to but that would be a mistake. I have to stay low, and anyway that may just be the car of the shooter. What would Dad have done? He'd have been patient. He always said, *more haste less speed.*

Sweat runs down into my ears, mingling with the plastic tubing of my hearing aids.

I need to make a dash for it. To get to my Hilux.

My pulse speeds up to a drumroll.

I get to my knees and lunge forward to my truck and feel the hiss of another bullet pass me. Fuck. I unlock and jump in and duck down on the front seats. Will he ambush me here? Will he shoot my tyres out? I stretch my arm and turn the key. Engine noise. I keep my head down. The noise of my wheels as I accelerate hard up the hill back toward the town I'm learning to fear.

No more bullets. Nobody driving after me.

I cough from the adrenaline and sit upright, my attention on my mirrors, my heart still pounding.

How many bullets was that? Three?

Mud all over the steering wheel.

I speed up to 120, hardly slowing to take corners, my truck flexing on its suspension. Up into Visberg town. Someone beeps their horn as I race pass Konsum and take the side-road up by Annika's place. I leave town and drive back round the long way toward Gavrik.

I try to hook up my phone to my hearing aids but my aids are too wet.

I put my phone on speaker. Two per cent battery.

'Thord, I've been shot at.'

'What? Where are you?'

'I'm okay.' My words spit out twice as fast as usual. 'I'm coming into the station.'

'You're not injured?'

'I'll be there in twenty. And—'

My phone dies.

The road back is dark. No streetlights in this part of the world. I can see nothing ahead and nothing behind. Darkness. No vehicles. Fringes of rough, unmanaged forest.

My breathing slows and so does my heart. Who the fuck shoots at someone in Sweden? In broad daylight? Blood in my mouth. I bit my lip falling to the ground. I'm cold with sweat and the adrenaline in my bloodstream is only now starting to fade. I turn the heated seat on. And the heated steering wheel. I'm shivering.

I pull up in the no-parking area outside the cop shop and open my door and run inside.

Thord's there on the public side of the desk.

'Come through.'

We pass through the keycode-locked door.

It's just me and him. No Chief, no Noora. Three cells and five desks. Filing cabinets. A Big Mac box on Thord's desk, with its fries carton flat underneath and his ketchup thimble stored neatly inside.

He places his hand on my shoulder. 'You say you got shot at?'

I nod and all of a sudden I want to hug him. Burst into tears. Collapse. But I hold it together and say, 'Visberg hill, close to the white-bike memorial. Three shots, I think.'

Chief Björn walks in carrying a mug of coffee with 'Miami PD' written on the side in big, blue letters. He raises his eyebrows when he sees my muddy clothes. 'Heard there was some kind of ruckus.'

'I got shot at.'

He walks closer.

'Out on the street?'

Thord turns to him and says, 'Visberg hill.'

'Boar hunt?' says the Chief.

'The bullets got close.'

'Sure can feel that way,' says the Chief. 'One time out in Utgard, few hunts back this was, maybe four years ago, might have even been five, I could've sworn a bullet sailed right through my cap.' He runs his fingers through his grey hair. 'We located said bullet after an hour or more of searching. Curious, I was. Couldn't let it go. Turns out I was more than twenty metres away from that shot.'

'Now, wait a—'

'Ain't calling anyone a liar or no such thing,' says the Chief, taking a sip of his coffee and recoiling from it like it's too hot. 'Not such an easy thing to judge, is all.'

'I was shot at.'

Chief scrunches his eyes together and scratches his head.

'You see the shooter, did you?'

'No.'

'Was it dark?'

'It was getting dark. All this happened less than an hour ago.'

The Chief nods and blows into his mug through puckered lips.

'Now, don't take this the wrong way but I got twenty-twenty vision and twenty-twenty hearing, if that's even the correct measurement, and I couldn't judge how close a bullet came to ending my existence. Police officer thirty-eight years, Chief for nineteen.

I'm a hunting man, shot my first elk at twelve with my granddaddy up near Östersund way. I'm not making no judgement one way or the other, but believe you me, it's tough to judge how close a shot came to hitting you.'

Thord offers me a Kleenex and I wipe my face and my neck and blow my nose.

'Chief's got a point,' he says.

'There were three separate shots.'

'It's hunt season. Boar and elk up by Visberg forest. This ain't Stockholm city,' says the Chief. 'Ain't even close. You had a scare and I acknowledge that. I'll even talk to the hunt boss out in Visberg to emphasise the need for good sportsmanlike conduct.'

'Hunt chief?'

'Edlund's his name. Dental man.'

Oh, great.

'Who do I go to if the police don't believe me?'

Chief takes a long swig of coffee and keeps it in his cheeks and shakes his head. 'Ain't a matter of belief. Not that simple, I'm afraid. It's more a matter of perception.'

'Maybe I'll call Falun police,' I say.

Thord puts out his hand but the Chief says, 'It's alright, you go right ahead. I'll let old Markus Carlsson know to expect your call, if you like. He's a fair man, Markus. Tough, but fair. I reckon he'd hear you out.'

Fuck this.

I turn to walk out and then I remember the note.

I check my pocket and drag out the folded front page of the *Visberg Tidningen* dated two weeks ago. It's damp and limp.

'Got this under my door earlier today. Pushed under, in the secure area of my apartment.'

Thord reads it and then walks over to Chief Björn and hands it to him.

The Chief puts on his glasses.

'Neighbourly dispute?' he says. 'You still live on Marksplatsen?'

'I moved.'

'New building, new neighbours. We'll look into this if you like.'

I stare at Thord and his radio comes to life. It's Noora's voice. Some kind of code. Thord replies with a code of his own and then turns to me and says, 'The constable will be here in a few minutes. End of shift.'

Noora and I head back to my place in the Hilux. I tell her what happened on the hill. I tell her about the Chief's reaction.

'I'm staying with you for the next few days,' she says. 'I already have two shelves in your wardrobe. I'm armed and trained. I won't let anything happen to you, you hear me?'

I nod and she places her hand on my knee.

I stagger upstairs to my apartment. The adrenaline has left my vascular system and I am barely a shell of a person.

Noora makes us both scrambled eggs while I shower. I come out in my robe with a towel wrapped around my head.

'Sit down,' she says. 'Thord's filled me in on the contents of the note.'

Eggs, golden and perfectly cooked. Silky ribbons and folds. Rough crystals of sparkling sea salt, cracked black pepper and tiny rings of sliced chive, all resting upon rough-cut sourdough toast. The steam rises up and I can sense the heat from the pepper.

I eat and she eats.

Then she puts me to bed.

Noora lets me rest my damp hair on her arm and she sings a nursery rhyme in Arabic. Something beautiful and soothing her mother sang to her as a child in Gothenburg. I try to forget the three bullets, the three near-death experiences. She sings and my eyes close.

28

Noora wakes me with a kiss to the forehead and I pull her in close.

An hour later I cook her American-style pancakes from a packet I bought in ICA Maxi last week. I add blueberries and syrup. They look pretty decent considering I made them. She makes lattes and we sit out on my little two-person balcony with blankets over our knees.

'Sunday brunch,' she says.

I kiss my fingertips and say, 'Out of a box, but still, they're pretty tasty, no?'

'Sorry I can't stay longer. Thord asked to swap shifts. He's got some kind of wedding-planning thing with Priest Kilby down at the Lutheran church.'

'It's fine.' I fold over a thick pancake and it splits open and the soft, fluffy insides emit steam into the cool October air. 'I'm not so shaken today. Maybe the Chief was right. Maybe the bullets were twenty metres away and I'm just being paranoid.'

'Call me anytime you feel you're in danger,' says Noora. 'Where will you be today?'

'I need to visit the Edlund golf club.'

She frowns. 'You trying to get your green card, Tiger?'

'Hell, no. Trying to interview Eva Edlund, boss of the club, on the pretence of a bullshit feel-good article about their philanthropic pre-Christmas gala dinner.'

'You got a problem with philanthropy?'

'Not always,' I say. 'But I reckon if the billionaires paid all their taxes there'd be less need for it. And less need for them to graffiti their names all over hospital wings and school libraries. If they just quietly paid what was due like everyone else manages to do, and they kept their names to themselves, I think the world would look a little better.'

Noora thinks about that.

'I've been sending files over to a psychological profiler in Uppsala. Smart guy named Westergren. Isn't it amazing what they can glean from bare-bones evidence?'

I stay silent. I just want her to keep talking.

She sips her latte and the milk stains her upper lip.

'For example,' she says. 'The way the killer dealt with the body. Severing the head *after* death. Taking it away. Working meticulously on the teeth. Painstaking work. Westergren thinks it suggests someone who may have killed before, perhaps multiple times. Someone whose crimes are escalating. A first-time killer is unlikely to have severed the head. They'd have been satisfied with the kill itself. And they certainly wouldn't have been so cold as to have worked diligently on a dead man's teeth.'

'You saying there's a serial killer in Visberg?'

She shakes her head. '*I'm* not saying it, the profiler is suggesting it's a possibility. That's all. And his conclusion isn't that this person has killed before, just that it's an angle we should look into. Westergren also made clear the killer didn't necessarily have any formal dental training. Could have been self taught through the internet or an international-correspondence course. Maybe some training overseas.'

'That doesn't help you much.'

She takes another sip of coffee.

'He thinks the most disturbing factor is the killer's display of trophies, I think that's the word he used. *Trophies.* Leaving the teeth and the head in plain sight. That he or she may have got more of a thrill mingling in a crowd and leaving those items, and then witnessing the crowd's reaction, than he did killing or working on the severed head. Westergren thinks he might be taunting the police.'

'Taunting?'

'Said maybe he's some kind of sociopath with a chip on his shoulder. Deep-seated issues with authority. Maybe he's trying to prove he's superior. Possibly had a childhood of juvenile offences, trauma, or else bullying or belittling by one or both parents.'

'Sounds like a normal upbringing to me.'

She kicks me gently under the table.

'I can't remember exactly word for word.'

'Can I see the profile?'

She shakes her head. 'No can do.'

'So what did you learn?'

'Sorry?'

'That you didn't know already, I mean. About the killer.'

She looks out at lovers' walk. At the trees turning red and the benches still sparkling with dew.

'We already know the perp is someone with access to a rifle. Someone with training, or experience handling a firearm and a chainsaw. Someone with physical strength, enough to carry both items, as the medical examiner states the beheading was carried out soon after the gunshot wound was inflicted. Likely someone local, who knows Visberg forest and knows all about Pan Night. An insider. Now we can add disturbed, bullied, and/or attention-seeking to the list. Unfortunately, that describes half of Värmland.'

I start to clear away the plates and Noora puts her hand on mine.

'I was thinking,' she says.

And then she smiles. A full, easy smile that reaches all the way up to her eyes.

'We both work long hours. Irregular hours. We both have diddly-squat in terms of savings.' She laughs. 'I'm sorry, this isn't sounding as romantic as it did in my head. What I'm trying to say is: Tuva, what do you think about us moving in together?'

I stand there like an idiot, plates in hand, staring at her.

Noora's smile flattens. Deflates.

'I mean, there's no rush, but—'

'No,' I say. 'It's just...'

It's just that I am completely terrified. I'm head over heels for you, I really am, but I need my own space. I'm too young, or too weird, or too pathetic. Almost definitely too selfish. I don't want you to see me when I'm sad. Or drunk. When I'm too lazy to do the dishes. When I leave the trash bags by the door for days and days.

'No big deal,' she says, helping with the plates, moving this awkward scene forward. 'No rush. Just think about it. I'm not down on one knee, Tuva. It's not a big deal.'

I take the plates inside.

Everything feels wrong.

Why am I so fucking awkward about this? Because if I relapse I don't want her to see me drink. I don't want her to see me game until 4am to keep the dark thoughts of Mum out of my head. The guilt. The knowledge that I didn't do enough for her. Didn't allow her to die with a simple, sincere word of love in her ear.

'I have to go,' says Noora, kissing me on the cheek.

'Let's talk about it soon,' I say.

'Sure,' she says, closing the door behind her.

What's wrong with me? Why do I sabotage every good thing that comes into my life. Like I don't deserve to be truly happy. Like I have to contain and limit any joy so it's manageable. Put it in a small box. I can't let go, just be in love, forget about the past. Why do I need to keep the world at a distance? Is it to stop myself from getting hurt? I get hurt, anyway.

I drive to Visberg. Empty. My guts dry and scratchy.

My dash reads eight degrees. I squirt my windscreen to remove the dead carapaces of insects, long deceased. Escapees from the forest, each one a victim of a head-on collision but their diminutive size means they're disregarded. Squirt, wipe, gone.

At eleven-twenty, I pass by Svensson's Saws & Axes. Closed. At eleven-forty, I drive past the white bike, past the cross, over the railway lines, past the bus shelter and up into Visberg. The sun is shining out from behind the giant roof bee. The sunny side of the street has a few people milling around. Pre-ordering takeout pizza or buying sweets from Konsum. The shady side of the street is completely deserted. The statue is taped off. The apple trees are almost completely bare.

I head on out of town, up toward the old, abandoned steel mill.

The sign to the golf club is split into two. On top it says, 'Edlund Golf' in gold script. Under that, a larger sign with bold print that reads, 'Strictly Members Only'. Maybe I'm small minded, but I really can't stand these places.

I drive through some kind of putting practice area with lots of holes and small flags. The car park is full. It's immaculate: no garbage, no single bush out of place. The cars are all expensive modern Volvos. Sleek lines and no bling. Stealth wealth. And when I say they're all Volvos I am not exaggerating. My muddy Hilux looks like a redneck crashed a banker's convention. It's me, and then I count seventeen, no, eighteen Volvos, each one of them new and sparkly clean. They do valet service here or something?

I walk toward the clubhouse, which is designed to mimic some kind of Bahamian hotel; all layered roof levels and covered verandahs. Except here they need outdoor heaters. Lots of them.

'Excuse me, ma'am. Are you a guest of a member?'

He's skinny and angular, with slicked-down short hair and light pink trousers and a check shirt. He's my age. He looks like a goddam extra from a '50s comedy.

'I'm here to see Eva Edlund.'

He nods and one of his eyebrows twitches at the mention of her name.

Pink trousers opens the main door for me.

'Take a seat here, please. Your name is?'

'Tuva Moodyson,' I say. 'You can call me Tuva Moodyson.'

He bites his upper lip and fixes his hair and walks off down a corridor.

Fuck me, this place is fancy. Tiled limestone flooring, bar at the far end, a locked-up pro shop and another locked-up pro office, whatever that is. Does a pro golfer really need an office? How much paperwork can there possibly be?

A couple walk past me, both in their seventies. She has blonde hair up in a bun and he's bald. They're both tanned, not from a sunbed, not even from a late summer break, but from spending time at their own apartment in Nice or Majorca. I can tell. The tan isn't hurried; it's been worked on and curated. They both scowl at me and he removes his golf glove to reveal an identical copy of the pinkie ring I spotted on Sven Edlund's little finger. The one with the woodcock.

'You found us alright, then,' says Eva Edlund, suddenly beside me. Then she says, 'Hello Diedrich, hello Susannah. Pleasant round?'

'Just glorious,' says Susannah. 'Seventy-nine.'

'Seventy-seven,' says her bald partner.

'That dog-leg on the fifth,' says Susannah.

'It's a rascal,' says Eva, turning to shake my hand. 'Would you like to come with me, Tuva?'

She walks and I follow. She's a little shorter than me but ten times more fit. She's wearing white trousers and a yellow, polo shirt with a blue cashmere sweater draped casually over her shoulders.

'I've set us up here so you can see the eighteenth hole. Do you play?'

'No.'

'Pity.'

We sit down outside on patio furniture, the expensive rattan type. There are heaters all around to keep the air at room temperature. A large, dark-green Bose speaker sits a little way from us playing anaemic jazz. There are others planted around and there are uplighters hidden among the clipped, green bushes and granite rocks.

'Still or sparkling?'

She's got both here waiting on the table, along with two tall glasses etched with the Edlund Club logo, each filled with ice and lemon.

'Sparkling, please. Do you mind if I record?'

I place my digital Dictaphone on the table.

'Well, I don't know, I...'

'Because I'm deaf,' I say. Nobody ever says no after that.

'Of course,' she says. 'I'm sorry.'

'Tell me a little background about the club, if you would.'

She stares at my ears. 'There was a less formal club here, erected in the '50s, quite a rough little nine-hole thing; shabby, open to everyone. But the current course and clubhouse were established in 2003. We're strictly members only.'

I look around at the crowd. They all look exactly the same. Easy smiles and big sunglasses. Pastel-green trousers and black-and-white golfing shoes. Caps and visors. More Ralph Lauren logos per square metre than perhaps anywhere else on planet earth.

'What is the membership criteria?'

'It's... confidential.'

I notice a figure walking toward the green on the eighteenth hole. It's Ragnar Falk, with a guy I don't recognise.

She talks more about how they're recruiting a new pro, how they have a new chef, bla, bla, bla. This place is WASP central. It's whiter than a goddam ski resort in Nazi Germany.

'Has the club been impacted by the Arne Persson murder?'

She looks aghast and leans in closer. 'No, of course it hasn't. This place is an exclusive escape from all that dreadful news. Look around you.'

Greens and fairways poisoned with weedkiller. Smug middle-aged golfers drinking spritzers and eating overpriced Waldorf salads. Some awful super-fit woman demonstrating her swing to a table of enthralled onlookers.

'Was Arne Persson a member here?'

'He was a plumber,' she says. Her eyes narrow.

'But I heard he was here a lot. Something to do with the sprinkler systems?'

She looks down at my Dictaphone and takes a sip of her sparkling water and then she coughs so hard people start to turn and look.

I look at them and gesture toward Eva and say, 'Too much gin.'

She goes bright red and turns and says, 'She's only joking,' and then turns back to me.

'What do you want?'

'You must know everyone in this town if you're the membership director for the club. If someone wants to get into this elite place, they need to go through you. I want to know if you have any theories, any useful gossip, regarding the vicious murder.'

She looks down at the Dictaphone and mouths the word, 'Off.'

I switch it off.

'Why on earth would I divulge theories like that to someone like you?'

'Because my investigations can help solve the crime. Help get justice. How about that? Or maybe because I have carte blanche to write whatever I choose about your golf club. That a good enough reason? I can write a glowing article that will not only be read by ten-thousand locals, but also online by other prestigious golf clubs in Gotland or in the expensive suburbs outside Stockholm. Or I can write something less…' I pause, 'less glowing.'

She frowns but Botox ensures it's not much of a frown. Her eyes are narrow slits of hate right now.

'Two things. Are you sure that contraption is turned off?'

I nod and show it to her.

'One. No member here is implicated in any way. We're a closed group. We know each other's business and many of us are in fact related. This is in many ways a family organisation.' She lowers her voice to a whisper but I can just about hear her. 'We know who's sleeping with who; when someone loses a significant sum of money on an ill-advised investment. There are no secrets here.'

'And?'

She sits up a little straighter. 'The Yugoslav pizza chef.'

'Kodro is Bosnian. And he's not the chef, he's the owner.'

She scowls at me. 'Have you researched his personal war-record? The man was investigated by the international-war-crimes tribunal in The Hague. He wasn't tried in the end but I'm told that decision was purely political. You look into what he was accused of and you'll find some very troubling similarities to the Arne Persson slaughter.'

'Okay.'

'Two. The Yugoslav is very close to the twin boys who own the computer-game café next door to his grease pit. Those twins were harmless enough before they met him. They used to play their dragons and dungeons games, playing cards mainly. But since the Yugoslav moved in next door they've been involved in extremely violent and sadistic online games. And the Yugoslav plays, too, after both shops have closed. Some kind of cult in there. They even have an interconnecting door between the buildings; they don't know I know but I do. The door connects their basements underground. Those two boys have been trained up like his personal soldiers. The three of them have turned into some kind of elite Yugoslav death squad.'

29

On the way out to the car park I pass six women who all look identical. Blonde bobs, well-fitted trousers, expensive leather trainers, navy-blue merino-wool sweaters, gold jewellery, designer sunglasses up in their hair. I can't help staring. They look straight through me and stiffen their smiles.

Volvo, Volvo, Volvo, my beloved Hilux. I jump in and speed off, leaving the Edlund cult – sorry, club – behind in my mirrors. Place makes me shiver. Entitlement, short grass and tiny little balls.

In the office I remove my aids and start digging. There isn't much noise in here, just Lena in her office talking on the phone to an old friend in New York. But I like the ritual. Aids out, tabs open, Word doc waiting.

There's nothing on The Hague international-war-crime tribunal website specifically mentioning Luka Kodro. Nothing at all. But I do find individuals with similar names indicted for crimes against humanity. Genocide and murder and ethnic cleansing. The shooting of civilians and the mortaring of villages. Rape. The establishment of concentrations camps. Men indicted from all sides. This horror took place in mainland Europe when I was just a kid. It's unthinkable that it happened at any time in history, but this happened in the '90s. And it's shocking that we don't really talk about it more.

I find some interesting long-form think pieces on *Hunted 2.0*, the game the twins apparently play. It's cited in papers calling for tighter regulation. There's one piece written by a South Korean professor explaining how these ultra-violent, ultra-realistic games are potentially dangerous. He doesn't know to what extent. He writes that it's a difficult thing to quantify. But he warns that the introduction of artificial-intelligence technology, creating AI enemies and ultra-HD lifelike avatars, and the widespread adoption of sophisticated, virtual-reality gaming hardware, may combine to create such a heightened and immersive gaming experience that users could, theoretically, have a tough time differentiating the real world from the world of games like *Hunted 2.0.* My default position is to leave gamers the hell alone. It's usually old dudes who've never even played on a Gameboy regulating what the younger generations should play. But the South Korean professor may have a point. Makes me think.

I draw a map.

Sometimes, especially with an investigation this complex, with so few clues, it helps me to sketch. I've seen large whiteboards over in the cop shop. Saw them during Midsommar when the police were out looking for Tammy and Lisa Svensson. Useful to have something visual to let a different quadrant of your brain mull over.

I draw Visberg like a spider in the centre of a vast web. Immediately around the statue where Arne's head was left on the anvil I mark out the square. The Hive dominates at the top. Then the Grill, the gamer café, the pharmacy and Konsum, all on the left of the map. Opposite, the dental surgery, the old newspaper-office, the pop-up shop, the clockmaker's shop and private basement museum. Then, spreading out, I note the golf club to the north-east, and the long, steep hill to the west. The bike and the approximate area where Arne's body was discovered. The clockmaker's house. The abandoned train tracks. The white-bike memorial.

There is a person – or maybe more than one person – living and working within this map who shot, dismembered, and posthumously whitened the teeth of a local plumber. That person, wielding a rifle and chainsaw, is still at large. They may be storing their weapons under their marital bed or in their basement or at their place of work. They may be keeping them in their Volvo so they can evade capture, if and when the police catch up with them. Maybe they've sunk the evidence in Snake River or in the depths of Utgard forest. A gun and a bloody saw and some tooth pliers and drilling equipment, and half a dozen or more elk skulls.

Lena opens the door from her office. She has her phone in her hand.

Her lips say, 'Call for you.'

I put in my hearing aids and give her a thumbs up. She puts the call through.

'Tuva Moodyson.'

'Ms Moodyson, hello, I'm glad I caught you. This is Margareta Sofia Erikkson from the Hive self-storage in Visberg town. How are things with you today?

'Fine. What can I do for you?'

'Well, I was talking to my son, and Emil told me you'd been making extensive enquiries round the town about this awful business. I wanted to, well, he wanted to…'

'Go on.'

'Do you have plans, Ms Moodyson? Sunday-dinner plans, I mean? It's just that we haven't had a chance to say our piece yet. Do you have any plans?'

'Dinner plans? I could come over to interview you, if you like.'

'That's all good and dandy, but Emil and I always share a proper hot Sunday dinner, have done ever since before his daddy passed. Call it six sharp?'

I look over at Lars's empty desk. Seb's empty desk. Maybe I work too much?

'I'll be there.'

'Very good.'

She calls off.

On the way out of Gavrik, I notice two pumpkins flanking the entrance to Grimberg Liquorice. One has an upturned, carved smile and the other has a downturned grimace.

The sky is the colour of cheap, laminated chipboard – a huge white slab of the stuff.

Chris Isaak on the radio. 'Wicked Game', the one from *Wild at Heart.* My driver's window is ajar. The steam from the sewage works leaches into the truck.

The music changes to some kind of Gregorian chanting. Humming and echoing like it was recorded inside a monastery. Or a cave.

When I arrive in the hill town, I see a horse in the town square. Sitting on top of it is Sheriff Harry Hansson, except today he's in his Sunday best and he really does look like a sheriff. Like some freak accident of space-time has dumped a man from Alabama or Mississippi into Visberg, Värmland.

I park up and walk over.

A young girl with pigtails pats the Sheriff's horse. The horse flares its nostrils and the girl does the same.

'Evening,' says the Sheriff.

'Nice horse.'

'Marsie's a fine specimen, alright. Of course, so was her mamma.'

The horse looks serene in this strange town. A beautiful creature with a chestnut coat and braided mane. The saddle is deep-brown leather and it looks oiled and well maintained. The Sheriff's boots are in the same condition. He has no spurs, but they wouldn't look out of place.

'Be a good girl and tell your pappa I'll be over at seven to collect my pepperoni with peanuts.'

Pigtails girl nods and skips across the road toward Visberg Grill.

'Luka Kodro's girl?'

'Youngest. Got one a little older as well. Both of them like the horses so I let them pet Marsie on a Sunday. No harm, no foul.'

'Any developments on the Arne Persson case, Sheriff?'

I know, I know. He's not a fucking sheriff. He's not any recognisable part of law enforcement whatsoever. But part of my job is to appease people like Harry Hansson. Oil the inner workings of the town. Grease them. Make things happen. If I call him 'Sheriff' he might tell me something. I don't really have a choice.

'Chief Björn tells me the forensic-science folks down in Linköping are hard at work on fibres and all sorts. You know they can get DNA from fabric these days? From the sweat or somesuch. They can tell who was dressed in what. You hear about it?'

'I hadn't.'

'Think about that next time you buy second-hand clothes. Think about that when you're checking out them pretty vintage dresses. You could be wearing evidence.'

I pinch my collar. 'All ICA Maxi specials.'

Sheriff smiles and nods his hat and says, 'Stay safe, Tuva.' And his horse clip-clops down toward the gamer café.

The flats above the ground-level shops have started to display their Christmas lights. They normally come out in November or early December but when there's been darkness, a local tragedy or an accident, they oftentimes get brought out weeks ahead of schedule. If the world outside is setting itself up to be black and cold, you have to do whatever you can to make life manageable. Some people light scented candles and bake cakes. They bring their SAD lamps out of storage and they buy themselves a challenging, new jigsaw puzzle. I game and I drink on weekends. Not weekdays, not anymore. I'm not sure if my drinking is a brain thing or a genes thing or what. But I had periods in London where I was taken advantage of. Weekends where I was left with an empty bank-account or purse. Mornings at the local clinic getting tested. Nights spent on friends' sofas to get away from obsessive men. I battled to get back control and now I'll fight to keep hold of it. Even if that means disappointing Noora. I'll explain to her why I'm weird. That it's me, not her.

I pick up a bunch of red roses in Konsum. They are blood-red, not bright red. These are dark, and every petal gives up its browns and its crimsons and its purples. A palette of mammalian blood that takes me back to that awful night in Visberg forest.

The town falls dark.

I cross over the street and almost get hit by a teenager on a high-pitch motorbike. He's riding too fast along with his mate. Tweaked engines and sturdy helmets. Rebellious but not too rebellious. Easy rider but not too easy.

The bee on top of the Hive spins slowly.

I notice the pigeon spikes all around the Hive's roofline. Thousands of upturned nails. A small songbird skewered on one, as if ready to roast over a naked flame; its feathers intact but its head reduced to a beautiful and delicate skull.

'Come in out of that cold,' says Margareta, opening the door, lit cigarette in hand. 'We have so much to talk about.'

30

Margareta takes my coat and ushers me through a door marked 'Private'.

She notices me sliding off my shoes and says, 'Oh, no, keep them on if you like, dear. We always do. Germs are good for you, I say.'

All of a sudden I lose my appetite.

'You eat meat, Tuva?'

'I eat pretty much anything.'

'Good for you,' she says. 'Pesky vegans get right on my tits. Emil, come in and say hello to Tuva.'

Emil approaches. He's in over-washed jeans, so pale they're almost white. Converse high-tops and a jock-style baseball jacket, the kind you see good-looking teenagers wear on American TV shows. His moustache has been oiled and the ends turn up slightly like a hairy smile.

'Hi, Tuva.'

'*Hej*, Emil.'

His wrists are covered with candy bracelets. Five or more on each arm.

'You kids sit down and get comfy while I finish off the meal.'

She leaves the room.

'You like *Cheers*?'

'Sorry?'

'*Cheers*,' he says. 'The award-winning American TV show.'

Actually I do. Saw reruns on YouTube back in my London university days. Flatmate used to watch them on her laptop whenever she was down.

'Yeah.'

He switches on the huge TV in the corner of the room. All the furniture is arranged to face it. The wallpaper is more like pub carpet: dark reds and greens and purples. A swirly, paisley pattern. Looks like fabric, like it's soft to the touch. The actual carpet is shag pile. Thick and soft. This kind of décor is unusual in Sweden, to say the least. Most people associate carpets with asthma. They see outdoor shoes inside and they associate that with 1950s English B&Bs, the kind with fluffy rugs under the toilet in the splash zone, and also, just for added pizazz, on top of the toilet-seat lid.

The theme tune of *Cheers* bursts out of the speakers and Emil switches the volume down.

'Sit,' he says, pointing to an armchair.

I sit and he sits in the next one over. There are three armchairs in this room, all pointed at the TV. No sofa. No bookshelves.

'Press the button,' he says. He presses his and his chair reclines and his feet shoot up on some fabric-sheathed platform.

I do as he says and smile as my chair transforms into a magnificent, kitsch thing, similar to the one Dad used to own.

'How long have you lived here in Visberg?'

'Since I was born,' says Emil.

Two small doors on the far wall burst open. Some kind of hatch. Margareta is there, cigarette in hand, pushing through two drinks.

'Bottoms up,' she says, and then she does some kind of move. I think she contorted herself to lift her bottom but the wall is obscuring the view.

Emil resets his chair and gets up to bring the drinks over.

'One for you,' he says, placing down my drink on a faux-mahogany shelf that swivels out from my chair. 'And one for me.'

His looks like Coke and mine looks like a margarita, with crushed salt or sugar crystals lining the lip of the glass. The liquid is semi-frozen. Nuclear pink. Finished with a slice of blood orange and a tiny umbrella, and a grape skewered with a cocktail stick.

'Chin, chin,' says Emil, his candy bracelet jingling on his wrist.

We watch the show.

Frasier's sat at the bar. The audience laughs. Emil sniggers. I take a sip. Sweet to the point of being too much, but it's not bad. Potent. I'll drink a third because I have to face that steep hill back down to Toytown later tonight.

Margareta carries through a silver tray. Three plates. She gives one to Emil, one to me, and takes one for herself. She hands out cutlery and paper napkins. We sit side by side. Three adults watching *Cheers* in a self-storage warehouse in hill town.

'What did you want to talk about?' I say.

'Shhh,' says Margareta. 'Eat up before it gets warm.'

I look at the shrimp cocktail. A shallow champagne glass filled with peeled shrimps and chopped lettuce. Five shrimp hang over the edge of the glass like pale fingers. The pink sauce is speckled with paprika.

'Mum's sauce,' says Emil, facing forwards, eating a shrimp with his fingers. 'Million Islands dressing.'

'Ketchup and mayo,' says Margareta. 'Plus a dash of Tabasco.'

Emil looks over at me, a drop of pink sauce on his moustache whiskers and says, 'Spicy.'

Margareta clears the plates and bangs around in the kitchen and yells 'Shit balls!' loud enough for me to hear it in here.

She brings through more plates and I say, 'Can I help you in the kitchen?'

'No,' she says. 'Sunday dinner is gospel in the Eriksson household. I cook, you enjoy.'

Another episode of *Cheers* starts.

'Series two, Mum.'

'Episode four. Some of Ted's best work,' says Margareta, walking in and placing down the plates.

'Mum loves Ted Danson,' says Emil.

'I could devour that man in one night,' says Margareta, holding a plate a little too limply and gazing at the TV. A French fry drops on my lap. 'I could eat that man up in one gulp. Just look at his jaw. He's a goliath of modern-day popular television.'

She snaps out of it and gives me my stone-cold plate.

'*Duck à l'orange*,' she says.

'Duck with orange,' says Emil.

Thanks Google Translate, I really needed that.

We eat and it's excellent. Crispy duck skin and a zesty, orange sauce. The duck is cooked slightly pink and the French fries are salty and crunchy.

'Delicious,' I say.

'Yes he is,' says Margareta, staring at the TV.

We eat and watch. The plates are removed. Ice cream is brought out. Margareta says, 'TV off, Emil. I must to talk to our house guest.'

He switches it off.

'You two carry on eating. Do you mind if I smoke? It helps me to think.'

'Sure.'

She lights up her cigarette – it's one of those thin, Parisian-style ones – and she smokes it with her back bent and her arm halfway up the chimney.

'Can I ask you,' she says, her hand up inside the chimney breast. 'Are you really a journalist or some kind of private investigator?'

'I'm a…'

She interrupts. 'I've seen the best. *Wallander*, *Sherlock*, *Murder She Wrote*. We're proud to say we watch a lot of award-winning television here.'

'I'm a reporter,' I say.

She takes a drag and blows the smoke up the chimney.

'Ragnar Falk never reported like you seem to be doing.'

'I'm most interested in the victims,' I say. 'Whether that's victims of an online scam or a traffic accident or a terrible murder. When I was fourteen my dad died.'

Emil stops eating his ice cream.

'When I was fourteen my pappa died.'

'Well, don't you two have a lot in common,' Margareta says, smiling.

I'd usually be reluctant to share, but I need whatever information this pair have. 'His death was misreported, you see. Journalists stated he was an alcoholic when he wasn't at all. One alluded to his blood-alcohol levels on the night of his accident. They made mistakes, and that was tough for my mum to endure. It was tough enough without that, but I think it probably tipped her over the edge.'

'She threw herself off the edge, did she?' says Margareta, cringing. 'Right off the edge, was it?'

'No, she just lost the will to live.'

'Thank God we had our favourite shows,' she says, looking at Emil. 'They got us through the tough times, eh, Emil.'

Emil nods.

When he eats his ice cream I can see just how tiny his teeth are. They look like milk teeth.

Margareta stubs out her cigarette and joins us. She starts shelling pistachio nuts into two bowls on her lap. She never seems to stay still for more than a few seconds.

'The murder of Arne Persson is my lead story and most likely will be for several issues.'

'Arne never deserved what came to him,' she says. 'People say this is like Emil's dad but it's no such thing.'

Emil looks at me. 'Pappa was an accident.'

Margareta uses her fingernails to pull apart a barely-open pistachio nut. 'Yes it was, Emil. A tragic accident. Shit…' She breaks her nail and bites off the torn end. 'There was no gunshot like with Arne Persson.'

'I slipped,' says Emil.

'Wasn't your fault in any way, honey,' says Margareta. 'Freak accident.'

'The saw fell on him,' says Emil.

'Accidents happen,' says Margareta. 'Anyone for a nut?'

We talk about Emil having to change schools and how the Hive was difficult for them to run until Emil was old enough to leave education and work full-time. How it was Emil's idea to increase prices for the larger, top-floor units by offering a new discreet, premium service up there to people who needed something similar to a safety-deposit service only on a larger scale.

'Those two pine-carving sisters are from your neck of the woods, aren't they?' asks Margareta.

'Alice and Cornelia? They're from Utgard forest.'

'Utgard used to be connected to Visberg forest back before,' says Emil. 'Learned it at school. Was all one huge forest until they felled to build the E16 motorway.'

'Those two sisters are more trouble than people think,' says Margareta.

'They're harmless,' I say. 'They're just eccentric.'

'We hadn't had a murder in Visberg for thirty-seven years until they both turned up. And it isn't normal, the things they make. Shouldn't be legal. Have you seen the little men? Some have dicks as long as pencils. Some have hairy backs and real teeth taken from God-knows-what animal. Ragnar Falk, he said he saw one with teats from a fertile polecat. Transplanted onto a pine troll. Teats!'

Emil smiles and looks at me then at his mother.

'All I know,' she says, 'is that they have rifles and they know how to shoot. They have sharp tools and it seems like they need human teeth a damn sight more than anyone else does around here. Nobody questions them properly because they're two little old ladies. Let me tell you, never underestimate an old lady. I should know. And I seen a similar episode of *Midsummer Murders* one time. You have to investigate the obvious suspects as well as the others. That's vital.'

'I guess the police need physical evidence.'

'Just look at their shop for fuck's sake.'

'Well, I'm not sure…'

'And they had that big fight with their landlord.'

'Go on.'

'Arne Persson. Clockmaker says they had a screaming match inside the shop and he overheard the whole thing. His basement museum runs under both units, you didn't know that, did you? Wasn't so much about the money as the terms of the lease. He even checked if they could operate a shop from one of our larger storage units, see'ns as they only need it a few more weeks. I said no, we're not that kind of operation, our insurance policy wouldn't cover troll making.'

'You must see all sorts, renting your units to random people to store their private belongings?'

'Oh,' says Margareta. 'You have no idea.'

Emil stands up and says, 'I could do my rounds now, Mamma. I could take Tuva with me?'

'You could,' she says. 'I suppose you could, honey.'

'Rounds?'

'Inspection,' says Emil, taking a long, black torch the size and shape of a truncheon from a desk near the TV. 'My job.'

'Take her,' she says, winking.

'What do you mean?' I ask.

'Emil walks round the corridors of the two lower floors each evening. Never the top floor, we leave that well alone as customers appreciate their privacy up there. Emil checks nobody has had a stroke or an accident lifting their stuff, that kind of thing.'

'Health and safety,' he says. 'You want to come?'

I think about it for a moment. I have a stungun in my handbag. And Emil's half a head shorter than me with milk teeth. I think I could take him.

'Sure,' I say.

Emil removes a master key from a locked cabinet and we enter the main building. It's cold and the lights flicker on and off.

'Old wiring,' he says. 'This place used to be a hospital for deranged children. And then a home for problematic juveniles. Don't talk, just listen.'

We creep along the corridor and he occasionally puts his ear to a locked room.

'Shhh,' he says.

We head through a door.

'Lights don't work through here,' he says, switching on his torch. 'You can hold my hand if you're scared.'

I'll hold your goddam neck if you try anything.

Emil unlocks a storage unit.

'Random check, we're coming in,' he says, knocking on the door. 'All in the terms and conditions.'

He shines his light into the small, windowless room. Cardboard boxes with black writing scrawled on the sides. I can see 'Ceramics' and 'VHS' and 'Mum's documents'. Makes me think of a similar storage unit I pay 300 kronor per month for in Karlstad. Mum's belongings in taped-up boxes. Photos of my grandparents. All of her old clothes folded into plastic containers. Her shoes. Her favourite woolly hat. Her books. Dad's brown boots. The dress she wore on their wedding day.

Emil locks up the unit.

We head upstairs.

'I need to get going soon,' I say.

'Got to finish my rounds,' he says, the torchlight bouncing off the white walls and illuminating his undersize teeth. 'It's my responsibility.'

We check one more, larger unit, full of paintings. Some of them framed, most just rolled canvasses.

Emil opens the last door on the corridor.

He shines his torch inside.

A dozen eyes shine back.

31

Emil slams the door shut.

'What was that?'

'Nobody in there. Nothing. Let's go.'

'Emil, there is something in there.'

He jangles the candy bracelets on his wrists, stretching the elastic before biting off one of the sweets.

'My job is to check to make sure nobody's had a fall or a heart attack. That's all. I can't snoop around if nobody needs my help.'

'Open the door again,' I say.

He frowns at me. 'I said no.'

'Open the door, I think I saw a body on the floor.'

He looks confused. 'There was no body.'

'Just open the damn door.'

He cracks the hard candy between his teeth.

'Why should I?'

'You want my number?'

He blushes and I point at the lock. He takes his master key and unlocks the door and pushes it open. He reaches too close to me looking for the switch.

The lights flicker on.

Heads.

Arranged.

Maybe sixty or seventy of them displayed in plastic boxes and on shelves. Some in cylindrical, glass jars. Others mounted on the wall. Most of them are skulls, bare bone. Small creatures: rabbits and mice. Some look fox-size or maybe badger-size. Taxidermy weasels and stoats. One with six legs and two heads. On top of the plastic boxes are deer skulls with small, sharp antlers. More like horns. And on the wall are the elk skulls. Seven. One with antlers and six without.

'What the fuck is all this?'

'There's no rule against it in the contract,' says Emil. 'No explosives or flammable liquids. No generators. No weapons. No stolen items. This unit has stored hunting trophies for years, no law against it.'

I approach a long elk skull.

'I'd say this was stolen.'

'You don't know that.'

'Look,' I say, pointing to its jaw.

Emil goes to touch the upper jaw-bone, but I put my hand in the way. 'This might be evidence. Don't contaminate it.'

I crouch to get a better look.

Perfect, gleaming white teeth.

One amalgam filling in a huge molar.

'This one has braces,' says Emil.

I check out the next skull and sure enough we have a moose here with braces.

'I didn't know elk get braces,' says Emil.

There's a Tupperware container of loose teeth and a box of disposable latex gloves. Unopened. Nothing else in the room.

Fifteen minutes later Sheriff Harry Hansson is taking a look in the unit himself.

'Thord will be here before the hour's out,' he says, turning to Margareta. 'Marge, who rents this unit from you and how long have they had it for?'

Margareta looks at Emil then looks at me.

The Sheriff puts his hand on his hip. 'Police will get the information sooner or later, best if I can tell them you assisted with the enquiries.'

'According to my files it was...' she pauses, 'Annika Persson.'

The Sheriff looks at Margareta and rubs his chin.

'Annika Persson, you say?'

'Since ninety-two.'

He rubs his chin some more.

'You do me a favour, would you, and lock up the external door until Constable Thord arrives from Gavrik police?'

Emil trots off to check units and knock on more doors. I see Sven Edlund, the town's only dentist, shuffling down the stairs, complaining as he goes.

Emil comes back and tells us the building is secure. Everyone else has left. Margareta offers the Sheriff coffee and he says, 'If it isn't too much bother, Marge.'

We drink the coffee by reception, not in the private apartment where I had dinner.

Thord arrives, and the Sheriff takes him up along with Emil.

Margareta says, 'You have a boyfriend, Tuva?'

'Nope.'

'Well, isn't that interesting news.'

Not really.

Thord comes back and talks in private with Margareta. He and I walk out together.

'This damn town,' he says.

The cider-scented wind catches round my neck and I pull up my collar.

'You ever seen anything like it?' I ask.

'What do you think?' He pauses and says, 'Sorry, I didn't mean to snap.'

I wave that away.

'What happens now?'

'This place is locked down until the forensics team arrive tomorrow morning and take samples. Can't do nothing else tonight. Keep an open mind, you hear.'

He walks me back to my Hilux. The tape surrounding the statue of Adolf-Fredrik Edlund flickers in the breeze and I wonder what he'd think of all this.

'Who the hell performs root-canal surgery on a goddam moose?' says Thord.

I have to smile.

'The shit I have to deal with,' he says.

'That a quote?'

'Don't you even…'

I look around at the pumpkins for sale outside Konsum and the plastic skeletons hanging in the window of the pharmacy. Over on the dark side of the square there's a large sign in the pop-up shop window written in red ink. 'ALL MUST GO.'

'This find going to be useful, Thord? The elk skulls?'

'I don't suppose so, I'm not that lucky. But it might be, I don't know. I'll talk to Annika Persson, check that the records are accurate. Maybe we'll get fingerprints or DNA or fibres, something we can connect to the earlier crime scenes. Can talk to other witnesses, check who saw who going into the Hive with large bags. Probably includes a lot of people, but we can start with that. We've already checked the alibis of all dentists and dental students in the Kommun. But this could have been a vet or a student, it could have been anybody. Thing I'm relieved about is that we've only got one body. It's in pieces, which is not ideal, but it's just one. Got the call from the Sheriff and I thought to myself, oh no, who this time? But he or she don't seem to have escalated, rather they seem to have gone backwards. From human victim to wild animals. And I for one pray to God that it stays that way.'

32

The town sparkles with frost.

I pass Visberg Grill, the two gamer twins sat in the window sharing a pineapple and crayfish pizza, and the night is silent. Down the hill, the asphalt still looks black but everything else is glazed. Ice crystals on thistles and dead birch branches. We're leaving autumn behind.

The white bike looks less ghostly tonight. Everything's turning white. It could be any other bike. I think about the person who created this roadside memorial. How they probably bought a brand-new bike for the purpose, maybe an exact copy of the one mangled in the hit-and-run accident. I think about how they must have wept, spray-painting each part of the bike in some backyard or field. White paint misting the air. Tears running down to dampen their face mask. And then loading it into a truck or a car boot. Driving out here a month or a year after the fatal crash. Choosing the spot. Resting the white bike against a tree stump. Leaving it there for eternity as a reminder. Then having to drive past it each day.

I should visit Mum and Dad in Karlstad Cemetery. I should go the day after Halloween. This week coming. All Saints Day, they call it. All Hallow's day. A time to remember. To light a candle and check in with the deceased.

There's a black Audi parked outside Svensson's Saws & Axes. I hit the brakes and slow to peek inside the store and my wheels lose purchase; I have to steer into the skid to correct it. It's the car from that awful night. The one that sped away.

Gavrik looks deserted. Why wouldn't it be? Cold night in late October with a murderer on the loose. Everyone's doors double-locked. Guns loaded. Windows secure. Knives taped under beds.

The twin chimneys of the liquorice factory stand tall and proud in the distance. Constant bystanders. They've seen it all before. They bear witness to our twisted Gavrik history.

Noora arrives at my flat shortly after I do.

'You look exhausted.'

'I need a shower.'

We embrace and she whispers into my ear, 'We need a shower.'

She means we haven't been as close this week as we usually are. Shifts and late nights. Homicide cases.

I run the water.

She lights the lemongrass candle on the sink, the one she bought me as a flat-warming gift, and then she turns off the light.

The room warms. It fills with steam. The faint rumble of an argument brewing next door. Noora walks out. A Robyn song starts up through my living-room speakers. I remove my hearing aids. Noora comes back in. Leaves the door ajar.

I just stand there.

She scrapes back the hair off my face. She smells of nutmeg. The heat in the room builds and the candle on the sink starts to crackle. Steam fogs the mirror. Noora puts her fingertips to my lips and drags them gently one way then the other. I kiss her finger. She moves forward and we kiss, with her finger still between our lips. I bend and kiss the nape of her neck. Fine down. The smell of coconut from her skin.

She moves closer to me. Heat between us. Her hip pressing between my legs. The sound of the water spraying behind. She pulls my shirt slowly over my head. I unbutton her shirt. The back of my knuckles caress her skin as I unfasten each button. The warmth of her. The shirt swings open and she wriggles out of it. We move closer together and she says, 'I missed you.' Heat where our skin meets. Pressure. Her lips at my earlobe. Me unbuttoning her jeans and her pulling down my trousers. She backs away and looks at my body and I let her. I open the shower door and we step inside. The water is slightly too hot. Noora takes shampoo in her hands and lathers my hair. She stands behind me, her body pushing into mine, and she rubs my scalp and rinses the foam from my hair. My neck bent. The spray pummelling the top of my spine. Her kisses touching my back, her hands on my hips, biting, pushing into me again, turning me around. I feel faint with the lack of air in here. She kisses my shoulders and moves her head down my arm. We entwine closer together. Wrapping together. Melting.

We lie on my bed in robes.

Her leg resting over mine. Flushed pink.

I'm heady. My mind free from all the thoughts of murder, and being a disappointing daughter, and whether this move back to Gavrik was the right thing to do. None of that. Not even Noora. Just me, feeling as light as a feather. Floating above the bed on a millimetre of fresh air. Released from mortal fear and angst.

We don't talk, we just lie still.

Noora is the best thing that has ever happened to me. She is probably the person I thought I would never find.

'Cake?' she says.

I smile and place my hearing aids back in and kiss her cheek.

'Thought so.'

She takes a frozen chocolate *Kladkaka* from the freezer and brings it to bed. We wait for it to thaw a little then eat it from the box with our hands. Dad always used to thaw it completely, then slice it up with a sharp knife and serve with lingonberries and whipped cream. Noora just tears off chunks and hands them to me.

'It's good,' I say.

'We found a tooth.'

'You found a what?'

'A new tooth,' she says. 'A loose one.'

'I thought the set in the pan was complete. Nothing missing?'

'That's what's worrying us,' she says, sitting up straighter in bed, placing her chunk of cake down on the cardboard box. 'Different set of teeth.'

'Shit. What does that mean? Animal or human?'

She cringes.

'Whose tooth is it?'

She says, 'No idea yet. We've sent it off to the national-forensics lab in Linköping. It was left on top of a pocket watch.'

'What do you mean?'

The song on the stereo ends and there's a silent pause.

'Hans Wimmer, the clockmaker, found the tooth sitting atop an antique pocket-watch inside his shop. A Longines. He went down to his basement, apparently he has a watch archive or something down there, and when he came back up there was a molar resting on a closed, silver pocket watch.'

'Think he's telling the truth?' I say.

'Why wouldn't he be? He brought the tooth directly to us, he didn't have to do that.'

I nod and the next song starts up.

'Chief thinks someone's testing us. Perhaps someone who is angry with Gavrik police department. Trying to make a fool out of us. Toying with us. Seeing if we're up to the job.'

'Prints?'

'Linköping will tell us soon enough. Listen, feel free to say no, if you like, but I need a favour. I have my mid-year appraisal coming up next week…'

'Nice timing,' I say.

She raises an eyebrow.

'I'm not as good at writing as you are. Take a look over the forms for me? Just a quick glance?'

'Of course,' I say, placing my hand on hers. 'Happy to.'

She looks pensive, pulling her robe tighter around herself.

'What?'

She swallows hard and pushes the chocolate-cake box away from her.

'They found something else on Arne Persson.'

'What is it?'

'I shouldn't be talking about it, so you have to keep this to yourself for now. Nobody else knows outside the police and it can't go in the paper. Can't even be discussed inside your office.'

I mime zipping closed my mouth and throwing away the key.

'White coats found a human hair not belonging to Arne. Found it on his severed head.'

'Whose?'

'Not that easy. Can't test for nuclear DNA, because there was no hair root. But the colour.'

I frown.

'The hair was red.'

33

I drive to the *Posten* office and the streets are full of coat-clad Monday-morning workers. One of the managers from the liquorice factory flashes his headlights at me and Mrs Björken from the haberdashery turns her face as I drive past.

The bell above the door tinkles. Empty biscuit-tin honesty box, a fresh stack of *Postens* for walk-ins, and the smell of ICA Maxi budget coffee coming from the kitchen. All feels reassuringly familiar.

I say hi to Nils and Lena then get to work. Writing up the story of elk heads, stolen and now recovered, but also building outlines for the peripheral stories around the murder case. Local readers don't just want forensics and police transcripts and maps of where the body was discovered. I've learnt all this to my cost. They also want threads connecting the story to the local community. A murder itself, never mind one with a beheading and ritualistic display, is difficult to digest. But interviews with local shopkeepers about Arne Persson's character, about his restored Chevrolet; interviews with players at his old chess club, detailing how highly competitive Arne Persson was when playing the game; snippets about how his late father was a doctor based in the asylum, now refitted as the Hive; photographs of Visberg town square, comparing the square in 1900 to the square in 2000 – that's what's fascinating for locals; it's what connects them to the heinous crime, what they need or want, or both. They deserve to be helped through this. Because they still have to live here once the slick-back journalists from Stockholm and Malmö have long gone.

I research DNA from human-hair samples. Noora's right. Of course she is. The hair itself, without the root, has no nuclear DNA, but it does contain mitochondrial DNA, which doesn't identify the person the hair came from exactly, but it does identify the common maternal thread. Who in Visberg has red hair? I google red-hair statistics for Sweden. Depends on your definition of red but the rates can be as high as thirty per cent. Nowhere higher in the world, save for the UK, Ireland and Holland. I get to work on a list. People I've seen in Visberg who have red hair. Julia, the receptionist at Edlund Tandklinik has red hair. I suspect Eva Edlund does as well, but she dyes it blonde, like all her fellow club members seem to. The wood-carving sisters have grey, scraggy hair. Tobias the hygienist has short, blond, hair. Sven Edlund's hair is black and grey, salt-and-pepper, as Tam would say. The gamer twins are both blond. Luka Kodro from the grill has jet-black hair. Ragnar Falk's beard and hair is as white as Santa's.

Lena's door bursts open.

Her mobile is pressed to her shoulder.

'Visberg,' she says. 'Get to Visberg now.'

I get up from my chair and Lena tells the person on the other end of the call that she'll call them back.

'Grave's been robbed in Visberg Cemetery. The Lutheran church. Get there and take photos.'

Of course I'll take photos.

'Whose grave?'

'Find out. Go.'

I grab the *Posten*'s proper camera, a digital SLR, and run out, almost knocking Lars over as I go.

'Easy,' he says.

I drive straight to Visberg with my radio on, scanning for news channels. Nobody has this story yet. Who was Lena talking to? Chief Björn? The Sheriff?

Past Svensson's Saws & Axes, up the hill. The curves and chicanes slow me down more than I'd like. You can't drive too fast up this hill. The bends are blind and the line down the centre of the asphalt is continuous. No dashes. No overtaking. This route is a health hazard.

Past the white bike, fresh white lilies or roses arranged in its basket. On past the destroyed bus shelter and the cross. My truck judders as I go over the old train tracks. I get to the town square and head on to the church. Short, stunted spire atop a white, wooden tower. A clock on each side. The date, 1798, under the green copper roof. Two police Volvos.

I park and run, with my camera switched on and ready.

Round the back I see three figures.

And a hole.

Earth mounded up each side; not neatly, it's a big mess. The gravestone is disturbed. It rests at an ungodly angle.

'No,' shouts Thord as I approach, his palm out.

I keep my finger on the shutter button but drop the camera to my hip.

'Okay,' I say.

I take a photo. Walk closer. Two magpies sit on the low perimeter wall watching events unfold. I take five photos. One magpie pecks at the other one and then they fly away.

'What happened?' I ask.

Thord runs to intercept me and says, 'We don't know yet.'

'Was anything taken?'

'This is a place of worship,' says Thord. 'Especially with All Saints Day coming up.'

'All Saints?'

'All Hallows Day.'

'Halloween?'

He shakes his head. 'American nonsense. All Hallow's Day, first of November. Time to remember the dead – and I don't mean skeleton outfits and horror movies.'

I try to look around him. 'Who's with you?'

He turns to face the open grave.

'Priest Kilby.'

'He's the priest in this town as well?'

'You don't get one priest per church anymore, Tuvs. Not all the way out here.'

'And who's she?'

'Johansson.'

'Who?'

'Karlstad homicide.'

'Homicide? For this? Who got dug up?'

He looks at me. 'Please, Tuvs. Some respect.'

'Who was it, though?'

He lets me step a little closer, then puts out his arm.

'That's close enough. Name on the stone says "Gustav Persson. Died 1999".'

'I haven't heard of him.'

Thord sighs. 'He was Arne's father.'

'Fuck.'

'Not here, Tuva. That language. Not here, not today.'

He rarely calls me Tuva.

'Sorry.'

'They must have been digging all night. Not easy getting down two-metres deep in the dark with spades and shovels.'

'Was there any treasure in the grave? Any jewellery? Gold watch or something?'

'Can't say,' says Thord. 'But my guts tells me that wasn't the motive.'

'What do you mean?'

He looks agitated. 'I can't say more at the present time, Tuvs. Not yet. I'll let you know when there's an official statement.'

I get escorted out of the graveyard. A journalist from Falun turns up and Thord tells him the entire site is out of bounds.

Who the hell would dig up a dead body that's been underground for decades? Why?

I drive to the town square.

Julia, the receptionist, waves to me from outside the pharmacy.

Her red hair glows orange in the sun.

34

'Julia,' I yell.

'I'm sorry, I'm late for work,' she says, with an apologetic look on her face. 'Catch up later?'

I get back into my parked Hilux and connect my laptop to my phone. This is my new reality. I need to work from Visberg each week, depending on what story is my priority. I have no office here. There's no budget for one even though rent is cheap. And there is no Starbucks or Espresso House. The Grill doesn't open until lunch. So this is my office space.

I can't even imagine what would drive someone to excavate a grave. Being in a churchyard at night with a spade, digging down deeper and deeper. The spade edge hitting something solid. Scraping away the remaining earth. Lifting the coffin lid. The grave I just came from – did they take something out of the coffin? A watch or precious item? A body part? For what? A DNA sample? Would there be any DNA left?

I email Sebastian with a list of research he can do, if and when he has time. Lena keeps nagging me to include him more, so I will. Research grave-robbing, pretty-boy. Knock yourself out.

I check in with Thord but the Chief picks up and he ends the call before I can ask if he has a statement on the grave disturbance.

Outside, a kid in an all-in-one zip-up suit picks up an apple almost as big as his head. The skin is brown and crinkly. As he holds it I can see liquid ooze from a tear at the base of the fruit. The kid's next to a bench where I saw two masked locals having sex on Pan Night. The kid holds the apple in between his mittens. He holds it close to his face. He opens his mouth and his teeth look just like Emil's. And then the kid's mother grabs the apple and throws it on the grass and it bursts. Half a dozen wasps fly out of it and the kid starts crying.

I lock up and walk over to the gamer cafe. No idea if Mind Games is open or closed so I try the door and it creaks open. Smells musty inside. Teenagers and takeout food and poor ventilation. Smells like home.

I pass through a corridor lined with black sheets and push through a curtain. Or maybe it's just another black sheet hung from the ceiling? Through another curtain, and another. Darker and darker. Deeper and deeper.

There are four people here gaming. Three guys and a woman.

One of the guys is wearing a virtual-reality headset and he's standing facing a wall, swinging his arms and ducking and yelling, 'Behind you, grenadier!'

The others are sitting in front of screens with their fingers on illuminated keyboards. They're wearing headsets with microphones. A fridge glows in the corner. It's stocked with Red Bull Extreme and other high-caffeine energy drinks.

'You won't get any sense out of him,' says one of the twins, still facing his screen. 'Playing since seven last night. He's lost down the rabbit hole.'

His brother is sitting on the far side of the room facing me. Even in this dark room I can see his eyes glow red in the glare from the screen.

I speak up. 'How much per hour?'

The twin keeps on playing for a few moments then smashes his fist on the table and throws off his headset and turns to me and says, 'Twenty kronor. Sit anywhere you like.'

I sit two screens down from the blue-haired woman. That's the etiquette. Always leave a space if you can. She's about forty, and she's playing UEFA World-Cup football or something similar.

The screensaver in front of me lists the specs of the computers. The speed of gameplay and the broadband levels. It tells me which games are available. Mostly ultra-violent shoot-em ups as far as I can tell. I load up a version of *Doom* I like.

One of the twins comes along beside me.

'You game, eh?'

I keep looking at my screen and pick up a sawn-off shotgun. 'What does it look like?'

He watches me play for a few seconds and then says, 'You hear about—'

His twin screams from the back of the room and a can of Red Bull flies past, hits the far wall and explodes.

'Fuck, David,' says the twin next to me.

More fists hitting desks.

David goes over and helps his twin to clean up with paper towels.

'You need to get out, brother. Clear your head. You should let me play on.'

David smacks him on the shoulder and Daniel heads back to the rear of the room.

'*Doom*,' says David, his eyes bright red, like an exotic rabbit that's been clubbing all night.

'Yup.'

'You gotta harness that temper, David,' says the blue-haired woman. 'Focus it on the game at hand. Channel it.'

David flicks up his middle finger behind her back.

'I saw that, nephew,' she says. 'Screen reflection, asshole.'

The clock on the base of my screen reads 11:59am.

'Grill just opened,' I say to David. 'Quick pizza? Might be able to swing you a discount advert in the *Posten* if you play your cards right.'

He yawns and scratches his nose and says, 'I got nothing better to do.'

Am I losing my touch? How about a little enthusiasm?

We walk outside and he shields his eyes with his forearm. He smells of supermarket deodorant and fabric softener.

'My first and favourite customers,' says Luka Kodro, inviting us inside with a sweep of his forearm.

'Hello chief,' says David, rubbing his eyes.

We sit down. David orders two Cokes with ice, and a Vegetariana with cranberries. I get a Spicy American Sausage. David taps his fingernails on the table fast like a drumroll. I stare at them and he stops and rubs his hands together instead.

'Too much caffeine? RSI?'

'What?' he says.

'Repetitive Strain Injury? I used to get that when I gamed too much.'

'You gamed too much?'

'Way, way too much. What were you playing in there?'

'Beta of a new Halloween game that drops tomorrow night. It's called *Massacre 31st*. Some zombie-apocalypse bullshit. But it's pretty realistic. They've made a good effort.'

'You gonna be busy tomorrow night on Halloween, then?' I say. 'Kids won't be out trick-or-treating?'

'Busiest night of our year if a decent game drops,' he says. 'Last year we got *Hunted 2.0*.'

'Never played it.'

He rubs his eyes again. 'Stick to *Doom*. Trust me.'

'Not good?'

Our pizzas arrive, hot and steaming.

'Thanks,' I say.

Luka Kodro and David exchange looks. I can't quite decipher it, but these two know each other well. Was that look a warning or an acknowledgement?

'*Hunted 2.0* is the best game I have ever played,' he says. 'Because it's ultralocal.'

I take a piece of charred sausage with my fingers and eat it.

'Ultralocal?'

'Swedish designer. Swedish made. It's modelled on the forests of Norrland. The early levels are all hunting groups. You start with smaller weapons and smaller game. Birds and rabbits. Work your way up to roe deer and beaver, if your aim's good enough, if you stick to the hunt etiquette. The guns change. Bigger calibre. You get to hunt wild boar, elk, brown bears even. It's incredibly realistic, that's the thing. You're involved in skinning, hanging, butchering, gutting. You get dogs you need to feed, and maps with hunting towers, but the graphics are so good it's like you're out there in Visberg forest. Everything is in Swedish which makes it feel real. I don't know how to explain it: the ferns, the ditches, the mushrooms. It's like you've walked out of town and started hunting.'

'Do you hunt for real?'

'You mean in the actual forest?'

I nod and eat a big mouthful of pizza.

'Hell, no, you crazy? You seen the mosquitos out there? Besides I'm not in any hunt team. It's all political bullshit run by the Edlund family.'

He tears the crust from his pizza and chews it with his mouth open.

'And the later levels?'

He looks coy. 'I dunno, your readers aren't going to understand if they start reading about that stuff.'

I sip my Coke. 'Okay then. Off the record.'

He looks excited, his red eyes widening. 'Shit gets real after a while. The hunters turn on the hunt leader, then on each other. Do or die. Kill or be killed. You need to make or find shelter. Fires are good, they recharge your energy levels, but they can also give away your position. There are crossbows and hammers and chainsaws, not just guns. Knives. Machetes. Hand-to-hand combat. Using each other as human shields. Last night when I was playing I couldn't kill a zombie bear until I gnawed the nose clean off his face. Once you get down to five players in one forest there's cannibalism, the collecting of certain animal and human bones, antlers, human skulls. All inside the forest. In hunting towers and by bonfires. You can't get out of the woods. It's all pine trees and hollows and Swedish road signs. Realest shit I ever played in my life.'

'My dad used to warn about ultra-violence,' I say. 'Talked about *A Clockwork Orange*.'

'An orange?'

'It's a Kubrick movie. Dad used to say that you can get hungry for more and more extreme things. Like an addiction. At some point you have to say no. Draw a line. Realise that it's enough.'

'Don't you dare tell my customers that,' says David, yawning, some gooey cheese coating his tongue.

'Arne Persson ever game in your place? Ever play *Hunted 2.0*?'

David shakes his head. 'Not welcome.'

'Why not?'

David swallows and then leans closer to me. 'He never had no kids of his own, so he went after other peoples'. You know what I mean?'

'That's the first I've heard of it.'

He eats more pizza and then drinks a mouthful of Coke to swill it down.

'Small town, back country. Folks don't talk to people like you.'

'What are you saying he did?'

'He was the scout leader back in the day. Back when Daniel and I were kids. You know the kind of man who wants to be a scout leader, right?'

Actually I don't.

'People used to say he preferred the blue-eyed boys. Never did a thing to me but my brother was convinced he was a monster. Whole town knows about it.'

Ragnar Falk walks past the window.

'Poor old fool,' says David, nodding at him. 'First his daughter gets killed and then you steal his newspaper.'

35

I spot Thord talking with Sheriff Hansson out by the bandstand so I pay for the pizzas and leave. I'm still processing what David told me about Ragnar's daughter. I never even knew he had a child. Losing my parents was tough in so many ways. It changed me, affected every cell of my being. But losing a child. What would that do to a person?

The clouds overhead are indigo and they are fit to burst. The wind swirls, blowing my hair in front of my eyes, and the bee on top of the Hive squeaks louder as it fights to keep turning.

'Tuva,' says Thord as I approach. He's standing with Sheriff Hansson. I don't like him calling me Tuva. It puts me on edge.

'Any news on the grave disturbance?' I say.

The Sheriff pulls a face like he just smelt something awful and Thord says, 'We're talking Halloween plans right now.'

'He thinks we should cancel,' says the Sheriff. 'I say let the kids have their night of fun. Ain't nothing but a harmless bit of pumpkin carving, apple bobbing, trick-or-treatin', old-fashioned tom-foolery. They need the escape at the moment, truth be told. Never had a single bad thing happen on Halloween in my town and intend to maintain that clean sheet.'

'We're going to have an increased police presence,' says Thord. 'You can write about that in the paper, that's on the record, let the locals know.'

'We want people to feel safe, see,' says the Sheriff.

'Patrols to ensure kids play in good faith,' says Thord. 'We don't want no drunk driving or vandalism.'

Or ritualistic mutilations.

'They gonna clean up the apple sludge round here, Sheriff? Looks like a farmyard after a rainstorm,' I say.

'That's the way the Edlunds want it,' says the Sheriff, his thumbs in his belt loops. 'Same thing every year. We spray down and clean up on All Saints like the start of a whole new year.'

'Each town does it their own way, I guess,' says Thord.

The Sheriff snorts. 'Well, *we* certainly do.'

The three of us stand still and watch as Hans Wimmer crosses the square holding a child's car seat. His frame is elongated, he's as tall as a church door. Wimmer places the car seat inside his Skoda, then checks the broken clock on the outside of his shopfront, then goes inside and turns the 'Open' sign until it says 'Closed'.

'He's a queer soul,' says the Sheriff.

'We don't say queer no more, Sherriff,' says Thord, shaking his head.

'We do up hill town. I don't mean nothing bad by it.'

The manager of Konsum steps outside. She counts the pumpkins by tapping each one on the green stalk, like a kindergarten teacher tapping heads while loading kids onto a bus for a school trip.

'I found out something new today,' I say.

'What do you want, a candy bar?' says the Sheriff.

'Ragnar Falk's daughter was killed,' I say.

'Oh, that,' says the Sheriff. 'Bad business that was.'

Thord looks at the Sheriff.

'You didn't know?'

Thord keeps on looking at him.

'Falk had a daughter, Johanna her name was. Sweet, polite girl. Anyways, she was riding her bike down Visberg hill, it's not a good road for a bicycle rider, especially not in elk-hunt season.'

The Sheriff turns a quarter way round to face the top of the hill. To look down it. The sky is darkening by the minute and a flock of birds squawk and fly off in one black mass, as if to evade the upcoming weather.

'It was a hit and run,' says the Sheriff.

'Damn cowards,' says Thord. 'Had one myself first year on the job, out west near Utgard forest, close to the river. How someone can cause destruction and then just up and leave, not face the music as it were, is beyond me. How do you suppose a driver like that would sleep at night?'

'Johanna Falk was thrown twenty metres up toward Gavrik town.' Sheriff Hansson scratches the groove above his lip with his fingernail. 'She was stone-cold deceased before she even got to the hospital, poor thing. Seventeen years old, if I remember right. Ragnar was there by her side on the road. And ever since he's kept a white bike at the exact spot she passed on.'

'They ever have any leads on who did it?' asks Thord.

'Back then it was Falun police in charge of us hill people, not your pappa, may he rest in peace.'

Thord nods his head slightly.

'Talk of youths out drinking and reckless, maybe some home-brew alcohol involved, or the liquorice liquor made by the stamper at the factory. "Old evil", she calls it. Almost lethal, or so I heard. But you know small towns as well as I do. Thing like that can be covered up real fast by the driver's father if he has more blind love for his boy than respect for justice. Maybe the car gets crushed over Utgard forest way at the scrapyard, some cash changes hands for a no-questions-asked service, I know those Snake River boys have done similar in the past. Maybe false alibis are provided or whatnot. Police found nothing useful and old Ragnar aged about ten years in one week. His beard turned white real fast, and the words in the *Tidningen* started to get more and more depressing. He focused on accidents and heart attacks and so forth. Didn't cover so many stories up at the Gymnasium school as he used to. Not with his daughter's friends still studying there. Couldn't face them, I expect. Couldn't see them still living and breathing. Young men and women with futures ahead of them. He couldn't write them stories much no more and that hit the paper pretty hard. People started moving over to the *Gavrik Posten*.'

I see Ragnar's office on the shady side of the square. The newspaper stuck inside the whitewashed shopfront. The lights off. The, 'No Cash Left on The Premises' sign taped to the door. The, 'For All Enquiries Call Lena Adeola at the *Gavrik Posten*' sign right underneath. His beard went white like Mum's hair did after Dad died. You might think things like that are myth and legend, exaggerations made by those left behind. But it can happen. Mum's hair turned white so fast. Started falling out in clumps as well. So our neighbour – the kind dinner lady who eventually fed me home-cooked meals and let me watch movies in her flat – bought Mum a silk pillowcase. Apparently they can help reduce the hair loss. Less friction, so she said. Mum never even took it out of the wrapping paper. She slept on Dad's old pillow instead. His pillowcase. She never washed it ever again. His tears and his sweat and his saliva in the cotton. His scent. The last of him for her to hold each night as she lay there awake trying to make sense of it all. The remnants of her husband. Of her love.

36

I work from my Hilux and research Johanna Falk's death. Thank God for Google.

It happened in 1994.

October 24.

According to the article in the *Värmlands Tidningen* Johanna was riding her bike down to meet her boyfriend by the lake in Visberg forest. She'd arranged for him to drive her back up the hill later that evening, on account of the hill being too steep to cycle up. According to the piece, she'd been hit by a vehicle that police estimated was driving at 60–80 kph. Visibility that night had been fair. No ice on the roads. Johanna was wearing a yellow coat. It doesn't mention helmets but I guess they weren't so common back then. Tragically. The piece says she was hit from the rear as she was descending the hill, and she was thrown some fifteen to twenty metres. Motorists found her lying in the road. Her bike had been thrown into the ditch. It says medics battled to save her in the ambulance, but she was declared dead on arrival at the hospital. It says she left behind her father, Ragnar Falk, aged forty-two.

What demon did this? Killed a young woman on a bike and then left the scene of the accident without even stopping to see if she was still alive? Without even calling 112 anonymously? What kind of animal?

By the time I close my laptop, Visberg square is dark and raindrops are beating down on my Hilux roof.

I scan around. The gamer café looks closed but it's probably open. Preparing for tomorrow night's Halloween launch of the new zombie game. I see Tobias, the hygienist, run away from Visberg Grill carrying two pizza boxes. He's also wearing an orange hat. That's what you get when everyone shops in the same store. The pharmacy is already closed. The Hive looks ominous, its black timber walls melting into the night. Its yellow-painted window frames reflecting back in the wet streetlight like dozens of identical, jaundiced eyes.

The dental surgery is closed. The newspaper office is closed. The pop-up shop is most likely closed, but I can't really tell as they never have any lights on anyway. The clockmaker's shop is closed and the battery-powered alarm clocks have been removed from the window display.

I think about the files in my office. On the computer, but also stored in filing cabinets near Lars's desk and near my desk. The clippings of major stories archived by Lena over the years: the reservoir flood of 1976, the Grimberg centenary, the Medusa murders, the visit from the captain of the Swedish ice-hockey team the year I arrived here, the Ferryman saga, the pile-up on the E16 in 2014. And my private files. Stories Lena and I decided not to run for whatever reason. Research that was too important to throw away. And then I look at Ragnar Falk's office again.

The wind and the rain drench me as I jog through the square. I pause for a moment under the domed shelter of the bandstand. Nobody around. Nothing here. Rain beating down on the roof. There are no lights on upstairs in any of the buildings on the dark side of the square. The block looks deserted. Falk lives upstairs but he must be out. I schlep through apple sludge and mud to get to the dental surgery, then walk round the back of the buildings. Back doors are easier to work on than front doors. I pass garages, car-parking spaces and salt bins. Some kind of small electricity sub-station humming away in the rain. The cover says 'Danger To Life – High Voltage. Keep Out'.

I think about the master key used by Emil Eriksson to open the Hive self-storage units. I think about how I gained access to Mum's locked trunks after she died. How I tried to force the mechanisms and actually succeeded with some of the smaller ones. But then I needed help with the biggest box. The one that contained all her most precious items. I found my answer on YouTube. There's something irresistible about a locked box. Some childhood fantasy of treasure chests and secret maps. That, combined with an insatiable hunger to find out more about Mum. And Dad. It seemed impossible to ask her to her face, back when she was alive. But I could find out for myself. You can discover pretty much anything on YouTube if you look hard enough. It is the present-day equivalent of the Library of Alexandria. I searched for how to pick a padlock, and within fifteen minutes I was in. The lock lying open and defeated by my socked feet. The smell of old paper. I took out each of the items and inspected them carefully. Mum and Dad's wedding certificate. A photo of her holding me on the day I was born. My crying was freefall at this point. I was using the silk pillowcase as a tissue, the one she never opened yet stored in her locked chest. Perhaps a gesture to the dinner-lady neighbour. Then I found Dad's knife from his boy-scout years, engraved with his initials. Her wedding bouquet shrivelled to a dry and crunchy mess inside a plastic ice-cream tub. I found a photo of Mum at a dance when she was young, laughing and messing around with her girlfriends, and I sobbed through my smiles. Then other photos I'd never seen before in my life. Her and Dad sitting on deck chairs on a beach somewhere. The note on the back said, 'Skrea Strand, Falkenberg '95'. When I looked through that chest I felt we'd been a family. The three of us.

The rain has saturated my hood and one of my aids is getting feedback so I slip both out and place them in my bra. Best place: warm and dry. Trick from my audiologist.

Two paperclips. I always keep a few in my coat pocket, along with a pen and a small notepad and couple of spare hearing-aid batteries. I bend one paperclip over onto itself and flatten it out. I straighten the other completely.

The wind catches round my neck and I look one way, then the other. I don't like being this vulnerable. Unable to hear someone approach behind my back or at my side. Unable to explain my being here. Unable really to justify even to myself why I'm standing behind an old newspaper office in murder town armed only with two fucking paperclips.

I insert the folded paperclip and hold it in place with my finger. There needs to be some rotational pressure on the lock.

Silence.

The raindrops bounce up off the pavement and dampen the underside of my coat. Inside my coat. Only Swedish rainfall can do that.

I rake the straightened paperclip back and forth, pushing it in to engage each pin within the lock mechanism, but also acutely aware of my back. My flanks. The people that could be observing me right now. Waiting for their moment to pounce.

I'm about to quit when something inside the lock gives. Thank god for the rehabilitated ex-con on YouTube thoughtful enough to share his lock-picking expertise. I slowly turn the looped paperclip and the padlock opens. Best thing about this is that when I leave I'll clip it locked again and nobody will ever know I was here.

I open the door and walk inside.

No more rain beating down on my head.

My phone is in my pocket and I can use the torch function if I need to but I'd rather avoid it.

A small kitchenette and toilet immediately inside the back door, then a staircase leading upstairs. I tiptoe toward the front of the building. The large room with Ragnar's oak desk in the centre. Framed stories on every wall. Some black and white, others in colour. All of them faded. I can see the town square through the large window, like I'm watching it on a cinema screen. Black trees glistening with sweet rain. Cars drive by, their headlights streaking in the murk. The neon sign from the Visberg Grill coming and going behind the apple tree branches as they sway in the wind.

I sit down on the floor shielded by Ragnar's desk and place my aids back in.

They're working fine.

The wind changes direction and rain starts to beat against the window.

I open the first filing cabinet. Accounts and other useless information. I keep looking, careful to drag open each drawer as gently and noiselessly as I can. It's difficult for me to judge if I'm doing this quietly so I have to work by touch. Vibration. The slowest and smoothest of movements. I think about Dad's mantra: *Slow is smooth. Smooth is fast.*

Archives covering the '70s. Then I find the '80s and we get colour print. Then the '90s. I pull drawers and open folders until I get to 1994. Cream-coloured folders like the rest. But then a red-plastic file with a rubber band around it.

I slump to the floor, my back to the desk.

Ragnar's own notes about the circumstances of his daughter's death.

Interviews with local residents. I can see shorthand extracts from chats with Eva Edlund and Margareta Eriksson. There are sketches and lists of cars owned by local people; the lists have cars and trucks checked off systematically. Registration plates and addresses. Lists of names with codes next to them. Notes cross-referenced with vehicles found up at Snake River Salvage, west of Gavrik. Then a short list of cars unaccounted for. Four names, all men.

The list is headed with the words 'Possible Murderous Drivers'.

Three names I don't recognise.

And one name I do.

Arne Persson.

37

I stare at Ragnar's handwriting. The ink has sunk into the paper from force, or perhaps he left the pen in place too long thinking about his dead daughter.

Ragnar believed Arne Persson killed his child.

The only light on the paper shines through the open footwell of the desk. Visberg streetlight illuminating the handwritten name of a mutilated man.

My breathing quickens.

The dust in the room catches in my throat and I have to stifle a cough. No noise, Tuva. No lights on, no noise, no movement visible to anyone in the square.

When did Ragnar work out who killed his daughter? Now, after all these years? Or is this an old note? The paper looks new. No yellowing or ink fade. But then it's been stored inside a file, not hung on the walls like his old front pages. Did Ragnar Falk shoot and behead Arne Persson to avenge his daughter's death?

I kneel and photograph the note but it looks black on my screen, so I open the filing cabinet and place the paper inside. I glance out at the street. Nobody. Apple-tree branches thrashing around, losing the last of their rotting fruit. I switch on my flash and take a photo. The cabinet does a good job of swallowing most of the light. I close the drawer as silently as I can.

Have to leave everything exactly as I found it. If Falk is a killer, I don't need him getting suspicious. I move the chair I nudged and I make sure my bootprints aren't clear in the dust.

The ceiling creaks.

Is that my hearing aids or was that actually a sound?

I stand dead still.

No noises. Silence. A car drives toward the shopfront and slows but then it drives on by. It's a black Audi. Eva Edlund's Audi.

Dust tickles the fleshy insides of my nostrils.

I pinch my nose and straighten up slowly.

As I stand, the sleeve of my jacket catches a coffee mug and time slows down.

I lunge to catch the mug but it's too late.

It hits the dusty floorboards and spins and ricochets but it does not break.

Another creak from upstairs. I can feel movement up there.

I lift the mug with my sleeve extended over my hand and I place it back on the desk how it was before. My heart's beating too hard. A damp spot on the floorboards. Cold coffee. Dust particles float in mid air and my heart pounds inside my ribcage.

I swallow.

The smell of old paper. Old wood.

And then the light in the stairwell turns on.

How do I explain this? I can't catch my breath. Will I even get a chance to explain? I step slowly to the door and hide behind it.

Ten clear creaks as he walks down the stairs.

The light comes on and I see the gleaming, metallic barrel of a rifle.

And then I see Ragnar in his nightshirt. He has red chest hair and his feet are bare. His skin is so dry it looks like scales: deep cracks up and down his heels.

The movement of the door and the man disrupts the dust and it tickles my nose.

Both nostrils.

I bite down hard on my tongue and squeeze my eyelids together.

Ragnar huffs and walks to the desk. He inspects the files and notes and then walks to the front door to check the lock.

I emerge from behind my door and step out carefully to the kitchen and then tiptoe to the rear door.

Do not squeak, please do not squeak.

It doesn't squeak.

I open it a crack and slip through and close it gently and replace the padlock.

Click.

Then I crouch and walk away. Not running, just walking. Casual.

Two figures emerge from the darkness, from behind the dental surgery, their shadows as long as two humpback whales.

'Hello, girl,' says Cornelia, the speaking one.

'Bad,' says Alice, shaking her head.

'Shhh,' I say, waving my hands around.

'Don't you dare shush me, girl,' says Cornelia.

'I have to go.'

I walk around them but they follow me into the town square. Alice is holding a bottle of something. Most likely home-brew liquor, strong enough to knock out a normal person.

'What do you reckon the girl was up to, Alice?' says Cornelia loud enough for me to hear clearly.

Alice blows a raspberry.

I stop and look back. 'Please.'

'Girl's polite,' says Cornelia. 'Them fancy big-city ways.'

They speed up. These two half-bald troll-carvers speed up and I look back in horror.

'What do you want?' I say.

'Stop running away, girl' says Cornelia. 'You ain't paid for your mask yet. One thousand.'

She's right. 'I'm sorry,' I say, handing over the cash.

'Ain't got no receipts, girl. We didn't see you, you didn't see us. Look.'

She points an index finger with no nail at her own shopfront. The window is full of trolls. Demonic little shin-high dolls with rat teeth and moustaches made from polecat bristles. One is a curvaceous, girl troll with bright blue eyes pointing in different directions. She has a thatch of dark hair between her legs. Looks like rat fur. They've carved the pine heartwood to form cleavage. Wooden cleavage.

'Thirty-one per cent off,' says Cornelia.

'Sale,' says Alice.

'One-day special on account of the date,' says Cornelia.

And then I see the bottle in Alice's hand. It glints in the streetlight.

It's not whisky or brandy. It's not moonshine or potato wine or homemade vodka.

It's a plastic bottle of Svensson's own-brand chainsaw oil.

38

My pillow alarm shakes me awake at seven.

I have the groggy remnants of a bad dream playing on loop in my head. I can't remember what happened but it feels like it lasted a day and a night. No recollection of the depth of the thing, but I do have an image in my mind's eye: Cornelia standing at the feet of Arne Persson, keeping lookout. Alice standing at the head end, one calloused hand gripping the pull cord of a chainsaw.

I shower and eat Coco Pops and then I grab my bag and head out.

Something on the mat by my door. Inside my apartment, next to the shelf where I leave my keys each night.

A postcard?

I bend down and pick it up, my hair still a little damp.

It's a card with a vintage image of Visberg on the front. The square is there, complete with bandstand and statue. The Grill is a pawn broker and the gamer café is a hair salon. Konsum is a greengrocer and the clock shop is a butcher. There are whole sides of pork hanging from hooks where the alarm clocks are now displayed. The ones Hans Wimmer takes in each night and probably keeps safe down in his basement museum. The Hive is not painted black and yellow, it's sickly green, and there is no bee on the roof. A cross is bolted above the door but I can't tell if it's religious or medical. There are bars on all the windows.

I flip the card over.

Anonymous.

No greeting, no signature.

Text printed by an old-fashioned typewriter.

Roses are red.
Violence is blue.
It's a heady time of year.
And I want you.

The hairs on my arms stand up.

Is this someone's sick idea of a Halloween prank? Because I can tell you, I do not need this shit in my life right now. I'm tempted to tear up the card but I stick it in my bag and leave.

Toytown is cold and there's still rain in the air. Clouds heavy and full right above us all. Waiting. Biding their time.

I go straight to the cop shop.

Deserted.

A bloodstain on the wall above a patch of shiny floor and a 'Careful Slippery' sign.

I take a numbered ticket and ring the bell screwed down into the pine counter. The door opens.

'Moodyson,' says Chief Björn.

'Can I talk to you, Chief?'

He looks at me with no emotion in his eyes whatsoever.

'Reckon you already are.'

'It's about Ragnar Falk.'

He swallows hard. 'Come back through here and let's do this properly. We got the heat on.'

I follow him through the key-code door.

'You manning the station alone?'

'Not exactly. Thord and Noora are in Visberg checking on one or two things. You drink coffee, do you?'

This is the first time he's ever offered me a cup of anything. Am I being accepted into this town, his town? Feels like it takes me a year to move forward one per cent.

'Yes. Yes, I do. White, no sugar, please.'

He looks at me with a face that says *do I look like waitress?*

'Over there,' he says, pointing to a kettle next to the sink.

I walk back toward the three cells and pour myself coffee into a mug that says 'Värmland's finest.'

When I get back to the Chief's desk, there's another dude sat next to him.

'This is Detective Shadid from Karlstad homicide.'

'Hello detective, I'm Tuva Moodyson.'

The guy just nods. Clean-shaven, navy shirt and navy trousers.

'Falk,' says the Chief.

I think about the paperclip attached to my coat sleeve. 'I've been researching historical events connecting certain members of the Visberg community to Arne Persson.'

The detective makes a note. The Chief looks at the note the detective made.

'And?'

'Ragnar's daughter was killed in a hit-and-run incident in 1994.'

The Chief leans back in his chair. 'That is correct.'

'I have reason to believe Ragnar Falk was investigating the accident over the years, as would be understandable.'

'I'd say,' says the Chief.

'Arne Persson was the individual Ragnar Falk suspected of driving the hit-and-run car that was never recovered.'

'Falk told you this, did he?'

'I gleaned it from the information available and from my extensive interviews of multiple Visberg residents.'

'You *gleaned* it?'

I nod.

'Gleaned it?'

I nod again.

The Chief says, 'I've reports from the neighbourhood-watch coordinator...' he takes a deep breath and then carries on... 'Coordinator, Harry Hansson, tells me Ragnar Falk suspects someone was casing his building yesterday evening, sometime between eight and ten.'

'Casing?' I say.

'Looking for possible entry points and exit points, with a view to a robbery or home invasion.'

'Good job their neighbourhood watch is so watchful, isn't it.'

The Chief looks down his nose at me.

I clear my throat. 'All I'm saying is please don't discount Ragnar Falk from your investigation just because he looks harmless and he's got a limp and a Santa beard.'

'That everything?'

'No. I got sent this.'

I take the creepy Halloween poem from my coat and place it on the desk.

The Chief reads it.

'Looks like you got yourself an admirer.'

The detective checks his phone, then writes a note on his pad and shows it to Chief Björn.

'Okay, Moodyson. We'll take all you said about Falk's daughter into account. I got to go now, I'm sure you'll understand.' He points to the door and I leave.

Outside, there's a guy walking around in double denim. He's pushing a sheepskin-fur-lined buggy and his toddler's wearing a full skeleton-sleepsuit. Black with white bones.

'Happy Halloween,' he says as I pass him.

His kid bursts into tears.

The bell tinkles above the door to *Gavrik Posten.*

Sebastian looks like a new penny. Fresh haircut, fresh complexion, freshly-ironed shirt. I haven't pressed a shirt since Mum's funeral.

'Luka Kodro,' says Cheekbones. 'The Bosnian pizza maker. He doesn't have any kind of gun officially registered, but I have it on good authority that he uses an old military gun in the woods for target shooting. Not hunting, just paper targets.'

'Good,' I say. 'What else?'

'What else?'

'Statements from neighbours? Anything from the police? Is it the same kind of weapon used in the Arne Persson killing? Who is the registered owner, if anyone? Rifle or shotgun or handgun? Ammunition he uses? What gauge is the barrel?'

'Right,' he says. 'Shit. Right, I'm on it.'

He runs back to his desk and starts typing something.

'You need help in Visberg tonight?' he says. 'Need back-up?'

Part of me wants to say yes, wants to say, just be there to watch my back. See what I don't see. But if I'm going to be living and working here for a while, and I will be by the look of my new contract, then I need Visberg locals to trust me. They have to see me as their go-to person. For their middle-of-the-paper slow-news-day features on their Buick restoration and their longest-ponytail-in-central-Sweden story, but also so they can fill me in on gossip and secrets when a major event takes place. I need to be their primary contact.

'I'm fine. You need to be here covering Gavrik Halloween. Has Lars talked you through how to use the DLSR camera in low light?'

Sebastian nods and looks disappointed.

I text Noora. *About what you said. Can we talk later tonight when I'm done?*

She texts back almost immediately. *Sure xxx*

And now I feel like a human again. Those three kisses. The ones I find awkward to write even though it's stupid that I'm awkward and even though part of me loves receiving them. Mum never sent any. Not on a card. She never sent me a card after Dad died, or sat me down for a chat. There were no messages to end with kisses. I reply to Noora with a single x.

Lars walks in.

'Mrs Björken from the haberdashery is livid.'

He removes his coat like a DVD on slow-motion setting. It gets tugged off his shoulders and each arm gets pulled through. He shakes the coat and straightens it then hangs it carefully on his hook.

'Why?' I ask.

He looks round to me, his bifocals misted from the October damp outside.

'Why?' he says.

Then he removes each boot and places it neatly on the shoe rack. One Velcro trainer on. Then the next. He pulls the first one off again and adjusts the strap.

'Tooth,' he says.

Sebastian looks confused.

'What?'

Lars saunters over toward the kitchen and says, 'Coffee in the pot, Seb?'

You could just check.

'Yeah, fresh in the pot,' says Sebastian. 'What tooth?'

Lars stops and turns around, standing in the doorway of Nils's office-slash-kitchen.

'Mrs Björken went in to get a cap replaced.' He puts his finger inside his mouth and checks on one of his own teeth and then looks surprised. 'Sven Edlund started the procedure as per expected.'

Lars stops talking and just looks into the middle distance.

Jesus Christ, just get to the fucking point, man.

'And...' says Sebastian.

Lars takes a deep breath. 'Apparently Sven Edlund left the room for a moment and when Mrs Björken looked up again it was Dr Eva Edlund wearing the face mask, holding the drill.'

'What?' says Sebastian.

'Well, she is a qualified dentist,' I say.

'Not practicing though,' says Lars. 'Besides, it upset Mrs Björken, because you don't expect a different face to appear looming over you when you're down in the chair, do you? A strange face and a drill making that awful, squealing noise. Mrs Björken put her hand in front of her mouth and refused to cooperate with Eva Edlund.'

'What happened?' I say.

'Sven came back and completed the procedure. He apologised and said he'd wanted his wife's opinion on the tooth, and that he should have let Mrs Björken know what was going on.'

'Doesn't sound like a front-page story,' says Sebastian.

'I never suggested it was,' says Lars. 'But as I mentioned, Mrs Björken was quite put out. Said the look in Eva Edlund's eyes would haunt her to the grave. Said Eva had an excited expression.'

I work on my outlines and type up interviews from my digital Dictaphone. Pot noodle at my desk followed by a Daim bar. Then off to Visberg.

I'm stuck behind a slow-moving mobile crane until I get to Svensson's Saws & Axes, where the driver pulls over because she's good enough to let me pass. The sky is white with dark-grey patches that move fast across the horizon. A deer lies dead on the side of the road, it's neck bent round the wrong way.

The rain starts coming down heavy when I'm halfway up the hill. The white bike glistens. The cross bears up to the weather, just like it's done for a thousand days before, except this afternoon it has a rainproof grave-candle flickering and spitting at the point where the cross meets Visberg mud.

The town hasn't transformed the way it did on Pan Night. It's still open to the outside world. No road blocks. The rain beats down and I park outside Konsum. A troupe of schoolkids wearing hooded raincoats carry their instrument cases over to the bandstand and shelter underneath it, their innocent faces lit by their phones.

In between me and them are dozens of bright-red toadstools. New arrivals in town. They've pushed up through the apple sludge and now they dot Visberg town square like it's plagued by acne. Or plague.

People milling around. Excitement in the air. A chestnut seller sets up and the rain makes his charcoal fire smoke and hiss.

I look around at the pizzeria and think about Luka Kodro's unregistered gun. Could it be a remnant from the terrible war? The gun he fired to scare away the bird that awful night? Could it be a weapon that has been used to end life back in the '90s, or more recently? Above the fogged-up restaurant window is a smaller first-floor window.

Behind the glass is a woman with two girls looking out at the square.

All three have bright red hair.

39

I work away in my new office, aka my Hilux. The upstairs window above Visberg Grill is empty now. The Kodro family are most likely preparing for tonight's trick-or treating.

I remember when Halloween first came to Stockholm in a big way. I was ten or so. It started with the cool kids – richer kids, who'd visited Disney World or New Orleans with their parents. Kids who travelled regularly to catch up with the relatives who moved to the US during the diaspora, when Sweden was one of the poorest countries in the Western world. Those kids started celebrating Halloween, and parents all over Sweden turned their noses up. American nonsense. Even though Halloween probably arrived in the US originally from Ireland and Scotland. Swedes said it wasn't Christian and that we should keep All Hallows Day sacred, even though most traditional Swedish holidays are about as Christian as a sacrificed virgin on a mountain to appease some god of harvest. But my first Halloweens were not good experiences. Mum wouldn't even consider it an occasion. Banned me from making so much as a homemade mask or a witch's hat from a cardboard cone painted black. Easter is for witches, so she said. Another oddball Swedish tradition that my London flatmates never really figured out. Easter? Witches? About as relevant as bunnies or chocolate eggs, I guess. And then, when I was old enough to disobey Mum and go out, I didn't really have any friends to trick-or-treat with. My deafness was an isolating factor but so was my individual situation. No dad. No mum able to pick me up or drop me off. No parent to sign release forms so I could go away on school trips. No guardian to pay for official school photographs or birthday gifts for schoolmates. I became quieter. Adept at living life in the corners and the shadows. Not making a scene. Just existing on the fringes and hoping for some better days in future years once I had full independence.

Well, here I am, motherfuckas.

I shoot off emails to Lena and Thord, and tidy up the timeline of events leading up to Arne Persson's murder that I'd like to include in next week's issue. It needs to be accurate but also sensitive. Local people don't want too much hard information. Nothing gratuitous. I'm not in this for clicks, I'm in it for the long haul.

A bang on my windscreen.

I wipe the condensation and strain to see who thumped the glass.

Red hair.

I turn my key one notch in the ignition and wind down my window.

'You need my garage again, Tuva?' asks Julia.

I smile and shake my head.

'No need tonight,' I say. 'Or is there?'

'No, no,' she says. 'Halloween is for kids, at least it is in Visberg. You eating before things kick off.'

I look over at the half-squashed clingfilm-wrapped meat-ball-and-beetroot sub I bought earlier today from the newsagent in Gavrik.

'That thing even edible?' she says.

'Not sure I can stomach another pizza,' I say.

'Sure you can.'

'In an hour, then? I need to work some more.'

She agrees and walks away.

I see Emil and Margareta Eriksson right in front of me. They place heavy, oversize pumpkins outside the entrance to the Hive.

Konsum still has a few uncarved ones left. There's something outside the pop-up shop glowing in the shadows but it looks too small to be a pumpkin. Too pale.

I do my rounds.

In Konsum I ask the manager about whether he's heard anything new about the murder. About the grave disturbance.

'All behind us, now,' he says.

'But nobody's been arrested or charged?'

'Best thing this town can do is move forwards. We'll be in the run up to Christmas after tonight. Busiest time of the year for us.'

I'm always stunned by this. How humans manage to view momentous events through the prism of their own daily needs and wants.

Sven Edlund walks out of his dental surgery carrying a bag of golf clubs, and then Tobias the hygienist walks behind him, carrying a slightly smaller bag. Is the Edlund's club open on Halloween? Is this Visberg festivity really just for children?

The kids in the bandstand are eating steaming chestnuts from paper cones. A black girl with white facepaint is tuning her guitar and it sounds awful through my aids. Behind the musicians is a bank of amplifiers, and the cables run out and loop through puddles. They're already half submerged in mud and rotten apples before the sun's even gone down.

I check in with Thord about the grave robbery.

'I still can't tell you much more, Tuvs.'

'You can but you won't.'

'I can't.'

'Was the head removed?'

A long pause. Sound of breathing.

'It was, I knew it was.'

'I didn't confirm anything,' says Thord. 'Do not write that in your paper. You understand me?'

'Elk skulls. A dead man's head buried two decades ago.'

'No comment.'

He puts down the phone and I notice the fog rolling in from the side streets. It's not dense tonight, but it makes Visberg look older than it is. A grainy, sepia photograph of itself.

I head over to the grill and it already smells like wood smoke and roasting meats of various kinds.

The window's steamed up and the huge plastic udders of ketchup and mustard and mayo are being refilled by Luka Kodro himself. He's wearing blue jeans and a white T-shirt as usual and he looks handsome. How the hell does he manage to never get ketchup stains on his pristine, white shirts?

Julia comes inside and we sit down.

'My boss is off to play golf in all this, can you believe that?'

'In the fog?' I say.

'In the fog. In the fine drizzle. On Halloween of all days.' She shivers for effect. 'No way I'd be out on an isolated windswept golf course today, even without a crazed killer on the loose.'

'No Green Card, eh?' I say.

She laughs out loud and I notice she has a gold filling at the back of her mouth. I rarely see them these days.

'Playing with his young protégé, Tobias,' says Julia. 'Thick as thieves those two.'

'Is Tobias a member of Edlund's Club?'

'He's working on it,' says Julia. 'That's the vibe I get, anyway. Doctor Eva likes him even more than my boss does.'

I make a mental note of all this. Like I'm building a delicate web of connections, trying to figure out how all the locals fit together. Who owes who what. Who needs something from who. Who's raging. Who's hurt. Who's infatuated.

'You out later to watch the kids get their candy?' I ask.

Julia screws up her nose.

'Join me if you like. We can walk around and you can tell me who's behind all the masks. I need to cover it for the paper.'

She shrugs with a smile. 'Sounds good. It's a date.'

Our pizzas arrive and we devour them. Something about the cold and the damp and the way I sense the atmosphere in this town turning again. The mood. As much as everyone tells me tonight will be an innocent, child-friendly PG13-night compared to what happened last week, I can still feel the charge in the air. The hint of danger. People here seem to be drawn to it.

We split the bill.

'No tip?' I ask.

'We don't really tip in Visberg,' she says.

'What about the waitress, though. She was really nice.'

'That's her job, I guess,' says Julia.

We walk out and I leave a 20 kronor note. You have to tip. You just have to.

The air outside is chill and it is infused with the scent of roasted chestnuts. The smell takes me back to London, to long winter walks along the south side of the Thames with my then boyfriend.

The band in the bandstand is playing 'Hurt' by Johnny Cash, or Nine Inch Nails, whatever, but the pacing is wrong and it sounds a little too slow. And it's already a slow tune.

There's a queue of teenagers outside Mind Games. None of them have bothered to dress up. The door says 'Welcome to the Halloween Zombie Feast. Doors open 19:00'.

'Nerds,' says Julia, elbowing me and then pulling on her orange, bobble hat.

'If I wasn't working tonight I'd probably be in that queue with them,' I say.

She looks at me. 'You? Seriously?'

We walk toward the statue of Adolf-Fredrik Edlund. The anvil sparkles after its recent deep clean. There are pumpkins all around the base and Sheriff Hansson is there in full uniform, with his star badge and beige shirt and brown tie and striped trousers and radio attached to his shirt loop. Outside the Hive, there's Noora talking to Hans Wimmer the Austrian clockmaker. Law enforcement are out in force. Or as much force as we ever have, all the way out here at the end of the world.

Noora looks over and narrows her eyes. Is she jealous of Julia?

The music changes to *Girl... You'll be a woman, soon*, and the boy singing has an exceptionally smooth voice. The beat vibrates through me and reverberates round the square.

More and more kids arrive. Some in groups, and other, younger children holding the hands of their parents. A tall woman wearing a *Scream* mask carries a doll close to her chest. I smile and of course her mask doesn't move so I don't know if she smiles back or scowls but the doll isn't a doll it's a real baby. Its own extra-small *Scream* mask tipped back to the rear of its head, its fat, ruby-red lips clamped to its mother's breast, its cheeks flushed from the cold air of hill town, or the warmth of its mother's sweet milk.

There's a pair of young boys in clown costumes complete with curly red wigs and they're collecting slugs from under the apple trees. One has almost half-filled a jam jar with black, shiny, engorged slugs, and the other is mixing them with his Halloween candy. All looks the same from where I'm standing.

Julia and I walk across the square and the music's too loud just here. The junior band is enthusiastically playing 'Jeepers Creepers', and an elderly couple wearing latex smiling-dog masks are dancing like they're eighteen all over again. Then the woman slips on the apple sludge and the music stalls and she's taken away by three men, the Sheriff overseeing them.

The pumpkins outside the pop-up shop aren't pumpkins.

The sign in the window still says '31% off. Closing It Down Sale', and the door to the shop is wedged open with an oversize *hustomte* troll, a regular, not a special, just one of Cornelia's, this one the height of my knee. The sisters are being less coy than usual. The window display is crammed full of expensive carved trolls. Specials. Some of Alice's finest work. They're lined up like a battalion of evil, pine men looking out at Visberg town square. What I thought were pumpkins are in fact carved turnips with mean little slits for eyes. They're small. Fist size.

The music changes to 'Somewhere Over the Rainbow'.

The fog thickens.

And then a gun goes off outside Visberg Grill.

40

People scream and throw themselves to the ground. An old man cowers behind me, using me as a human shield.

Sheriff Hansson walks over to the Grill.

I see Noora with her hand on her gun.

Hans Wimmer climbs out of his old Skoda and puts his hands up into the cold autumnal air. Must be nine-feet tall with his hands up. Taller than a bull elk.

The Sheriff talks to him and then turns and says, 'Just a car backfiring.' Then he stands on top of a bench and cups his palms around his mouth and yells, 'Nothing to be afraid of, folks. Backfired is all.'

The volume in the square slowly increases to normal, like a dial being turned. Some take this as their cue to head home, but the older teenagers are emboldened. Like they survived something. Two of them start kissing outside Konsum: a boy with thick blond hair and a girl dressed as a fairy.

I take photographs and then I walk over to the Sheriff.

'Sheriff.'

'Damn old vehicles,' he says. 'Scared some of these people half to death.'

A figure emerges from behind an apple tree wielding a chainsaw. It's not turned on. It's quiet. The Sheriff says, 'Excuse me, Tuva,' and walks to them and tells them to take the chainsaw home. I can read his lips from here because he's directly under a streetlight. The person removes their Freddy Kruger mask. It's Margareta Eriksson from the Hive. He tells her that bringing out a chainsaw isn't appropriate right now, not out in the town square.

Margareta walks away, back to her storage units and her carpeted apartment, and someone else yells out, 'Killjoy!'

The temperature drops and the apple slime beneath my boots begins to sparkle.

Fog pumps in from outside the town like waves breaking on a shore.

There are high-pitched screams from moped engines as teenagers race round the back of the dental surgery to where I picked Ragnar Falk's lock. Low-cc motorbikes with good-looking kids, the girls on the back, the air thick with anticipation, mixed with the kind of adolescent cool I've never even gotten close to. It's like watching a movie. The girls' bare arms wrapped around the boys' waists. It looks like the boys are the ones in control, but they're not really. The helmet visors reflect orange light from flickering pumpkin lanterns. The band plays 'The Sound Of Silence' as the town soundtrack.

A girl in school uniform with sunglasses and a white cane says, 'Trick or teeth?'

'It's trick-or-treat,' I say.

'Trick,' she says.

I just walk away.

There's some kind of apple-bobbing contest going on outside the pharmacy, so I wander over and photograph it for the paper. The apples look too perfect: red and grass-green things grown in New Zealand and flown over wrapped in tissue paper, while their acidic Swedish cousins rot on branches directly opposite and then fall down to be consumed by wasps from the inside and rats from the outside.

A kid dressed as a ghost almost chokes. Either because he swallowed water or else he bit into one of the apples. They still have their labels on. He receives a sharp punch to the back that does the trick.

Noora walks over and says, 'You see anything out of the ordinary you report it to me.'

Well, okay, love of my life, great to see you too.

How does she manage to do this? To separate the different chambers of her world like this. Is it coldness or just professionalism?

The streetlights flicker on and off and she says, 'End of the line.' And then she goes off to help a desperate mother who can't find her son.

The wind picks up and a large apple falls from a high branch and breaks open on a bench. Must have been one of the last on the tree.

Four men walk past me, each one holding a *tunnbrödsrulle* hotdog. They smell incredible. Pork sausage and Norrland flatbread and shrimp salad and mash potato and ketchup. Food of the gods. One of the men is Daniel from the gamer café. Shouldn't he be hosting the game launch tonight with his twin?

I approach the chestnut stall.

It says 'Kristersson's Nuttilicious Delights. Established 1899' on the side of his cart.

'Mind if I take a photo?'

'What do I get out of it?' says the grey-haired stall owner.

'Free advertising, I guess.'

'You gonna buy nuts?'

I take the photo. He looks stern in his stained leather apron, holding a sharp, metallic scoop. His grey hairs fall across his face so the photo only picks out one of his eyes.

I relent and buy a portion of chestnuts and walk away. They're hot and they smell delicious. Sugar and earthiness. More memories of midnight walks by the Thames on nights with no breeze and no chill in the air. The lights from riverside buildings reflecting in the tidal waters. The buzz of traffic on nearby bridges. Sirens in the distance. Barges taking London's waste slowly out of town. The feel of a man's hand in my own for the first time that year. The sense of what might come to pass.

Two women walk by wearing police-uniform fancy dress, but with short skirts.

I don't want to linger by the bandstand because the music's too loud to be comfortable. They're playing an excellent Nick Cave song and there's a bony black dog sat close by, and he's howling his duet with his neck bent up to the sky.

The fog thickens.

I can see the Konsum side of the street pretty clearly, but the dark side is almost invisible. I take a few photos, adjusting my aperture to take account of the lower light. No heads on anvils and no teeth in pans. Just a backfiring Skoda. Maybe they were right. Maybe Halloween here is a gentler affair, designed mainly for the local kids. Maybe hill people exorcise their demons and get out all their pent up frustration on Pan Night each October.

Murder slugs glisten black on the wet grass.

A boy walks past me holding a bright-red toadstool covered in white dots. It's as big as his face. Most of the other town-square toadstools have already lost their shape. They've gone from round to flat. They've released their spores. Millions of microscopic particles now float around in the low mists, ready to create new fungi next year. I can smell them. Some lethal, some delicious. The air is heavy with fungal spores and chestnut smoke, with innocent laughter and the sickly scent of decaying fruit.

Julia joins me with her own chestnuts in hand. She's peeled them and they look like shrunken brains. A woman walks past the dental surgery with black Grimberg salt-liquorice coins taped over her eyes and Julia says to me, 'Well, that's in poor taste.' I have to say I agree. Julia chases her and tells her so. The woman unpeels the coins from her eyes and eats them in one mouthful.

'It's not funny,' Julia says.

'I agree,' says the woman.

We walk past the side of the dental surgery onto her street. There are more people wearing fancy-dress cop costumes now. I count nine just in this corner of the square. Maybe twenty in total.

Beneath a streetlight in the distance a figure stands erect wearing a top hat.

A small man heads out in that direction. It's Emil, I can see his moustache whiskers in the glare from the light.

'You want a *tunnbrödsrulle?*' asks Julia. 'I'm starving.'

It happens in seconds.

I see the man in the top hat seize Emil. He lifts him clear off his feet and throws him to the ground.

'Hey!' I shout.

'What is it?' asks Julia, turning to look.

The man in the top hat holds Emil by his ankles and begins to drag him toward the kerb. Emil screams obscenities at him, his head banging on the road with every bump.

'Fuck,' says Julia. 'That looks real.'

'Stop.' I yell, running toward them. The tail-lights of a car flash on and off. Its boot pops open.

Julia yells 'Police! Over there!'

The man's car starts up.

He picks up Emil and Emil starts punching and kicking him. His top hat stays on the whole time. He's wearing a cheap plastic pig mask, the kind you see at a fairground. The man lifts Emil and dumps him into the boot of the car and slams it shut and drives off.

I run after it and photograph the car.

The fog fills in the gaps.

They're gone.

41

Other people arrive. Fake cops and skeletons. One woman wearing a white nightie with a huge, red, painted smile. From under her skirt is some kind of imitation umbilical cord. It's connected to an antique doll that drags behind her.

The band starts playing 'Hallelujah'.

Noora speeds past us in her police car, the tyres squealing and smoking on the asphalt.

'What do we do?' asks Julia by my side. 'Can we help?'

'You stay right here,' says a deep voice from behind me. It's Sheriff Hansson and he has his hand on his radio. 'Police from Falun coming in from the other side to intercept. You leave them to stop the car.'

'They have Emil,' says Julia.

'They?' says the Sheriff.

'One person started the car when the top-hat guy dragged Emil into the boot. There must be two abductors.'

Sheriff turns and talks into his radio. When he's done he answers questions from trick-or-treaters, carpenters and call-centre workers, with masks perched on top of their heads and fear in their eyes. Then Sheriff Hansson turns back to me and mutters under his breath, 'I told them yesterday we should cancel. They never listen to me.'

Did he tell them that?

I get quotes and statements, but most people just want to get back to the perceived safety of their homes. Their warm beds and their locked doors.

I drive Julia back to her house, and she says, 'Can you just wait a sec until I'm inside and I've checked all the rooms? It'll just take a minute, and then I'll signal so you can get back home. I'm a bit shaken is all.'

'Sure.'

She unlocks her door and goes inside. The ground-floor light comes on. I see her silhouette move across the room. I lock my truck from inside. The upstairs light comes on. Both lights. Then she appears in the front door and mouths, 'All okay. Good night.'

I set off home and there are two cop cars in Visberg town square with their lights on. More of a show of force than anything else, as the car with Emil in the boot will be long gone by now. Luka Kodro is casually drinking a small cup of espresso outside his café, wearing just his white T-shirt and jeans. A man behind him is wiping down tables. Luka nods at me as I drive past.

Down the hill and through the fog. I'm starting to think it was a bad idea coming back up north for this promotion. I managed to get out and then I came back like an idiot. For a job. For friends. For Noora.

Across the old train tracks and past the cross.

The white bike has either fallen over in the high winds or else it's been pushed. I should get out and fix it but I can't be outside the truck on this hill on a night like this. Not after I was shot at. I'm not an idiot. I cannot end up in the boot of some maniac's car. Won't let it happen.

I drive on.

Past Svensson's Saws & Axes.

The twin chimneys of Grimberg Liquorice look inviting and I've never had that feeling before in my life. They're usually foreboding. The scale of them and the way their shadows cast all the way down Storgatan, the longest street in town. But tonight they pull me closer, like identical lighthouses calling out, saying, *this way wanderer, seek safety over here.*

I hope this is a new missing-persons case; resolvable, not another murder. I cannot countenance the idea of a fresh, severed head. The killer posturing. Taunting. Teasing us all with his or her brilliance. Poor Emil. The tone of his voice when he was dragged away. The sight of his head hitting the kerb. Who the hell pulls someone by their ankles? You drag with your arms looped under the armpits surely? Something biblically horrific about a head scraping along the ground. The disregard for life or well-being. The ritualistic animalness of it all.

Gavrik is quiet and it looks peaceful tonight.

Straggler trick-or-treaters, older kids, wandering along Eriksgatan with plastic buckets full of candy. Dude on a bike with a bag of Tam's takeout food swinging from his handlebars. One girl on a scooter. Two adults, probably parents not wanting to appear too protective, hovering twenty metres behind their offspring.

I get to my building and park. There's a passive-aggressive building-chairman message stuck to my mailbox with tape. It says, 'confirm your attendance at the bi-annual building deep-clean on November 15 by no later than 17:00 on Friday'. The 'no later' is underlined in red ink. Twice.

I'm weary climbing the stairs. The light on our floor is fine but the stairwell light blinks on and off. Why don't you focus on that, building chairman? And why don't you stick your head up your ass while you're at it?

Inside.

I double-lock my door and send my photographs from tonight to Thord at his official police-email address, like the Sheriff asked me to. They're not hi-res but when I zoom into the photos I can see the car is dark blue and the registration plate is either missing or else it's been covered over. The top-hat man looks strong. The boot sits open, a coil of blue rope visible in the boot light. And the look on Emil's face says, *what the hell is happening to me and why is nobody coming to help?* It says, *don't hurt me.* It says, *do not kill me.*

Why did they kidnap him, of all people? Emil seems harmless enough. Sure, I didn't appreciate his less-than-subtle candy-bracelet routine, but he didn't touch me. Nobody in Visberg has ever said a bad word against him. Did he do something? Was he to blame somehow for his father's accident? Or did he *know* something?

There's an argument flaring up in the next-door apartment again.

No bangs on the walls this time, but swearing and screams. Crying. If it wasn't for little Dan and the fact I can remove my hearing aids whenever I like, I'd probably move. In fact I'd definitely move.

I check my fridge. A lettuce that has turned urine-yellow. Why do I buy salad just to let it rot? Half a carton of milk and half a carton of *filmjölk*, the sour milk my London flatmates never really grew accustomed to. Sweet, soft cheese, known as *messmör*. It tastes like tangy caramel. A bar of Marabou with digestive pieces. No alcohol. Two bottles of Coke – it tastes so much better from real glass bottles. And a box of long-life UHT orange juice. I close it and open the freezer. Lots of snow, the kind you don't want in a freezer, and a half-eaten box of fish fingers. I take them out and then there's a knock.

On my internal door?

I think about the threatening front-page note. And the postcard with the poem. Someone from inside the building, or at least someone who has the code?

Another knock.

Two more.

I swallow hard and take the stungun from my handbag, the one Benny Björnmossen gave me.

'Hello?' I say.

'It's me, dickhead.'

I open and Tam's standing there, shivering and holding up two bags of Thai food.

I breathe a big sigh of relief and let her in and double-lock the door.

She looks at the folded, cardboard box of fish fingers on the counter and points to it. 'That's why I'm here, see? Panang or Pad Thai?'

'Pad Thai.'

She sets it all up on my kitchen table. Plastic cartons of steaming, perfect rice-cooker rice. Cardboard boxes of spring rolls, so crispy the thin batter has bubbled in the fryer and the bubbles have been frozen in time, ready to crunch and burst inside my mouth. Prawn crackers in a greasy bag. Both kinds: white and spicy. Her curry and my noodles. We sit down and she says, 'Fucking Halloween. Brings out the worst in teenagers. Did in me, anyway.' I start chopsticking hot noodles into my mouth. They're glossy and fresh, flecked with red chili and leaves of bright coriander. The spice is a balm. I'm heated up from every angle.

'A man was kidnapped in Visberg tonight,' I say with my mouth full. 'Just off the town square.'

Tammy swigs from the alcohol-free beer she makes a point of drinking when she's with me to make me feel more normal. She says it's so she can drive but I know she does it for me, because the fridge in her flat is stocked with them whenever I go over there. She's not driving *then*, is she.

'I heard,' she says. 'Worked at the self-storage place?'

I nod. 'Owner's son.'

'Police will find him.'

I wrinkle up my face like, *maybe they will but maybe they won't.*

'They found me, didn't they,' she says, and suddenly I feel like a Grade-A idiot for not connecting this to her abduction over Midsommar.

'Fingers crossed,' I say.

My phone vibrates on the table.

'If Noora's coming over,' says Tam, looking at the phone. 'Then I'll go. It's no problem.'

'She's asked to move in,' I say.

'How do you feel about that?'

'Terrified,' I say.

The message is from Sebastian.

It says police have taken in a suspect for questioning.

It says they're talking to Ragnar Falk.

42

I'm at the police station before 8am. Four other journalists stand outside, two of them recording pieces to camera. An outside-broadcast van with a dish on its roof. One woman from *Svenska Dagbladet* waiting outside my office, probably trying to talk to Lena.

Thord lets me into reception and locks the door behind me.

'Here we go again,' he says.

'What do you mean?'

He pushes the vertical strip-blinds apart with the biro he keeps behind his ear and says, 'This media circus. No offence.'

'None taken.'

'We can't talk in the main office. We've got company from Linköping, Karlstad and Torsby. Full house. Let's talk in there.'

We walk through to the press-conference room. There are cycling-proficiency-advice posters on the wall and a range of unstamped, unsigned certificates spread out on a table.

'Bicycle bullcrap,' says Thord. 'Most of the kids round here have a motocross bike or an EPA tractor. But we gotta tick those boxes.'

He makes a *tick* action with his index finger.

'Any news on Emil Eriksson?'

He shakes his head. 'Not yet, I'm afraid. Not much in the way of CCTV or traffic cameras way out past the hill town. Ain't got so much as a speed camera, despite all the fatal RTAs and maimings they had up there over the years. We've got help doing door-to-door enquiries and we've got experts making what they can from your photos. I'm obliged to you for that. They can zoom in and work out all sorts, even from a grainy image. Improve the quality on their computers using specialist software. Sometimes I feel like those boys and girls with the gadgets solve all the crimes these days, and I'm just paid to sit here and hand out goddam certificates to any kid who can make it down Storgatan without falling off his BMX.'

Thord smiles to himself but he looks tired.

'Ragnar Falk?' I ask.

'We've been talking to him and some others. Trying to piece together exactly what the hell is going on over at Visberg. Chief reckons we might have some boundary changes after all this is said and done. He reckons that'd be a good thing.'

'What do you mean?'

'I mean he's not too keen on policing that town no more is what I mean.'

'Do you think Arne Persson was the hit-and-run driver that killed Ragnar Falk's daughter all those years ago?'

'Don't matter so much what I think, Tuvs. Matters what Ragnar Falk actually did. Chief doesn't seem to like the idea much, but then Ragnar ain't got no clear alibi for the night of the murder, or for this Pan Night just gone either.' He turns to check the clock on the wall, then turns back to me. 'Who did you see around last night in Visberg town square?'

'It was difficult to tell, I—'

'Stupid masks and grown men dressed up like babies and skeletons, I know what you mean. But did you see anyone who could not have been involved, is what I'm asking you? Anyone I can discount from my enquiries for the abduction at least?'

'I saw the Sheriff and Noora.'

He gets out his pen and then looks up at me. 'Well, I don't reckon we need to get alibis from the Pope or the Queen of England, but go on.'

'I think the gamer twins were in their café hosting a new game launch. One of them, at least.'

'You think or you know?'

'Think.'

He grumbles something.

'I was standing with Julia Beck, the receptionist when it all happened.'

'Dental receptionist?'

I nod.

'Go on.'

'I saw Hans Wimmer the clockmaker, but that was a while before the abduction.'

'Still useful – now I know he was in the area.'

'Margareta Eriksson got sent home by Sheriff Hansson for having a chainsaw as part of her Halloween costume.'

'For having a what?'

'A chain—'

'I heard what you said.'

'And the Grill owner Luka Kodro was sat outside his restaurant about fifteen minutes after the abduction happened.'

'Was he, now?'

'Yeah.'

'Fifteen minutes. You sure about that?'

'Might have been twenty. Maybe twenty-five.'

'What was Kodro doing?'

'Drinking coffee.'

'Anyone else there with him?'

I think about that and then I shake my head. 'Maybe someone clearing tables. That's it.'

'You've done good.'

'What do you have for me?'

He scratches the stubble on the side of his face. He hasn't had time to shave today.

'The grave incident up at the churchyard.' He sucks his upper lip down under his bottom lip and shakes his head. 'I gotta tell you, we didn't need all this right now.'

I wait for him to go on.

'The head was removed from the coffin. Would have been just bone by now, so I'm told. Just a skull, pretty much.'

'Are you connecting this to the Arne Persson murder?'

'Officially? No. Unofficially? What do you think? Listen, I gotta go now, Tuvs. Watch yourself in hill town. Take pretty boy with you. Watch your back.'

I walk out and a photographer from one of the national tabloids takes a picture of me and I scowl at him.

The window of *Gavrik Posten* has a crack in one corner. It's been taped on both sides with packing tape. I go inside and the bell tinkles over the door.

'What happened?' I ask.

Sebastian looks up from his screen and says, 'Halloween kids.'

'Lena in?'

'She's got a mammal-gram; mobile place in ICA car park. Big truck.'

'A what?'

'It's a...you know,' he blushes and points to my chest. 'Mammal-gram.'

'It's called a mammogram, shithead.'

'That's what I said.'

I make us both a fresh pot of coffee.

'How long have you been in?'

'Since seven-fifteen,' he says. 'Lena gave me a set of keys.'

'Early bird,' I say.

'I think I've found something but I keep hitting a brick wall.'

I hand him a mug of coffee and perch on the edge of his desk.

'I've been searching for combinations of terms connecting the recent attacks and incidents. Cross-referencing Visberg with Arne

Persson and Visberg with "teeth" and so on, trying to get the algorithms to do some work for me.'

I gesture for him to get to the point.

He sips his coffee and says, 'Got a hit on page seven of the results when I raked through "Visberg", "teeth" and "skull".'

'Yeah?'

'Hans Wimmer.'

I put down my coffee.

'I'm listening.'

Sebastian locates the tab on his computer. 'It's a blog post from seven years ago. The blog's been deleted, but I can still see the gist of it by searching around it and looking at the guy's social media.'

'What guy?'

'An independent watchmaker from Amsterdam.'

'Amsterdam?'

'He visited Visberg to look at Wimmer's clock museum, apparently. One of the finest collections of organic clocks in the world.'

'What's an organic clock?'

He beckons me over to look at his screen and then he switches tabs.

'Antique clocks made out of organic materials,' he says. 'Bones and human tendons, that kind of thing.'

'Okay.'

'Guy visiting, Dutch guy, watchmaker himself, used to work for a big Swiss brand, he made some kind of official complaint on a horology forum. That forum no longer exists. This Dutch guy's social media no longer exists. His blog no longer exists. It's like he's been wiped from the surface of the Earth.'

43

I ask Sebastian to research deeper into the complaint against Hans Wimmer. To find the missing blogger. I tell him not to hesitate to contact the police if he comes across something important and can't reach me. A murder and an ongoing abduction case. Time is of the essence.

The drive to Visberg feels longer than ever. Away from the motorway and the pulp mill and the police force. Away from the transport connections to the outside world. If Visberg still had its train line I'd be a lot more comfortable about the place. As it is, I feel like I'm strapped into a capsule, about to launch into deep space.

My dash reads four degrees.

A woman walks out of Svensson's Saws & Axes carrying a brand-new petrol chainsaw. She waves to the guy in the shop and loads the saw into her Honda.

As I approach Visberg hill I take in the enormity of the elk forest. A mountainside smothered with pines as tall as church steeples. Sure, it's divided by a twisty road and that adds a veneer of safety, an illusion of civilisation, but it's just Utgard on a slope. Square mile after square mile of elk-infested pine insanity. A maze designed by some architect of chaos to maintain the darkness within.

I turn on my heated seat.

The outer fringes of the woods look like an army assembled. A line of warriors from a different age, commanded to hold their ground, come what may. Stand still until you're told to charge.

Someone's propped the white bike back up and I'm happy about that.

Past the cross, over the old tracks, up on top of the summit. The bee spins and people buzz around the square walking their hunt dogs and drinking strong Swedish coffee from their own personal ICA thermos mugs. I pull over outside the Hive. There are four municipal gardeners in dark green uniforms and they're jet-washing the apple sludge from the pavements and raking up the layer of organic filth from the grass. The sun is shining on the Konsum side of the square. The clock outside Wimmer's Clocks is still not working.

I get out and notice the crowd outside the dental surgery.

'Glad you're able to join us,' says Julia, her hair glowing in the sun like strands of spun gold.

'What are you doing?'

Eva Edlund muscles through the group and looks up at me with her ice-blue eyes and her perfect, blonde bob. 'This is the official search party. We're looking for Emil Eriksson.'

'Looking for him here?'

'This is just the rendezvous point,' says Eva with a disappointed expression. 'Search starts once everyone arrives.'

Sven Edlund looks stern, his hunt dog straining on its lead. Neither looks like they want to be here. In fact, the hound seems desperate to investigate the basement of the dental surgery. It's pulling so hard on the leash its eyes are starting to bulge in their sockets.

'Adolf,' says Sven Edlund. 'Sit. Sit down, boy.'

Oh, nice choice of name, meathead.

The dog sits but its nose is still twitching in the direction of the surgery basement.

A chill runs through my body. At this moment the town feels wrong, it feels toxic. Like just standing here should come with a health warning.

Dozens of identikit people arrive in their Volvos. This is Edlund's golf club displaced to the town square. They kiss each other on the cheeks and one woman shows off her new boots.

'Dubarry,' she says. 'They're from Ireland.'

Annika Persson arrives and receives pitiful looks from the Edlunds.

The four municipal gardeners rake and brush and hose away the dead and dying fruit. The jet-wash guy is pushing a tidal wave of red toadstools, dead sticks and fermented apples toward his truck.

'I can make flyers,' I say. 'I've made them before. Flyers with Emil's photo. Contact details and social-media information. Maybe someone else could start a Facebook page?'

Sven sniffs. 'Best talk to Margareta before you graffiti the whole town with leaflets. Make sure that's what she wants for her son.'

The assembled search party walks off, half of them down the hill, half in the direction of the abduction point near Julia's house. No sign of the Sheriff. Maybe he's in Gavrik helping police. The real police.

I walk to the clock shop, curious after what Sebastian found out from that missing Dutch blogger. There are no clocks in the window display, and the sign on the door reads, 'Tempus Fugit. On Vacation'.

I text Sebastian *Any more info on Wimmer?* He responds almost immediately *Working on it.*

The door to the pop-up shop next door creaks open.

'Don't just stand there looking gormless, girl. Give me a hand.'

Cornelia Sorlie is trying to push a wheelbarrow through the door but the door keeps self-closing. I hold it wide open for her.

'Where's Alice?' I say.

'None of your concern where Alice is.'

I look into the wheelbarrow. It's full of trolls, each one swaddled individually, like babies in soft fleece blankets. A barrow full of carved miniature people. One has painted red cheeks and a real hair moustache. Blond. Tiny white teeth. Another has a huge mouth with fat, red lips and a swollen tongue, probably ripped from the mouth of some Utgard mammal. The sisters once told me they bulk-buy their teeth off the internet, mostly from Eastern Europe. They told me they're not expensive.

'You want me to help you with your van door?' I ask.

'No, girl, I don't.' She gestures with her head. 'Taking these specials to my storage lock-up. But you can help me get in if you don't got better things to do.'

I walk with her and she is strong. I can see the muscles in her shoulders through her overalls as she pushes the troll barrow.

'Is Alice okay?'

She grunts and says, 'Not her best self, Alice. Hospital keeps on taking the skin off her flesh.'

'Skin?'

Cornelia slows when she gets close to the kerb. As the barrow bumps down onto the road, the doll eyelids of one of the trolls pop open and the eyes beneath are shrivelled. They look like old grapes. Some kind of wild-animal eyes shrunken deep into their carved pine sockets.

'Growths,' says Cornelia. 'They cut 'em out, but I ain't optimistic, girl. It's a bad state.'

'I'm so sorry,' I say.

She pushes the barrow up the far kerb and along the side of the Hive and she says, 'Yeah, you ain't the only one.'

'Main entrance?' I ask.

'I go in the back way,' she says. 'Top floor. I can take it all from here, girl. And don't go blabbing your mouth about what I told you. Alice is stronger than an elk in August.'

She walks away, the wheel of her barrow squeaking in time with the bee on the roof. So Cornelia and Alice have a unit up in the exclusive, private upper floor. Makes sense, I guess.

I go round to the main entrance.

Door's locked.

I ring the bell and wait and then ring it again.

Margareta comes over. She looks older than before. Sick with worry. The door opens.

'They found my Emil?'

'They're out looking,' I say. 'They'll get him back to you.'

She rubs her palms up and down her face and says something I can't decipher.

'We should have been taking soul cakes to the grave of his late father today,' she says, crossing herself. 'We do it every year, like clockwork.' Then she looks up at the ceiling and shakes her head. 'What the hell have I done to deserve all this?'

'None of it's your fault,' I say. 'Emil will turn up soon. My best friend went missing back over Midsommar and she came back unscathed.'

'Food-truck girl up Gavrik way?' she says.

'Yep.'

Margareta nods and lights up a cigarette. No strategic smoking with her head up the chimney now, she just lights up with her back to a non-smoking sign, her '70s weave underneath an illuminated fire-escape sign.

'I can make flyers and maybe coordinate some social-media campaigns if you like?' I say. 'If you can let me have a recent photograph of Emil, I can put a piece in the paper as well.'

'Front page, is it,' she says?

That strikes me as an odd question, but I guess she's in shock. 'Most likely,' I say.

She nods and swipes through photos on her phone.

'How about this one?' she smiles and shows me the screen. It's a photo of her and Emil standing on the roof, backdropped by the giant, turning bee. Margareta takes up most of the photo.

'It's a beautiful picture,' I say. 'But do you have one just of Emil?'

She exhales smoke through her nose and swipes again, shows me one of him, and then I help her email it to me.

'I'm sure we'll find him,' I say.

As I open the door to return to the square I hear the theme tune of *Cheers* start up in the other room. The TV volume must be extremely loud. Is there someone else in the owner's apartment? Or does Margareta have it playing constantly on a loop?

I step out onto the pavement. The sickly smell has intensified, like the jet-wash water is churning the mud into some kind of poison cider.

The Sheriff's car turns up and parks. He gets out.

'Poor kid,' he says as he looks over at the Hive.

I shake my head. 'Dragged off the street like that.'

'I've known little Emil Eriksson since he was knee-high to a cockroach.'

'Grasshopper,' I say.

'Not Emil,' says Sheriff Hansson. He never got that big.'

There's a screech from above and a white owl lands on the roof of Sheriff Hansson's taxi. The owl has a rat in its talons. Some kind of sewer rodent, still twitching with the last electronic pulses of its life. The owl looks at us calmly and then she digs her curved beak into the neck of the rat and she feasts.

44

The Sheriff tries to scare the huge bird away, but the owl tells him to go to hell. She takes her time with her hard-won rat. She pulls at it with her beak and she eats. And then, when she's done, she flies away, leaving a bloody mess on the taxi roof.

'Pest,' he says with his fist in the air. 'Goddam buzzard.'

It was an owl. Even I know that was an owl.

A lady in her fifties wearing a floor-length coat steps up to the Sheriff and says, 'Are you working today, Harry? Could you run me down to the churchyard, I'd like to pay my respects. Fixed price if you don't mind, I don't trust the meter.'

The Sheriff mumbles something I can't understand and then opens the back door for her. Guess he doesn't get hailed down in the street much in this town.

Tobias the hygienist is standing outside Konsum with one of the barbers from down Annika's street. The barber's wearing a white apron and his hair is oiled and combed perfectly. The man is a walking advert.

'None of this happened here till she took over Ragnar Falk's newspaper,' says the barber. I can read his lips pretty well from here.

Tobias rolls his eyes and says, 'Not sure we can blame the newspapers for all this.'

'Not the newspapers,' the barber says, pointing at me with a long finger. 'Her.'

Tobias says something I can't make out and then he says, 'Emil will turn up soon.' 'He'd better,' says the barber. 'They had enough tragedy in that family these past decades.' He looks over at the Hive. 'Emil's pappa never deserved that end.'

'When was that?' asks Tobias.

'Before you were even a twinkle in your daddy's eye,' says the barber. 'Poor man lost his head on the diagonal, not that the angle makes it better or worse.'

I pass them by and the barber kind of hisses at me and I give him a poisonous stare that says *do not fuck with me, old man. Not today.*

The gamer café is busy. I can tell because of the roars and screams emanating from inside. Sounds like there's a massacre going on inside Mind Games, and in a way, I suppose, there is. A virtual-reality massacre, unthinkable just ten years ago. Violence depicted so authentically I saw a guy about my age run out last night and vomit in the square. And yet as abhorrent as that kind of gaming sounds to some people, I've completed enough *Doom* levels to know how addictive it can be. How you can lose track of time. Lose track of your own moral compass.

The Grill chef is placing blankets over the backrests of all the chairs outside the pizzeria. It's a Swedish thing. Back in London I'd ask for a blanket outside a bar or a restaurant and I'd be met with a puzzled expression every time.

Luka Kodro opens his door.

'Tuva Moodyson,' he says. 'Early pizza? Spicy American Yankee Sausage?'

'Too early, even for me.'

'Coffee then?'

'Sure.'

Luka makes some gesture to his chef and his chef brings out a pot of black coffee and two smaller pots of hot milk. I place a blanket over my knees. Luka does not.

'What do you make of all this?' he says.

'Emil getting abducted? I have no idea why anyone would want to do that.'

He nods and sips his coffee.

'Men do strange things when they're angry.'

'So do women.'

He smiles and nods and then thinks about it some more and nods even harder.

'Is your newspaper getting to the bottom of this? I for one would like to go back to business as usual.'

'The police have leads, so they tell me.'

He looks over at the shady side of the street.

'Let me guess. Ragnar Falk, because his daughter was killed by a stupid, reckless driver, and now police realise it was probably Arne Persson who did it.'

'Did he do it?'

'How would I know? Back then I'd hardly even heard of Sweden.'

I think about the war-crime-tribunal documents I read through.

'Talk to me about what happened to your hometown before you left.'

He shakes his head. 'There is not enough time in the world.'

'Try me.'

He sips his coffee and crosses his arms. No tattoos. Tanned skin. The chiselled forearms of someone who has always worked with his hands.

'What nobody here in this country understands is that it could happen here. You all think it couldn't, that you're a superior people, a more civilised population. But this country is five bad decisions and one charismatic leader away from it. Same as every other country on the planet. And when things turn, they turn fast. The ethical code of a society changes so quickly nobody can keep up. The unthinkable becomes just an order. A rational revenge. I sit here some nights after we close and watch boys go into the café next door, pretending to be soldiers. Killing make-believe men for fun.

It's never fun. I see the bloodlust in their eyes. But the truth is that they will not be the soldiers fighting for local hills and local bridges if things ever do turn. They think they will fight, but they won't. It's the quiet men who fight. The stoic women who keep armies moving. A teacher may command a hundred men to recapture a field he once took students to for a study session on rock formation. He might fight against one of those students. He may have to shoot that student in the head. Worse, even. The computer-game boys next door will be hiding.' He looks down into his coffee cup. 'Men fighting for a hill. For what?'

'I can't imagine.'

He raises his eyebrows for a moment and then they drop down again. 'I don't like what has happened here in my town. Men going missing. Men being cut up.' He shakes his head. 'My chef is a Kosovan. My business partner is a Serb. But we're all Swedes. We don't want to see things go back to darkness.'

'Do you know who is responsible, Luka?'

He shakes his head and drains the last of his coffee. 'I'm not in the inner circle, Tuva. I'm no Edlund. If they stopped to imagine their precious, golf course dug up for mass graves they might change their priorities. Accept outsiders into their town. Be more forgiving of whatever went on in the past.'

Hans Wimmer arrives in his Skoda and walks into his clock shop.

'Now, he is a serious man. Mark my words.'

'Why do you say that?'

'I have seen men like him before. I have marched alongside them. I have stood witness.'

I look Luka straight in the eye to judge his reaction and then I say, 'Did you have anything against Arne Persson?'

He smiles and looks up above the restaurant.

'No,' he says. 'You see, Tuva. Most men don't realise that most of their days are already behind them. They don't realise how few lie ahead. But I see that. I see.'

45

I call Sebastian about Hans Wimmer and the disappearing blogger.

'Nothing more yet. I'll get back to you.'

Half of Visberg is pristine. Short grass. Jet-washed benches shining in the light. Bare apple trees. Not a toadstool in sight. The other half of the square is still full of pectin sludge. Like the streets of Paris before the centuries-old water system cleans the gutters each morning and flushes the night filth out into the Seine.

There's a 'Missing' poster taped to the statue of Adolf-Fredrik Edlund. It looks homemade. Probably by Margareta – a desperate mother begging for her only child to be returned to her.

Hans Wimmer's watching me from inside his shop. He turns the sign over from 'Tempus Fugit. On Vacation' to 'Time rests for no man. Open'.

I walk to the shop and notice the sisters have vacated the next-door unit, the shop owned by the late Arne Persson. The grotesque masks fashioned from boar hide are gone. The standard trolls made by Cornelia are gone. And the nightmarish specials crafted lovingly by the calloused hands of Alice are gone. The only thing I can see in the window is a remnant of the sign. It had read, '31% Off'. Now it just says, 'Off'.

The door to the clock shop opens and beeps.

'Have they found Margareta's boy yet?' asks Hans Wimmer, pushing grey hairs behind his ears.

'Not that I've heard,' I say.

'Oh dear.' He looks around the square, at the municipal gardeners and the Grill and Konsum. They're starting to put out Christmas wreaths already. One part of the year melts into the next. Then he stares over at the Hive. 'Oh dear,' he says again.

'May I come in? I might want a watch for my girlfriend.'

He looks startled. 'Your...' He pauses, computing this. 'Very good. Of course, please do come inside.'

I make a point of looking at the Seikos and the Timexes for a while.

'Do you have anything Swiss made?'

'Watches over there,' he points to the corner cabinet. 'Swiss clocks downstairs. I have to keep a selection of haute horology pieces in for the Edlunds in case they drop in.'

'Swiss clocks, please.'

He looks at the 'Clock Museum' sign attached to a chain hanging across the stairs down to the basement. 'You want a Swiss clock for your... I'm afraid they're very—'

'Just been promoted,' I say. 'It's burning a hole in my pocket.'

He removes the chain and says, 'I'll need to lock the main door and close up if you want to go down there. No telling who'd come in if I left the shop unattended.'

I swallow and check the stungun in my handbag. All present and correct.

'Sure.'

We walk down.

It's not as I expected. There's a wall of clocks on pillars and in glass cabinets, but otherwise it's a mess down here. A kids street-map rug and a *Bamse* bear jigsaw, half completed. An iPad charging by the wall. A blackboard with a picture of a smile.

'Squatters?' I say.

'The kids play down here when I'm working sometimes. I can't close the shop when the schools close for the day – I'd go bankrupt within six months.'

'Are these for sale?' I ask, pointing to the clocks.

'Would you ask that in the Louvre or the Metropolitan Museum of Art?'

The Louvre, this is not, mate.

'Sorry.'

'All of the clocks on this wall are museum-quality artefacts. I act as caretaker and so, I hope, will my family one day. But the clocks on that table are for sale to the public.'

I take a look but they're all boring gold-plated carriage clocks and wall clocks. It's the museum pieces that catch my eye.

I point to one.

'A sealskin clock from Norway,' he says. 'Baby seal. I have to keep it oiled.'

I point to another.

'Early example of a Jaeger LeCoultre Atmos clock. Almost perpetual – it derives its energy from changes in atmospheric temperature.'

I pass by a sundial and a pendulum clock and a wooden cuckoo-type clock covered in hair.

'Hair?'

'Ponyskin. Rough hair.'

I approach a clock in a glass case, pointed away from me.

'Ah, that's a rare tusk clock. One of the finest ever made.'

I walk around the container. Its corners are the tusks of a walrus. The clock is framed by the sharp incisors of a big cat, I'm not sure which kind. 'What are they?'

'Hippo tusks and then horse teeth inside.'

'And around the clockface itself?'

'Two complete mouthfuls of human teeth. All mid-eighteenth-century peasant teeth.'

I stare at him.

'They're two-hundred-year-old teeth. Call your policewoman girlfriend if you'd like her to inspect them.'

There's a bloodstain or a paint stain on the beanbag near the blackboard. Hans Wimmer opens a door I hadn't noticed before, a door to another staircase leading lower still. A basement beneath a basement.

I jog to the stairs and say, 'Thanks then,' and run up two at a time.

A stumble toward the top and I grab the chain to steady myself and it cuts my index finger. The wind has picked up outside and the apple trees are thrashing around. I try the lock but it's fixed so I can't open it.

A bang downstairs. The sound of an engine starting.

I fumble with the door and after a while it gives and I step out into the cool November air.

Eva Edlund appears as if from nowhere.

I suck the wound on my finger.

'Was it you who defaced the Edlund family statue with that pamphlet?'

'Oh, come on.'

'Keep them to the benches and shops, please. The statue is a protected monument, just ask the Kommun.'

'Can I ask you a question?'

Eva squints.

'Have you seen Hans Wimmer's kids recently?' I can't get the image of the bloodied beanbag out of my head. 'I'm just checking up on them. Making sure they're okay.'

'His *children*?' she says, looking up at the broken clock outside the shop. 'Hans Wimmer has no children.'

46

Eva walks off in her chequered golf trousers. She glances back at me.

Hans Wimmer has no children? What about the toys? The car seat?

I turn to face the clock shop and the closed sign is back on the door. 'Tempus Fugit. On Vacation'. The sign across the stairs down to the basement is swinging back and forth. Doesn't feel right. And his house is closest to the original murder scene.

Maybe there are kids around but they're his step-children. Would Eva know every aspect of his life? Maybe he has a girlfriend who has kids?

Noora's on the other side of the square checking someone's driving licence.

I run over.

She ignores me and tells the guy from Svensson's Saws & Axes to drive more slowly, especially now we're in November. He looks at her like, *I'll do what I want*, and then gets back into his pick-up truck.

'Got a sec?'

She nods and we walk over to the bandstand.

'Search party found a black hat near the old steelworks,' she says.

'Emil's?'

'Nope. They got over-excited and called Chief Björn, they even demanded a CSI team, you believe that? Margareta Eriksson says he never even owned a black hat.

'Hans Wimmer,' I say.

We sit down on chairs under the canopy of the bandstand.

'I haven't got long,' she says. 'What about him?'

'He has kids' toys in his shop basement and also in his house deep in Visberg forest. But Eva Edlund just told me he has no kids.'

'I heard this one already.'

'What?'

'Back at Easter time, I think it was. Saw him fixing his car seat and buying chocolate eggs in Konsum. I'd just started here, so I was asking Thord about all the local characters, anyone with previous, anyone who stands out. All part of the job. He tells me the clock-maker has no children. He just has toys lying around in case a family comes into his shop or to his house.'

I wrinkle up my face.

'Maybe it's good business, letting the parents browse watches longer, keeping the rugrats happy,' she says. 'Or maybe it's creepy. I don't know. People gotta do what they gotta do to get through from one year to the next. Everyone's dealing with something.'

'I'll send you over some information Sebastian dredged up about a missing Dutch blogger. Let you see what you think.'

She nods her head.

'And we need to talk,' I say. 'About the flat and—'

'We will,' she says, and she places her hand on the edge of my chair so our little fingers touch. There's a jolt. A transfer of heat and electricity. I don't want our hands to move. Ever. In this strange little hilltop town I feel good right now, our hands fused, hers and mine. I just need a little time to figure things out. I know I love her but what I can't work out is how to proceed. How not to screw things up.

'Interpol officer visiting Gavrik today,' she says. 'Investigator.'

'About Emil?'

She shakes her head.

'Officially here for the grave disturbance.' She checks her phone. 'There's a web connecting Visberg to older crimes across half of

Europe. Chief knows more about it than I do. Sorry, Tuva, I have to go.'

I move my hand a little so that two of my fingers rest on hers.

'Not here,' she says, her face softening, her lips curling into a shallow smile. 'We'll talk soon. Don't worry.' She winks at me. 'We're good.'

She walks away.

We're good. Thank God for that. Maybe in a year I'll be ready to live under the same roof with her. Maybe only nine months. After I get my habits in order and my life set straight.

I climb into my truck and turn on the heated seats and call Sebastian.

'Interpol officer in town. The grave robberies,' I say.

'Okay.'

'Find out exactly who it is and what cases they've worked on in the past. Cross-reference with potential suspects of the Arne Persson murder and the Emil abduction. Let me know if you pull up anything connecting back to Wimmer, the Edlunds or watchmaking. Get back to me with details as quick as you can.'

I go to ring off, but he says,'Tuva. Margareta Eriksson's been here in the office this past hour.'

'Was she giving her statement to the Chief?' I say.

'Lena says Margareta's agreed to give up all the names of the private leaseholders of the top-floor units in the Hive. The premium units. Lena reckons locals are fuming because they should have been confidential in perpetuity. They have paperwork to prove it. Locals say she might lose half her business.'

I look over at the Hive and there are people filing into the rear doors with suitcases and flat-pack cardboard boxes. There's a hatchback being loaded up half out of view.

'Thanks for telling me. Get back to me as soon as you hear more.'

Maybe he and I can be a team after all. If I'm working remotely more from now on, Visberg, and even further afield, bigger stories, covering anything in Sweden that Lena will sign-off on, maybe this set up will be good for the both of us. Maybe my boss is a goddam genius.

The last member of the municipal clean-up squad hoses down her shovel and packs all her gear into her truck. Wheelbarrow, jetwash, rake. The woman's wearing a baseball cap but she looks a lot like Luka Kodro once she's removed her muddy overalls. Jeans, tan, white T-shirt. Like a younger, skinnier version.

I update my spider diagram of people connected to Arne Persson and people connected to Emil Eriksson. There are too many overlapping connections for it to be helpful. It's a Venn-shaped mess. The reality of any small town in the middle of nowhere. Everyone's linked to everyone else. The secrets are everywhere and the lies get looked after and nurtured by each successive generation.

The Sheriff parks and gets out of his taxi cab.

I run over.

'Sheriff.'

He's not wearing his beige shirt with star badges. He's not wearing his brown trousers or utility belt or polished, black boots. He's not got a radio hooked through his shoulder loops. He's in hunting gear. Green-brown mottled camouflage trousers and a jacket that smells like rotting bear flesh.

'What can I do for you?'

He pulls his rifle bag out the back of his car and unzips it and checks what's inside and zips it up again. There's a pair of pliers half in and half out of the bag. He puts on an orange hat that says Svensson's Saws & Axes.

'You going out hunting?'

'Searching for Margareta's boy,' he says. 'But my nephew a few towns north reckons he heard wolves out last night. Between you and me I don't think he'd know a wolf howl from a badger grunt but I'd rather be prepared.'

I hold my jaw, the molar pain throbbing like a second heartbeat.

'Get that seen at if I was you.'

Not here, mate. Not a bloody chance. I'll be making my next appointment in Karlstad even if I have to pay double for the privilege.

'Edlunds dental surgery is shut,' I say. 'They're all out searching. Julia and Tobias, Eva and Sven. All out.'

'Could try in there,' says the Sheriff, pointing his rifle in the direction of Mind Games.

'Gaming will take my mind off the pain, but I need to fix the root cause, pardon the pun.'

'You mean soda pops?'

'I mean root-canal work.'

'That's what I'm talking about. David the twin done completed three years before he quit to set up that computer-game club.'

'Who did?'

'Young David. His brother never got the grades, not such a bright spark, that one, but David's a clever boy. He can't fix your problem maybe, but he can take a look for you. He fixed a filling for me sometime last year when the Edlunds were off at their fancy island house out East.'

'He did?'

'They sell the emergency filling kits in the pharmacy next door. David helped me out free of charge, he did. Said he needed the practice and then he never even charged me. Said it was absolutely his pleasure.'

47

I make my way over to Mind Games.

Outside the front door is a young teen wearing a hoodie. She's buying roleplay cards from an older girl. I think they're Luka Kodro's kids, one of them at least. The younger girl passes the older girl a 500 kronor note. The older one passes her two cards.

My phone rings and the girls notice me and walk away.

'Tuva Moodyson.'

'It's me,' says Sebastian. 'Listen. I talked to Gavrik Hotel. The owner owes me a favour. Asked about guests who checked in today and described the Europol woman but she told me they only had one guest check in, so no need to describe her.'

I move so my back is to Mind Games. I watch the town square, as clean and shiny as a movie set. Like nothing bad ever happened here.

'Woman's name is Erika Smith.'

'Hotel gave that up?'

'Like I say, they owed me. She's based out of Jonkoping.'

'I'm listening.'

'I've been researching her past cases, where her Instagram posts have been sent from, landmarks, Facebook check-ins, trying to figure out what she's working on.'

'Good.'

'Not much to go on, she's quite discreet. But there is a recurring theme, from interviews and her social media. She's spent a lot of time this past year in Estonia. I'm guessing she's working on something connecting Estonia and Sweden.'

'Wait a minute.'

I take the phone from my ear and turn it on to speaker mode.

'You there?' he says.

'Wait.'

I search for 'Estonia' in the notes function on my phone. There is a link somewhere. I heard someone mention that country this past week.

'Are you still there, Tuva?'

Luka Kodro walks past me holding hands with one of his daughters, the one with two new cards.

I find the note. The highlighted section.

'Shit,' I say.

'What?'

I turn off speaker mode and turn the phone to my ear.

'Hans Wimmer,' I say. 'The Visberg watchmaker, clockmaker, whatever he calls himself. He lived in Estonia for four years.'

48

'You saying Wimmer is a grave robber?'

'I don't know what I'm saying. You find more on Wimmer's history. Cross-reference with Estonia and that missing Dutch blogger, the one who visited the clock shop and then disappeared. Call me back as soon as you find something.'

He rings off and then my phone rings again.

'What is it?'

'Tuva?'

A woman's voice.

'Sorry, yes. Who is this?'

'It's Daniel's mamma.'

I think of the gamer-café twin.

'Okay?'

'I got your number from the internet. Could you babysit Dan tonight, just for an hour?'

Wrong Daniel.

'Can't tonight, sorry. Could you use a service?'

She goes quiet.

'What time?' I ask.

'Seven to eight. I promise I won't be late this time. I wouldn't ask if I had any other choices. He's so happy with you.'

I get butterflies at that comment. He's happy with me.

'Sure,' I say. 'I can do seven till eight.'

I see Luka Kodro walk to the back entrance of the Hive without his daughter. He moves toward the door leading up to the premium first floor. And then a dark van pulls up. Four men step out, all with shaved heads, one of them holding a pair of pliers with rubber grips. They follow Luka into the building.

The air cools. There is no fog today, the square is crystal clear and the benches are clean. But it is cold. Feels like it could snow.

An old man with a long, leather jacket walks past me toward the Grill, dragging a broad snow shovel behind him, the sharp edge scraping the pavement.

I step into Mind Games.

Black curtains. The light falling away with every metre, every turn.

The place is full of young adults. It smells like takeout pizza. Faces glow in the screen glare. A guy in the corner gives military commands to his teammate in a controlled tone. The teammate yells back, 'I don't got a grenade!'

I find a twin. No idea which one it is.

'Daniel?'

The guy keeps playing his game, his headset on at a jaunty angle.

'Incorrect.'

'David, sorry.'

He looks up. 'Oh, it's you.'

His T-shirt says 'Eat the Rich'.

'We're full right now. The new game, you see. Come back in half an hour, maybe an hour to be on the safe side.'

'I don't need a computer.'

He frowns at me and stands up. Someone brushes past him and trips and stumbles into me.

'What do you need then?'

'I'm writing a story for the paper. On job opportunities and young entrepreneurs in rural communities.'

His frown intensifies.

'I heard you trained as a dentist for a while before opening this place.'

He rolls his eyes. 'You heard wrong.'

A guy in the corner screams 'Watch my back, fuckboy!'

'You didn't train?' I ask.

David walks toward the Red Bull fridge next to the till and the display counter with the Dungeons and Dragons cards.

'That life is not for me. This is for me.'

'You didn't enjoy dentistry?'

'I make good money doing this and I get to game for twenty-four hours a day seven days a week if I feel like it. Early access to games most people will never even hear about. Can you do that as a fucking orthodontist?'

'I guess not.'

His eyes are red.

'Sorry, I'm just tired. I got good grades at school, that is true. My parents were pissed when I left early, but this way I get to work with my brother, which we both like. We always work really well together.'

'Someone told me you do procedures in a back room here.'

'Oh, did they?'

'You don't?'

He smiles. 'No, Tuva, I don't. If there's an emergency I might be able to help out, but these days I'm too busy for any of that. Look around you.'

I look around.

'You see any other business within a hundred kilometres of this place thriving like this, do you?'

He has a point.

'I gotta get back to work if you don't mind.'

He sits back down and unpauses the game he's playing.

I step out into the light. Six or seven flat snowflakes fall to the earth. Not a blizzard, not even a snowfall. Just large flakes floating down like magnolia petals.

I reach into my pocket to get my keys.

There's loose gum in there.

And something unfamiliar.

A tablet?

I take it out.

No. Fear surges up from my stomach. I'm holding a small white tooth.

A milk tooth.

49

Oh, no.

Is this one of Emil's teeth? Proof of life or proof of…?

I turn the tooth over in my fingers.

Or could this be from the robbed grave? A leftover tooth from Arne Persson's skull?

No. It's Emil's. I don't know how I know, but I do.

A gunshot booms from down the hill and ricochets round the town square. It's not loud but it's clear. Like a warning shot.

I look around trying to work out who put this inside my pocket. How? When? One of the twins? Someone else in Mind Games?

The snowfall stays constant. The lightest of flakes. One here, one there. Nothing settling on the pristine square.

Someone's taunting the police and they're taunting me. Playing games. I think someone in Visberg has an issue with authority.

I call Thord at the station.

'Gavrik police, Chief Andersson.'

'Chief, it's me, Tuva.'

He grunts his hello, then says,'Constable Thord isn't available.'

'I'm in Visberg and I've found a tooth in my pocket.'

'You found a *what* in your pocket?'

'A tooth. Looks like a child's tooth.'

He's quiet for a moment.

'How'd it get in there? Who's tooth is it, Moodyson?'

'I have no idea.'

Another gunshot. Then another.

'Can you bring it straight on over to the station and I'll pass it over to the forensic team. Try not to touch it or...' He pauses. 'Just keep it safe but leave it alone.'

'On my way.'

'Oh and Moodyson.'

'Yeah?'

'You seen the watchmaker today, Wimmer, his name is. You seen him around Visberg town?'

'I did earlier. Think he's still inside his shop.'

'Okay, then. If I'm not here when you arrive, someone else will have to process the item.'

He rings off.

You work as a journalist in LA or Cairo and you'll rarely get close to the actual crimes, the actual evidence. It's the opposite here. The town is so incredibly small and cut off that I get hands-on with crime scenes and I get too close to perpetrators. That's the deal with small-town journalism: the big stories are few and far between, but when they break you're right there in the middle of it all.

An expensive-looking minibus drives round past Konsum. The writing on the side of the bus says 'Edlund's Private Members Club'. It parks by the rear of the Hive. Six women and one man step out. All blond, all in golfing gear. They look around then disappear into the building.

More gunshots but they're further away this time.

Ragnar Falk limps out of his old newspaper office and turns towards the Hive as well. Fuck me, everyone in this town is more focused on emptying their private storage units than they are on finding poor Emil.

I feel the tooth through the fabric of my jacket but I try not to touch it directly.

There's a new sound coming from the forest down the hill. Sounds like trees being felled. Sounds like screaming chainsaws.

The streetlights are on and the air feels close to zero.

I get to my truck and start the engine. Heated seats on. Heated steering wheel on. I sync my hearing aid to my phone and set off. My dash reads zero degrees.

Feels like this whole town has something to hide today. Like there are groups and partnerships beneath the surface, secretive, closed communities with their own agendas. The sky may not be as dark as on Pan Night but this is worse. Clandestine chats and people emptying God-knows-what from anonymous storage units.

I leave the town behind and start my descent. Even with studded tyres, my truck slides and slips. The rain from earlier has created pockets of black ice in the dips and flatter stretches. Ice that'll dump you straight off the road into a ditch or a pine, or off a ten-metre granite cliff.

It's just before six. I'll get to the cop shop, leave the tooth, then get back to take care of little Dan for an hour. I'll cook him, fuck knows, whatever's in my fridge. Or I'll take him to the drive-thru. His mamma can't complain see'ns as I'm getting paid nothing for my trouble. And then a talk with Noora. A proper talk. Set the record straight and make up. I'll play that song she likes. The French one I can never remember the name of.

My phone rings.

Someone's whispering, but I can't make out the words. Either a bad connection or a prank call.

'I can't hear you,' I say. 'Speak up.'

Still nothing. Heavy breathing. I can't make out a single word.

'Call me back,' I say, and then I end the call.

Two seconds later my phone rings again.

'It's me,' says a small, breathy voice. 'Julia.'

The tiniest of whispers.

I slow to 10kph.

'What's wrong? You okay?'

'Help.'

I slow down even more. I can't pull over just here, so I increase the volume of the call.

'Where are you, Julia? What's wrong?'

'The old train tracks,' she says. 'He's here. Watches…' Her voice breaks up. 'I've called the police but they'll take too long. Help me, Tuva,' she whispers, her voice cracking with fear.

'Train tracks? Where exactly?'

I hear her gasp and then there's a deeper voice in the background.

'He's coming back now,' she says, her voice cracking.

'Train tracks north or south of the road? How far in?'

'I don't know,' she whispers. 'I don't know. About a mile. North of the road, I think. Please, hurry. Help.'

'Hans Wimmer has you? Has he hurt you?'

'Not Wimmer,' she says. 'It's Emil.'

50

Emil?

How is that possible?

I think about his candy bracelets. About his clumsy flirting. His head bouncing off the pavement as he was dragged away screaming on Halloween. How did I get this so wrong? What the hell is he trying to do with Julia? How many people are involved in this?

A flurry of snow blows in from the side, and the surface of the road is painted with diagonal, white stripes. The wind pushes and pulls at my truck.

I see the train tracks ahead as I head down the hill. The barrier that is no more. The clear corridor free of pines to each side of the road. I slow down and indicate. I turn right.

The truck judders as it leaves the asphalt. This feels all kinds of wrong. You don't drive along a train track, it's just not a good idea. The rails are rusted and the wooden sleepers are starting to rot down. I drive at 10kph, careful not to wreck my tyres on the rails.

The trees thicken either side of me. The sky is truly dark here, even with my headlights on full beam. It's like navigating through an inkwell.

The metal studs in my tyres crunch each time they hit the steel tracks.

I turn on my radio but it's all white noise. I'm too far from civilisation. Too far from antennas and other people.

There are flashes of crimson-red up ahead. Wet, glossy, red spheres gleaming in my lights. Funghi. The evil Disney toadstools. Fly agaric. They manage to look delicious and lethal at the same time. Like toffee apples with crisp, red caramel on the outside, each white dot a pristine cyanide pill.

Emil, with watches? Is that what she whispered? It was difficult to hear her. Does Hans Wimmer have something to do with this?

A car up ahead.

Parked.

And an abandoned train-carriage next to the car on a piece of siding.

It's Julia's green Renault; the driver's side door is wide open.

I slow down.

I stop my Hilux.

My phone has reception even here, thank God. Julia's called the police but I'll call them again as soon as I know her location. I take my stungun and my knife from my bag.

I open my truck door but stay inside. Have to be careful. Take my time. *Slow is smooth and smooth is fast.* The noise from the forest is immense. The branches whip this way and that in the gale-force winds. Sounds like a furious ocean.

I step down onto the tracks. I'm parked right on them, like a suicide waiting to happen. This feels like a bad rollercoaster-nightmare or a virtual-reality video game I can't switch off. One of David's specialist VR games but the headset is locked securely onto my head.

No sign of anyone.

I leave my truck door open and walk toward the Renault. My heart's beating so hard I can feel it. The wind chills my nose and moves my hair over my eyes.

My Hilux headlights illuminate the scene in harsh, white light. The green Renault and the abandoned, rusted, train cargo-carriage with graffiti all over its solid sides.

I get to Julia's car.

Her keys are on the ground, half submerged in mud.

Shit.

The police are on their way. They'll be here soon. I'll have back-up anytime now, back-up with guns and training.

I hold out my stungun in front of me like a dagger.

I'm trying to listen out for her whispering, but the wind makes my aids whistle and squeak. The feedback is unbearable.

Where is she?

Maybe I'll go back to my Hilux and lock the doors. Stay inside until help arrives. But what if he's hurting her? What if help will be too late?

There's a thing in the trees.

It's a deer or an elk – something wild, with eyes reflecting back in my headlights.

Ten or fifteen-trees deep. It's not a deer, a deer would have skipped away as soon as I arrived. It must be an elk. The eyes are level with mine so it's standing in a hollow. Two shining eyes in a sea of absolute darkness.

Cold water drips down my back. Sleet mixing with sweat and freezing to my skin.

'Julia,' I whisper.

Nothing.

I creep around the front of her car. Shadows here, a black area my headlights can't reach. The abandoned train-wagon looks rusted to the spot, its name and logo long covered with myriad graffiti tags and a layer of pollen.

A crow caws and flies overhead; broad, black wings flapping and gliding.

I step on a toadstool and it collapses under my boot.

'Julia?'

Slugs all around me, the ground covered with them. Brown ones and black ones. Glistening.

I crouch down to look underneath the train carriage.

Beer cans and one broken watch. A thousand more slugs.

'Julia? Are you here?' my whisper is taken by the wind and sent crashing through the pines into deep forest.

I touch the carriage.

The rusted surface is rough on my skin. The dry pollen feels like moth-wing residue between my fingertips.

She's not here. Could she be at another point on the tracks? Did I misunderstand her instructions. My breath clouds in front of my face. I'll head back to my truck and wait there, doors locked, stungun ready, until the police arrive. I'll call Luka Kodro to come help me.

There's a noise.

A squeak.

I stop dead.

'Julia?' I whisper.

The noise is right at the limit of what I can make out. In the darkness, in the forest, I can't pinpoint where it's coming from. Behind me, up in a tree, further away.

'Where are you?' I whisper.

'Help me,' she says.

Holy shit, she's inside the carriage.

I look around for Emil. For anyone else. Anything else.

Something runs across the tracks further up the line and stops still to stare back at me. It's a small deer. Her ears turn in every direction but her head remains as still as if it were cast from bronze and mounted on a plinth in the town square.

The deer bolts and I move my head closer to the gap in the carriage door. The only door I can see.

'Julia?'

'Please,' she says. 'Don't wake him.'

I put my hand to the door and it creaks as I drag it open. It slides but it's so rusty I can't stop it from making a noise.

'Shhh,' she says, louder than before.

I get it open far enough so I can climb up. I squeeze through sideways.

'Julia?'

It's dark inside. Pitch black. Echoey.

'Tuva,' she whispers.

Lights flash on all around me. Spotlights and halogen, security lights, so bright I have to shield my eyes.

The door slams shut at my back.

She's right there in front of me.

Sat behind a desk with a laptop.

'Welcome to Visberg Tandklinik.' She says. 'Do you have an appointment?'

51

'What?'

'I said, do you have an appointment?'

She checks her laptop. Her orange hat is sat next to it.

'Where's Emil?'

She points behind me and suddenly there's an arm at my neck. He's got my head in an armlock and I'm squirming around. Knife. Stungun. I try to reach for it but his arm has dug deep into my throat. I cough and gasp for air. Just need to get into my bag. I twist and jerk myself and my arm finds the leather of my bag. He starts pulling it from my shoulder but that's fine, because now I have my stungun in my hand.

My bag falls and I see my hairbrush skid across the train carriage. There's some kind of plastic sheet on the floor?

I press the button on the stungun and jab it into Emil's groin. I miss the groin but get his hip. He yelps. But nothing else. No stun. No wounded man convulsing on the ground. I press the button again and jab it into his thigh. Nothing. Like sticking someone with an iPhone.

Julia's watching all this calmly from behind her desk. Her face is devoid of emotion. She's tidying the dental-floss samples next to her laptop and she's looking me straight in the eye.

'Help,' I gasp.

She nods and checks something on her laptop.

I'm dizzy. I try to pivot to throw Emil off me, to make him lose balance, but I'm losing my strength. He's holding me in a vice-like grip and my head is completely still.

My vision blurs at the edges but I take in the room.

Windowless.

Walls made from white shower curtains hanging from the ceiling.

A table with neat stacks of magazines and four green plastic garden chairs in a row. A fishtank full of pondweed. An empty water dispenser.

'Help,' I say but there is no noise. My head feels like it's going to collapse in on itself. I'm getting tired.

There's a poster advertising mouthwash directly behind Julia. And some kind of framed certificate.

The police will help me.

They'll be here soon.

My body starts to go limp.

'Just relax,' says Julia. She types something on her laptop and I smell Emil's sweat as his body tightens behind mine. Everything goes dark. 'Oh, look,' she says. 'I've found your appointment.'

52

My eyelids are heavy.

I wake up alone.

The ceiling is white and there's an office lamp pointed at my head.

I gasp and sit bolt upright.

Only I can't. I can't move at all. I strain my eyes to look down at my body. Silver duct tape secures my wrists to the white plastic arms of a sun lounger. My chest is taped down. My waist. My thighs. My knees. My ankles. I can wiggle my boots but I cannot move my head. Tape around my forehead and around my neck.

'Help!' I scream. 'Help me.'

I start to hyperventilate. To panic.

I go to scream help again, but no noise comes out.

What do they want with me?

I try to slow down my breathing. The air tastes stale. Old. The smell of decay. But everything looks clean and sterile. The ground is covered with dark-green tarp sheets. The stool next to my sun lounger has wheels on its feet.

I strain my arms to break free from the tape but it's too tight. So many rolls of tape just to keep me here on this lounger. I thrust and kick and thrash but the lounger merely nudges a centimetre. Can I topple it? Can I get it to a wall and rub the tape against something abrasive?

No.

I can hardly move it.

So thirsty. My lips are dry.

The sun lounger has either been attached to the ground or else weighed down. I have so little mobility on this reclining chair. I can't turn my head. I can't raise my hand. I can't turn my hips. Like I've been buried in a skin-tight coffin, six feet underground.

Stay calm, Tuva. Think. The police are on their way. You just need to think.

Except of course they are not on their way. Of course they're bloody not. That's what Julia told me to lure me here. Nobody's on their way.

I suck in air through my nose.

My bag. My phone. My knife.

I look around trying to strain at my bindings. If I turn my head a few degrees, the tape pulls at my forehead so much it feels like it'll rip the skin off and reveal the flesh beneath. But I can see most of the room. Not what's behind me, though. I can't see that.

On my left side hangs a white shower curtain. Next to my left hand is a small, round table with a plastic cup of water and a bowl. Then the floor-standing anglepoise lamp. And another lamp attached to some kind of battery pack. Then a candle in a candlestick.

'Help.' I scream.

Nobody comes.

The shower curtain on my left blows in the breeze.

If I look at my feet, I can see a plastic patio table with an expensive-looking camera and a plastic demonstration model of a jaw, complete with teeth. Then to my right is a laptop on another table. The laptop is covered with clingfilm.

I swallow hard and shout, 'I need water.'

Doesn't feel good to be left in here alone. I need reassurances. To start negotiating my release somehow.

Next to the laptop is a lightbox, the cheap battery-powered kind you can display messages and emojis on. If I strain my eyes in their sockets I can see the edge of something white behind me. Another shower curtain, perhaps.

How long was I out for? A minute? An hour? Did they carry me in here and tie me up? What else did they do to me? I look down my body. I'm fully clothed. I'm not in any physical pain, apart from a burning sensation on my forehead from twisting against the heavy-duty duct tape.

Why is Julia doing this with Emil? Is this connected to his father's accident? Did he fake his own abduction?

I try to twist my wrists, to make some space, to open up a gap between my skin and the tape.

The air moves.

The shower curtain dances in the breeze and Julia walks through in her uniform.

'The doctor will be with you in a moment.'

She smiles and clips an X-ray image to the front of the supermarket lightbox.

'What? You have to let me go, Julia. Loosen my wrists. I can't feel my fingers.'

She smiles and says, 'It's normal to be anxious before a procedure like this. Try not to worry, we'll take great care of you.'

She pats my shoulder and walks out.

53

What the hell is this? Some twisted game of doctors and nurses? I push with my legs, the strongest part of me, and try to buck against my restraints, but I'm stuck here. Trapped. The blue-and-white-striped chair-cushion is visible between my boots. I curl my fingers over the lounger armrests and pull and my chair collapses to horizontal.

Movement to my left.

Julia walks back in. No, wait, it's Emil.

Only it's not.

'How have your teeth been, Tuva?' says Tobias, the hygienist, dressed in a dental uniform with some kind of microscope attachment stuck to his forehead. 'Any discomfort I should know about?'

'Tobias, please. You have to let me go.'

'Well,' he says. 'Let's take a look, shall we?'

He sits on his stool and then turns to check the X-ray images on the ICA Maxi lightbox. Then he starts typing something on his laptop, pressing the keys through the clingfilm.

'Please,' I say, on the verge of tears.

He ignores me and types some more.

'Don't worry, you're in good hands.'

I scrunch my eyes tight.

'See this,' he says, pointing to the lightbox. 'That's the tooth in need of root-canal work. Your old dentist mentioned it, I believe? We dentists call root-canal science *endodontics*.'

The bad smell behind my head intensifies. Like an old garbage can left out in the sun.

'Let me go now,' I say. 'You can't keep me here against my will.'

He looks sympathetic and says, 'This is a common attitude towards root-canal procedures. It can be daunting, I know. Traditional dentistry, the kind still taught in the schools arrogant enough to deny me entry, is well behind the times. Don't worry. Medical science, especially in the experimental sector, has come a long way since the old days. With the kind of new techniques not yet adopted by Sven Edlund and his generation, we can make this procedure almost painless.'

'You're not a fucking dentist.'

He frowns at me and points to the stitched badge on his uniform.

'Maybe this will assuage your doubts.'

It has the word *Doctor* before his name.

'Or this?' he says, pointing to a framed certificate next to his laptop. Like something you'd get for swimming twenty-five metres.

'I won't open my mouth,' I say.

He chuckles.

'In fact, I've already had all the root-canal work done,' I lie. 'Had it done in Karlstad.'

'Well, we can check that, can't we. Now, just put your mind at ease and relax.'

He walks over to washing-up bowl and washes his hands with water from an Evian bottle. Then he steps to a box on the wall and takes out a pair of latex surgical gloves. He puts them on. Then he washes his gloved hands, the latex squeaking as he works the soap through his gloved fingers. He comes closer and moves the microscope on his head over one eye. The eye looms huge right in front of me.

'Open wide, Tuva.'

54

I keep my jaws clamped shut.

I bite down so hard that my teeth start to ache in their sockets. The blood pumps inside my temples and my body goes cold.

Get the fuck away from me.

'Open wide for me, if you would.'

He stares at me. One normal eye and one giant one. He has a metal stick in his hand, with a small round mirror on the end.

'Don't be concerned, Tuva. I just need to have a look around.'

He's patient. He pushes with his feet and his wheelie-stool slides over the dark-green tarp to his laptop. The tarp rucks under the wheels. If I strain, I can just about see him in my peripheral vision.

Tobias glides back to me.

'Let me talk you through the procedure to ease your nerves. Would that help?'

I shake my head but it hardly moves. I'm stuck to a plastic sun lounger in the recline position, trying to communicate with a delusional monster, and I can't talk, and I can't even shake my head.

'Excellent,' he says. 'First things first. I need to inspect your teeth and gums. There's one tooth at the back there, next to your wisdom tooth, that's been causing you some distress, I hear. We dentists call that tooth the "second molar".'

I groan but the groan is muted with my lips tight shut. The noise feels animal. It reverberates through my skeleton.

'After I take a look I'll use some local anaesthetic. You've had that done before I expect, if you've ever had a filling. I don't yet have your full notes from your old dentist. Have you had local anaesthetic before, Tuva? Not allergic to anything, are we?'

He moves his chair back.

'Don't fucking touch me,' I say, before clamping my jaw closed again.

He looks over. 'You'll hardly feel a thing, I assure you.'

I snort in and out through my nose. The air is cold and it stinks. Something sour. Old mince.

'Okay, let's try this one last time, Tuva.' He places a syringe and needle on a small tray. The tray itself is covered with clingfilm. 'Open wide.'

I clamp my jaw even tighter shut and I close my eyes. Then I panic and open them. He's just staring at me blankly.

'Nurse, please,' he says in a calm voice.

The shower curtain dividing the train carriage moves and Julia walks through with the top end of a thermos mug. What the hell is she going to do with that?

'Here you go, doctor.'

She passes the thermos to Tobias and he takes a sip and says, 'Roasted almond milk?'

She nods.

He smiles. 'Thank you so much.'

I strain at my ankle tape but it won't budge. Why am I not stronger? In my head I am the strongest beast on the planet, capable of bursting out of these bindings, but in truth I am locked down here, in the middle of Visberg forest, with a man playing dentist in a rotting train carriage.

I convulse. It's a half cry that I choke back down.

Tobias is washing his gloved hands again. I've never seen a dentist or doctor do that.

'I just need your assistance for a few minutes, if you're not too busy, nurse?'

Too busy? Are they for real? Like there are families in the other room, the one with four patio chairs and a tank of dead, floating fish. Too busy?'

'Of course, doctor.'

He comes behind me and I cannot see him. I lift my chin as far as I can off my chest and bend my head back and strain my eyes in their sockets. But I can just see the train ceiling.

She unwraps something.

Rustling paper or plastic.

Tobias says, 'Please, Tuva. It'll be much more pleasant for all of us if you can cooperate. Now. Open wide, please.'

I can feel the sweat leaving my pores, even though it must be five degrees inside here. I'm hot with fury and panic and chilled to the bone, all at the same time.

'Open,' he says.

'No!' I scream.

And then it's happening. Julia's hazel eyes joining Tobias's cyclops giant-eye directly above my face. Her fingers pinching my nose. How many more senses can they deprive me of? I look at her with pure, distilled hate. Venom. My body tenses against its restraints and in my mind's eye I lift from this sun lounger and I slap her right across the face.

How did it ever come to this?

Her fingers squeezing my nostrils so hard they might bleed. Him staring at me. Waiting.

I open my mouth a millimetre and breathe.

Tobias sees my chest move up and down and then he pushes his fingers into the corners of my mouth, like I'm a cat who needs to swallow a worming tablet.

My mouth opens and I start to gag.

Her hands are still on my nose.

I feel suffocated.

Locked down.

My mouth opens wider and I taste his latex gloves. Some kind of powder coating.

I open my jaws more.

And then I bite down on his fingers as hard as I can.

55

He lets out a yelp and the pleasure that gives me is indescribable.

How do *you* like it, shithead.

Blood erupts from his finger and drains down his latex glove. His uniform has a red trickle up its sleeve and it's almost straight. Like a stripe. Like a conscious design decision.

He runs his finger under the tap and Julia looms right over my face. She has a clipboard over my mouth, so I can't bite her or spit at her. She says, 'A doctor like Tobias. The skills he has. The artfulness of his fingertips. I cannot believe what you just did.'

'It's nothing,' says Tobias, applying a plaster and a new glove. Washing the glove. 'A shallow cut, that's all. Now, nurse, if you could be so kind as to bring me the speculum,' he pauses, 'and your gun.'

I scream as loud as I can, 'Help me. Help! I'm inside the train! Help me!'

But my voice echoes inside here, bounces off the walls and falls back down to me.

'Only the deer can hear you out here, Tuva.'

Speculum? No.

'No,' I say. 'Let's talk. I can help you. I have money.'

'He's a doctor, Tuva,' says Julia, walking back in with a gun in one hand and a plastic speculum in the other. 'He doesn't need your money.'

'Open wide, please.'

I open my mouth.

They didn't even need to threaten me with the speculum or the gun. I'm not sure which is worse to be honest. I can't countenance either.

'I'll just insert this gently. Let me know if it's uncomfortable.'

It's a mouth speculum. Some kind of spring-loaded mouth-opening device made from clear plastic.

'Speculum,' I say, but it's undecipherable.

'Just relax,' he says.

My mouth is wide open. I push at the plastic with my tongue to check if I can push it out of my mouth without the use of my hands. I reckon I can.

'No, no,' he says. 'One moment. Tiny adjustment.'

He opens it wider and locks it with a screw.

I can't spit it out.

My jaw is locked open and I am taped horizontally, looking up at one oversize eye.

I try to shake my head.

I can't.

I try to move my arms.

I can't

I try to talk.

I can't.

He disappears from view for a few seconds.

Police. A hunt team. Sheriff Hansson. Sebastian. Anyone. Come now and end this hideous farce. I beg you.

Tobias holds up a narrow syringe and pushes the plunger.

A dribble of clear liquid squirts from the needle.

'Now, hold still,' he says. 'Little scratch.'

56

I brace myself. Every muscle I have turns rigid like steel. He is not doing this with my consent. I loathe every cell in his body.

I can feel the needle pierce my gum.

'Another little scratch.'

I tense up again. How do I know it's dental anaesthetic? What if it's poison?

I start to pant, my breathing out of control.

'All done,' he says. 'Now we must wait a few minutes to ensure the anaesthetic is effective.'

He leaves the room.

I feel it. One side of my tongue goes numb. The tooth that's been aching these past weeks stops hurting. My mouth feels larger on that side. Distant from me.

I swallow and the plastic mouth opener creaks.

My mouth and lips are dry. I need lip balm. I see dust flakes floating around in the harsh lamplight and imagine them floating down into my gaping mouth. Like I'm a fish caught on the shore as the tide goes back out. Some idiot fish waiting for a fly.

I listen out. My hearing aids are fine. They haven't beeped any battery warnings and they didn't loosen or fall out of place during that horrific headlock. My blackout. How long did that last for? Minutes? Longer? I want to know. I demand to know the details. There is a black space in my memory, a void, for the first time since last Christmas. It wasn't long after Mum died. The fish fingers for

Christmas dinner. In bed. The XL bottle of vodka and the miniatures. The paralysis. The complete loss of Boxing Day. Unconsciousness and self-loathing.

Gunfire outside.

One shot.

I try to scream but the mouth retractor and the anaesthetic turn my efforts into a pathetic bark.

Julia comes back in.

She says, 'Easy, Tuva. Let's get you a sip of water, shall we?'

She has some kind of flexible hamster-cage drinking-straw attachment on the end of a bottle of mineral water. She bends the straw attachment so the tip grazes my lower lip.

'Ready?'

I can't nod so I try to say yes with my eyes.

She squeezes and I drink, gulping it down. Desperate. Fucking livid.

'Help me,' I say, but with this thing in my mouth it's just two noises separated by a pause.

She smiles and leaves.

I have an itch on my eyelid. Really it's the least of my troubles but I've never been in this situation before. It's driving me crazy. I need to scratch my own eyelid. I need to move my finger.

I start straining my muscles systematically. You won't find me dead here. You will not visit this trainwreck in ten years' time and find a skeleton with perfect teeth strapped to a goddam sun lounger. It won't happen. I tense my legs. I strain with my arms. I twist my head. The tape is starting to loosen a little in places. Either that or I'm imagining it. Or I'm just getting colder. That's what happens when you start to freeze. Opposite of bloating or swelling. If it gets even colder tonight, maybe I'll shrink down even more.

I stare up at the ceiling. My jaw is aching now. It's not normal having it wedged this far open for this long in a never-ending silent scream. This technique is not taught in dental schools.

My thoughts turn to my parents. Dad. Please. See me here. Now, in this godforsaken place. Follow the train tracks. Do something if you can. I'm desperate. I can't imagine what these two will do. I can't read them.

What about hunt dogs? There's something stinking in here, or maybe it used to be here and it's been moved. Someone else in my position? On this reclining chair? What happened to them? Is this where they brought the head from the grave? Oh, God. Maybe the dogs will sniff it. Maybe the hunt dogs will bring their masters here. And they'll surely be armed, those men. Maybe Luka Kodro will discover this place. I'd like him to find all this. If there was one person in the world I'd choose to deal with Tobias right now, it would be Luka Kodro.

Julia walks over and hooks a suction tube over my lower lip.

I move my tongue over my molars and it is completely numb on one side. It feels broader than usual. Heavier.

I strain my knees up off the striped cushion. A millimetre at a time, Tuva. *Slow is smooth. Smooth is fast.*

Tobias walks in and pulls some kind of rubber sheet over my damaged tooth.

'It's a barrier,' he says. 'To isolate the molar.'

Julia moves the suction tube slightly and for the briefest of moments it gets stuck on my lip and she lets out a little giggle and moves it and says, 'Sorry.'

'Music?' says Tobias.

I say, 'No,' but it's just a noise.

He says, 'Excellent.'

He uses his phone and then the music begins.

Wagner.

'Ride of the Valkyries'.

'It's called "Ride of the Valkyries",' he says.

I know what it's called.

He washes his gloved hands once again.

And then he starts up his drill.

57

The sound is head-splittingly shrill.

I usually remove or turn off my hearing aids for dental work. In public, I only really take them out for swimming, concentrating in the office – and dentist visits.

I can't feel the pain but I can sense it through that grinding noise and I can taste it in the chemicals on my tongue, and I can see it in the one oversize eye of this imitation dentist. His face is so close to mine I can smell him. His breath is filtered through his face mask but I can still smell it. The faint mintiness. And I can feel it washing over my lips and my chin in waves.

Is he getting a thrill out of this?

The drilling intensifies. I scrunch up my eyes and the noise softens a little and moves away.

'Is it your hearing aids?' says Tobias, removing the drill. 'I'm sorry, I should have thought of that before. Would you like me to remove them until the procedure is over?'

I stare at him, my jaw clamped open. I hate being horizontal like this. Locked down. The vulnerability makes me furious and I have no way of releasing that fury. I try to eject the hooked-on suction tube from inside my teeth but I can't do it. I try to shake my head and the duct tape allows a small shake. A tiny movement from side to side.

'Yes?' he says. 'Okay. Nurse, would you help me with that, please.'

He waits there, drill in hand. I can't move my head so my eyes swing from right – to keep a look on him – to left, to see her. She probes my ears. She pulls the earpiece from my inner ear and I want to bite her hands off. How dare she touch my aid. They are more personal to me than she could ever understand. She moves around the back of me and I roll my eyes up to try to keep her in my vision, but she goes. Then she's with Tobias. She removes my right aid and the world turns silent.

Burst in. Now. Do it. Police, dogs barking, highly trained people with guns drawn. Do it now.

Nothing happens.

I can't move or hear or speak.

He says something. I see his mask moving as he talks but I can't hear him and I can't read him. He pulls down his mask.

'Sorry,' he says. 'I'm going to open up the tooth itself now. Just let me know if you need more anaesthetic.'

I start to cry. I don't want to give them the victory but I can't stop myself. I jerk my body up and down, move my arms and hips as much as I can, tense every muscle in my body.

'Easy,' says Tobias. And then he replaces his mask and the drill grows as it moves closer to my wide-open mouth.

My jaw hurts.

The gums beneath my lower-front teeth hurt from the hooked-on suction tube.

The tooth he's drilling into does not hurt. I can't feel pain, but I can feel the drill probing deeper and deeper. Through the enamel. Through the dentine. The sound of it. Vibrations coursing through my skeletal system. The water vapour inside my mouth.

And then his drill hits my nerve.

58

My face twists and contorts with pain.

The intense misery of it. Like needles being pushed up inside my jaw, inside my sinuses, all the way to my brain.

He backs off.

There is a fine spray of blood on his pristine white mask.

Julia comes round to look at me and she says, 'The doctor will give you a little more anaesthetic for the pain.'

She smiles. She actually smiles.

He injects me again. Further back into the gum around my wisdom tooth. I want to tell them to stop. I want to plead with them, strike some kind of desperate bargain. But my words are just noises and they would ignore them anyway. It's like I'm still trapped inside one of the new virtual-reality games people play at Mind Games. Still have the headset locked onto my skull. Some under-the-counter extreme-horror game they bought from overseas playing on a loop. A world I cannot leave. Something so nightmarish that the twins argued with each other over whether or not they should release it to their customers.

Tobias works away at my hollowed-out tooth.

I lose track of time.

He consults the X-ray images on the ICA lightbox, and then he removes his mask.

'That's the worst part over. I hope it wasn't too uncomfortable?'

He tilts his head on an angle.

I just stare at him. A snared animal caught in his trap.

'I'm going to flush the hollow tooth with antiseptic, and then probe for the deep nerves in each of the roots. Would you like more music?'

Fuck off.

'Okay, then.' He puts on some kind of music. Wagner again, perhaps. I can't tell.

I close my eyes tight shut. It feels like his drills and instruments are probing so deep into my jaw they may come out inside my throat or through my chin. The noises and sensations and vibrations are exacerbated.

The light levels change in the room.

I snap my eyes open.

But he's just adjusting his anglepoise lamp.

He washes his gloved hands again and says, 'I think this will be a fine result.'

I turn my ankles to try to loosen the duct tape. I pull my wrists up and down. Twist my hips. Arch my back. No progress.

'Nurse, could you give the patient some water, please.'

Julia moves the suction pump around inside my mouth vacuuming up debris and saliva. She squeezes drops of water from her hamster-drink bottle and I swallow them. Everything tastes wrong. Blood mixed with banana-flavour antiseptic liquid. And the tooth feels so hollow, like there's a draught inside it. Like the wind blows over it and down inside the cavity.

Little Dan. I should be babysitting him right now. Watching *Back to the Future* or *Ghostbusters* or *ET*. Any one of dad's old movies that I still watch from time to time because he loved them. I still laugh at the same scenes he laughed at. The same lame jokes. I cry where he cried. I can still feel him behind me on the sofa when I get to the end of *ET*. His hand on my shoulder. My hand on his hand. Him telling me it's not sad, it's happy, through his own tears.

'In normal circumstances,' says Tobias, enunciating clearly with his lips. 'I'd wait a week…' I can't decipher his next few words, and then he says, 'Start filling in a few minutes.'

I wriggle my wrists. I twist my forearms. The duct tape is loosening a little but it doesn't help me. Just millimetres. It'd take me days to work these loose. Weeks.

And then I feel something digging into the underside of my wrist.

Hurting me.

Scratching me.

It's a paperclip.

It's the paperclip I used that night to pick Ragnar Falk's lock.

59

'Do you mind if I photograph your tooth? We dentists need your approval these days.'

I nod.

Because I want him to focus on my mouth. Not my right hand. *Take as many photos as you like.*

My hand is bucked, my fingers bent beneath my palm. I can reach the paperclip with the tip of my middle finger. I try to coax it out of my sleeve, but my fingertip is too sweaty to get purchase. The flash of his camera goes off in my face and I close my eyes against the white. I strain my hand, the tendons stretched, and manage to get the end of the clip under my finger. More flashes in my face from the camera. Slowly, I drag the paperclip out along the lifeline of my palm; the cool steel moving over the grooves and valleys that some people believe predict my life and my death.

Another flash.

He moves the camera in closer and I just want to bite the lens off it.

My jaws ache so much and the anaesthetic is starting to wear off. That smell in the room. The chill in this place. The cramp in my left thigh from being taped down like a butterfly pinned into a frame.

A gunshot outside. At least I think it is, but it's difficult to tell. I hope it is. Come this way, team. Hunt inside this horror of a train carriage. Release the dogs and pull your triggers. End this.

He washes his gloves again and says, 'I'm just going to…' And then his eyes widen and he says, 'Would you like your hearing aids back in, now the drilling phase is over?'

I nod as hard as I have ever nodded. My head only moves slightly up and down but it's enough.

'Nurse, please.'

She walks in through the shower curtain. Her hair glows red in the anglepoise light. She puts in my aids and her fingers feel clumsy and intrusive. Too much touch around my lobes. Too much probing. I'd bite my tongue if this mouth retractor would let me.

'Now, that's better,' he says. 'I'm going to clamp this around your tooth so I can create a permanent crown. Let me know if it's uncomfortable.'

Nothing about this is comfortable. My cramp, my jaw ache. The fact that I need to pee. The pain in my jawbone from the tooth root being removed. Whatever he did to the nerve.

Julia sucks out my mouth with the tube.

'If only your father could see you now,' she says to Tobias.

Tobias looks at her and smiles and says, 'Batteries.'

She hooks up a rechargeable lithium-battery pack to one of the lights.

'Hold quite still,' he says.

Bastard.

He clamps something round my tooth. It's not painful but I can feel the pressure of it. An alien thing in my mouth.

He mixes some kind of compound with a small plastic spoon.

I have the paperclip now. My hand is flat on the lounger-chair handle and the clip is under my middle finger. I move it up. Slow and smooth. I push my arm and I take the clip in my fingers and Julia leaves. He's mixing the compound. I take the paperclip in my fingers while he's staring into my wide-open mouth. I open it with my fingertips and it feels wonderful. There's a surge of adrenaline in my body. Adrenaline mixed with hope. Keep looking into my mouth, you beast. Do not stop. I manage to get half of the clip open. My fingertips ache from the contortion. Everything aches.

He adjusts the suction tube and then starts applying the cement or whatever it is to my tooth. Scraping and scratching. Adjusting. I have the pin. It's full-length now. Almost straight. Julia walks back in.

'I'll leave this for five minutes to set a little and then I'll check your bite.'

That means this plastic retractor will be removed from my mouth at last. I could cry with relief. He walks through the shower curtain with her.

Focus, Tuva.

I move the folded-out paperclip so it points into the pad of my index fingertip and I stab the other end into the duct tape wrapped around my wrist. I stab and stab. Dozens of tiny holes. Scratches on the silver tape. I want the holes in some kind of line to weaken the integrity of the tape so I keep stabbing. My eyes are straining down to my hand and the suction tube is pulling saliva from around my tongue.

They're kissing in reception by the fishtank full of dead, floating fish. I can hear them. The noises. The groaning. Are they having sex back there?

I keep stabbing. I manage to get through so deep in one spot that I stab the skin under my wrist.

Blood.

Please, don't have hit a vein. Please don't let this alert Tobias. Will the tape soak up the blood? Will it drip onto the tarp?

The shower curtain opens and Tobias is standing there, the faint smudge of apricot lipstick on the edge of his mouth.

'Nurse, please.'

Julia walks in, smiling, her hair a mess.

'Please, remove the speculum, if you would.'

I let my hand go limp. There's no visible blood, nothing to give the game away.

She unscrews the clamps, holding the spring-loaded mouth retractor in place. The hard plastic scrapes over my teeth as she removes it.

I close my jaw and open it again. I move it from side to side, relishing the movement. The freedom. I blow air from my mouth and swallow down the bitter fluids inside my mouth.

'I need to check your bite,' says Tobias. 'You're not going to do what you did last time, are you?'

'No,' I say. and I mean it. As much as I want to bite his fingers off, I need to focus on escaping from this hellhole.

'Very good,' he says. 'Open wide, please.'

I open my mouth and he moves a small piece of cardboard or something over my teeth.'

'Wider, please.'

I open wider.

And then, as if in slow motion, I drop the paperclip and it falls to the floor.

60

'How does that feel?' He removes the cardboard thing from my teeth.

'Good,' I say.

Did he notice the paperclip? Did he hear it? Will he see it down on the tarp, shining up at him?

My lip begins to wobble.

'Are you cold?'

I nod my head.

I'm cold but that's not it. I'm terrified. Exhausted. Too alone here. How will I rip apart this duct tape now?

'Nurse.'

She arrives and Tobias asks for a blanket.

'I'm sorry about the heating in here,' he says. 'This surgery is only temporary.'

What kind of delusion?

She brings in a white fleece blanket and places it over my legs.

'My hands are very cold,' I say.

She pulls up the blanket to cover my hands.

'I just need one more photograph, if that's okay?' he says. 'I like to document my landmark firsts, for my own records.'

I open my mouth a little.

'Wider, please.'

I open it wider.

He photographs the tooth, the flash exploding inside my mouth. His breath mingling with mine. The smell of the room catching at the back of my throat.

'That's your first procedure over,' he says.

I look at him.

'Thank you. Can I pay now?'

He smiles and then half laughs.

'We still have the main procedure to complete,' he says. 'The root-canal work was for you. That's done now and I think you'll find it was done very well. The next procedure is for me, if I'm completely honest. No other payment will be required.'

'No,' I say, more of a whimper than a word. 'I'm too tired. I can come back another—'

'Don't worry,' he says. 'You just lie back and let me worry about it.'

I'm getting hot under the blanket. Fear and dread fuelling me, the energy building beneath the fleece.

'Nurse, please.'

Julia arrives.

'I'm ready to begin the main procedure.'

She looks excited.

Then she steps behind me and moves a curtain or something. I can't see her but I can hear her. Like the drawing of a pair of curtains.

Tobias swallows and moves his blood-splattered mask over his mouth and nose.

He's looking at whatever is behind me.

'We're going to need a fresh speculum, nurse,' he says. Then he looks at me and says, 'Don't worry, this one won't be as far back in the mouth. We won't have it locked open so wide this time. I'll do what I can to minimise any discomfort.'

'No.'

'You have nothing to worry—'

'I'll come back another time,' I say. 'I promise I will.'

Tears roll down my face.

'It's not that—'

'Please.'

'You don't need to worry, Tuva,' says Julia. 'The doctor won't—'

I cry more.

'Show me,' I say. 'Move the chair at least so I can see.'

Tobias shakes his head and then he picks up a hand mirror from next to the laptop. He wipes it with his sleeve and holds it up.

It takes a few moments for me to see what's reflected back at me. Something on an identical sun lounger. Same striped cushion. Same duct tape.

My breathing quickens.

'No, please.'

I tense at my taped arms. My hips twist left and right.

'Oh, God. No.'

61

Emil's lying out cold on the sun lounger behind me. His full moustache. His small frame. Some kind of liquid pooling under his body and collecting in the tarp sheet.

'What have you done?' I ask.

'The best thing is if you can focus on the main—'

'Help me!' I scream.

'We're the ones who are here to help,' says Julia, as she gazes admiringly at Tobias.

Tobias puts down the hand mirror and once again I can't see behind me.

Don't notice the paperclip. Do not see it.

'Speculum, please, nurse.'

She moves closer with the plastic mouth retractor.

My old anaesthetic is wearing off more now. I can feel the pain rising up in my jaw.

'No,' I say. 'Please, Julia. It's enough now.'

Tobias skips through music on his phone. Chooses some kind of upbeat swing tune, and then he washes his gloved hands again in the washing up bowl.

'This will be the most important procedure I have completed to date,' he says.

Julia's hands hover close to my mouth.

'Open, please.'

'No.'

Tobias says, 'Open wide, please.'

They both loom over me. I can see the capillaries in the whites of his eye. The ice-cold blue around his pupil. A sty developing on his upper lid.

He holds his fingers out in a pincer shape and I open my mouth.

What they don't know is that the tape around my right wrist is starting to tear. I am stuck down to this chair at every major body joint: head, shoulders, wrists, chest, hips, knees, ankles. But with one more flex of my right wrist I could free that hand. They don't have that information. Now I have to figure out what I can do with just one hand.

Julia hands Tobias a new tray and says, 'Doctor.'

He takes it.

There's a scalpel and a pair of pliers and a fresh syringe and needle.

'What are you doing?' I ask, but with this thing in my mouth the words are undecipherable.

Tobias says, 'Are you curious? I'll fill you in. Tuva, are you familiar with the term *allotransplantation*?'

I move my eyeballs from side to side to signal 'no'.

'Exactly,' he says. 'And neither is the rest of the world. Not even most mainstream dentistry. But they will be after today.'

I tense my ankles but the tape is secure.

'Live transplantation of a living tooth, complete with blood supply, from one human to another. The Pharaohs used to receive teeth from their slaves in ancient Egypt, did you know that? And wealthy Europeans even received teeth from domestic workers. It fell out of fashion but, in my opinion, with modern 3D scans and so on, it represents the future of sound dentistry. We transplant corneas and skin grafts. Livers, kidneys, and hearts. So why not teeth?'

I start to choke and Julia unscrews part of my mouth retractor so I can close and open my mouth. I swallow and say, 'You can't do this. I can't have a dead man's teeth.'

Tobias looks offended. 'Tuva, you misunderstand. For a start, this patient is not deceased, merely heavily sedated. It's essential that his teeth have living nerve tissue and blood flow. And secondly, you won't be receiving his teeth. He only has infant teeth. It's he who will be receiving yours.'

62

I scream and they hold down my head.

They insert the mouth retractor again and screw it open. Not as wide as before, but still too wide.

I make a solemn pledge to save Emil somehow. To overcome this pair. When I move my wrist I can feel the tape stretch and tear. There is hope. Not much but there is some.

'Insert the speculum into the mouth of patient C, please, nurse.'

She walks away leaving me here with Tobias.

I listen as she inserts the retractor. I listen to the plastic scrape against his teeth. I hear her turn the screws to lock it into position.

'He won't be needing suction, nurse. This part won't take me more than a few seconds.'

Tobias leaves my field of vision but he's taken the scalpel and pliers with him on that clingfilm-wrapped tray.

I can't see what they're doing.

'Hold the patient's head steady, please, nurse,' says Tobias.

What are they doing?

'One,' says Tobias. And I hear metal on metal. A quiet groan of exertion. 'Two,' he says. 'All done.'

He glides over to me on his wheelie stool. In his hands is the small metal tray. The scalpel is clean and looks unused. The pliers have blood on them. The needle is unused. There are two small teeth lying next to the needle.

I screw up my eyes as tight as I can. I will not allow Tobias to implant one of my teeth into Emil's mouth. It's evil.

'I understand your reservations,' says Tobias. 'But we can't make a dental omelette without breaking a few teeth, now, can we? These two,' he points to the tray, 'were milk teeth. Straightforward to pull. Yours, on the other hand, will be rather more challenging.'

I start bucking against my chair. Too exhausted from all this. I feel like I'm going to pass out.

'Nurse.'

He hands her the hand mirror.

'It won't take long,' she says, holding up the mirror. 'And when it's over, you'll get a gift from the doctor.'

She points the mirror so I can see Emil.

He has a trickle of blood flowing out of the corner of his mouth.

Behind him sits a half-deflated bladder-balloon.

Unpainted.

Rotting.

That was the terrible stench.

And the source of the liquid pooling under Emil's unconscious body.

Next to the mirror I notice Tobias squeezing anaesthetic from the needle.

'Little scratch,' he says.

63

Tobias injects anaesthetic into the gum on the other side of my mouth. I need to be patient. Bide my time.

'I'll let that start to work and then I'll be back in a few moments to start the transplant.'

He smiles and pulls his bloodstained face-mask down under his chin.

I stare up at the ceiling.

The shower curtain separating this part of the carriage from the fake reception area ripples as he passes through and I yank up my wrist. I heave at the tapes, lifting my hand, straining, and the tape rips. I drag my wrist back and forth and free my hand completely from the sun-lounger armrest.

Stay calm.

Keep quiet.

I shake my wrist around to get the blood flowing again and then I put my free wrist under the blanket and pull off the tapes on my left hand. I have to be careful not to make too much noise. They rip. I now have both wrists free. Hidden by the blanket, I rip off the tapes securing my chest, waist and hips. I can't reach the knee or ankle-tapes without pulling off the tapes securing my head to the lounger. I still can't sit up. But I'm free now, from neck to hip. Do I untape the rest and run for it? They've got a rifle in reception and there's no other way out that I know of other than through the door I came in by. If I let him transplant one of my teeth into Emil's mouth what will happen to me afterwards? Will they sedate me like they did with Emil? I can't believe they'll just let me go and tell my story to the police. More likely they'll do to me what they did to Arne Persson.

Tobias walks back in with Julia close behind.

I keep my arms on the armrests, exactly like they were before, the blanket covering my sliced-through duct tape.

My jaw is wedged open with the plastic mouth retractor. Tobias's one eye approaches and looms over me again. He moves his mouth mask into place. It sucks in and blows out with each of his breaths.

'Let me know if you can feel this.'

He pokes my gum with a sharp metal instrument.

I can't feel it.

'Ouch,' I say.

He looks into my eye and says, 'More anaesthetic, please, nurse.'

She leaves and my head clears.

He turns to change the music on his phone. From something Russian to German opera. Mahler, I think.

I lower my right hand from the blanket and pivot my elbow.

The tray is right there.

I pick up the scalpel as quietly as I can. My head is still clamped in place, my jaw is stretched wide open, my ankles are bound. He turns toward me and I stab the scalpel up and round into the underside of his neck. Plunging it in as deep as I can. He doesn't scream, he whimpers. He goes down, his hand clamped around his neck. Blood gushes out from the wound. The green tarp turns glossy. I pull the retractor out from my mouth and place it on my chest and then I slice at my head-tapes with the scalpel and pull out clumps of my own hair, along with tape. I kneel up. There's a groan, but it's not Tobias. It's Emil. He's waking up. I sit and slash at my ankle tapes.

I'm free from the lounger.

The music plays on. Oboes and violins. Trombones. Kettle drums.

Emil's eyes are wide open. Looking around. His jaw retracted. Panic. Blood in his moustache whiskers.

I put my fingers to my lips. 'Shhh.'

He looks as terrified as I feel.

I search the room for some kind of weapon – a bat or an iron rod – but there's nothing. I only have the scalpel. It's pathetically small.

I try to peer around the edge of the shower curtain into reception. My heart's beating and my jaw is numb. I could bite off my tongue and swallow it without even knowing.

Emil groans again.

My heart feels like it's beating at twice its normal speed.

I can't even look at Tobias.

Julia's at her desk, sucking up anaesthetic from a vial into a syringe with a fat needle. The fish float dead in the fishtank. The magazines are stacked into three neat piles. Some on fishing. Some crossword puzzles. Some on the Swedish royal family.

I look down and the green-tarp floor is covered in blood now. A river of it.

I have to focus.

Julia isn't looking this way. She's still concentrating on the syringe.

The door's right there.

Two metres from where I stand.

I'll spring to it and then I will flee.

No other option.

Tobias cries, 'Help,' and I see Julia's face turn in my direction. She drops the syringe and it falls to the ground. I burst through the shower curtain and Julia picks up a handgun I never even noticed before from beside her laptop. I keep on running. I scream, even though I don't want to. Too much fear and too much pain. Exhaustion. I've seen too much.

'Stop!' she yells.

I lunge for the door.

It's locked.

'Stop right now, Tuva, or I will shoot.'

Her voice is shaky.

I swallow hard and turn slowly to face her.

She moves toward the shower curtain, her gun trained on me the whole time. Her hands are quivering. She looks into the makeshift dental surgery and lets out a yelp.

I see something in her eyes. A blackening.

I push the bolts on the door and it slides open. I'm sorry, Emil.

There's a loud click from behind me.

No bullet.

I glance back to see her trying to fix her gun. Take the safety off. Reload. I don't know.

I jump down onto the weed-covered gravel by the tracks.

Darkness and freezing-cold forest air.

My Hilux is right there but I don't have the key. It looks safe that way but I know it's a death trap.

Fog everywhere. Thick fog like dry ice.

I run. Like a hunted deer, I flee into the mists, into the pines. I run five-trees deep. Ten-trees deep. Fifty-trees deep. My feet are soaked with bog water and my jaw feels like it's dislocated. Eventually I stop and cower behind a broad beech tree, panting. I can't see Julia. But I can see lights. In the distance, splintered through the trunks. Blue flashing lights. She's either called an ambulance for her sick lover or else the police have found this hellhole.

There are shouts and commands and I can't make out the words but I recognise a voice.

Noora's voice.

The smell of pine needles, wet with moisture.

Without even thinking I find myself running back toward the train carriage. I should cower down and hide but I have to warn Noora. And Thord. Warn all of them. They could be walking into a trap in that abandoned carriage.

I crash through dead branches and get whipped in the face by wet branches.

Two police cars on the tracks, one either side of my Hilux. The glossy pine walls reflect the blue lights, and the cold fog drifts through the tree trunks on the wind.

'Wait!' I scream.

My hearing aids aren't working properly. Too wet. One's squealing.

Noora looks round toward me and I keep on running.

I see Thord approach the carriage with his gun drawn, the muzzle pointed down at the ground.

'Wait!' I yell. 'They're armed.'

Thord turns to face me and, as if in slow motion, Tobias steps down onto the tracks. His white dentist's jacket is red.

'Police,' shouts Thord.

Tobias has a towel or a sheet wrapped tight around his neck. He's holding his rifle by his hip. He starts to raise it so the butt rests against his shoulder.

Noora fires.

Tobias falls to the tracks.

64

I collapse onto my bed.

Spending most of this morning at the police station giving my statement to Chief Björn and some suit from Karlstad homicide was exhausting. Reliving it all. Every detail. I only really spoke about it yesterday. About the train. But in my head was a hideous collage of the headless man in Visberg forest, Pan Night and the anvil, Emil being dragged away into the fog by his ankles. The unravelling horror of it all.

I rest my head on the pillow and stare at the photos on my bedside table. The one of Mum and Dad. The one of me and Tam down by the reservoir. The one of Noora smiling, showing off her one perfect dimple.

My hearing aids are out and I feel numb.

It's like this every time I experience something traumatic. Before, I'd try to get back on my feet and go to work. I'd get out for a walk, try to reinstate my faith in humanity. I'd try to climb back on the metaphorical horse. But now I know better. It takes time. Now I know you stay numb for as long as you need to. I'm letting the shock drain out of my cells. I've hit the 'restore to factory settings' button and I'm lying here in standby mode.

Lena walked me over to the police station this morning. She didn't say much, she just kept her hand loosely on my shoulder, in a manner that said, *if you fall down, I am right here beside you.* She picked me up after I was finished talking about that carriage, that sun lounger, the noise of the dentist's drill. She walked me home and made sure I was okay. Lena's never been a mother, but really, she has. She's been a mother in an unspoken way. A mode of caring particular to her and her alone. One day I'll thank her properly, if I can find the words.

It's getting dark outside.

Winter is approaching and the light is leaching from the spore-filled skies. Outside in Gavrik town people are discussing how much more firewood they need for the white months. They're stocking up on snow shovels and de-icer and rock salt in ICA Maxi. Down-filled coats are being taken down from attics. This morning, one woman passed me and Lena on Storgatan and she had a bright-blue plastic sled under one arm and a red-faced toddler under the other. The Grimberg-factory janitor will soon start salting and gritting the area in front of the twin chimneys. He'll carry on doing that every day for the next six months.

Text on my phone from Noora.

I put my aids in and switch them on and they play the familiar jingle.

I wash my face with cold water and take a deep breath and look at myself. The corners of my mouth are red from the plastic retractor. Aside from that I'm physically okay. I'll survive.

Noora knocks on my door and I undo both locks and let her in.

She's wearing her royal-blue fleece and jeans. She holds out her arms and I walk to her and we stand there for a long time. Her soft cheek against my dry cheek. Her arms around my shoulders, but looser than a normal Noora hug. That's how she is. Noora knows I've been strapped down and locked up. So her embrace is lighter than usual. I don't feel trapped. I feel safe.

'How are you doing?' she asks.

Big sigh. 'I'll be alright in a few days.'

'Have you eaten anything?'

I shake my head. 'Tam's bringing something over for me. For you as well, if you're hungry.'

She smiles.

We both sit down at my IKEA kitchen table.

'Are *you* okay?' I ask. 'Did you get questioned?'

'There's always an investigation after you discharge your service weapon,' she says. 'Due process. It's vitally important that these things are looked into.'

'But it'll be fine?' I ask.

She nods. 'It'll be fine. Lots of paperwork and I can talk to a police psychiatrist if I choose to. Especially as this was my first. But I'll be fine.'

I shake my head. 'It's like they really believed in their lie. Like they thought they'd set up a dental surgery.'

'I don't know,' she says. 'He was determined to carry out procedures. From what we've seen and heard so far, it's possible she was obsessed with him and he was obsessed with being a dentist.'

'Why, though?'

She takes off her fleece and hangs it on the back of her chair. 'Between you and me, Tobias's father and grandfather were both dentists. His grandfather even patented some kind of denture. They were well respected and they were both well known in their field. But Tobias never got the grades. He tried as hard as he could, but he never got into medical school for dentistry. Tried to circumvent it by using his father's credentials, by applying to medical schools in Eastern Europe. They all rejected him.'

'But that doesn't explain...'

'His parents were disappointed in their only son and they didn't hide it well, according to Ragnar Falk. Ragnar knew Tobias's father a little back in the '80s. And Ragnar has some theory that the Edlunds only made things worse. The way they go on about being qualified doctors all the time, even Eva Edlund, even though she's never practiced. Ragnar thinks the anger built up over time. Every day, seeing their certificates framed on the wall. And Sven wasn't exactly a considerate boss to Tobias. Dismissive, Ragnar said.'

'It's weird what makes people do extreme things.'

'It's been mentioned that Tobias and Julia were in a coercive relationship of some kind, that he was controlling and she was susceptible after a string of bad break-ups. The Chief says her parents weren't a good example to her. Julia grew up watching, day after day, her mother doing everything for her father, yearning for his approval, his appreciation, and never really getting it. Tobias was clean cut, never really stood out in a crowd; but underneath it all, a nasty piece of work.'

'Chief Björn told me he's dead.'

She nods. 'Tobias was pronounced dead in Falun hospital. He died from the gunshot wound, Tuva, not from the blade injury.'

'I know. The Chief told me.'

'You didn't kill him.'

'I know.'

She places her hand on top of mine. The warmth of it. The pad of her index finger strokes the nail of my ring finger. Her chair squeaks as she moves it closer and we sit there melting together, our shoulders crumpled into each other.

And then I feel it. The cycle of these things. How good follows bad follows good. We will be happy, Noora and me. We will muddle through in our own way. In our own time and on our own terms.

'Tobias and Julia had been stealing medical supplies from Edlunds Tandklinik for months,' she says. 'Stored some of them in the Hive.'

'Chief said Emil Eriksson will be okay,' I say.

'I don't know about *okay*,' she says. 'What he went through in that train. Being sedated over and over again in that cold carriage, deep in the pines. But yes, he's in a stable condition. Physically he should make a full recovery. Mentally, only time will tell.'

The Chief told me they used a remote car-starter the night they abducted Emil. Made it look like one man and a driver. But all the time the accomplice was Julia and she was watching the whole scene with me.

'Is there any sign of Julia?'

Noora pulls away.

'Not yet. She escaped into the fog. The size of Visberg forest didn't help, nor the fact that we didn't know at that point that we were dealing with two perpetrators. We spent too much time trying to save Tobias and look after Emil. I regret not tracking her sooner.'

'You think she's still in Visberg?'

I think about the white bike. About the clockmaker's house deep in the woods, the one with no windows or doors on the ground floor.

'Dalarna police traced her debit card being used in a machine 150km east of here a few hours ago. They're on her tail.'

'I hope she gives herself up.'

'I hope so, too,' says Noora. 'We're still trying to piece together why they targeted Arne Persson. We know Tobias's father was friends with Arne years ago and then the friendship ended suddenly. Karlstad homicide have found plans made months ago. Plans to practice before the transplantation attempt. They said it was as if Tobias had designed his own curriculum, his own dentistry education.'

A knock on the door. Noora answers and it's Tam standing there with sleet in her hair, holding three plastic carrier bags of hot food.

'I got fuel,' she says, kicking off her boots, placing the bags down next to the sink. She comes over to me and I stand up. She looks up into my eyes and says, 'Are you sure you're alright?'

I smile and say I'm fine.

She puts her hands on my cheeks and I recoil a little at the coldness.

'Sorry,' she says, rubbing her hands together. We hug and she whispers, 'Are you okay, though?' and I nod.

'Right,' she says. 'Pad Thai, panang, and Thai green curry. My three bestsellers. All made with VIP spicing. No mild, Scandi bullshit. Two bags of white crackers, two bags of chili crackers. Lots of rice. I brought paper plates and cutlery so no washing up required. Dig in.'

We do.

The food is delicious. We're all ravenously hungry, but I eat carefully because of my tooth.

'Will a real dentist re-do the root canal?' says Tam.

I flinch at the memory. 'Maybe,' I say, glancing up at the clock on the wall.

'You tired?' says Tam. 'Shit, I'm keeping you up. You must be exhausted. I'll get off home.'

'No,' I say. 'It's not that. Let's eat together, but there's someone coming over at eight. Young man called Dan I'd like Tam to meet. He made me a handsome 'get well soon' card according to his mum, and he wants to give it to me in person.'

'You got competition,' Tam says to Noora.

'He's seven,' I say.

'I'll keep my eye on him,' says Noora.

'The doctor who saw me last night said the tooth looked okay. Checked for wounds or infections, gave me some anti-bacterial stuff. Said I could see a dentist today if I wanted.'

They both look at me.

'I don't want to see a dentist for a very long time,' I say. 'The tooth feels okay. The procedure never hurt that much and I got the feeling Tobias actually did a decent job. I'll get X-rays but I don't want any work done anytime soon.'

'Ratshit bastard,' says Tammy.

There's a quiet knock at the door.

'There's the new boyfriend,' says Tammy, winking at Noora.

I stand up and open the door.

But it's not little Dan with a 'get well soon' card.

It's Julia, with soaking wet hair. Before I know what to do, she aims her gun and pulls the trigger.

And all at once, my world changes.

Acknowledgements

To my literary agent Kate Burke, and the team at Blake Friedmann: thank you.

To my editor Jenny Parrott, and the team at Oneworld: thank you.

To my international publishers, editors, translators: thank you.

To Maya Lindh (the voice of Tuva): thank you.

To all the booksellers and bloggers and reviewers and early supporters and tweeters and fellow authors: thank you. Readers benefit so much from your recommendations and enthusiasm. I am one of them. Special thanks to every single reader who takes the time to leave a review somewhere online. Those reviews help readers to find books. Thank you.

To @DeafGirly: thank you once again for your help and support. In many ways your opinion matters to me more than anyone else's. I continue to be extremely grateful.

To Sweden: what a place! Thanks for welcoming me in.

To my family, and especially my parents: once again, thank you for letting me play alone for hours as a child. Thank you for taking me to libraries. Thank you for letting me read and draw and daydream and scribble down strange stories. Thanks for not censoring my book choices (too much). Thank you for allowing me to be bored. It was a special gift.

To my friends: thanks for your ongoing support (and patience, and love).

To Mary Shelley and Irvine Welsh: I read *Frankenstein* and *Trainspotting* back-to-back as an awkward teenager. The books blew my mind. Thank you.

Special thanks to my late granddad for teaching me some valuable lessons. He taught me to treat everyone equally, and with respect. To give the benefit of the doubt. To listen to advice even if you don't then follow it. To take pleasure from the small things in life. To read widely. To never judge or look down on anyone. To be kind. To spend time with loved ones. To keep the kid inside you alive.

To Bernie and Monty: what can I say? I'm lucky. You both make me happy. Thank you.

To every shy, socially awkward kid: I see you. I was you. It will get easier. I promise.

To my wife and son: Thank you. Love you. Always.

TUVA MOODYSON BOOK I

Selected for ITV's Zoe Ball Book Club

'The tension is unrelenting, and I can't wait for Tuva's next outing.'
Val McDermid, author of *Still Life*

'The best thriller I've read in ages.'
Marian Keyes, author of *Grown Ups*

SEE NO EVIL
Eyes missing, two bodies lie deep in the forest near a remote Swedish town.

HEAR NO EVIL
Tuva Moodyson, a deaf reporter on a small-time local paper, is looking for the story that could make her career.

SPEAK NO EVIL
A web of secrets. And an unsolved murder from twenty years ago. Can Tuva outwit the killer before she becomes the final victim? She'd like to think so. But first she must face her demons and venture far into the deep, dark woods if she wants to stand any chance of getting the hell out of small-time Gavrik.

TUVA MOODYSON BOOK 2

Winner of Best Independent Voice at the Amazon Publishing Readers' Awards 2020

'A complex plot suffused with the nightmarish quality of *Twin Peaks* and a tough-minded, resourceful protagonist add up to a stand-out read.'
Guardian

'Scandi noir meets Gormenghast. Just wonderful. Can't get enough of Tuva Moodyson.'
Mark Billingham, author of the Tom Thorne Novels

TWO BODIES

One suicide. One cold-blooded murder. Are they connected? And who's really pulling the strings in the small Swedish town of Gavrik?

TWO COINS

Black Grimberg liquorice coins cover the murdered man's eyes. The hashtag #Ferryman starts to trend as local people stock up on ammunition.

TWO WEEKS

Tuva Moodyson, deaf reporter at the local paper, has a fortnight to investigate the deaths before she starts her new job in the south. A blizzard moves in. Residents, already terrified, feel increasingly cut-off. Tuva must go deep inside the Grimberg factory to stop the killer before she leaves town for good. But who's to say the Ferryman will let her go?

TUVA MOODYSON BOOK 3

Longlisted for the Theakston Old Peculier Crime Novel of the Year 2021

'Eerie, unnerving and buckets of fun.'
Observer, thriller of the month

'BRILLIANT central character.'
Ann Cleeves, author of the Vera Stanhope novels

FEAR

Tuva's been living clean in southern Sweden for four months when she receives horrifying news. Her best friend Tammy Yamnim is missing.

SECRETS

Racing back to Gavrik at the height of Midsommar, Tuva fears for Tammy's life. Who has taken her, and why? And who is sabotaging the small-town search efforts?

LIES

Surrounded by dark pine forest, the sinister residents of Snake River are suspicious of outsiders. Unfortunately, they also hold all the answers. On the shortest night of the year, Tuva must fight to save her friend. The only question is who will be there to save Tuva?

WILL DEAN grew up in the East Midlands and had lived in nine different villages before the age of eighteen. After studying Law at the LSE and working in London, he settled in rural Sweden where he built a house in a boggy clearing at the centre of a vast elk forest, and it's from this base that he reads and writes. His debut novel, *Dark Pines* (Point Blank, 2018), was selected for Zoe Ball's Book Club, shortlisted for the *Guardian* Not the Booker prize and named a *Daily Telegraph* Book of the Year. The second Tuva Moodyson mystery, *Red Snow* (Point Blank, 2019), won Best Independent Voice at the Amazon Publishing Readers' Awards, 2019. *Black River* (Point Blank, 2020) was longlisted for the Theakston Old Peculier Crime Novel of the Year Award, 2021. Will is also the author of *The Last Thing to Burn* (Hodder, 2021).

Will loves to hear from readers. You can find him on Twitter and Instagram @willrdean, as well as speaking regularly about reading and writing on YouTube under the name Will Dean – Forest Author. **#TeamTuva**